CALLING
THE
CIRCLE

ALSO BY HEATHER W. COBHAM
Hungry Mother Creek
The Mother Tree

CALLING THE CIRCLE

BY
HEATHER W. COBHAM

Book design by Nathan Bauer

Cover design by Kylie Sek

ISBN-13: 978-0-9914085-2-8

For all the women who have helped expand women's rights, whether in the public forum, or quietly within their own homes and communities. Thank you for your courage and sacrifice.

HEATHER W. COBHAM

CHAPTER 1

A ridge of bark pressed into Chapawee's back, its pressure familiar and supportive. She lifted her right hand and traced a thick root from the trunk of the live oak to where it entered the earth. For the past three years she'd sat alone with the Mother Tree. Solitude was a comfortable companion, but she was nearing the end of her life, and yearned to sit here in a circle of women once again.

Soon, the heat and humidity would keep everything still, but for now the forest was full of activity. The squirrels rustled leaves in pursuit of one another. The kingfisher called further up the creek, and the insects hummed as the sun began her assent. Chapawee leaned away from the Mother Tree and lifted her thick, silver and black braid so the breeze could cool her neck. Tears pooled in the corners of her eyes and she tried not to blink, hoping to hold her grief in place. The tears overflowed and slid down her cheeks, despite her best efforts. Past the saw palmettos, the ripples in the dark water of Hungry Mother Creek divided the morning light into a thousand suns.

Years ago Chapawee had sat here in a sacred circle with her mother and sister, as well as a mother-daughter pair that lived on the Bay River, about twenty miles away. The two families, both descendants of the Neusiok Indians who had lived here hundreds of years ago, would gather at the solstices and equinoxes; the women for cooking and circle time, and the men for hunting and fishing. The other family eventually moved away and Chapawee's daughter and niece joined Chapawee, and her mother and sister in the circle. Her daughter left when she married a Coharie Indian, and her niece died in childbirth. For twenty years after her mother's death, only she and her sister, Kanti, sat by the

Mother Tree. And now, for the past three years Chapawee had sat here alone. Almost a full generation had passed since there'd been a true circle of women next to the tree.

Another tear escaped. Chapawee stood and faced the Mother Tree, an embodiment of the Great Spirit. "Help me call the circle. I need the connection and wisdom of other women."

Chapawee took a pinch of tobacco from the pouch around her waist. Inhaling its sweetness, she laid it at the base of the Mother Tree as an offering, confirming the intention to find others to join her circle.

But who would she invite? The closest Indian tribe was the Coharie, a hundred miles away in Sampson County where her daughter lived. Perhaps, instead of searching for Neusiok descendants, she should invite women who'd also grown up on the banks of the Neuse River, no matter their heritage. The wind picked up slightly and Chapawee heard the upper branches of the Mother Tree rattle and hum in agreement with her decision.

After observing the colored and white women, she knew they had their own rituals for connecting, so hopefully, once they were seated together in a circle, it would feel familiar. Chapawee wrapped her arms around the trunk of the Mother Tree in gratitude. Today she'd received validation it was time to call the circle, and soon, which women to invite would become clear.

Her eyes were dry now, and her shoulders relaxed. Instinctively, she searched for large stones to line the clearing around the Mother Tree. Rocks were sparse, and it took over an hour to find stones big enough. Perspiration moistened her hairline and neck, and dripped between her shoulder blades. When Chapawee was finished she'd placed twenty stones, each the size of a loaf of bread, in a circle that began, and ended with the Mother Tree.

Chapawee stepped back and smiled. She'd gathered the stones for a circle, and now she would gather the women.

***

Tonight was opening night of the James Adams Floating Theater, and Hodges Street pulsed with life as people made their way to Oriental's harbor front. Vivi and Goldie weaved through the crowd, past couples arm-in-arm, children running and laughing, and horses carrying people from farther out in the county. Folks in this rural community were hungry for entertainment, and Vivi was hungry for a distraction.

"Momma, look!" Goldie pointed towards the harbor. "There's the showboat."

The James Adams Floating Theater was a barge over 100 feet long with a low draft that allowed it to ply the shallow waterways of eastern North Carolina. It didn't have its own propulsion, and two tug boats were anchored beside it.

"You could fit twenty of Daddy's fishing boats onto that one."

"Well, not twenty, but at least four or five," Vivi said and brushed a dead leaf off the shoulder of Goldie's pink smock dress. "Were you in the woods in your good dress?" Vivi asked.

Goldie grinned sheepishly and then ran ahead when she saw her best friend.

"Wait for me at the ticket window," Vivi yelled.

Usually Goldie's excitement was infectious, but tonight Vivi was immune. For Goldie's sake she acted the part, something she'd perfected the past year. In fact she did it with Bubba, and occasionally her mother. She was so practiced at playing roles to keep others happy that she could be an actress on the floating theater.

A seagull reprimanded Vivi with a harsh call. It swooped close to her head and then landed on the roof of the showboat. Vivi tucked a stray curl under her felt hat, and resolved to enjoy the evening.

3

She scanned the crowd for her mother who was meeting her and Goldie for the show. Seventeen years after her father's death, Vivi still had to remind herself that her mother would be alone. Daddy had been over six feet tall, and if he'd been here tonight, he would have spotted her already, waving, picking up his pace to greet her, his face barely able to contain his smile. At least that's how she imagined it.

She was eleven when he died, the same age Goldie was now. He'd be seventy if he were here today. A knot in her chest tightened. Vivi instinctively reached for Bubba's arm but he wasn't here either, still out in the sound netting for shrimp. Last year he'd scheduled his fishing around the showboat and they went as a family. He'd gotten as excited as Goldie about the entertainment and the novelty of a floating theater. After the show Bubba had entertained them with his renditions of the songs and acts, but that was before, before his brother had drowned.

"Vivi, Vivi! I'm over here." Her mother's voice interrupted her thoughts and Vivi veered left.

She was an inch taller than her mother, and bent slightly to give her a warm hug. "Mom, you look lovely." Her mother, Etta, was 48 but looked more like Vivi's sister thanks to how easily a few gray hairs blended into her blonde, and how conscientiously she'd protected her fair skin through the years. Goldie had the same coloring as Etta, while Vivi had her father's olive complexion and chestnut-colored hair.

"Now we have to find Goldie," Vivi said, and linked her arm through her mother's.

The theater was larger than any building in Oriental, seating up to 500 people in folding opera chairs on the main floor. The walls were white, with blue and gold crown molding. Generators under the stage provided electricity for the huge chandelier that hung from the ceiling and the smaller ones attached to the wall. Windows on both sides of the boat were open to the breeze, which tempered the August heat.

Vivi pointed. "I see three seats together, there, in the middle."

Goldie picked up her pace. "Yeah! That's close to the stage. Hurry before anyone else gets them."

They slid past the folks sitting at the end of the row to the three center seats. Goldie twisted to look behind her for her friends and then scooted forward to peer into the orchestra pit, her joyful anticipation needing a physical outlet. Goldie's enthusiasm, paired with the concentrated excitement inside the theater, were difficult to resist and Vivi smiled. She looked at the program and hoped tonight's show would give her a reason to laugh and enjoy herself. Since Bubba's brother drowned last September, things at home had been heavy. Bubba had been the joy and light of the family, but that ended when they buried his brother. Now Bubba was absent, either out fishing, or in the haze of moonshine.

The lights dimmed along with Vivi's thoughts. Goldie leaned back in her seat, her eyes transfixed on the stage. The curtain opened and the melodrama, *Mabel Heath* began.

***

Vivi glanced at the program. It was the last scene before intermission. She didn't want to miss the specialty acts performed during the break, so slipped out to get lemonades before the rush. The curtains closed and the lights came up just when Vivi returned to her seat.

Goldie took a sip of her lemonade. "Momma, can I go find my friends?"

"No, sweetie. Stay here with us to watch the specialty acts." Vivi looked at her program.

"A woman named Adelaide Thornberry is going to sing in just a minute."

Goldie plopped down into her seat with resignation, but was immediately engaged when the performer slipped from behind the curtains onto the stage. She was striking, with auburn hair rolled into a pompadour around her face and then pulled into a chignon at the nape of her neck. She was slightly shorter than Vivi, with curves that were showcased by the emerald silk evening gown, adorned with rhinestones.

Adelaide smiled at the audience and then began a raucous rendition of "Oh That Beautiful Rag". Vivi laughed and clapped with the others, and was awed by this woman's confidence and the joy she transmitted to the crowd. The song ended and it took a minute for the applause to die down. The singer settled herself on a stool in the middle of the stage. The second song was a ballad, "When I Lost You", and the contrast in style between it and the first song was startling. Her sweet, haunting vocals entranced Vivi until she was aware of nothing but that voice and the woman in the spotlight. For a moment their eyes met. Vivi's heart beat against her ribs and a flush crept up her neck. The knot in her chest loosened.

Vivi looked again at her program. Who was this Adelaide woman? When Vivi lifted her eyes back to the stage Adelaide was looking directly at her. She had blue eyes. Vivi held her gaze a moment, then looked away, confused by the connection she felt. She shook her head to clear her mind. It wasn't the songstress, but the song and the lyrics she connected to.

"I lost the gladness that turned into sadness, when I lost you."

The song ended and Vivi exhaled, unaware she'd been holding her breath and sitting at the edge of her seat. Adelaide started the next song and lifted her gaze over Vivi's head, gesturing with her arms and moving her hips in time with the upbeat tempo. The music and the song pulled Vivi into the moment, and here, she was happy.

Adelaide bowed and disappeared behind the curtains, just as the lights blinked to indicate intermission was over and the play would resume.

"Mama." Goldie tugged at her sleeve demanding her attention.

"Vivi, are you alright?" her mother asked over Goldie's head.

Vivi took Goldie's hand and said, "Yes. Yes. I'm fine. That music put me in another world."

"I know," her mother replied. "She's a talented singer."

"Can I go get a cookie?" Goldie asked, already standing with her hand out for the money.

"There isn't time." She picked up Goldie's lemonade from the floor. "Finish your lemonade and we'll have a cookie when we get home."

The second act began, but Vivi had difficulty paying attention. The sound of Adelaide's voice and the last line of her ballad played on in Vivi's mind. It felt like only a moment had passed when the curtains closed on the play. The lights came up and the entire company performed a song for the grand finale. Vivi kept her eyes on Adelaide, trying to discern her voice from the ensemble. When the song ended, their eyes met and for that instant, and everything else dropped away. Vivi clapped until all the performers left the stage.

Vivi, Etta and Goldie followed the crowd to the exit. Goldie swung her arms, imitating the dance steps in the finale and Vivi hummed the tune from the last song.

"It's nice to see you smiling," her mother said to Vivi.

Vivi's smile broadened. "The play was middling, but the music was magic wasn't it?"

"It appears it was for you, dear."

The three of them stepped into the night air and a light breeze cooled Vivi. Goldie ran to find her friends.

"The air feels good," Vivi said. "It was getting stuffy in there."

"Looks like some of the performers are enjoying the air too," her mother said, pointing to the right.

Before she turned her head, Vivi knew Adelaide would be there, and her intuition was confirmed when she saw the auburn hair. Vivi stopped to watch Adelaide, who clapped her hands and then leaned over, holding her stomach in laughter.

Her mother touched her elbow. "Are you coming? We better collect Goldie."

"Mom, can you keep an eye on her for a minute? I want to thank the woman who sang 'When I Lost You.'"

"Sure. We'll meet you in front of the general store."

Vivi walked against the flow of people and made her way towards the performers. The rhinestones on Adelaide's dress flashed when she stepped into the light of the gas street lamp, and Vivi was suddenly self-conscious in her plain cotton dress. She swallowed hard and wished for one more sip of Goldie's lemonade.

Adelaide turned in her direction. Vivi caught her breath at the same moment Adelaide's face lit up.

"You came," she said, as if they'd had a conversation about this meeting. Adelaide took both of Vivi's hands in hers.

Vivi had to look away from Adelaide's blue eyes or release her hands, because the combination made her lightheaded. She opted for the latter and crossed her hands over her heart and said, "I came to thank you for your voice, the songs. They . . ." How could she put her feeling into words? "They filled an empty place inside me and . . ." Vivi hesitated again.

"You merged with the music?" Adelaide asked. She had a strong northern accent that hadn't been evident when she'd been singing.

Vivi nodded her head in agreement. "Yes. That's a good way of putting it. For a moment it was just your voice and the music, and my worries fell away."

Adelaide smiled at her. "Art at its best transforms us, just as you've described, and your words are the highest compliment I could have received tonight." Adelaide looked over her shoulder at the other performers who were walking back to the showboat.

"I'd better go, but thanks for taking the time to speak to me." Adelaide paused. "What was your name?"

"Vivian Gibbs, but people call me Vivi."

"Vivi," Adelaide repeated, holding her hand out for Vivi to shake. "I'm Adelaide. It's nice to meet you." Without letting go of Vivi's hand she continued. "We'll be here in Oriental for a week. Please come back if you're able. I'd love to see you again."

Adelaide squeezed Vivi's hand, gave her one last smile, and walked quickly to catch up to the other performers. Vivi watched Adelaide's long, thick hair, released from the chignon, swing across the middle of her back. She took a breath and smiled. Maybe she should return for another show.

***

Vivi pushed a small plate of oatmeal cookies towards Adelaide. She wanted to touch her arm to prove she was real, but resisted. It was hard to believe this beautiful woman, who'd enchanted her with her voice and songs just a week ago, was now sitting at her kitchen table. Adelaide took a cookie from the plate and ate half of it in one bite.

"Oatmeal is my favorite," she said and then took another bite.

"Mine too. So how are things?" Vivi asked. "Are you settled at the Central Hotel and in your new job as manager there?"

"Yes. I've unpacked, and the room is large enough that I could create a small sitting area beside the fireplace. It's still a hotel room, but I made it as homey as I could." Adelaide paused and took a sip of her lemonade. "So far, I enjoy my job as manager. It's nothing complicated, and the accounts end is similar to keeping the books for my father's business."

"I know the owner was relieved to find you after the other manager rushed away to care for her dying mother. Do you know how long she'll be gone?"

Adelaide took another bite of her cookie. "I have no idea, but for my sake I hope it takes a while. I think I'm going to enjoy the pace of living in Oriental."

"What made you leave the showboat to stay, besides finding a job? With all your experience, and the opportunity to travel, it's hard to understand what Oriental has to offer you."

Adelaide stared into her lemonade and then lifted her face to Vivi. The pause before she answered was only a few seconds, but it felt longer and Vivi shifted in her chair, uncomfortable being the object of Adelaide's full attention.

"Well, you for one reason," Adelaide said.

"Me?" Vivi asked and took a sip of the lemonade. It needed more sugar.

"Yes. Taking the job with the James Adams Floating Theater was an impulsive decision, and I quickly realized I didn't like being confined to a boat, or someone else's schedule. I'm used to being in charge of my day." Adelaide twirled a piece of hair that had escaped from her French braid around her finger. "When I met you after my show, I knew we could be friends, and having lunch with you, Goldie and your mother, confirmed that, so Oriental seemed like a good place to jump ship."

"But, Adelaide, staying in Oriental also sounds like an impulsive decision. I'm surprised they let you leave the showboat. You were the most talented performer they have."

"Thank you for that vote of confidence Vivi, but I wasn't a lead in the play and they can easily absorb my absence. I will miss performing though. When I'm on stage, I lose a sense of myself, and merge with the music and the audience."

As Adelaide talked, it seemed like she was transported to the stage. She lifted her chin and her chest swelled as if to take a breath for the next note. "But the satisfaction from performing wasn't enough to counter the restrictions of life on a showboat." Adelaide leaned across the table towards Vivi. "It also feels frivolous to be on stage when social issues need to be addressed."

Social issues? Vivi kept this thought to herself to avoid looking uninformed, but her face revealed her question.

"Women's suffrage, Vivi," Adelaide said. "In Boston I was part of the Boston Equal Suffrage Association for Good Government. Our goal is to put a state suffrage amendment on the ballot. When I left Boston, I was burned out from all the work and so little progress. But now I miss it. Do you have a suffrage association here in Oriental? Maybe I could help."

"Not that I'm aware of," Vivi said, ashamed to admit she'd hardly given this topic any thought. She and her mother had only discussed suffrage in passing, and mostly in jest when they'd fantasize how different the country would be if women made all the decisions.

"Looks like I can be of help! I'll ask around to see if anyone knows of a local suffrage organization."

"If you're ready to go back to that work, why stay here? Seems like a big city would be a better place."

"Working on suffrage is only part of my reason. I'm not ready to go back to Boston. Too many people," Adelaide paused, "and memories. I want to experience life in a small town, with a slower pace."

Adelaide confidently followed her heart where it led her, both on and off a showboat and this amazed Vivi. She wasn't sure if she'd ever done that, except for marrying Bubba, and that wasn't turning out as planned. "You are bold," Vivi said. "Is your father still living? What does he say? And I'm sure you have a suitor. Will he come here to retrieve you and escort you back to Boston?"

Adelaide laughed, pushed back her chair from the table and folded her arms across her chest. "My father made me this way. I have three older brothers and by the time I came along he and mother treated me practically the same. He worries about me, but never stands in the way of what makes me happy. As far as a suitor, I've had my share, but eventually they've all tried to change me, to reign me in, and I won't have that. I'd rather be alone than the handmaiden to a husband."

Vivi fell silent and tried to assimilate what Adelaide had said. Adelaide's perspective didn't fit her understanding of a world where you needed a man. It'd never crossed her mind that a woman would choose to be unmarried. The greatest holes in her life were left by absent men, her father in death and now Bubba in his moonshine. But to choose to be without a man, at least a husband, that was a new idea.

Vivi thought of life without Bubba and felt an immediate sense of relief, followed by guilt. She didn't want to be without the Bubba she'd fallen in love with, just the Bubba that was here now. As if on cue, Goldie ran through the back door and over to Vivi. "Momma, I found a baby turtle outside. Can I use one of our crab pots for a cage so it can be my pet?"

Vivi's heart filled. If Bubba wasn't in her life she wouldn't have Goldie, and Goldie was definitely worth any price she had to pay.

"Goldie," Vivi said, "where are your manners? Please say hello to Miss Adelaide first."

Goldie took a breath and smoothed the front of her gingham dress. "Good afternoon, Miss Adelaide." Goldie inched towards the back door. "Do you want to come outside and see the baby turtle?"

Adelaide laughed and met Vivi's eyes. "That's up to your mother."

Vivi stood and took a cookie over to Goldie. "Miss Adelaide and I will be out after we finish our drinks. Go see if you can find the mother turtle down by the water. If you can't, we'll talk about adopting the baby."

"Yes, Ma'am," Goldie said. She ate her cookie in two bites and sped out the back door.

"I love her joy and curiosity," Adelaide said and took another sip of lemonade. "I bet you were the same when you were her age."

Goldie was eleven, the same age she'd been when her father had died in front of her. The lemonade glass slipped from Vivi's hand, sloshing lemonade onto the table. Vivi remembered those last moments with her father. They were seated across from one another at his desk, both writing, he a letter to his brother, and she in her journal. The rest of her memories were fragmented, her father slumped in his chair and the terror when she couldn't wake him, her mother, crying beside her father's body and the smell of the roast burning in the oven.

Adelaide took her hand. "Vivi, are you OK?"

The warmth and pressure of Adelaide's hand was a comfort. She met her eyes and they were full of concern. "Do you need to lie down?" Adelaide asked when Vivi remained silent.

Vivi took a breath to unknot her vocal cords. She squeezed Adelaide's hand slightly. "No. Sorry I startled you. Your comment took me back. And yes, in August of my eleventh year I was like Goldie. Life was full of joy and new discoveries, both in nature and in all the books I read from my father's library." Vivi paused. "But then in October, my father died of a heart attack right in front of me, and that changed everything."

Vivi did her best to hold back her tears, but several slipped out. Adelaide leaned towards her and with her free hand gently wiped them away. With that simple gesture Vivi felt acknowledged, and understood, something Bubba hadn't done for her in a long time.

"Is everything all right, Vivi?"

Vivi tensed and immediately pulled her hand away from Adelaide's when she heard Bubba's voice. She turned towards the door and said, "Bubba. I'm fine. This is a surprise. I didn't expect you home for another week at least."

Bubba leaned in the doorway and his gaze went to Adelaide and then back to her. His brown cotton work shirt was rolled up to his elbows revealing deeply tanned forearms and hands. He hooked his right thumb under his suspender. "Joe fell and broke his arm and couldn't work. We came back early so he could see Dr. Purdy and I could find another crewman."

Bubba looked over at Adelaide again and Vivi snapped to her senses. She hadn't seen Bubba for over a week while he'd been fishing near Ocracoke. She wasn't giving him much of a homecoming.

Vivi stood. "Well I'm sorry about Joe, but happy to see you." They each took a few steps towards the other and then Bubba removed his straw hat and enveloped her in a hug. She lay her head on his chest and breathed in the fish, salt, and sweat smells on his shirt. He was five inches taller than her and his chest was broad and thick with muscle, just like when they'd first met as teenagers. She pressed into him and prayed he wouldn't drink this time while he was off the boat.

Vivi stepped away from Bubba and gestured to Adelaide who was now standing. "Bubba, this is Adelaide Thornberry. She's a singer from the showboat that was here last week. She's going to stay in Oriental for a while."

Adelaide stepped towards Bubba with her hand outstretched. "It's a pleasure to meet you, Mr. Gibbs."

Bubba shook her hand. "Likewise, Miss Thornberry. You don't sound like you're from around here. What makes you stop off in Oriental? I'm sure there're more interesting places you could have picked."

Adelaide laughed and flung her braid off her shoulder to her back.

"That would be a Boston accent you detect, and I needed a break from performing. The first night the boat was here I was drawn to this town, or maybe it was the water, or the friendly people. I'm not sure, but when I saw the flyer advertising the temporary manager position at the hotel, I knew it was meant to be."

Vivi felt Adelaide's gaze on her, but she looked straight ahead at Bubba, relieved Adelaide hadn't mention suffrage, or that meeting her were two of the reasons she chose to stay.

Adelaide continued, "Being here is like finding the piece of a puzzle you've been searching for and pressing it into place. Anyway, I have a job that includes room and board at the Central Hotel, so I'm here for a while."

She walked to the back door. "I'd better head back, and give you two some time."

"Don't leave on my account," Bubba said. "I've got a few more things to get off the boat." To Vivi he said, "I kept some shrimp for us to have for dinner tonight."

Adelaide already had the door open. "No. I need to go."

"I'll walk you half-way home," Vivi said. "Maybe we can find Goldie on the way and see if she found the mother turtle."

Outside, Bubba veered right to their pier and his boat and then turned back towards them. "Nice to meet you, Miss Thornberry. I'll see you shortly, sweetheart," Bubba said to Vivi.

Adelaide and Vivi headed around the front of the house to the street. "Thanks for having me over," Adelaide said. "It was nice to meet your husband too. Is he often away fishing?"

"Yes, we're apart a lot, especially this time of year, but that's the life of a commercial fisherman. He works hard to provide for our family." That much Vivi could say with conviction. Thankfully Bubba's drinking hadn't interfered with his work.

"I've made the choice to be single for now," Adelaide said, "but the stability and comfort of having someone to share life with must feel good."

Vivi wasn't sure how to respond. And thankfully didn't have to when Adelaide continued. "Can you visit me at the hotel sometime this week? We could have tea on the porch or go for a walk by the river."

"I'd love to. I'm preparing for the start of school, but could stop by in the late afternoon, on my way home one day."

"Mama," Goldie called from behind them.

Vivi and Adelaide stopped and turned back to see Goldie running full speed towards them. Her dress was splattered with dark brown, pluff mud. She stopped short in front of the women. "Daddy's home early and we're having shrimp for dinner."

"I know, sweetie. We just saw him at the house."

Goldie held out a Scotch Bonnet shell. "And look what he brought back for me. It was in one of the shrimp nets."

"That's beautiful," Vivi said, taking the shell and turning it over. She held it out for Adelaide to inspect as well. "Now say good-bye to Miss Adelaide and go help your father unload his boat. I'll be right back and we'll start cleaning the shrimp."

Goldie nodded her head to Adelaide. "Bye, Miss Adelaide." She hugged Vivi and then ran full speed behind the house towards the dock.

Adelaide laughed and they continued their walk. "Does she ever slow down?"

"Oh yes. She's probably been lying in the mud watching that turtle quietly since we last saw her. When she's interested in something she'll slow down and give it her full attention."

"Like you with your father's books," Adelaide said.

Vivi stopped. "Yes. I suppose she is like me in that way. And Adelaide . . ."

"Yes?"

"Thank you for . . ." Vivi hesitated. "Thank you for your kindness when I spoke of my father. It's not often that I let myself think about him."

Adelaide slipped an arm around Vivi's waist and they began walking again. "I'm happy you shared that with me. You shouldn't stop yourself from thinking about your father. I'm sure he was very important to you."

Vivi didn't agree with Adelaide. Thinking and talking about her father only made her sad, and that's exactly what had happened today in the kitchen. "I'd better turn back here, so I can help Goldie clean the shrimp."

"Sure," Adelaide said. "Thanks again for a lovely afternoon. I look forward to seeing you this week."

"Me too," Vivi said.

Vivi slowed her pace on her way home. What an interesting woman; an unmarried singer and suffragette from the north. They were different in many ways, but it was easy to be with Adelaide. She was even comfortable enough to talk about her father, which rarely happened.

The afternoon sun was intense and Vivi paused in the shade of an oak tree. Her week ahead would be full with school preparation, but seeing Adelaide again gave her something to look forward to.

CHAPTER 2

Chapawee covered the last collard seed and sat back on her heels. She'd been on her hands and knees for over an hour planting her fall garden of collards, lettuce, cabbage and some garlic and cilantro for herbs. She wiped her brow with a rag and stuffed it back into her dress pocket. September was only a few days away, but the temperatures were like mid-July in her sunny garden plot.

Chapawee crawled into the grass. Maybe she should stretch her legs out before standing. Frustration crawled through her body. Why couldn't she stand up as effortlessly as she used to? She took a breath, put her legs out in front of her, and wiggled them back and forth to get the blood flowing. She was older and had to do things differently. Being angry only make things worse.

The south wind picked up and cooled the bare skin on her neck and arms. Chapawee leaned back on her hands and noticed the sky, cobalt blue with white clouds puffed like cotton bolls ready for harvest. She lay down on her back, hands folded beneath her head, and watched the clouds shapeshifting, a cotton boll, a turtle and then two jellyfish.

"Chapawee!"

Chapawee sat up on her elbows with a start. Her neighbor, Cora, was charging towards her.

"Cora, what's wrong?" Chapawee asked, sitting upright.

"Oh thank God." Cora put her hands on her knees to catch her breath. "I was coming over to see you and spotted you laid out by your garden and thought . . ." Cora stood up straight and looked towards the creek.

Chapawee smiled and finished her sentence. "You thought I was dead."

"Yes."

"Well, Cora, if one day you find me dead, laid out beside my garden in the sun, you'll know I died happy. Please take care of my garden if that happens. I'd hate it to go to waste."

That would be a lovely way to die, Chapawee thought to herself. She'd prefer that scenario to lying dead under her wool blanket in her cabin. She moved to her hands and knees to get that thought out of her head.

"Since you're here, Cora, can you give me a hand and help me up?"

Cora was ten years younger than Chapawee, and still strong and sturdy. She took Chapawee's left hand and helped her to stand.

"Thank you," Chapawee said, brushing dirt off her dress. "You came at the perfect time."

Cora squeezed her hand. "We have a knack for doing that for one another, don't we?"

Chapawee nodded. "Let's sit on the dock and catch more of the breeze."

The dock had one boat slip for the jon boat Chapawee used to fish and crab, and to run out to the Neuse River for summer sunrises. Her father had built the first dock in this exact location sixty-some years ago when her family arrived on Hungry Mother Creek. It'd been replaced multiple times, sometimes board by board, and sometimes in its entirety after a hurricane.

Chapawee sat at the end of the dock, splashing her feet back and forth in the water to clean off the garden dirt. Cora plopped down beside her.

"You reckon we'll be able to get up from here?" Cora asked, laughing.

Chapawee slapped the top of the piling beside her. "I use this for support and haven't been stuck out here yet."

They sat for a while in companionable silence, Chapawee gently swirling her feet in the water and Cora humming a tune Chapawee didn't recognize, but found comforting. The river grass clicked and rustled in the wind, providing percussion to Cora's song. The afternoon waned and the sunlight softened as it filtered through the trees behind them.

"I've been alive fifty-nine years," Cora said, staring out at the water, "and I still have difficulty reconciling how the world can be beautiful and peaceful like this, and cruel at the same time." Cora's hand lightly fingered the scar that circled from her upper back around to the front of her neck.

Chapawee laid her hand over Cora's, brown skin on black. They knew each other well enough that they didn't have to speak of the trauma they'd both endured.

"That's the way of nature. We can have this," Chapawee said, spreading her hands out in front of her, "or we can have a squall with lightning and high winds."

"I understand that, but what about people? Some are filled with love and others hate, and some are indifferent – not contributing to evil, but not fighting it either."

Chapawee took a breath. "We can't change what others choose," Chapawee said, tucking a loose hair back into her braid, "but when I feel hate rising, I do my best to change the story I'm telling myself which justifies that feeling, though I often fail." Chapawee closed her eyes to appreciate the warmth of the afternoon sun on her face.

"You're right, but God knows I'll have a hard time finding a story that'll convince me to be loving towards some kind of people."

"Not hating someone doesn't mean you have to be friends."

Cora laughed. "Thank goodness for that."

Chapawee brought her braid around her shoulder and brushed the end of it across her palm. They lapsed into comfortable silence again and stared at the water. An expansion in Chapawee's chest told her what she needed to do. She released her braid and turned towards Cora.

"Cora?"

Cora lowered her gaze to Chapawee.

"I'd like to ask you something."

Cora nodded. "Go ahead."

Her certainty vanished. "Do you remember me talking about sitting in a circle with my mother and sister?"

"Sure," Cora said, and then laughed. "I've never told you this, but when I was little, I would sneak through the woods and spy on you when you had your circle."

"So what did you think?"

"I was only about ten and didn't know much. I just thought it was something Indian women did, kind of like my momma would sit in a circle and quilt with some of her friends. I saw the five of you pick up some stick from the middle but I never heard anything you said. A few times it sounded like you were singing something and that scared me and I would run off."

Chapawee laughed. "Those were some of the chants from our tribe."

"Guess you don't do that anymore, now that your sister has died?"

"No. I sit by the tree we used to gather around by myself, but it's not the same. I miss sitting in a circle with other women." Chapawee paused. "What I'd like to ask you is, would you join me in a new circle?"

"But that's for Indian women. Why do you want a colored woman in your circle?"

Chapawee's back hurt from angling herself towards Cora and she shifted to look at the water. A heron strode gracefully in the shallows on the other side of the creek.

"It's true that I've only had a circle with women from my tribe, but there's no taboo against allowing others. There are no Indian women to invite. I'm the only one here."

"But why now?" Cora asked. "Maybe since your people are gone, it's time for the circle to end."

Cora's words knotted Chapawee's stomach. Her reaction solidified her commitment. The circle could not end.

"Cora, have you ever had a deep sense of knowing about something? You didn't need language to think it through, you just knew?"

Cora tilted her head to the right and thought for a moment. "Yes, and one of them was marrying Jeremiah. As stubborn as we both are it didn't make sense for us to marry, but I had that sense of knowing you're talking about, and that sure turned out well." Cora leaned back on her hands and laughed. "Not that we haven't had our differences."

"So you do know what I mean," Chapawee said. "That's how I feel about the circle. I'm meant to do this, and pass the tradition along for women in the future."

"I guess I could come and try it," Cora said, and slapped a mosquito on her arm. "But what exactly do you do? When I was young, I figured it was like an Indian church where you worshiped your gods."

Chapawee kicked the water with her feet. "It's kind of like that, but mostly it's about having a place to speak your truth, tap into your inner wisdom, and have support from other women."

"Chapawee, I already have that with you. Why do I need the circle as well?"

"Imagine the power of sitting, not just with me, but with four women. The connection would be multiplied that much more."

Cora took a deep breath and looked out at the water. "OK. You've convinced me to give it a try."

"Wonderful. Our first circle will be the Saturday after the equinox, at sunrise."

"Who else will be there?" Cora asked.

"I'm still working on that. I hope to invite at least three other women, so you'll find out when you arrive."

"Very mysterious, Chapawee. There's no witchcraft I hope, because if my preacher found out I was involved in anything like that, I'd be thrown out of church for sure."

Chapawee laughed. "No. We're not casting spells or making potions. But women speaking their truth and accessing their wisdom may scare men in the same way."

The two friends locked eyes. "We don't have to worry about that since no men will be there," Cora said.

Chapawee nodded.

"Guess I better get home and heat up some supper." Cora pulled herself up to standing using the piling for support.

Chapawee did the same. "Thanks for coming by. I'm happy you'll be a part of the circle."

"You're welcome. I'll give it a try . . . for you," Cora said, and led the way down the dock.

At the garden, they paused before parting.

Cora smiled. "Have a peaceful evening, Chapawee."

"You too, my friend."

Chapawee watched Cora walk down the worn path between their properties and into the woods that separated their homes. The sun was setting, and Chapawee looked to the west instead of returning to her cabin. The Mother Tree commanded her attention. It was a black silhouette on the orange and pink canvas of the evening sky. The air was still, and the water a mirror that bathed everything in the color of dusk.

The quiet, the light, and the energy of this liminal time of day drew Chapawee to the Mother Tree. She walked the short distance between her garden and the cleared patch in front of her sacred tree. The sky dimmed, and violet, indigo and navy pressed the orange and pink into the horizon. Chapawee took a breath and lifted her arms overhead. She began a slow, marching dance around the circle that she'd marked with stones. She chanted in her mother tongue, the feel and sound of the words a comfort. Chapawee's tempo and volume increased, and her focus narrowed to the movement of her body and her voice. The words and sounds tumbled out easily and the spirit of her mother and sister were with her as she chanted to call the circle once again.

**

One by one, Vivi opened the windows of the second-story schoolroom that had been closed since the first of June. The room smelled musty and was as hot as a furnace, thanks to the trapped August heat. The southwest wind coming through the windows didn't do much to cool the air, but at least got it moving. Vivi loosened the first few buttons of her blouse and rolled her sleeves to her elbows for some relief.

Regardless of the heat, she had work to do and so walked to the trio of boxes by the door. Thank goodness Mr. Woodard had brought them up for her because she couldn't have managed them alone. They were full of new schoolbooks for the 1914-1915 school year. She needed to transfer these to the bookshelves, and then box up the old ones. At three o'clock, the teacher from the colored school was coming to pick them up.

Vivi piled all the new books on the floor. She'd address these later, but wanted things ready for the teacher's arrival. She organized the old schoolbooks into the boxes; history, math and science books were followed by reading primers, children's stories and finally some poetry books, novels and biographies suitable for the upper school students.

Vivi surveyed the bookshelves. She'd kept some of the classics and her favorite authors but was she giving away too much? She looked into the boxes and took out *Pride and Prejudice*, and a book of William Blake's poetry and returned them to her bookshelf.

The breeze lured Vivi to the south-facing window, which also provided a good lookout for the colored teacher and she sat on the windowsill to wait. What was her name again? Vivi pulled the letter from her skirt pocket and looked at the closing: Sadie Bell. Vivi had seen Sadie at a school board meeting, but they'd never spoken. Her letter requesting books was their first contact. Vivi felt good about helping the colored school which had only been open a few years.

The warmth and silence lulled Vivi, and she leaned her head against the window frame, savoring the absence of tension. When Bubba was home, he tried to hide his drinking and she tried to ignore it, hoping time would solve their problems. Slowly, their marriage was slipping into the sinkhole created by their avoidance. Vivi did her best to hide her anger and loneliness from Goldie, but when she was alone, the empty spot carved by her father's death, once filled by Bubba, pained her as intensely as the day he had died.

The clip-clop of hooves brought Vivi back to the present and she saw a cart, pulled by a mule, turn the corner. Seated on the bench were a colored man and woman. Vivi stood when the cart stopped in front of the general store. It must be Sadie and her husband. The school room was above Mr. Woodard's General Store and it would be easier if Vivi were there to greet them. Mr. Woodard wouldn't be an issue – he took colored people's money as easily as whites' – but someone else in the store might question why they were here.

Vivi met Sadie and her husband on the porch of the general store. Sadie was a few inches taller than Vivi and close to the same age. Vivi held out her hand. "You must be Sadie. I'm Vivi." In her peripheral vision she saw several white patrons in the store watching her through the window.

Sadie stepped forward and took Vivi's hand. Her handshake was firm. "Yes. I'm Sadie Bell and this," she said, looking to the man beside her, "is Lucas, my husband. I thought we'd need him to help move the books."

Lucas wasn't much taller than the women, but was broad and solid with muscle. He smiled at Vivi, took off his hat and nodded at her. Vivi returned the smile. "Nice to meet you. Your cart should be fine parked right there. Follow me upstairs to the schoolroom. The boxes are packed and ready to go."

Mr. Woodard intercepted Vivi before she started up the steps. "Everything OK, Miss Vivi? Do you need me to help?" he asked.

"I don't think so. I'm giving some schoolbooks to Mrs. Bell, and her husband," she said, motioning to Lucas, "he'll help us carry them. I'll let you know if we need you."

"OK. I'll be right here," he replied, and moved away from the steps.

Sadie, Lucas and Vivi stepped around the boxes sitting at the door of the schoolroom. "Here you go," Vivi said and gestured towards the boxes. "I hope they'll be useful even though they're five years old." Vivi looked up and met Sadie's eyes. They were light brown and flecked with gold.

"Five years old is better than what we've got," Sadie said. "Thank you for agreeing to pass these on. It'll be nice though when the school board decides the colored children deserve brand new schoolbooks too."

A blush crept up Vivi's neck and deepened the red already there from the heat. She couldn't hide from the fact that she and her students were treated differently because they were white, an uncomfortable truth she'd tried to dilute by donating her books.

Lucas placed a hand on Sadie's upper arm and said, "But the kids will be excited to see these books to start their school year." Sadie relaxed under his touch and squatted to look through the boxes.

Vivi sat on her knees beside Sadie and asked, "Which grade levels do you work with?"

"I teach the 1st through 4th grade and the principal takes 5th-8th."

"I mostly work with the elementary too," Vivi said and reached into the box in front of them. She pulled out one of the reading primers. "The children learned a lot with this one. I think there are five copies in here."

"It doesn't matter how many. We're used to sharing," Sadie said.

Vivi noticed Sadie's eyes go to the bookshelves behind her, mostly empty now except for the books she planned to keep. Sadie stood and walked to the bookshelf. She removed the book of poetry by William Blake.

"William Blake. One of my favorite poets." Sadie turned the pages slowly.

William Blake was also one of Vivi's favorites – the reason she'd kept the book.

"'He who binds himself a joy, does the winged life destroy. He who kisses the joy as it flies, lives in eternity's sunrise.'" Sadie closed her eyes after she read and said, "I love how poets can distill complex and ineffable truth into four simple lines."

"I know. Sometimes I lecture for thirty minutes and I'm not sure if I've said anything substantial, but can read a poem in thirty seconds that bursts with meaning."

Lucas bent down and picked up one of the boxes. "I'll let you ladies talk poetry, and get these boxes down to the cart."

"Thank you, Lucas," Vivi said. "Do you have that book of poetry?" she asked Sadie.

"No, but I have a journal where I record my favorite poems."

Vivi reached down to the bottom shelf and pulled out *Leaves of*

Grass, by Walt Whitman. She handed it to Sadie along with William Blake's collection. "Please. Take these with you to use. Your love of poetry may rub off on your students."

"Are you sure?" Sadie asked. "What will you use?"

Vivi thought of her bookshelves at home and her mother's house, the time she'd passed as a child reading in her father's study and the hours she'd spent reading to Goldie. Books were a staple in her life, like coffee, water, and johnny cakes on Sunday morning. She'd never thought of it as a luxury.

"Please, I want you to have them," Vivi said. "I taught William Blake and Walt Whitman last year and won't need them this semester." Vivi also knew she could talk with Hilda from the women's club and they'd help her get more poetry books. She wondered if they donated books to the colored school too.

"Thank you," Sadie said, and wedged the books into the side of the last box.

Lucas stepped into the classroom. His shirt was wet and clung to his chest, and sweat rolled from his hairline down both sides of his face. He pulled a red bandana from his pocket and mopped his brow. "Glad this is the last one," he said, bending to pick up the box containing the poetry books.

He set it in the cart next to the others. "Thanks for helping, Lucas," Vivi said. "I'm sorry my husband wasn't here to give you a hand." Bubba was still home looking for a new crewman, but she hadn't been able to find him this morning to ask for help.

Lucas retrieved his hat from the seat of the cart and tipped it again at Vivi before putting it back on. "I was happy to help." He reached over and pinched Sadie on her arm. "Not that I had much of a choice anyway."

Sadie swatted his arm and smiled. "Come on, Mr. Bell. Let's get these books to the school so we can get home. The kids are probably wearing their granny out."

"You have children?" Vivi asked as Sadie stepped up into the cart.

"Yes. A son and daughter, Rose and Jake. Rose is eight and Jake is five. I'm sure they've depleted my mother's energy by now."

Vivi smiled. "They must keep you busy. I just have one, Goldie. She's eleven."

Sadie nodded, but didn't add more.

"It was nice to meet you both." Vivi shifted from one foot to the other, unsure of what to say next. Their schools were only a few miles apart, but would they have an occasion to speak again?

"Have a good afternoon," Sadie said, ending Vivi's dilemma. Lucas slapped the reins against the mule's neck and they drove off.

Vivi watched their cart heading west until they were almost out of sight. The positive feeling she'd expected was absent. Sure, she'd made a difference for this school year by donating the books, but it wasn't solving anything long term. Sweat ran down her back and urged Vivi inside, out of the heat. She wouldn't solve these problems standing on the porch, and needed to finish organizing her books so she could meet Adelaide at the hotel for an iced tea. The thought of Adelaide counterbalanced her discomfort and she hurried upstairs to finish her work.

***

It was too hot to light the stove so Vivi set out a simple, cold supper of ham, potato salad, sliced tomatoes and some biscuits left over from breakfast.

"Goldie, please come in and set the table."

Goldie sat on the back steps staring out at Camp Creek.

"Goldie," Vivi repeated.

"Yes, Ma'am."

"Have you seen your father lately?" Vivi had been home from her visit with Adelaide for over an hour and hadn't seen Bubba.

"No. Not since lunch."

Vivi turned away so Goldie wouldn't see her anger. Bubba was probably drinking.

"Want me to go out to his boat and tell him dinner's ready?"

"No. He'll turn up when he's hungry enough."

Vivi didn't want Goldie to see her father drinking, and he probably wasn't on his boat. In early spring she'd gone to the shed they had at the edge of their property. While she was rummaging for the garden tools she found a pile of empty bottles under a burlap sack. There was a chair that hadn't been there before, pulled near the small window that looked out at the creek.

During the fall and winter she'd tolerated Bubba's moods, withdrawal, and the alcohol on his breath at night, but it'd been almost a year since his brother had drowned. She and Goldie needed him. That night she'd confronted Bubba about the shed, accusing him of choosing to sit there, instead of spending time with her and Goldie. He got defensive and said he needed time alone to deal with his brother's death, something she wouldn't understand as an only child. Since then, she didn't speak about his drinking, and he didn't speak about his brother. There was less conflict, but no connection. Together they managed the household and cared for Goldie, but otherwise Vivi was alone.

"Here are my beautiful girls."

"Hey, Daddy."

Bubba's speech had an exaggerated precision that Vivi knew was an attempt to hide his slur. She took three glasses from the cabinet and neutralized her facial expression before turning. "Goldie, put these glasses on the table and we're ready to eat."

"Hey, Vivi. How was your day?" Bubba took an awkward step towards her, his arms open. The green eyes that used to light up when he saw her, were tinged with red. Vivi stepped around him and placed three dinner plates on the table. She would ignore the fact he was drunk, but couldn't bring herself to hug him.

Bubba dropped his arms and plopped down hard in the chair at the head of the table. Vivi prayed he made it through the meal without a major gaffe. After having her childhood shattered by heartbreak, she desperately wanted to protect Goldie. Goldie had noticed that her father had been more quiet since Uncle Ray had died, but nothing else, and Vivi didn't want to say anything disparaging about Bubba to her.

"How was school today?" Bubba asked Goldie after everyone had filled their plates.

Goldie cocked her head to the side. "Daddy, I don't go back to school until next Tuesday, after Labor Day."

"I was the one who went into school today. Not Goldie," Vivi said, keeping her voice even.

"Oh." Bubba reached for another biscuit and knocked his glass of water over, drenching the food on his plate.

"Dammit!" Bubba jumped up and threw his napkin on the table.

Vivi swooped in with a towel, aware that Goldie was sitting stock still in reaction to Bubba's curse, something she wasn't accustomed to hearing.

"I'm not hungry anymore," Bubba said at the threshold of the back door.

Part of Vivi wanted him to leave, but another wanted him to finish out their dinner as normally as possible.

"Bubba, it was only water. We have plenty of food. I'll fix you another plate."

"Water." Bubba spit that word out like poison and Vivi tensed. "It was water that killed Ray."

Vivi opened her mouth to say something to calm him, but Bubba cut her off. "And one year ago today Ray drowned, but it doesn't seem that you care," he said directly to Vivi. "You couldn't even give me a goddamn hug or ask me how I was doing." Bubba stormed out the back door, past the pier and in the direction of the shed.

Goldie hadn't moved from her place at the table and now fat teardrops fell onto her plate. The sight of them incensed Vivi. Goldie ran upstairs and slammed her bedroom door before Vivi could comfort her. His last words echoed in her mind despite her anger. "You couldn't even give me a hug, or ask how I was doing." Perhaps she played a role in Bubba's behavior too. Vivi silently cleared away their uneaten dinner.

CHAPTER 3

The minister's voice rose and fell. Vivi tapped her feet to stay awake, and stared at the rainbow the stained-glass window had thrown on the floor beside her. She panned the sermon for gold, keeping the nuggets about grace, and letting the sin and judgment fall through. There was enough suffering in life, and she wanted God to lift her above this, not exacerbate it.

The wooden pew was uncomfortable, and Vivi shifted, her shoulder brushing her mother's. Her mother leaned into her, a gentle acknowledgment, but kept her eyes on the minister. Her mother was always there. Even after her father's death, she never got so mired in her grief that she couldn't comfort Vivi. She also didn't lower her expectations of Vivi after her father died. In fact, more was expected because there were only two of them to care for the home, garden, horses, and to figure out how to pay their bills. Several times, Vivi had tested her mother, shirking a chore or not coming home for dinner, but she was disciplined with more tasks, or even worse, a day without reading.

She'd quickly learned that fulfilling her responsibilities earned her freedom. Vivi smiled. Maybe her idea of God was based on her mother; unconditional love, and the capacity to forgive, with expectations to do your best and contribute. Vivi's smile faded. If she was honest, her recent behavior in her marriage didn't follow her mother's example.

The people in the pew in front of her stood, startling Vivi. Had she missed the benediction? And what about the last hymn? She didn't remember standing to sing, but if she hadn't her mother would have prompted her.

"You were day-dreaming again, weren't you?" her mother asked.

"I guess so," Vivi said. The church hummed with quiet conversation as congregants made their way out. Vivi leaned into her mother and whispered, "I tried to pay attention but my thoughts were distracting." And because of them, I'm actually leaving church with something to think about, Vivi mused to herself.

At the end of the pew Vivi's mother turned back and said, "You're like your father that way. Maybe you should write down some of your thoughts. Share them with others."

Vivi unconsciously gritted her teeth. This wasn't the first time her mother had encouraged her to write. "I'll think about it, Mom. It's hard to find the time with work, Goldie, and now that Bubba . . ." She didn't finish her sentence. Her mother knew what she was going to say.

Vivi and her mother walked side-by-side towards the double doors of the church, wide open to the morning sun. They walked into the light as they left, and Vivi smiled at the paradox. In front of the church they shook hands with the minister and Vivi watched for Goldie in the crowd of children coming from the side door.

"Vivi, you know your ability to write is a gift. A gift your father also had."

She wasn't giving up on this topic, Vivi realized.

"It would be a shame for you not to use it. And, if you get those thoughts out of your head, maybe you'd pay more attention to the moment you're in." Her mother took her arm for emphasis.

Goldie broke away from her friends and joined them. "What's for lunch? I'm starving."

Vivi silently thanked Goldie for the interruption. Her mother's words hung in the air though, and Vivi batted them away, not sure she wanted to commit her thoughts to paper.

***

Chapawee leaned into the broad trunk of the pine and watched Etta's house. Vivi was there for Sunday lunch, and Chapawee was waiting for them to come outside when Vivi left.

Shortly after she'd set the intention to call the circle, Chapawee thought of inviting Etta and Vivi to be a part of it. Etta was close to her daughter's age and they'd occasionally played together when Chapawee and her husband took fish to Etta's father, who ran the fish market.

Their families' lives intersected regularly because of the trade, but also when Etta's mother exchanged coffee and cornmeal for Chapawee's vegetables and herbs. After Etta's husband died, Chapawee reinstated this exchange, and occasionally left a rabbit or fox she'd trapped so Etta and Vivi would have fresh meat. In the last few years Chapawee's garden had shrunk and she had less to share, but Etta continued to be generous with her gifts of staple foods. Through this exchange, she and Etta already had a connection, and though Chapawee didn't know Vivi well, she wanted to include her to maintain the mother-daughter relationship that'd always been a part of the circle.

Chapawee hoped the right words of invitation would come to her today. They came easily when she talked with Cora, but Cora was like a sister. A screen door creaked and Vivi, Goldie and Etta came out onto the front porch.

Chapawee walked across the street, self-conscious about approaching Etta's home. She was Indian, and Etta was white, and walking up to the front porch on a Sunday afternoon was different than delivering vegetables at sunrise. Chapawee thought of the Mother Tree, her sitting there with her sister and mother, and her stride lengthened. This was what she was supposed to do.

Etta saw Chapawee approaching and waved. "Chapawee, what a nice surprise to see you." She descended the front porch steps and met her in the front yard. "We've just finished lunch but there's plenty if you'd like some."

Vivi and Goldie came up behind Etta, and Chapawee smiled at them.

"Goldie," Vivi said, "this is Miss Chapawee, one of grandmother's friends."

Goldie didn't move and Chapawee felt her appraisal and the questions she was too polite to ask. Most likely she'd never seen an Indian before.

"It's nice to meet you Goldie," Chapawee said. "I appreciate the lunch invitation Etta, but I came to talk with you, and you too," she said, looking at Vivi.

Etta and Vivi exchanged questioning looks and then Etta said, "Of course. Please come up to the porch and sit. Goldie, why don't you go inside and read something from your grandfather's library?"

"But why can't I stay?" Goldie put her hands on her hips for emphasis.

"Goldie, listen to your grandmother." The screen door slammed behind Goldie and she stomped down the hall.

Etta motioned Chapawee to one of the chairs on the front porch and she took the other, while Vivi sat on the porch swing. "Is everything all right?" Etta asked. "Do you need our help?"

Chapawee was bothered that Etta thought she was here to ask for something, but then their relationship had always been based on the exchange of goods and nothing deeper. She took a breath and created a moment of silence so her words had a space to fall.

"In a fashion, you can help. You can help me continue a ritual that's been a part of my family for generations."

Etta and Vivi leaned towards her.

"When my parents moved to the Neuse River, my mother continued the practice our people had of women meeting in council, in a circle, where leadership was equal and shared, where women could discern what was best for them, their families and their tribes."

Chapawee paused to make room for the questions she saw on Etta's and Vivi's faces.

"Just the women met?" Vivi asked.

"Yes. Only the women."

Etta reached out and took Vivi's hand. "Like us, Vivi. We were only two, but you and I made many decisions together, without a man, after your father died."

Chapawee saw the connection between Etta and Vivi. She'd made the right choice. The way of the circle would come naturally to them. "My mother called the first circle beside the live oak near our cabin on Hungry Mother Creek. Since I was a young woman I've sat there with my mother, sister, daughter, niece and other Neusiok women, but now everyone is gone and I sit there alone." Chapawee paused. "The power is stronger when other women are present."

With her hands held out in front of her, palms upward, Chapawee said, "I'd like to invite you to join my circle by our sacred tree, the Mother Tree."

Vivi and Etta looked at one another and back at Chapawee. She knew she'd taken them by surprise. "I'm sure you have questions."

Etta began. "I'm honored for the invitation, but we're not Indian. This is not our tradition. I don't know. I'm Christian and . . ." Etta hesitated. "It wouldn't be right."

Vivi answered before Chapawee could. "Mother, you just said that you and I did things similar to the circle, so how could it be wrong? I don't hear Chapawee saying we have to renounce any of our beliefs. Am I correct?"

Chapawee smiled at Vivi's enthusiasm. "Yes. You are. The circle is not about a set of beliefs. The circle is a place to speak truthfully, set intentions, and find solutions. You tap into your inner wisdom using the energy of the women present, the women who've sat there before, and the Great Spirit, or what you call God."

"You've been there many years all alone," Etta said. "Why do you need the circle now?"

Chapawee sat back in her chair. She hadn't expected to talk about this. She looked Etta in the eye. "Etta, my time here is short, and before I die, I must teach the way of the circle. The Mother Tree, the ground around her, and the waters of the Neuse are sacred and I don't want women to lose this connection after I'm gone." After a pause to let these thoughts settle, Chapawee continued, "The circle meets at sunrise on the solstices and equinoxes, just four times a year. The fall equinox is next Thursday, but we'll meet Saturday morning when you're not teaching, Vivi."

Chapawee knew they wanted to confer, but since the equinox was less than a week away, she didn't want to leave without an answer. Chapawee waited. The porch swing creaked with the gentle motion Vivi created. Etta drummed her fingers on the armrest of her chair and the silence between the women lengthened.

Finally, Vivi planted her feet to stop the swing and said, "I can't speak for Mother," she glanced towards Etta, "but I would be honored to be a part of your circle."

Chapawee exhaled. She and Vivi immediately looked to Etta.

Etta looked towards the street and then at Chapawee. "I'll come next Saturday and then see after that."

Chapawee bowed her head slightly and said, "Thank you." She looked at Etta. "You know where my cabin is. We'll meet there and walk to the Mother Tree. If you leave at dawn you should arrive at my place just before sunrise."

Chapawee stood and the other women followed. "I'll see you next

Saturday," Chapawee said, then walked down the steps into the yard. Her nerves, held at bay on the porch, released and she wiped a drop of sweat from her brow line. She'd called the circle and all the women had agreed to come next Saturday.

The first step was complete.

"Chapawee," Vivi called.

Chapawee paused and turned back to the porch.

"Will there only be the three of us at the circle?"

"No. There will be five women." She waved goodbye and walked quickly to the street, avoiding further questions. She was clear about who needed to be in the circle and wanted the five of them to be seated by The Mother Tree, inches from one another, before they could make a judgment about who she'd invited.

***

Vivi watched Chapawee walk away and turned to her mother. "I wonder who the other two women will be?"

Etta sat down and Vivi sat beside her in the chair Chapawee had vacated. "I don't know. I think Faith Stevens buys herbs from Chapawee sometimes. Maybe she'll be one of the other women, but I can't imagine who else would be willing to do this."

Etta paused and Vivi used this chance to speak. "I know you're hesitant about going Saturday, but I'm intrigued. Chapawee said the purpose of the circle is to speak truthfully, set intentions and find solutions. I want things to be different in my life, but I get busy and never make any changes." She was going through the motions of life, waiting for Bubba to stop drinking before she could be happy. "Maybe a circle of women could help me."

Vivi knew what her mother was going to say. "But Vivi, that's what church is for. I wonder what Preacher Bray would say about us sitting in a circle with an Indian woman?"

Vivi stood and opened the screen door. "Goldie! Finish up what you're reading. We're leaving in a minute." She turned back to her mother. "First of all, if we don't tell him, I highly doubt he'll find out and second of all, if he does, there's no reason to be upset. If sitting in a circle of women is threatening to him, then his beliefs are not as strong as he professes."

"Vivi," her mother said. "I know you've never gotten as much from his sermons as I have, but there's no need to be disrespectful."

Vivi didn't want to quarrel. They'd had similar versions of this discussion over the years and it never changed their opinions or experiences in church.

"Mother, thanks for agreeing to go to the circle." Vivi embraced her and then stepped back and held both her hands. "See how you feel Saturday and if you're uncomfortable you don't have to go back again."

Her mother smiled and squeezed her hands. The screen door slammed.

"What were y'all talking about with the Indian woman?" Goldie asked.

"I'll tell you on the way home," Vivi said.

Goldie took the porch steps two at a time. "I hope Daddy's awake when we get there so we can go fishing."

"It's almost 2 o'clock. Of course he'll be awake," Etta said.

Vivi heard judgement in her mother's voice. She rarely talked with her about Bubba's drinking, partly because of her habit of ignoring it, and partly because of the shame that she had chosen a husband who didn't live up to her father.

"He didn't feel well this morning and slept for a few extra hours," Vivi said. "Goldie, don't forget to hug your grandmother good-bye."

Goldie ran up the steps to hug Etta. "Thanks for lunch, Grandmother.

If I catch fish later, I'll bring you some."

Etta kissed Goldie on her cheek. "I'll look forward to that, because you always catch something."

"Bye, Mother. I'll see you Wednesday night at church and we can set up a time to leave for Chapawee's on Saturday."

Goldie ran ahead, now focused on fishing with her father this afternoon. Chapawee's description of the circle monopolized Vivi's thoughts. Speak truthfully. Set intentions. Find solutions. Something needed to change to relieve her sense of emptiness and improve her marriage. Maybe the circle would help.

In the past month, she'd met Adelaide and now had the invitation to Chapawee's circle. These events were a variation from the routine that had numbed her. Vivi's mind hummed with possibilities, and for a change, curiosity fueled her thoughts instead of anxiety. She lifted her skirt and ran to catch up to Goldie.

CHAPTER 4

Chapawee lit the kerosene lantern and took it outside to her porch railing. She imagined the women wouldn't arrive until there was more light, but just in case, this would show the way. The sky was clear and speckled with stars, and the air held the crispness of fall. A faint glow emanated in the east and Chapawee hoped that Etta, Vivi and Sadie were starting the ride to her cabin. It would take about twenty minutes on horseback from town, although Sadie had a shorter distance living just outside the town limit. Cora, her neighbor since she was a child, only had a short walk.

Cora, Etta and Vivi had come to mind quickly, but it had taken longer to find the fifth woman for the circle. Five women easily created the shape of a circle, whereas four formed more of a square, and the energy didn't flow as well. Chapawee mentioned her dilemma to Cora who immediately suggested Sadie. Despite only having casual conversations with Sadie at the colored general store, she trusted Cora's intuition. Thankfully, with some persuasion from Cora, Sadie agreed to come.

Chapawee went back inside and opened the door of her pot-belly stove to watch the flames. She needed something to calm her unsettled mind. At sunrise, a circle of women would meet again around the trunk of the Mother Tree. These women were not Neuseiok, and it was her responsibility to teach them the way of the circle. She couldn't do that with thoughts darting around like bees in a frenzy. She needed to be calm, focused, and able to connect with the Great Spirit and the energies of her ancestors.

It was difficult to discern the best ritual for women who'd never gathered in a circle before. What was second nature to her, would be foreign to them. She remembered going to the women's circle when she was only four or five, sitting silently beside her mother or playing with her sister nearby. When she first participated as a young woman she was familiar with what would happen in the circle, and because she was with family and women she'd known all her life, trust was easily established.

Things were very different this morning. The women were not all related, part of the same tribe, or even the same skin color. She would be the only Indian, Sadie and Cora were colored, and Vivi and Etta were white. She was unaware of any time where Indian, white and colored women interacted in a truly equal setting. Cora was in a subservient position with the white woman she kept house for; she'd seen Sadie and Vivi together, but it was when Sadie had collected the white children's secondhand books. Sadie had the need and Vivi fulfilled it. Of course, Chapawee had known Etta for over twenty years and they were friendly and helpful with each other, but nothing deeper than that.

Chapawee stood and paced her kitchen floor. Had she made a mistake? Would she be able to create a supportive environment that connected the women? Selfishly, she wanted to experience the power of sitting in a circle again, but she also wanted to pass the sacred work of the circle forward, and use it to help the women see their differences as a strength, not an obstacle.

Chapawee paused and peered out the window beside her front door, but no one was in sight. It would work as long as the women connected to their true feelings, and then had the courage to share them. She hoped that filament of personal truth would weave the women together, and they would see past skin color and stereotypes, and connect as humans.

A movement caught Chapawee's eye and Cora walked into the circle of lantern light on her porch. Chapawee opened the door to greet her and heard the thump of horse hooves close by. Her heart rate accelerated in anticipation. She'd called the circle, and they were here. Now she must trust her instinct and the guidance of her ancestors to make it a success.

***

Vivi tucked her legs beneath her and smoothed her dress over her knees. Chapawee had warned them that they'd be sitting on the ground so she had worn her most simple dress and, thankfully, had thought to bring a light shawl to ward off the cool morning temperature. To Vivi's immediate right was Sadie, the colored schoolteacher she'd met a few weeks ago, and to her left was Chapawee. On the other side of Chapawee was Cora, Chapawee's neighbor, a colored woman also. Vivi had never seen her before, but Chapawee said she worked as a domestic for the Swindell family here in Kershaw, so she probably didn't come to town much. Next to Cora was Vivi's mother, who looked calm and assured despite the deep reservations she had about being here.

The woods beside Hungry Mother Creek were glowing in anticipation of the sunrise. Chapawee bent over the fire laid in the middle of the circle and brought it to life with an ember from her kitchen stove. Vivi sat silently with a mix of unease and positive expectations. Just sitting in the woods at sunrise was a new experience for her, therefore being here with her mother, two colored women and an Indian woman was surreal. She remembered the words Chapawee had used to describe the circle: "a place to speak truthfully, set intentions, and find solutions. A place where you tap into your inner wisdom using the energy of the women present."

She looked around the circle at Cora, Sadie and her mother. No one made eye contact as they watched the flames take hold at the base of the fire. How would Chapawee take this group and create a connection?

Except for Vivi and her mother, there seemed to be more differences than commonality.

Chapawee finished with the fire and took her place in the circle. All the women's eyes went to her, waiting for instruction, but Chapawee was silent. She held a thick stick, shiny and worn from use. Vivi shifted her weight under her, uncomfortable sitting on the ground, and with the silence. She was used to quiet in the evenings when Bubba was on the boat, and Goldie was asleep, but to be in the presence of others without interacting felt unnatural. Chapawee's chest rose and fell with her breathing and Vivi took this as unspoken instructions. She closed her eyes and focused on the sounds around her, the crackle and pop from the fire, the rustle of leaves, and the birdsong that reached a crescendo with the morning light.

"Thank you, ladies, for coming this morning."

Vivi opened her eyes.

Chapawee continued. "I imagine sitting here for the first time feels uncomfortable for you all, but to me it's a great comfort. The women of my family have been gathering in a circle beside Hungry Mother Creek for over fifty years." Chapawee pointed to the live oak directly across from her. "This is The Mother Tree, also a part of the circle. She was a sprouting acorn the first spring we met and by the second spring she was almost four feet tall. My mother took her presence as a sign we'd selected a sacred spot for our circle. We named her The Mother Tree, knowing she'd be here long after we were gone and would continue to mother the circles that sat beside her."

Vivi glanced at her mother, knowing the talk of a tree as a mother would disturb her. She caught her mother's gaze and held it for a few seconds and then she looked at the tree. She'd only thought of a tree as a tree, a beautiful creation, but not possessing the animate qualities of a mother. She stared at the bark on the trunk, the lower limbs reaching

45

just above Sadie's head and thought of the cross on the wall at church. Perhaps this tree served as a symbol for the Indians, like the cross did with Christians.

Chapawee pointed east, which was in front of Vivi, and just off to her left. "The sunrise has reached us," she stated, and as if her words had summoned it, the sun elevated above the trees on the other side of the creek. "It's time to begin."

Vivi's heart rate picked up. Begin what? Maybe she'd made a mistake accepting this invitation and pressuring her mother to attend. Would she be able to speak truthfully with women who were from such different backgrounds? Sadie repositioned herself beside Vivi who wondered if she had similar doubts.

"I've shared with each of you the essence of the circle," Chapawee said, redirecting Vivi's attention. "The focus of each gathering is a ritual which changes based on the seasons and the needs of the women present. The common factor in any of these rituals is to speak truthfully, from your heart. This opens the door to your inner wisdom. Today is the first time we've sat together, and for some of you it's the first time you've met, and I thought a simple ritual would be best." Chapawee paused and looked around the circle, making eye contact with each woman. "I ask that each of you share a word, or short phrase that best describes where you are in life, or how you've been feeling. If something just popped into your mind, then you already have your answer."

Vivi swallowed. How did Chapawee know that a word had immediately come to mind? She needed to think about this more. That word didn't make sense to her.

Chapawee held up the stick she'd been holding and said, "This is our talking stick. Whomever has the stick is the speaker and has everyone's attention. When the speaker finishes she puts the talking stick back into the circle for the next woman. When each of us shares, there will be no comments, judgments or questions, only the power of your words being received by the circle, and of course, The Mother Tree," Chapawee said with a smile, and pointed the talking stick towards the tree.

"We'll start with ten breaths in silence, four for the four seasons, five for each of us present and one for The Mother Tree. I'll start with the talking stick and when I'm done whoever is moved to speak will pick up the stick to share."

The fire had died down and Chapawee added several sticks and a split log from a pile just behind her. Vivi kept her eyes on the fire and tried to focus on counting her breaths but her racing thoughts distracted her. This was different from anything she'd ever done. She'd been part of a circle at church but they focused on a Bible verse or parable, or church activities. If they spoke of personal things it was related to what they were doing, not how they were feeling. In fact, she rarely discussed her interior life with anyone, except on occasion with her mother, but even then she put a positive spin on things so as not to make her mother worry. Would it be safe to be fully honest here? Part of Vivi wanted to run back to her horse and ride away.

Chapawee cleared her throat and picked up the talking stick. "Before I share, I want to acknowledge that it may be difficult for you to not respond to what the others say. Our instinct is to offer solutions, or comfort, and that does happen in the circle, but with silence and presence, not words."

Immediately Vivi thought of her and her mother sitting on the front porch or by the fire in silence after her father died. No words would have eased their pain, but their silence and companionship did. With that memory, Vivi's shoulders relaxed and she took a deep breath. Maybe this wouldn't feel as foreign as she'd thought.

"Now, on to the ritual and how I'm feeling at this point in my life," Chapawee said. "The first word that came to me was ancestor. I want to be a good ancestor, and leave wisdom and knowledge as my legacy. I also realize that soon I will join my ancestors and I'm trying to befriend death rather than fear it."

What did she mean, "befriend death"? Vivi thought. She'd never heard anyone talk about death this way. Fighting to stay alive, not surrendering, was the message she'd received, but at her age, with Goldie to care for, that perspective made sense. What about her father? Did he have the choice to fight or befriend death, or did it swoop in and claim him with no options? Vivi struggled for her next breath. She'd been there with him and all she remembered was that he was there and then he was gone.

"One of the reasons for calling this circle is to pass along the tradition, and teach you about its power," Chapawee said, drawing Vivi's attention back. "I hope this sacred ritual on Hungry Mother Creek will continue for years to come." Chapawee raised her eyes toward the sky. "And personally, I want to experience the power of the circle energy again. Sitting here under the Mother Tree with a circle of women opens me up in a way I can't replicate alone, and connects me to my ancestors who've sat here before." A blue heron honked by the creek and Chapawee bowed her head slightly and placed the stick near the fire in the center of the circle.

The women held the silence. Vivi reviewed what Chapawee had shared and wondered how sitting in a circle with four women she barely knew would help her connect to her ancestors. It didn't seem logical, but then Vivi remembered the comforting sense of her father's presence when she would read or write at his desk after his death. That wasn't logical either. Maybe what Chapawee was talking about was similar, and Vivi should experience the circle before she passed judgment.

Sunlight from the east lit the lower half of the woods and in contrast to the silence amongst the women, the air around them was alive with the morning cacophony of birdsong, squirrels dashing through leaves, and a hawk calling in the distance.

Maybe because it was closest to her, or because she was the next eldest, Cora leaned in and retrieved the talking stick. She sat cross-legged, with her dress pulled over her knees and her eyes lowered. Finally she glanced up at Sadie, and Vivi saw something pass between them she couldn't interpret.

In the silence, Vivi studied Cora. She was slightly older than her mother, maybe late 50's and at the back of her head was a bun with wisps of gray hair scattered amongst the black. The sleeves of her dress were pushed up to her elbows, revealing muscled forearms. Cora looked over Vivi's head into the woods behind her.

Finally, Cora took a breath and began. "Content. That would best describe my life now. Since I was five, helping my momma keep house at the Kenan plantation, I've worked from sunup to sundown, and often into the night."

The word plantation pierced Vivi. Cora, almost the same age as her mother, had been born into slavery. Even with her father's death, Vivi's life was one of relative ease compared to Cora's. Guilt and shame competed for her attention, but she refocused on Cora's voice, honoring Chapawee's instructions.

"Since Mr. Swindell died three years back, my work has been lighter. Miss Betty is happy eating leftovers for supper, and I leave before dark. I have time to quilt and make supper for me and Jeremiah. He's home from the lumber mill before I even get there, so for the first time in our lives we have time and energy to enjoy evenings together."

Cora paused, looked down at the fire and then back into the trees behind Vivi. "I guess that's it. I'm grateful for the peace and simplicity in my life now."

Sadie repositioned herself, drawing Vivi's attention. She noticed Sadie's hands were clenched into fists and her chest rose and fell with deep breaths. Sadie looked her way and immediately unclenched her fists and folded her hands in her lap. Vivi looked back at the fire but remained aware of Sadie beside her. She recognized the look Sadie had on her face. She was bursting to say something but holding back. This was easy for Vivi to see because it was something she did daily with Bubba, holding back the questions and complaints.

In the silence Vivi wondered if she should talk about her marriage, but kept returning to her first reaction when Chapawee posed the question of where she was in life. The other responses that came to her later were the well-rehearsed answers she usually gave when asked how she was, but Chapawee had made it clear that speaking the truth was what made the circle special.

Her mother leaned in and picked up the talking stick which surprised Vivi. Because she'd influenced her mother to come, she'd expected her to wait to speak. She wondered what her mother would share, and expected it to be similar to Cora's feeling of contentment, or even happiness. Her mother was always optimistic and it was she Vivi sought out when she herself was sad or discouraged.

Etta turned the talking stick vertically and draped her hands over the top end. Her blonde hair glinted in the sunlight now streaming through the trees. She looked directly at Vivi for a moment and then said, "Chapawee, thank you for that question. I'm asked almost every day, 'How are you?', but never with the sincerity and intention that you did. It made me reflect more deeply."

Her mother had had the same reaction she'd had, Vivi thought. That the circle required more than the socially expected response.

Etta dropped the talking stick into her lap. "If I'm honest, I would have to say I'm lonely."

Vivi's breath caught in her throat. Her mother had never said this to her. She saw Goldie almost every day after school, and Vivi and her mother went to church together and shared several meals a week. How could she be lonely?

Her mother continued as if she'd read Vivi's mind. "Vivi, please don't feel responsible. I cherish time with you and Goldie, and wouldn't change that for the world, but I can't expect you and Goldie to meet all my needs."

What other needs could she have? Vivi immediately thought to herself, but then realized her mother was also a woman, not just a parent and grandmother. Vivi rarely thought of her mother from this perspective.

Her mother continued, "My husband James died seventeen years ago, and although I'll never replace him, I'd like someone to share my life with." Etta paused and looked into the fire. "Even more intimate friendships would be nice. I speak with women, my neighbors and other church members, but there's no one with whom I have a deep connection. It began after James died. I was busy raising Vivi and taking care of our home, land and animals and didn't have time to socialize. I also think that as a single, young widow I was seen as a threat by other women, or at the very least an inconvenience."

Vivi thought of her blossoming friendship with Adelaide. It filled a place in her that she hadn't realized was empty, and her mother wanted to fill that same void in herself.

"Now don't get me wrong, I have much to be grateful for, but loneliness is always in the background of my life." Etta dabbed the corner of her left eye and cleared her throat. "It's a relief to speak about it. Now that I've acknowledged this, I hope to make some changes."

Etta nodded her head to Chapawee, and smiled as she lay the stick beside the fire. Vivi watched her mother and wondered why she'd never shared this with her.

The women held their silence and Etta's words settled. Something in the circle shifted for Vivi after hearing her mother speak so honestly, and she imagined that Chapawee and Cora had done the same. Chapawee placed another split log on the fire. Vivi watched the flames leap and dance in the breeze and made the decision she would share what had first come to her mind, even if she didn't fully understand what it meant. Yet before she could reach for the talking stick, Sadie picked it up.

Sadie sat with her back straight and firm, and twisted the talking stick in her hands. Her rhythmic exhalations and intense gaze into the fire made Vivi wonder if Sadie had the same conundrum of whether to share the deeper truth, or stay safe with the superficial.

Sadie and Cora locked eyes and then Sadie said, "Thank you, Etta. Your honesty has given me courage to do the same."

Sadie had addressed her mother with her first name. The muscles in Vivi's neck and upper back tensed in response. She'd never heard a colored woman address her mother that way, and it was uncomfortable, but why did she expect anything different? Did she think her mother deserved more respect than Cora or Chapawee just because she was white? Her immediate reaction to Sadie's words was answer enough, and Vivi stared into the fire, acknowledging the prejudice she'd tried to hide by being nice, and helpful. It was yet to be determined if the circle would assist her in speaking the truth, but it certainly helped her to acknowledge it.

Sadie tapped one end of the talking stick on the ground. "I am," she paused, "frustrated. I'm frustrated that the children I teach have a schoolhouse that leaks and is so cold in the winter that we must keep our coats and gloves on. And though I'm grateful to Vivi for the used schoolbooks," she said, looking at her, "why do I have to ask the white teacher for her cast-offs? Why don't colored children deserve new books like the white ones? Why does my husband get half the price for his handmade furniture when it's twice as good as any white man's? And how do I explain to my children, the sign by the harbor that says, 'No livestock or coloreds allowed in the water'?" Sadie's voice gained volume with each item she listed.

A weight sat on Vivi's chest, and sweat rolled down her back despite the cool morning air. She thought about Goldie getting secondhand books or being denied the ability to swim in the harbor to better understand Sadie's intensity.

Sadie took a deep breath. "This is not a comfortable emotion and I don't want to dwell here." The women kept their attention on Sadie, and Vivi tried to release her reaction to what Sadie had said to listen deeply, as Chapawee had described.

"I want to use my frustration as motivation to address these injustices, but then I feel insignificant. How can a colored teacher in the rural south make an impact? I guess hopelessness lies beneath my frustration."

Sadie's posture collapsed from an arrow into a curve and she placed the stick between herself and Vivi.

The air palpated with the powerful truth Sadie had shared. Vivi had never heard a colored woman speak like this. She knew it took courage to say what she did, and trust that the women would honor her words and keep them safely in the circle.

Vivi looked at The Mother Tree, knowing she was the only one left to speak. She took a breath and considered what she would say. To honor the circle, the other women, and herself, she must speak the truth. Vivi made eye contact with Sadie and then picked up the talking stick that was waiting for her.

The sun warmed the left side of Vivi's cheek and she let her shawl drop to the ground. A fish jumped in the creek and the morning unfolded with her usual grace, a contrast to Vivi's internal state. She grasped the talking stick for support.

"I'm . . ." Vivi's voice cracked and she cleared her throat. "I'm a little nervous."

Vivi paused and looked out at the water, then continued. "Disconnected. That was the word that immediately came to mind when Chapawee posed her question. I wasn't going to share that because I didn't understand what it meant, but as I've held that word, disconnected, while you all spoke, I know it's the truth."

Vivi rubbed the talking stick gently, and the stubs where branches had once been pricked her palms. What should she say next?

"Disconnected. When I say that aloud I see how it applies to my life," Vivi paused, "and especially to my marriage." She looked around the circle, expecting to see judgement, but there was none. She continued. "I'm completing the tasks expected of me as a wife, mother, teacher, but I'm not engaged with what I'm doing. There's no joy associated with most things, satisfaction occasionally, but no joy. I want to be passionate, excited, and playful, in all areas of my life, but I'm not."

Vivi paused and thought of listening to Adelaide sing and the time they'd spent together. She was more alive with Adelaide, but how could she replicate this in daily life, when Adelaide wasn't around?

"Another word that comes to mind as I speak is boredom. Nothing seems to engage me, and I'm not sure if I need to change my perspective or change how I spend my time or maybe both."

Vivi looked down at the talking stick but no more thoughts presented themselves and she laid it close to Chapawee. The women held the silence, and the truth of what she shared settled over her. She would have expected to feel embarrassed or even ashamed, but instead a buoyancy rose in her chest. It was hope. Giving voice to what she'd been hiding gave her incentive to make things different, despite not knowing where to start.

A log burned through its center and collapsed into the fire, sending sparks into the air. Vivi threw dirt on an ember that landed in front of her. The silence lengthened and all the women looked towards Chapawee, waiting for direction.

***

Chapawee kept her eyes closed. She wasn't ready to break the silence because that was what connected them, and the energy they'd created by speaking truthfully and listening deeply. It was salve to her soul after years of sitting alone by The Mother Tree. She wondered if the others could feel it.

Today was the first circle for the others and Chapawee reminded herself that she was also a teacher. She opened her eyes and took Vivi's hand with her right one and Cora's with her left. Instinctively the other women clasped hands and closed the circle.

"Thank you for your presence this morning," Chapawee said, releasing Cora's and Vivi's hands. "Please keep what's been said this morning in confidence. Take the truth of what you've shared, and ask for clarity about how to proceed. If you're willing, I look forward to sitting with you again in December, on the winter solstice."

Etta and Vivi walked directly to their horses, awkwardly wishing the other women a good day, and then left. Cora and Sadie were behind her, talking in hushed voices.

In the circle, everything had felt right, but now she questioned herself. After they broke the circle there was silence, not the easy conversation she, her sister and mother would have. But then, these women had just met.

"Chapawee," Sadie said, interrupting her thoughts.

"Yes?" Chapawee replied, walking back to where Cora and Sadie were standing.

Neither woman said anything. Cora looked down at the tip of her boots, poking out from under her skirt and Sadie looked over Chapawee's head.

"Is everything alright?" Chapawee asked. "I'm grateful you both came and hope you found some inspiration from our time in the circle."

Sadie took a breath and looked directly at Chapawee. "Thank you for inviting me, and I can see how sitting in a circle is meaningful to you, but I don't know if I can be a part of this again."

Chapawee's heart tightened. Sadie continued. "When we were in the circle I got caught up in the moment and all your talk about speaking truthfully, and I did that, but now I regret it. What if Vivi goes back to the superintendent and tells him of my views and discontent and I get labeled a trouble-maker and lose my job?"

Sadie undid the top button of her blouse. "The whole point of the circle as I understand it is to be honest, but I don't think it's in my best interest to be honest around white women I hardly know." She wiped her forehead with a handkerchief she had in her skirt pocket.

Sadie paused and looked at Cora who remained silent. "And Cora, well, tell Chapawee for yourself."

Chapawee stepped closer to Cora. "Do you feel the same as Sadie?"

Cora nodded in agreement. "Chapawee, you and I've been neighbors most of my life and I know Sadie from church, so I'm comfortable with you two, but I've never met Vivi and Etta. Unlike Sadie, I was on guard the entire time I was in the circle, and because of that I wasn't honest."

Chapawee's heart sank. Had she imagined the connection, her desperation for a circle clouding her perception?

Cora continued, "I was honest about my work. It's the least demanding job I've ever had and for that I'm grateful. But the reason

Jeremiah is home before dark, is because he can only work part of the day because of the back injury he got working on the chain gang fifteen years go. If it wasn't for our sons sending money from Baltimore, we couldn't get by." Cora looked away from Chapawee. "And how can I be content when my boys aren't here? I'd give up that extra money in an instant to have them closer, but there's more opportunity up north."

"I know you miss Abe and Titus. Why didn't you share all this in the circle?"

"Same as Sadie. I can't trust those white women. They seemed kind, but I don't want to complain and draw attention to myself. Jeremiah complained about his wages and the next thing you know they arrested him for stealing a hammer from work and put him on the chain gang."

Cora touched the thin scar that curled around her neck. "I've seen black folk do what's right, and ask for what they deserve, and it doesn't usually end well. I'm with Sadie. I don't know if I can be in this circle with white women, and honor your tradition of truth-telling."

Chapawee took several deep breaths and looked into the woods towards The Mother Tree.

"I can understand why you feel this way. Maybe I should have told you that Vivi and Etta were coming, but I thought you might decline if you knew this."

Sadie and Cora both nodded in agreement.

"I called the circle for my benefit, but also to ensure this ritual isn't lost. I hoped that in the safety of the circle, we could learn to trust one another, and see that although our life experiences are different, we share similar struggles, joys and dreams. I want our circle to build a bridge. Our strength as women is greater when it's combined."

Sadie walked to her horse and untied the reins from the hitching post. "You make a good point, but it seems idealistic that the five of us sitting in a circle as equals will make any difference in the larger world."

"Yes. It is idealistic," Chapawee said and took a few steps closer to Sadie. "But change has to start somewhere, and it might as well be with us. Why don't you both think about this, wait and see if Etta and Vivi maintain the confidentiality of the circle, and then let me know before the winter solstice if you plan on returning."

"That works for me. How about you, Cora?" Sadie asked, mounting her horse.

Cora kicked a rock with her foot and looked at Chapawee. "For you, I will give it some more thought."

Chapawee bowed her head in gratitude. "I'm happy to discuss this more if you need to."

"Thank you," Sadie said. "Bye, Cora. See you tomorrow at church." Sadie turned her horse down the path and trotted around the bend.

Chapawee walked to Cora and took one of her hands. "Thank you for telling me how you feel. I hope you will reconsider."

"I'll let you know when I make my decision." Cora squeezed her hand. "But nothing will change our friendship."

CHAPTER 5

Vivi looked at her watch and then ran the last block to Lula's tea shop to meet Adelaide. She'd been anticipating their meeting all week and couldn't wait to tell her about her experience at the women's circle. With the tea shop in sight, Vivi slowed down and repositioned a bobby pin in her Gibson roll, to capture hair that had escaped during the day.

The front door of Lula's was wide open, taking full advantage of the Indian summer temperatures on this early October afternoon. Vivi pushed opened the screen door and immediately saw Adelaide at a table in the back corner. She was wearing a light blue jumper dress with a white blouse underneath. Even in her most casual clothing, Adelaide looked glamorous compared to Vivi in her schoolteacher attire. Adelaide's face lit up when she saw Vivi, and her heart somersaulted. It'd been a while since Bubba lit up like that when she walked into a room. Adelaide stood when Vivi reached the table, and they embraced briefly.

"Vivi, I'm so happy to see you. I know we've both been busy with our jobs and you with Goldie and Bubba, but I've missed you."

Vivi reached over and squeezed Adelaide's right hand. "And I've missed you. We'll have to figure out a way to see each other more regularly. I have a catalog of things I've been saving to share with you."

The waitress arrived with a tea pot, and two cups and saucers on her tray which she placed on the table.

"Would you ladies care for a scone or one of our oatmeal raisin cookies?"

"No thank you," Vivi said. Tea was enough of a splurge.

"Oh, come on," Adelaide encouraged. "A bit of scone would be perfect. My treat. What kind do you have?"

"Apple cinnamon and fig walnut," Maribel said.

Adelaide looked at Vivi and simultaneously they replied, "Fig and walnut?" and then laughed at their coordinated answer.

The waitress left and Adelaide said, "I've got lots to tell you too, but you start." She poured tea into their cups.

"Remember the circle of women Mother and I were invited to join by Chapawee, the Indian woman?" Vivi asked.

Adelaide nodded her head. "Yes. How was it? It sounded mysterious, meeting at sunrise in the woods."

"It was. I was nervous, but also excited to do something I've never done before."

Adelaide leaned forward. "Who else was there? What did you do?"

Vivi shared the details of that morning, who was there, the history of the circle and the ritual. She left out what the others had said to maintain confidentiality, even though this meant she couldn't use Adelaide to process her reactions to what Cora and Sadie had shared.

"Oh, I love the ritual," Adelaide said. "And may I ask what you shared?" Adelaide's blue eyes stared intently into Vivi's.

Vivi was moved that Adelaide was interested, but sharing words heard only by the circle would violate the trust Chapawee wanted to establish. "We keep the details of what we discuss confidential, but I will say that our friendship provided inspiration for what I shared."

Adelaide smiled. "Well, I'm glad to hear that." She took a sip of her tea. "The silence and how you spoke in turn at the circle reminds me of my Quaker meeting."

"Are you a Quaker?" Vivi asked. She'd heard of some Quakers across the river, but there was no Quaker meeting here, and she knew little about them.

"Yes. Since I left Boston I've only found one Quaker meeting and that was in Elizabeth City, just a few stops before I arrived here. I miss sitting in silence with others and feeling the spirit move amongst us. I wonder if I could go to your next circle."

Vivi tensed. She adored Adelaide, but had already connected to Chapawee, Sadie and Cora, and of course her mother, by the ritual they'd shared. She knew Adelaide's presence would alter things, and if she was honest, a part of her wanted to keep Adelaide to herself.

"We don't meet again until the solstice in December, but from what Chapawee said part of her criteria for invitation was a connection to this area and the Neuse River."

Adelaide laughed. "In other words, no Yankees."

"Well, she didn't use those exact words, but that does sum it up," Vivi said, joining her in laughter.

Vivi took a sip of tea and then lowered her voice and said, "Please hold what I've said in confidence. Some people wouldn't like white, colored and Indian women meeting like this, and I don't want to put any of us at risk, especially Sadie, Cora and Chapawee."

"Of course." Adelaide sat back when the waitress placed the scone between the two of them. After she left, Adelaide continued, "But it's ridiculous you have to think like that. You should be able to spend time with whomever you choose."

Vivi thought about that for a minute. She supposed Adelaide was right, but it had never crossed her mind to spend time with colored women or to be friends with them.

"But Adelaide, this is the South and coloreds and whites have always had separate lives. Even though the experience was positive, it still felt uncomfortable to sit with women of different skin colors."

Adelaide rolled her eyes. "It's not quite this bad in Boston. The white supremacists down here are scared for you to have an opportunity to know your colored neighbors because it wouldn't take long to realize their intellect, hearts and souls, are similar to yours, while also recognizing they bring unique gifts to the world."

Vivi looked around the tea shop to see if anyone had heard Adelaide. Two other tables were occupied, but the women by the door and the couple on the other side of the shop were engrossed in their conversations. Vivi broke off a piece of the scone and washed it down with the orange pekoe tea.

"But the separation between colored and white is entrenched here," Vivi said, "and I'm ashamed to admit that I've never really questioned it."

Before she could finish her thought Adelaide interjected, "Well, I hope you are now!"

"I am." Vivi thought of what Cora and Sadie had shared in the circle. She'd never put herself in the shoes of colored women and tried to understand things from their perspective, until now.

"Are you OK?" Adelaide asked. "You've sure gotten quiet."

"I'm fine, but I'm questioning the beliefs I've grown up with." Vivi took a breath to regain her composure. "My parents taught me to be kind to colored people and help where I can, because they had a more difficult station in life, but . . ." Vivi stared out the screen door and saw a colored woman walk by, holding her young daughter's hand. They couldn't come in for tea and a scone. Why hadn't she thought this was wrong until now? Vivi tapped her fingers on the table.

After several minutes, Adelaide gently covered Vivi's tapping fingers with her hand. "Vivi, you don't have to solve anything today. Your shift in perspective is enough for now."

Adelaide's hand allayed her churning thoughts. "Thank you." She drank the last of her tea. "Well, enough about me. My brain hurts from thinking," Vivi said, and smiled at Adelaide. "What's happening with you?"

Adelaide finished her half of the scone and said, "Well, nothing as intense as a new world view." She squeezed Vivi's hand and then released it. "I've missed performing, and I've decided to have a one woman show. All my gowns and sheet music are with me, and I found a place to perform."

"Pickles Hall?"

"Yes, although I'm not a fan of that name." Adelaide swept her arm above her head, pointing to an imaginary marquee. "Adelaide Thornberry, live at Pickles Hall. Sounds more like an establishment of ill repute," she said playfully.

"Hey! Don't make fun," Vivi said with mock consternation. "Mr. Pickles is well-known in town and helps support the theater, so they named it in his honor."

"Well that's good to know," Adelaide replied with a chuckle. "Anyway, I spoke with the manager and he remembered me from the showboat. I've reserved it for the third weekend in October, a rehearsal Friday and a show on Saturday night."

"Adelaide, that's wonderful! I can't wait to hear you sing again."

"If you're willing, I'd like you and Goldie to help me backstage with my costume changes."

"Oh I'd love to," Vivi said, sliding to the edge of her seat, "and Goldie will be thrilled. We've never been in show business before."

Adelaide poured them more tea and Vivi checked the time. It was already four, but she still had an hour until she needed to pick up Goldie at her mother's.

Adelaide slapped *The Bayboro Sentinel* from her lap onto the table and pointed to a small story in the bottom right corner. "Have you read this? The North Carolina Equal Suffrage Association wants to add more chapters. We need one here. The women I've talked to in passing seem woefully uninformed about women's suffrage. We could change that."

Vivi glanced at the headline. "How do you have the time to think about all these things, racial issues, women's suffrage? By the time I get home from work, take care of Goldie, Bubba, our house and garden there's no time left to change the world." Until the women's circle, she hadn't even taken the time to change herself. Changing social issues had never crossed her mind.

A blush worked its way from Adelaide's neck to her checks and she ran her hands through her hair that was loose and lying over her right shoulder. "I'm sorry, Vivi. I wasn't judging you. I guess I take my time and freedom for granted." She looked down at the empty scone plate. "I don't have a family, or a job that changes people's lives like yours. It's my way of contributing to the world."

"But your songs, Adelaide. They're your contribution."

Adelaide smiled and for a second time placed her hand over Vivi's. "Thank you. I love performing, and hope I make the moment better for those who hear me, but that's not creating lasting change."

Vivi thought about how Adelaide's voice had stirred her heart that night on the showboat, and now, how the warmth of her hand did the same. She met Adelaide's eyes. "I don't agree. I think one experience, even if fleeting like a song, can create lasting change."

"You know, you make a good point," Adelaide said, releasing her hand, "and it supports why we need to start a chapter of the Equal Suffrage Association. A speaker we sponsor, a petition we start, or a news article we write, may be all it takes to change someone's mind about women's right to vote, and if we get the right, we have the power to change laws." Adelaide's face glowed and Vivi absorbed her enthusiasm.

"But Adelaide, do you believe that women should be in politics? Isn't that for the men?"

Adelaide laughed. "It's been for the men until now but that doesn't mean it should stay that way. Women are just as capable as men. Look at your mother. She finished raising you and has taken care of herself all alone. And you, you've got more education than most men around here. You teach children to read for goodness sake, manage your household, and mother Goldie. Women really are more than prepared to vote in my opinion."

Vivi smiled. Adelaide should be a lawyer, given the way she argued her views. She was right though. Vivi managed their household, their budget, Goldie. She was even in charge of the education of most of the children in town. It made sense she should have a voice in who was elected, and the laws that would impact her and the children.

"Let me think about it, Adelaide. I don't have much extra time and I know Bubba wouldn't be happy about me getting involved in politics."

Adelaide pushed her chair back from the table and put a few coins beside the tea pot. "But what would make you happy?"

This question caught Vivi off guard. She couldn't remember the last time someone asked her what made her happy, but she did remember her intention in the women's circle, to be more passionate and engaged in life and here was an opportunity.

"Yes, Adelaide," Vivi said, placing her napkin on the table, "I'll help you."

***

The October sun warmed the decaying leaves on the forest floor, and Chapawee breathed in the musky scent. She squatted, and pulled some weeds near a lettuce plant, watching for Cora out of the corner of her eye. They were meeting to collect wild carrot, a remedy she and Cora sold to the local women, white and colored. Twigs snapped behind her and Cora burst from the woods between their properties in a lope.

"Sorry I'm late. I was quilting and lost track of time." Cora stopped in front of Chapawee and adjusted the burlap sack strung around her shoulder.

Chapawee laughed and quickly embraced her friend. "You're here now, and you gave me time to soak up this gorgeous fall afternoon."

It was three o'clock and the sun was almost at the tree line. The forest on the western side of the path to Kershaw Road glowed. Chapawee spread her arms wide and asked, "Doesn't everything look dipped in gold from the afternoon sunlight?"

Cora laughed. "It sure does, not that I have experience with things dipped in gold."

"You've dipped fabric in goldenrod dye haven't you?"

"Sure. Lots of times," Cora said.

"Well then, I'd say you do have the experience."

They turned left onto Kershaw Road and walked west.

"We have plenty of experience with gold when you look at it that way."

"Sure do," Chapawee said and stopped by a patch of brown, wild carrot plants. She pinched off one of the heads. "We all end up like this," Chapawee murmured, holding up the dry, dead flower, "no matter what kind of gold is in our life."

"So true, my friend," Cora replied, pinching her own dead flower head and dropping it into her sack.

They were silent, and the only sound was the snap of flower stems and the crunch of leaves under their feet as Chapawee and Cora stepped further into the underbrush beside the road. The meditative rhythm of her task, the warmth of the sun on her back and Cora's presence filled Chapawee with contentment. She paused a moment and turned her face towards the sun. Despite all her loss, her husband's early death, her daughter moving away, and the deaths of her mother and sister, there was still abundance in her life. She had to remind herself of this daily. It would be easy for what was absent in her life to overshadow what was present.

"Cora," Chapawee said. "Let's leave plenty to reseed, and move to the patch on the other side of the road."

Cora nodded and crossed the dirt road. They continued their rhythm of picking the dead heads and dropping them into their sacks for another fifteen minutes. Chapawee wanted to ask Cora her thoughts about the women's circle, but decided to wait since it'd only been a week.

"I've got all I can carry," Cora said, holding out the burlap sack for Chapawee to see.

"Me too. Let's head back, and while we still have daylight, we can collect the seeds."

At Chapawee's, they walked to the back of her cabin to the wooden table she used for working with her herbs and medicinal plants.

Cora threw her sack on the table. "A bag of dried flowers is way lighter than one filled with cotton."

Chapawee didn't say anything. She was lucky she'd never had to pick someone else's cash crop. Her family had always grown, trapped or caught what they needed to survive, and traded the remainder for the staples they couldn't grow. If they needed extra money for something, her father occasionally worked a season for Mr. Wade who used to own Magnolia Bend Plantation. Now Chapawee supplemented her income with the money she made from her natural remedy. It wasn't much, because she gave away more than she sold, but it helped. She was teaching Cora what she knew, so she could continue this work when Chapawee was gone.

The shadows lengthened. "Cora, let's see how much we can get done before dark. We may have to finish tomorrow."

They each picked up one of the small cotton drawstring bags

Chapawee had left on the table. Once again, Chapawee sank into the rhythm of her task; pick up a wild carrot flower head, shake it to release the seeds into the cotton bag, throw it in the basket beside her. She'd use the dried flowers to start her fire for the rest of the fall.

"How much do you think we'll need this year?" Cora asked.

"I don't know," Chapawee said, never taking her eye off the task in front of her. "We'll harvest what we can and when it's gone, it's gone. Of course we'll hold some back for emergencies."

"Of course," Cora replied, pausing to lean into her hands and stretch her lower back. Cora put her hand in the bag and sifted the seeds through her fingers. "It's amazing what these tiny seeds can do."

"Yes. They give a woman a choice," Chapawee said, stopping to wiggle her fingers which ached from the tedious work. "I'm grateful to the first ancestor who listened to the voice of the wild carrot and understood its power to prevent pregnancy."

Cora playfully held a dried flower head to her ear. "I don't hear the wild carrot voice. Wonder how your ancestors did?"

Chapawee laughed. "It's a little more intuitive than that, but once we had the knowledge it was passed from mother to daughter."

"And to next door neighbors," Cora said and bumped her hip into Chapawee's as they continued their work.

Chapawee smiled. "Yes, and neighbors. Of course my daughter knows, but she's moved away and when I'm gone, Cora, you will continue this work and teach the next generation."

"Chapawee!"

Chapawee and Cora stopped their work at the sound of a woman's voice.

"It sounds like Jacqueline," Cora said and cinched the drawstring closed on her bag.

Chapawee nodded and stepped to the side of her cabin. "Jack, we're back here."

Jack came around the corner and immediately bent over with her hands on her knees to catch her breath. The neckline of her sack cloth dress was damp with sweat.

"Lord, child, did you run here?" Cora asked. "Is everything all right?"

Chapawee didn't know Jack well, only that she kept the books for Israel, the man who ran the colored general store. She purchased a large quantity of Chapawee's remedy to sell quietly to the colored women.

"I'm fine. I came to see if you had this year's supply of your remedy. A young girl needs one of your teas by tonight."

"Who?" Cora asked, locking eyes with Jack.

"I promised not to share her name," Jack said. "The man is threatening to hurt her family if she tells anyone what's happening. I'm just glad she trusted me to help so she isn't totally alone."

Cora slammed her fist into the table and Chapawee's anger boiled inside. She knew what this meant. Most likely the man was white and had the power to harm the girl's family if he chose to.

Cora paced a few steps towards the creek and then back to Jack and Chapawee. "Will it never end? If this girl tells the truth, she and her family will be punished." Cora glared over Chapawee's head into the woods. "Honesty makes no difference to the white man. My father was whipped, and my husband put on a chain gang, despite the fact they told the truth. Generation after generation this continues."

Cora marched down to the creek. Her anger coiled like a water moccasin ready to strike and Chapawee was glad she'd stepped away. Her anger was a distraction from how they could help in the moment. "Jack, we've just begun to gather the seeds, but I have enough to give you some. Do you have something to carry them in?"

Jack handed her a small handkerchief which Chapawee laid on her work table. She carefully measured out seven teaspoons of seeds from her drawstring bag, tied the handkerchief into a bundle with a piece of twine and gave it back to Jack.

"Thank you, Chapawee. I don't have the money now but . . ."

Chapawee held up her hand. "I won't accept any money for this. I'm happy to help. Now do you remember the steps?"

Jack nodded and said, "Chew one teaspoon today, and then a teaspoon daily for the next week."

"Yes," Chapawee confirmed. "Or she can grind a teaspoon and make a tea if the seeds are too bitter to chew. Remember to steep the tea for at least fifteen minutes."

The sun was close to the horizon now, and Chapawee wished she had her shawl. "Jack, you'd better head back. It's almost dark."

Jack held the bundle tight in her right hand. "Thank you, Chapawee. And Cora," Jack said, "try to release some of your anger. Being angry about what white men have done in the past lets them control you in the present, and I know you don't want that." Jack turned and walked quickly towards Kershaw Road.

Cora crossed her arms over her chest. "Hmph. Seems to me if I let go of the anger and move on, they win."

Chapawee emptied the flower heads left in Cora's sack into her own and then handed Cora's back to her. "Jack doesn't mean you should accept and give in. She just doesn't want to see you so upset."

Cora took her sack from Chapawee. "I don't know how you do it, Chapawee. Terrible things can happen, yet I rarely see you angry. Troubled and upset, yes, but not angry. How do you do that?"

Chapawee leaned into the work table, and looked west down the creek. Cora stood beside her waiting for her response while the horizon transformed from yellow to orange to pink. Chapawee kept her breath slow and steady.

"Cora, I'm sure you remember I was more outspoken in my younger days." Cora nodded. "And you also know that my husband, Kuruk, was a man of two natures. Some days he was patient and loving, and others angry and defensive. I quickly learned if I responded to his anger with my own, things got worse, nothing was resolved, and our daughter, Tayen, would be terrified, not only of her father, but of me too."

Cora nodded. "You had your hands full with Kuruk."

"Anyway, being married to him trained me to keep my anger inside. I feel it Cora, and if I sat here thinking on the white man that violated the young girl Jack is helping, I'd have trouble keeping it inside, but I choose not to give that man space in my thoughts. He's not worth it and it doesn't help the poor girl. But our seeds will."

"You're right." Cora brushed a tear from her cheek, and Chapawee knew Cora's fiery anger had cooled into black coal. "Reckon I should get home," Cora mumbled and took a step in the direction of her property.

Chapawee put her hand on Cora's arm and said, "Go home and have a nice supper with Jeremiah. Don't sit in these bad feelings all night. It will only exhaust you and take away what power you do have to make a difference."

The women walked slowly towards the edge of Chapawee's property.

"What power, Chapawee?" Cora asked, looking straight ahead. "An old Indian woman and an old colored woman have no power to change the white man's world."

They paused at the woods between their homes. "That may be so, but we must take control where we can, and it might not change the whole world, but we can change the world of one woman at a time and that's at least something."

It was too dark now for Chapawee to see Cora's expression, but she hoped her words had helped.

"Guess that's better than doing nothing." Cora sighed. "I'll come over in the morning and we'll finish harvesting the seeds."

"See you tomorrow."

In an instant, Cora's tall frame was absorbed into the darkness.

CHAPTER 6

The house was quiet and Vivi sat alone at the kitchen table which she'd converted into her desk for the evening. She pulled the kerosene lamp closer to the paper and reread her last sentence. *So, if you believe in a woman's right to vote and want to help this cause, please meet at The Central Hotel, Thursday, November 19 at 6:30pm.*

She was working on a flyer to encourage women, and men if they chose, to help start a chapter of the Equal Suffrage Association in Oriental. Adelaide would mention this at the end of her one woman show next weekend and they'd hand out the flyers as people left.

She read what she'd written so far and her stomach flipped when she thought of others reading her words. Would the flyer inspire people to come to the meeting? Comments on her students' work and letters to friends were the only times she'd shared her writing. She was nervous about others' judgment, both about the quality of her writing and the topic, as there was little talk of women's suffrage here in Pamlico County. Would the local women embrace the cause, ignore it, or label her a radical for pursuing this?

The bench on the back porch creaked as Bubba sat down to take off his boots. He was humming, and Vivi hoped this was the result of a good mood, and not the influence of whisky.

Bubba burst through the door in his socked feet. "Hey, Vivi. You waiting up for me?"

He took a few steps in her direction and that was enough for her to know he was drunk. The past year she'd become an expert in reading his body language, speech and eyes to know how much he'd had to drink.

"I'm working on the flyer we're handing out at Adelaide's show next Saturday." She neatened her papers into a pile.

Bubba stood behind her and placed his hands on her shoulders. "That meeting about women voting? Vivi, I don't see why you want to do that. Don't you have enough with teaching, Goldie and keeping our house?" Bubba paused and rubbed her shoulders. "And what about me? I need your attention too."

Bubba leaned down and kissed her neck. She instinctively tensed, but he didn't seem to notice. His lips worked their way around to the other side of her neck and then he gently tickled her ear with his tongue. His right hand slid down from her shoulder to caress her breast.

She could only grip the edge of her chair. Why couldn't she melt under his touch like she used to? Why didn't she crave the feeling of his skin on hers? Was it his drinking or had her feelings changed? She placed her hand over his and removed it from her breast.

Bubba let out a snort and walked around the table to face her. "Goddamn it, Vivi. What's wrong? We haven't been together in months, but you always have time to play with Goldie or go traipsing off with your new friend, Adelaide." He took one of her hands from her lap and held it between his palms. "But what about me? I need a part of you too."

Vivi's eyes filled with tears. She wanted to feel differently, and it pained her to see Bubba's longing. She knew how she should respond, but her heart and body were indifferent. Bubba reached up and wiped a tear from the corner of her eye. "What's wrong, sweetheart?"

It was difficult to believe he was sincere when he slurred his words. She looked over Bubba's head at the stove and remembered how Adelaide had wiped her tears. Why had that been more comforting than her husband's touch?

Bubba released her hand and sat down in the chair across from her, waiting for her answer.

"I don't know what's wrong." Vivi hated to lie, but knew that discussing their marriage when he'd been drinking would not be productive. She placed her papers into a large flat envelope. "But I do know that working on this flyer, and playing a role in women's right to vote has enlivened me in a way I've never felt before. But maybe it's taking too much of my attention."

After speaking her truth in the women's circle, it was now painfully clear when she avoided it, and this was one of those times. But what was the point in being totally honest with Bubba when he may not even remember this conversation tomorrow?

"It's late." Vivi stood and pushed her chair under the table. "Let's go to bed."

Bubba nodded and followed her to the stairs. He stumbled behind her and then caught himself with the banister. Vivi swallowed the lump in her throat.

***

"Can I run on to Grandmother's?" Goldie asked as she and Vivi rounded the corner of Midyette and Church Streets.

"Sure, sweetie. But don't forget to knock. She's not expecting us."

Goldie ran ahead, and her hair glinted in the sunlight. Time passed so quickly, Vivi thought. It didn't seem that long ago that she'd made this walk with a baby carriage, and now from the back, Goldie looked more like a young woman than a child.

A gust of wind surprised Vivi, and almost blew the large envelope she was carrying out of her hand. It contained the final draft of the flyer advertising the first meeting of the Equal Suffrage Association. Besides the time, date and location, she'd written two short paragraphs to entice women to come. Would her words move people to participate, or would she be judged for putting time into this effort?

Vivi slowed her pace to think about how she'd talk with her mother this morning. She and Adelaide had each contributed ten cents towards the printing costs for the flyer, but they needed five more and Vivi was going to ask her mother to help. She'd never asked for money, but hoped that because she was sharing her writing for a cause her mother supported, she'd consider it.

Vivi walked into the house she'd grown up in, and on the way to the kitchen was drawn to her father's study. It hadn't changed much since he'd died. She saw a book on the table beside the wing-backed chair and imagined her mother sat there to read.

"Vivi?" her mother called from the kitchen. "We're back here."

"Be right there," Vivi said.

She continued to stare into the study and could see her father sitting at his desk, writing. His pipe would be in his mouth, even if it wasn't lit and he'd look up and smile when he noticed her at the door. Most times, he'd wave her in and that was her cue to pull the chair from the corner and place it at his desk, directly opposite him. Two thick ledgers provided a booster seat to help her reach the desk. Without a word, her father would slide paper and a pen to her and she'd write as well. Sometimes it was a story she'd make up, and other times a narrative of what she'd seen outside or what she was learning in school.

Her mother's arm slid around her waist. "I thought you may have stopped here," she said and pulled Vivi closer. "I still miss him every day. When I look at you, and of course Goldie, I know he's been gone a long time, but when I sit in his reading chair in the late afternoon, I feel like he was just here, and is absent only for a short trip."

Vivi hugged her mother and then leaned against the doorframe. "I was remembering when I'd write with Daddy at his desk."

Etta smiled. "I'd walk by and see both your heads bent over your papers, and not a sound in the room but the scratching of pens."

Vivi knew what the next sentence would be and this time she had an answer.

"Vivi, you really should make some time to write again. Your dad saw your talent when you were young and I've seen it grow as you've aged. It'd be a shame if you didn't share it with the world."

Vivi lifted the envelope up and held it in front of her chest. "Well, I have written something and I'd like you to look at it."

Etta clapped her hands. "Oh, Vivi. I wasn't expecting this."

The tea kettle whistled from the kitchen and Goldie ran down the hall. "Grandmother! The tea water is ready!"

"Goldie," Vivi said. "Please don't yell, and you are perfectly capable of taking the kettle off the stove."

"Yes, Ma'am."

Goldie turned to run back to the kitchen, and the whistling ceased.

Etta smiled. "There's no middle ground with Goldie. She's either at full speed or not moving."

"Yup," Vivi said as they walked to the kitchen. "Sometimes it's a challenge, but I never want her to lose her curiosity and energy." Like I did, Vivi thought. Was it because her father had died or just a product of growing up and becoming a wife and mother?

Etta put the envelope on the table and went to the stove. "I'll make us a cup of tea and then I want to see what you've written."

"Wait," Vivi said. "Let's look at it now. I don't want to risk spilling tea on it before I take it to the printer."

"Oh, Vivi, you're printing this for others to read? Now you've really got me curious." Etta sat down and slid the papers from the envelope.

Vivi sat beside her at the kitchen table and Goldie stood between them.

"It's not much, Mom. Just a few paragraphs to encourage people to come to a meeting about women's suffrage."

"Women's suffrage? I haven't heard anyone talk much about that in Oriental."

"Exactly, and we need to. Adelaide and I want to start a chapter of the Equal Suffrage Association. We're going to hand these out after her show next weekend, and post a few around town."

"Hmm," was all her mother said. After a moment of silence while she read, Etta lifted her head. "This is wonderful. It's clear and convincing, which is perfect, because I'm sure many women, and especially the men, haven't given the topic of suffrage much thought."

"Thank you," Vivi said and then pointed to the blank spot in the corner of the page. "I have the emblem for the Equal Suffrage Association to go here, and the American flag will go here." She indicated the bottom right corner.

Goldie picked up the flyer to inspect it. "Can I go to the meeting too?"

"No. It's just for adults, and your focus needs to be on school," Vivi replied. She retrieved the flyer from Goldie and placed it back in its envelope.

"Goldie," her mother said, "the persimmons on my tree are ripe. Can you pick some and maybe we'll make jam this afternoon, if that's OK with your mother."

"Sure," Goldie said. She took the basket her grandmother offered her, the back door slammed and she was gone.

After serving their tea her mother sat across from Vivi and smiled. "You know it makes me happy that you're writing?"

Vivi nodded.

"In the circle you said you felt disengaged and bored with life, and now you're writing, working with suffrage and have a new friend in Adelaide. Looks like the circle helped you make some changes."

Vivi paused and considered her mother's words. "You're right. The circle made me aware that if things are going to change, I have to do something different. Saying yes more often has helped, and ignoring the voice that talks me out of doing new things," Vivi lifted the envelope with her flyer, "like writing."

"Yes, opportunities are always there, we just have to take them."

"And what about you, Mom?" Vivi reached across the table and placed her hand over her mother's. "Have you found opportunities to build new friendships?"

Was it her imagination or was her mother blushing?

"Nothing major, Vivi, but I did let Ben walk me home from church last week. He's been asking almost every Sunday for the past few months."

"Ben? You mean Mr. Whitehurst who owns the Central Hotel?" Vivi thought of her mother linking arms with this man instead of her father and pursed her lips to hold back the first words that came to her. She was being selfish.

"Yes. He makes me laugh and was a perfect gentleman. And Vivi," her mother said, leaning towards her, "no one will replace your father. He was the love of my life, but I'm ready for some companionship."

"And you deserve that." Vivi took a sip of tea. "It seems we're both making different choices after speaking truthfully in the circle."

"It does. I have to say it's surprising that something as simple as Chapawee's ritual can have such profound effects." Etta picked up the envelope containing Vivi's flyer. "And here's the proof."

Vivi took a breath. "Yes. But I do need some help with that."

"Of course," her mother said. "What can I do?"

"Adelaide and I are each putting ten cents towards printing the flyers, but to print one hundred, we need another five cents."

Vivi hesitated and in that pause her mother interjected. "Of course I can help with the money, and this is the perfect opportunity to talk with you about something else." Her mother stood and said, "Let's go sit in your father's study to discuss it."

A wave of dread washed over Vivi and her hands tingled with pins and needles. What was her mother going to say?

Vivi walked carefully to avoid spilling her tea, and sat in the chair across from the wing-back reading chair where her mother was seated.

Etta's eyes filled with tears and Vivi's anxiety escalated. "Mom, what's wrong? Are you OK?"

"I'm fine," her mother replied. "Don't worry. My tears are for something good. I didn't expect to get emotional, but it involves your father . . ." Her voice trailed off.

My father, Vivi thought. He'd been gone seventeen years, seventeen years as of last week to be exact. What could her mother have to talk about that involved him now? Vivi looked past her to the window that was cracked open. The curtain, beige with blue clipper ships, fluttered in the breeze.

Vivi took a deep breath and tried to relax her shoulders. "Mom, you definitely have me curious. What do you need to tell me?"

Her mother took a drink. The clink of her cup hitting the saucer startled Vivi. "Relax, sweetheart. I know it's difficult to talk about your father, but this is good, so let me get started."

Vivi sat back in her chair and twirled a strand of her hair.

Her mother continued. "I've told you that your father had been having chest pains for a couple years before he died, and was concerned he would die before you were an adult."

Vivi nodded and took the handkerchief from her skirt pocket to dab the corner of her eyes.

"What I haven't told you, at your father's request, is that he set up a trust fund for you. I've been the executor of it. Until now."

Vivi's mind swirled with questions and she sat forward in her chair.

"What? A trust fund? Why are you only telling me now?"

"Oh, Vivi, it was difficult keeping this from you. There were many times I wanted to, especially when I knew your money was tight, but your father was very specific with how the money was to be used and I had to honor that."

"Daddy left me money, but didn't want me to have it until seventeen years after his death? This doesn't make sense."

"It's not about the date, Vivi. It's the circumstances. Your father wants you to use this money to . . . wait." Her mother walked to the desk and removed a thick envelope from the top drawer.

She sat back down and said, "This is the legal document written in your father's words, and of course he and I had several discussions about it so I was clear on his intentions."

Vivi focused on her mother's voice and deepened her breaths.

Etta pulled the papers from the envelope and turned to the second page. "Oh, here it is. 'My wife, Etta Mann Perkins will be the executor of this trust and will only use the funds to help further the education of my daughter, Vivian Ray Perkins.'"

Her mother looked up from the papers. "I used this money to pay for you to go to teacher's training school."

"Oh," Vivi said. "I'd always wondered how you'd managed to save enough for my tuition. It would have taken a lot more seamstress work than I saw you doing. But how come you didn't tell me then?"

"Let me finish reading and you'll understand. 'The executorship will transfer to my daughter, Vivian Ray Perkins, after she reaches the age of 21, and at the discretion of my wife, Etta Mann Perkins. This fund is to be used to educate my daughter's children and to support causes that improve the quality of life and well-being of others.'"

Her mother looked up and their eyes met. Now Vivi understood the timing. Her interest in women's suffrage had prompted her mother to share this now.

"Vivi, your father was clear with me. He didn't want you to know about this trust and feel pressured to find a cause. He wanted it to happen naturally, and now it has. We'll go to the bank next week and transfer the executorship and then you can use the money how you see fit to start the local chapter of the Equal Suffrage Association. But," her mother continued with a more serious tone, "the trust specifically says that the money is to be used only for philanthropic purposes, or for Goldie's education, and not for everyday expenses." Vivi nodded in agreement and Etta continued. "And as you know, last year our legislature gave married women the right to control their own money, so only you have the power to use this. Another reason this is a good time to transfer the fund to you."

Vivi sat back in her chair to process this information. Her mother hadn't said anything about the fund for seventeen years; her father had been thinking of her as an adult woman, even when she was only eleven. Now she and Adelaide had the funds to help the suffrage effort and there was money for Goldie to go to college if she wanted to. Vivi looked out the window again. The same tree stood there and the sky was still blue, but the world felt different. "Mom, I'm at a loss for words. Maybe with this I can make a difference in the world, other than teaching children."

Her mother broke into a smile. "Yes, and that's part of why your father did this. He wanted to give you every opportunity to share your gifts with the world and make a positive impact. Money certainly makes this process easier."

Vivi's emotions were escalating but she couldn't discern exactly what she was feeling. Needing a physical outlet she walked to the window and opened it wider. The breeze cooled her skin but did nothing to stop her emotions.

"Are you OK?" her mother asked.

Vivi opened her mouth to say she was fine, but a sob beat that untruth. Her father had believed in her. He knew he may never know her as an adult, but had seen her potential when she was only eleven.

Her mother was beside her and Vivi turned into the arms that were waiting to comfort her. Etta didn't say a word, just rubbed her back.

Vivi was embarrassed she was crying, but couldn't stop, and soon her mother's shoulder was damp. After several minutes she stepped back and blew her nose in the handkerchief.

"I'm sorry for getting upset, Mom. I know you were happy to tell me this."

Her mother's cheeks were wet too. "Sweetheart, you don't have to apologize. I expected you would react this way. I've given you a lot to think about it."

"What made me cry," Vivi said, her voice cracking, "is knowing Daddy believed in me. He set those guidelines for the trust with faith that I'd have something to contribute to my community. Now I'm more passionate about doing the suffrage work so I can make Daddy proud." This is what she'd been missing since her father died and Bubba had been drinking. She needed someone besides her mother to believe in her. Adelaide did, or she wouldn't have asked her to work together on this cause, and now there was evidence that her father had too.

Vivi's mother touched her arm. "Your father would be proud of you no matter what. Do the suffrage work for yourself. Because it's what you believe in."

Vivi put her hand over her mother's and Etta continued. "That's part of the reason he didn't want you to know about the trust, because he knew how much you liked to please him and you'd pressure yourself to do what would make him happy, not you. Your happiness is all he and I have ever wanted for you."

The screen door slammed and Goldie burst into the study with the basket, overflowing with persimmons.

Before either of them could say anything, Goldie asked, "What's wrong?" Vivi looked at her mother and they smiled at Goldie's perception.

"Everything's fine," Vivi said. "Grandmother and I were talking about my daddy, and it made me miss him and feel sad."

Goldie gave Vivi a hug. "I'm sorry, Momma. I'm sad when Daddy's gone for a long fishing trip, but he always comes back and your daddy can't."

"You're right," Vivi said, keeping an arm around Goldie's shoulders. "But today I feel closer to your grandfather than I have in a long time, and that makes me happy too." All those years avoiding tears and thoughts of her father had actually blocked a positive connection with his memory.

"Come, ladies," Vivi's mother said. "Let's clean these persimmons and make some jam. It was one of your grandfather's favorites, Goldie."

"Mom, I'll be back to help shortly, but I need to drop this off at the printers by noon so they'll be ready for Adelaide's show next weekend." Vivi picked up her envelope from the kitchen table.

"Of course. We'll get started and be here when you get back." Etta pressed a nickel into her hand. "There you go, and come Monday we'll get things taken care of at the bank."

"Thank you." Vivi hugged her mother and said quietly, "Why don't you invite Ben to our Sunday dinner tomorrow after church?" Etta nodded and continued sorting the persimmons.

"Goldie, listen to your grandmother and I'll be back shortly."

Vivi headed towards Broad Street. She looked at the envelope in her hand. She was taking her writing to the printer and soon others would read it, and she had money to organize a chapter of the Equal Suffrage

Association. Invigorated by her excitement and the cool fall breeze, Vivi picked up her pace. Maybe she'd have time to stop by Adelaide's at The Central Hotel and give her the good news before she went back to her mother's.

CHAPTER 7

Chapawee made a small bundle of rue herb and hung it on a nail above her workbench. The October sun wasn't as intense as a couple weeks ago, and there was still a chill in the air despite it being late morning. Chapawee's hands were tired from her tedious work, but she only had a few more bundles to make and she'd be finished by the time the sun dipped to the west.

A sound caught her attention and Chapawee paused her work and stood perfectly still. She cocked her head and closed her eyes. What was it? She heard it again. It sounded like someone mumbling and then she heard a snap, like a stem breaking. Someone was in her front yard, but they hadn't announced themselves like most of her friends or customers. Chapawee walked to the edge of her cabin and peered around. Immediately, she ran towards her garden. A woman was tromping her lettuce and mumbling to herself.

"What are you doing?" Chapawee yelled when she got to the edge of her garden.

The woman turned around and Chapawee winced when the woman's left boot flattened a bunch of red leaf lettuce. She looked to be in her early fifties. Her brown hair was pulled neatly in a bun, and pearls encircled her neck and wrist, and dotted her earlobes. She was well-dressed and held white deerskin gloves in one hand, and a small leather handbag in the other. Chapawee wondered how in the world she had got to her cabin looking so put together, except for the dirt and lettuce leaves on her boots.

Before Chapawee could say anything else the woman yelled, "You're the witch doctor preventing me from being a grandmother!"

Chapawee took a deep breath to ground herself. She didn't flinch at the words, but at the deep sadness beneath the woman's anger. She reached her right hand out to the woman. "Here, let me help you out of my garden so we can discuss this."

The woman put her hands on her hips and smashed more lettuce with her right boot. "I will not. Something in your garden is keeping my daughter from getting pregnant."

"Ma'am," Chapawee said through tight lips. "That's lettuce you are stomping on, which most definitely is not interfering with you being a grandmother."

The woman looked down at the lettuce and then around the garden as if seeing it for the first time. She ignored Chapawee's hand and stepped out. Chapawee tried not to let her eyes stray to her demolished crop of lettuce. Hopefully she could salvage it later.

"Where is it?" the woman demanded. "Where is the plant you make your potions from?"

In all her years of providing her remedy, Chapawee had never had anyone confront her like this. Usually women approached her shyly, paid for the remedy and quickly left. No one had ever blown in like a hurricane demanding answers. Chapawee briefly looked up and watched a flock of migrating seagulls to calm herself.

"Ma'am," Chapawee said politely. "I'm Chapawee, and who might you be?"

The woman slipped her gloves back on and said, "I am Mrs. Livingston. Lucy Pott's mother."

Ahh. Lucy, Chapawee thought. She'd stopped by last week for her remedy and had been a regular customer for a while. She couldn't remember exactly how long.

"Five years," Mrs. Livingston said, completing Chapawee's memory. "For five years my daughter has been married, and still, no grandchildren."

Mrs. Livingston narrowed her eyes at Chapawee, who instinctively took a step back. She looked over Mrs. Livingston's head for a horse or carriage, but didn't see one. How in the world had this woman got here?

"Last night we got into another argument," Mrs. Livingston continued. "Lucy said she was tired of me always asking if she was pregnant. She told me she was taking something that wouldn't let her get pregnant, and I should stop asking." Mrs. Livingston's voice cracked and she swallowed hard. "She wouldn't tell me what she was using or where she got it, but I asked around and all the information I gathered pointed to you, the Indian woman on Hungry Mother Creek. So here I am at the source to rectify this situation."

"With all due respect, Mrs. Livingston," Chapawee said carefully, "I believe Lucy is the source. Even if she did get something from me, it's her choice, not mine, and not yours."

Mrs. Livingston threw her handbag down in disgust. "You're an evil woman, Chapawee, trying to take God's will into your own hands."

"If it's God's will for all women to have children then why did he make plants that interfere with that?" Chapawee said calmly.

Mrs. Livingston's neck and face flushed red and she snatched her handbag from the ground. "There. You said it. There is a plant here you've been giving to Lucy."

Mrs. Livingston walked towards the garden again. "Which one is it?" she asked. "Oh, you're not going to tell me. I should destroy the whole garden."

"Wait, Mrs. Livingston. Let me show you what's in my garden. Here's red leaf lettuce, some collards and cabbage." Chapawee pinched off a sage leaf, rubbed it between her fingers and held it up for Mrs. Livingston to smell. "Some sage for cooking. No potions growing here.

I eat what I grow and share some of it with friends, so destroying my garden isn't going to help your cause."

They stopped at the edge of the garden and Chapawee said, "I suggest you talk with Lucy, understand her perspective, and then find another purpose for your life besides being a grandmother."

If Chapawee could have pulled those words back into her mouth she would have. Mrs. Livingston wasn't ready to hear the truth yet.

The blood drained from Mrs. Livingston's face and she was silent. Chapawee's words hung in the space between them, waiting for Mrs. Livingston to accept or repel them. The high-pitched call of an osprey punctuated the silence.

Finally, she took a breath, removed her gloves and pointed a finger in Chapawee's face. "This, is not about me," Mrs. Livingston spat out. "This is about God's plan and how you're interfering with that by giving some Indian medicine to my daughter."

She stepped around Chapawee and walked towards the water and the back of the cabin. Chapawee blocked her way, not wanting her to see the drying rue herb. "Mrs. Livingston," Chapawee said, walking away from her cabin towards the woods and the Mother Tree. "Let me walk you around my property and you will see for yourself there is nothing unusual here."

Mrs. Livingston tromped beside her and Chapawee couldn't restrain a smile when they walked past the yellow, flowing rue herb growing at the edge of the woods. The wild carrot seeds were easier to transport, but if she ran out of them, rue herb was her back up remedy. They turned left at the corner of her cleared land and headed back to the path that led to Kershaw Road, giving the garden a wide berth.

When they'd completed their walkabout, Chapawee said, "You've wasted your time. Coming here to destroy some plant isn't going to achieve your goal. As I said earlier, your best option is to accept Lucy's decision."

"I will not accept Lucy's decision to stray from God." Mrs. Livingston removed a bill from her purse and held it in front of Chapawee in both hands.

The bill wasn't familiar. Chapawee studied it and saw it was ten dollars. She knew what was coming next, and imagined roots growing from her feet into the ground.

"How about I give you this and in return you stop giving Lucy your potion?" Mrs. Livingston said, her voice now dripping with honey instead of arsenic.

Even though that would buy Chapawee enough food to last till spring, she didn't even consider it. "No. Keep your money. I'm not interested."

Mrs. Livingston looked over her shoulder at Chapawee's cabin and then back at Chapawee. "It sure looks like you could use this money. What if I give you another ten dollars once Lucy is pregnant?"

Now it was Chapawee's face that flushed with anger. She would never sacrifice her character and the trust of her customers. "Mrs. Livingston, I said no. I think it's time you leave. Here's the path out to Kershaw Road."

Mrs. Livingston stuffed the money back into her purse and snapped it shut. "Well, I see why you live like this," she said, waving her hand in the direction of Chapawee's property. "You don't know a good proposition when you see one."

Chapawee put her hand in her pocket and rubbed the sage leaf between her fingers. They were standing only three feet apart but simultaneously living in separate worlds. "Can I walk you to the road?"

Mrs. Livingston picked up either side of her dress with her hands and marched defiantly to the worn, dirt path. "No. I'm fine and my husband is waiting at Kershaw Road with our automobile. Your little path was too narrow for it."

Thank goodness for that, Chapawee thought, imagining a Model T stuck in the middle of her garden.

After a couple of steps Mrs. Livingston turned around. "Don't think you've heard the last from me, Miss Chapawee. There's no telling how many babies you've kept from being born. You belong in jail and I'm going to make that happen. Mark my words."

Some of the men making those babies belong in jail, not me, Chapawee thought. She wasn't doing anything that women hadn't been doing for hundreds of years, but a brief wave of anxiety washed over her. She knew Mrs. Livingston was a woman used to getting her way.

The garden was a mess. Did she even have the energy to salvage it? Chapawee threw her shawl on the ground and knelt by the first row of lettuce. *I'll work on this row, and then take a break for lunch.*

Some leaves were torn away and she set those aside to eat. Others were only flattened and she gently pushed more dirt around the base of the lettuce head, and later she'd get water from the creek to refresh them. Thankfully, the rest of the garden had been spared from Mrs. Livingston's boots. Chapawee crawled on her hands and knees out of the garden. She bent her right knee and placed her right foot firmly on the ground. She took a deep breath and pushed herself to standing. I may need to make a cane to help myself get up, Chapawee thought. It was hard to believe she was old enough to use one. Inside she still felt like she was twenty-five, but her body was definitely looking more like her grandmother's.

"Hey, old woman."

Chapawee turned when she heard Cora's voice.

"You must have read my mind, Cora," Chapawee said, and took a few steps to get the blood flowing back to her legs.

"What in the world happened to your garden?" Cora asked when she got closer. "Did a bear get into it?'

"Well, something like that," Chapawee said. "Come back to my cabin and I'll tell you all about it."

Cora and Chapawee sat on the front steps of her home eating apples while Chapawee shared the events of the morning.

When she had finished, Cora's face was solemn. "Do you think we should stop making the remedy this year?" Cora asked. "Mr. Livingston owns the lumber mill in town, and with his money and influence, could certainly create trouble for you if he wanted."

Cora stood and paced in front of the cabin steps. "Jeremiah was put on the chain gang because a white man didn't take kindly to his words, and I have no doubt that you'll end up in jail if Mrs. Livingston takes this cause up with her husband."

Cora plopped back down beside Chapawee. "I'm scared for you, and me too. Maybe we need to forget all this, and burn the remedy we've already collected."

"I'm hoping things will blow over," Chapawee said, "but Mrs. Livingston definitely needs someone to blame for not being a grandmother."

"I'm just glad she only took her aggression out on your lettuce," Cora said.

"Me too."

Chapawee took another bite of her apple, and they sat in silence for a few minutes. Her brain was spinning. Was the threat of jail realistic? Should she carry on as usual, or burn everything like Cora suggested? But all women deserved a choice, and especially those who'd been assaulted, like the young woman Jack was helping.

"Cora, can you take Monday off from work?"

Cora turned on the steps to look at her. "I could try. Why? What plan are you hatching?"

"Today is Saturday. If we work the rest of today and all day Sunday and Monday we can finish harvesting the wild carrot seeds. You can take half over to Jack to sell at the general store and I'll hide the rest behind my wood stove. If someone comes to investigate and sees the rue herb, I'll say I'm drying it to ward off mosquitoes next summer."

"I don't know . . ." Cora said.

"Cora, if Mrs. Livingston is set on me going to jail, she'll find a way, no matter what I do. With her husband's money to back her, she could say I'm selling lettuce for birth control. I say we finish the harvest, and carry on as usual." Chapawee stood and faced Cora still seated on the steps. "I want to live what's left of my life on my terms, not motivated by the fear of what may happen."

Saying those words out loud energized Chapawee, and her heart opened as she released the fear. This was the right choice. "So, are you ready to collect the last of the wild carrot from the meadow beyond the Mother Tree? No one will see us there."

A southwest breeze blew several leaves along the ground between Chapawee and Cora and the sulphur smell of pluff mud permeated the air. Chapawee left Cora to think, and gathered her sack from the back of her cabin. When she turned from picking it up, Cora was there.

"You're old and small," Cora said playfully, "but strong in spirit. Hand me my bag and let's go."

CHAPTER 8

Vivi took Goldie's hands and they danced together to Adelaide's version of "The Good Ship Mary Ann." They were enjoying their first experience as backstage hands. Goldie especially loved moving around during the performance instead of sitting.

Goldie dropped Vivi's hand and ran to the thick, velvet curtain and peeked through it for the hundredth time. "Momma, I see Daddy, and Grandmother and Mr. Ben on the second row."

Goldie released the curtain and continued to dance alone in the small space between the curtain and the dressing rooms. Vivi was glad Goldie didn't tamp her enthusiasm by being self- conscious, but knew that would most likely happen in the coming years. Through the slit where the curtain met the wall, Vivi saw her mother, in the new blue dress she'd bought for the occasion, smile at something Ben whispered to her. It was strange to see her mother with another man, but she'd been more excited about tonight than Vivi had seen her in a long time, and that should take precedence over Vivi's discomfort. Bubba had tried to use the fact Ben was accompanying her mother as a reason to stay home, but Vivi convinced him it was important to be here to support Goldie's backstage efforts. Despite his resistance, he seemed to be enjoying himself and tapped his hand on his thigh in time with the music.

Vivi stepped back from the curtain when Adelaide introduced her next song. "Goldie, this is the last song before intermission. I need to make sure Miss Adelaide's dress for the second act is ready. You wait here and pull the curtain closed when she finishes."

"Ok," Goldie said, shaking her hips as she stood in place by the curtain cord.

Vivi laughed to herself. Goldie certainly provided extra energy backstage. She looked into the dressing room to be sure everything was in place; dress, shoes, hat, stage makeup. It was all there.

The audience broke into applause at the end of the song and Goldie pulled the thick cords with all her might, jumping with each pull. A few seconds later Adelaide came through the side curtains.

Instinctively, Vivi gave Adelaide a hug. "You were wonderful, and the audience loves you!"

"Thank you," Adelaide said and fanned herself with a copy of the program that she took from Vivi's hand. "I'm happy to be back on stage."

"I can tell," Vivi replied.

Adelaide's cheeks were flushed from the heat of the stage lights, her eyes sparkled, and a smile filled her face.

"You are a beautiful woman," Vivi said, immediately self-conscious at her honesty.

Adelaide took her hand and they walked to the dressing room. "You're sweet to say that but it's probably just the lighting and make-up."

Goldie came into the dressing room. "The lights are on and people are walking around. When do you go back on stage?"

"In fifteen minutes. Let's get me out of this dress and into the green one for my second act."

Adelaide turned her back to Vivi so she could unbutton her dress. Vivi worked her way down Adelaide's spine, undoing the tiny pearl buttons of the sky-blue evening gown. The top of the dress opened slightly and exposed smooth, pale skin at the base of Adelaide's neck. You could tell she'd never spent time on a boat, or bent over in a garden. Vivi's gaze lingered on that small patch of perfect skin.

The unbuttoning work wasn't strenuous, but heat moved up Vivi's torso, into her chest and then flushed her cheeks. Besides helping Goldie dress, she'd never been this intimate with another woman. Maybe if she'd had a sister this wouldn't feel so unusual. Adelaide seemed accustomed to it though, probably from her years of performing and being backstage with others in various stages of undress.

As soon as Vivi reached the last button, Adelaide leaned forward and slid her arms out of the sleeves.

"Goldie," Adelaide said, "help pull the dress over my petticoats and I'll step out of it."

Goldie jumped to work, and Vivi filled two glasses with water from the pitcher on the dressing table. She handed one to Adelaide after she stepped out of the dress, and drank the other herself.

Adelaide sat down in the straight-back rattan chair beside the dressing table. "I need a minute to cool down before I put on my other dress. Vivi, the flyers are ready to go?"

Vivi pointed to a thick package wrapped in brown paper on the corner of the dressing table. "Yes. As soon as you finish and make the announcement about our meeting, I'll come from backstage, give you half the stack and we can hand them out."

"Perfect," Adelaide said. "Thank you for taking our idea and making it a reality."

Goldie, who'd gone back to peek out the curtain again, came into the dressing room. "Miss Adelaide, people are sitting back down. You better get a dress on. You can't go out in your petticoat." She laughed at that thought and took the green dress from the back of the chair where Vivi had laid it earlier.

"Goldie, you're a good stage manager. You should work on a showboat like me."

"That would be fun. Can I do it? Momma, you can come too!" Goldie said with exuberance.

Adelaide stepped into the green dress that Goldie held for her and looked directly at Vivi. "I would go back on the showboat in a second if you and your mother would come with me."

Vivi's stomach filled with butterflies. She held Adelaide's gaze until Adelaide turned so Vivi could button her up. What an adventure that would be, and for an instant Vivi thought of the freedom of being on the boat; no lesson plans, no navigating Bubba's moods, just spending every day with Adelaide. Vivi finished the last button and then took the thick, grosgrain ribbon from either side of Adelaide's waist and tied a bow. The gold of her wedding band caught Vivi's eye.

"That would be fun, Goldie, but wouldn't you miss Daddy and your grandmother?"

"Yes, Ma'am. But maybe we could go for just a little while, like Daddy does when he's on the boat."

The small band Adelaide had cobbled together for the show began the introductory music for the second act.

"Now back to work," Vivi said and neatened Adelaide's skirt over her petticoat. "Let's get you ready for the stage."

Adelaide squatted to look at herself in the dressing table mirror, patted the powder puff across her forehead, nose and chin and then placed a jaunty green hat on her head.

"OK, stagehands," Adelaide said playfully. "Let's finish this show with a bang."

Vivi watched Adelaide transform into her stage persona and she strode confidently out of the dressing room.

Goldie walked along beside her as if she were also going onstage.

"Goldie," Vivi whispered, "remember your job?"

"Oh, yes, Ma'am," Goldie said and twirled to the beat of the music over to the curtain cords. Adelaide nodded at Goldie and she pulled the cords again.

The second act took less time and soon Adelaide was on her last song. The band faded their music until the only sound was Adelaide's voice holding the final note. As soon as she finished she spread her arms and bowed deeply. The audience erupted into applause.

Vivi and Goldie watched from backstage. "Momma, when should I close the curtain?" Goldie asked, her hands poised on the ropes.

"Wait until Miss Adelaide and I are giving out the flyers," Vivi said. The applause died down and Adelaide thanked everyone, which was Vivi's cue to retrieve the flyers from the dressing room. She untied the string and removed the brown paper that protected them.

Vivi stood for a moment looking at her words on the page. In a few minutes others would be reading them. Her stomach flipped with a mixture of fear and excitement.

"And while I have your attention . . ." Vivi heard Adelaide say. There's no turning back now, Vivi thought. Time to hand these out.

Vivi stood beside Goldie and waited for Adelaide to finish.

"Our country has fought against taxation without representation, but now it collects millions of dollars in taxes from women who are not allowed representation. Young men of twenty-one can vote, while the teachers who taught them to read the ballot may not, and the women serving our community in every uplifting moral and social enterprise are also denied this fundamental right of democracy. Who can justify this inequality in treatment? Women deserve the right to vote and that's why Vivian Gibbs and I are organizing a meeting for women, and men too, who are interested in starting a local chapter of the Equal Suffrage Association, to add our efforts to this worthy cause. Please take a flyer if you'd like to attend our meeting next week." Adelaide paused. "And thank you again for coming tonight." She waved to the audience and bowed slightly at her waist.

The change in the audience's mood was palpable. The enthusiasm for the music and Adelaide's voice evaporated immediately with the talk of suffrage, and all that was left was an awkward silence. Vivi pushed through her unease and stepped onto the stage. She handed Adelaide half the stack of flyers.

The house lights came up and Vivi walked down the steps to the right of the stage. Before she had a chance to hand out any flyers, her mother came up and hugged her.

She whispered in her ear, "I'm proud of you honey. I know there're women here who are interested, but not showing it because their husbands don't approve, but don't be intimidated."

"Thanks, Mom. Adelaide certainly didn't get a warm reception once she started talking about suffrage."

Her mother didn't answer and gently pressed her hand into the small of Vivi's back, propelling her forward. She heard the stage curtain close behind her and knew Goldie had followed her instructions.

Bubba stepped into the aisle and gave her a kiss on the cheek. "I'll wait for you outside."

"OK, but please check backstage for Goldie if she's not out here in a minute."

Someone tapped Vivi's shoulder and she turned to find Kathryn Dodson, the mother of one of her students standing beside her with her hand out. Vivi smiled and handed her a flyer.

"Thanks, Vivi," she said, "I'll do my best to be there." Kathryn turned and walked away with her head down, reading Vivi's words.

Vivi took a breath and slowly made her way through the departing crowd. She didn't thrust the flyer towards anyone and waited until she caught a woman's eye or someone approached her. When she got to the front door of Pickles Hall, she stood there to catch people as they left.

Her vision of passing flyers out, one after the other, didn't materialize and she struggled just to make eye contact with people as they were leaving. She only gave out five or six.

"I'd like one, Mrs. Gibbs."

Vivi flinched at the voice of Mr. O'Neal, the superintendent of Pamlico County schools. He snatched a flyer from her stack before she could hand him one, and read it while standing in front of her.

"Did you write this?" he asked, peering at her over the top of the paper.

"I did," Vivi said. Her voice cracked despite her best efforts to not appear nervous.

"Be careful, Mrs. Gibbs. Don't let your attention to this lost cause impact your teaching."

"Of course not. After my family, teaching is my first priority. I'll be doing this in my spare time."

"You make sure of that," Mr. O'Neal said. He put on his bowler and then slid the flyer into the front pocket of his coat. "I'll be keeping a close eye on you, and the school board will be hearing about your new interest."

He turned and left, and Vivi stood there wide-eyed. Was he threatening her? It'd never crossed her mind that working on women's right to vote would impact her job. He acted as if she couldn't focus on teaching as well as the suffrage movement, when in fact, women were masters at juggling the needs of multiple people and causes. Her initial anxiety coalesced in her solar plexus and transformed to anger.

His treatment wasn't fair. She had the right to support whatever cause she chose in her time away from work. Plenty of men in town were active in politics and it didn't impact their job. Why was it different for her?

Someone tapped her arm and Vivi roused herself from her thoughts and handed a flyer to the woman in front of her. The woman quickly folded the paper into a small square and tucked it into the bodice of her dress. She winked at Vivi, who immediately understood the unspoken message.

The theater emptied and Adelaide joined Vivi at the doorway. Like Vivi, Adelaide still had a thick stack of the flyers.

Just an hour ago, Vivi had been excited about taking her first step in the women's suffrage movement, and hopeful her words would make a difference, but it seemed nothing had been achieved tonight. She blinked back tears of disappointment, but Adelaide must have seen them because she immediately put her arm around Vivi's shoulders.

"What's wrong?" Adelaide asked, squeezing her shoulder gently.

Vivi slipped her arm around Adelaide's waist. "I'm sorry."

"There's nothing to be sorry about. Now tell me what's wrong." Adelaide stepped away from Vivi and looked directly at her.

"I'm disappointed. I had visions of us running out of flyers for our meeting. I thought women would be enthusiastic and asking us lots of questions, but instead we've only had a couple women quietly take an interest. And look," Vivi said holding up her papers. "We practically have all these left. Money wasted."

"Oh, Vivi. Don't let this get you down. I should have prepared you. Even in Boston, where people are more progressive, suffrage isn't a popular issue. I'm not surprised by the response." Adelaide took Vivi's left hand. "It just reinforces that our work is important. Oriental needs more education about women's right to vote."

"Thanks for saying that. Do you think we'll have enough interest to start a chapter of the Equal Suffrage Association?"

"Absolutely. We'll post your flyers around town and take some to the Women's Club."

Vivi thought of Sadie and Cora from the circle. Would they be interested in women's suffrage? She wasn't sure about Cora, but given Sadie's passion for equality, she most likely would.

Before she could talk with Adelaide about this, Bubba came and stood beside her. "Be careful," he said, his voice containing genuine concern. "I heard what Mr. O'Neal said and it appears most people here don't agree with you and Adelaide. Promoting a woman's right to vote may be asking for trouble." Bubba put his arm around Vivi's waist. "I don't want anything to happen to you."

"What's gonna happen to Momma?" Goldie asked.

"Oh, nothing is going to happen to your mother," Adelaide said. "Goldie, thank you for all your help tonight." She turned to Vivi. "Can our backstage help come to my reception at the hotel tonight to celebrate?"

"Thank you," Vivi said, "but we can't. Goldie needs to go to bed."

Adelaide's face fell. "Oh, Vivi, surely Bubba can do that. You have to come. I won't feel like celebrating if you're not there. Please come just for a little while. The guys from the band will be there and a couple people I've met at the hotel. It won't last long."

Vivi was torn. She knew Bubba wouldn't be happy if she went, but the sincerity with which Adelaide asked her warmed her heart.

Vivi turned to Bubba and saw him take a deep breath, but he didn't say anything.

Goldie crossed her arms over her chest. "That's not fair. I worked hard tonight and should be able to go to the party too."

Vivi put both her hands on Goldie's shoulders. "You were a wonderful help. How about Miss Adelaide and I take you out to the tea shop next week to celebrate instead?"

"But I want to go tonight. I can skip church tomorrow if we stay out late."

"No. Tonight is for adults, and I'll only be there a little while." Vivi locked eyes with Bubba. "You've outgrown bedtime stories, but I bet your father will tell you one of his fishing tales before you go to sleep."

She was thankful Bubba hadn't been drinking tonight because she wouldn't have had this option otherwise.

"Come on, Goldie," Bubba said, holding the theater door open. "Looks like your momma's making all the decisions now, so we better get on home like she said."

Vivi's stomach burned at the tone of his voice. Maybe this was a mistake, and then she looked at Adelaide whose eyes pleaded with her.

"Bubba, I've only made the decision to celebrate Adelaide's performance. I'll be home shortly."

Bubba nodded but didn't say a word. Goldie watched their interaction and then linked arms with her father. "Come on, Daddy, we'll make some hot chocolate and then you can tell me the story about the whale you saw."

Vivi smiled, despite being frustrated with Bubba. It would be good for him and Goldie to have some time alone. Goldie adored his undivided attention, something that hadn't happened as frequently since his brother died.

Goldie and Bubba walked away and Adelaide immediately gave her a big hug. "Thank you. I would have been lonely without you. Now, let's gather my things from the dressing room and get to the hotel."

It was nine o'clock and the town was quiet when Vivi and Adelaide left Pickles Hall. The cool air provided no relief for Vivi's turmoil. Bubba was right. She had taken charge and made her own decision about tonight. Both Bubba and Adelaide wanted her to come with them, and she'd chosen Adelaide. Should her family always come first?

The dress from Adelaide's first act was draped over her left arm and she gathered the end of it in her right hand to keep it from dragging on the ground. Vivi balanced the remaining flyers on top of Adelaide's hat box and followed her across Broad Street.

"I'm glad we only have to walk across the street," Vivi said at the bottom of the hotel steps.

"And I'm glad you're with me," Adelaide replied.

Maybe it was the lights on the porch, but Adelaide's face glowed. To have someone look at her like that made Vivi feel like the center of the universe.

The front door of the hotel opened and the trumpet player from Adelaide's band said, "Here she is. The lady of the hour. Come in. Come in." He held the door open for Vivi and Adelaide.

They quickly went back to Adelaide's room and deposited her things. When they returned to the lobby, Sarah, the piano player handed them each a glass of punch. Vivi took a sip, and when her stomach burned, she realized it contained alcohol. She searched for a place to set her glass down. It felt hypocritical to enjoy the punch when she berated Bubba for doing the same, although one celebratory drink was different from getting drunk.

"Sarah, it's good to see you," Vivi said. Sarah was a couple years younger than Vivi and they'd been in school together. "I remember you playing the piano for our school plays. You've stayed in good practice. You were wonderful tonight." Vivi looked at Sarah's left hand to see if she were married and without her husband too, but there was no ring.

"Thanks," Sarah said. "I haven't performed in a while except Sunday mornings at the Methodist church, but that's not quite as festive as this one's performance." She pointed playfully at Adelaide.

Vivi scanned the crowd for Ben, who lived in one of the suites, but didn't see him. He'd walked her mother home after the show and Vivi wondered if he was still there. Had her mother invited him in?

"Let's make a toast," the trumpet player said, bringing Vivi's attention back to the moment. He raised his glass. "To Adelaide."

Vivi raised her glass and Adelaide pulled her close, her hand firmly on Vivi's waist.

The toast continued. "Thank you for your amazing performance tonight. Your songs and spirit provided a welcome distraction to our little town."

Vivi didn't hear the rest of the toast. She was only aware of the warmth of Adelaide's hand on her waist and the thrill of being out on her own, not as Bubba's wife, or Goldie's mother, just as Vivi. She slid her arm around Adelaide, letting her hand rest on the gentle curve of Adelaide's hip. The toast ended and Adelaide held her glass up to clink with Vivi's. Without removing their arms from one another's waists, they toasted.

After the toast, Adelaide mingled with the band members and a couple of hotel guests who'd joined the party. Vivi stayed at the edge of the room chatting with Sarah. Out of the corner of her eye she watched Adelaide flit around, socializing with ease. That was something that didn't come naturally to Vivi, not that she had the opportunity to practice much. Most of her social events were family gatherings or church-related.

Sarah's voice faded into the background, as Vivi realized with a pang how different she and Adelaide were. Adelaide would surely grow bored with her and Oriental, and leave. The evening's magic evaporated and an overwhelming sadness enveloped her. Tonight wasn't her real life, and Adelaide wasn't going to stay forever, so she shouldn't get used to this.

"Vivi, are you OK?" Sarah asked and touched her on the arm.

Vivi blinked and looked at her. "I'm fine."

"You were staring off into space with the saddest expression."

"I'm sorry," Vivi said, taking a deep breath to regain her composure. "I was worrying about Goldie. She's not used to going to bed without me. I better get home."

"I understand," Sarah said. "I'm glad we had time to catch up. Say hello to Bubba for me."

Vivi didn't want to make her exit dramatic and slipped out of the lobby to Adelaide's room to retrieve her coat and the rest of the flyers.

"Why are you leaving?"

Vivi spun around when she heard Adelaide's voice.

"It's only 10 o'clock. Stay. Have another drink. I'm done mingling and want to spend time with you."

Vivi gathered her coat in front of her. "I need to check on Goldie."

Adelaide walked towards her and calmly took the flyers and her coat from her hands and laid them on the bed. She put both her hands on Vivi's shoulders and said, "Goldie is asleep now, dreaming of showboats. Now, tell me why you're leaving."

Vivi couldn't look Adelaide in the eye and gazed over her left shoulder out into the hall. She was embarrassed by the truth and a lump blocked her throat.

Adelaide squeezed her shoulders. "I'm a stubborn Yankee and I'm not moving until you tell me."

Vivi had to smile at Adelaide's comment, and immediately her throat cleared. She looked into Adelaide's eyes. "I was having a fabulous time, but it's only one night. At some point you will go back to Boston, and my life will return to the way it was. I don't want myself to get used to this, when it's only going to end."

Adelaide slid her hands from Vivi's shoulders down her arms and then held both her hands. "Vivi, you can't live this way. All we have is the moment, and every moment ends. If you don't allow yourself to be happy tonight, when will you?"

"I thought it would hurt less when you leave, if I didn't enjoy it as much while you're here." Somehow this had made sense a few minutes ago.

"Anticipating sadness doesn't decrease its intensity, and as far as me leaving, I have no plans for that. We have lots of work to do here together."

Vivi knew Adelaide was right, but this was how she'd been living her life, anticipating the next bad thing and not allowing herself to be happy. Maybe that needed to change. Vivi smiled. "You're definitely a stubborn Yankee, but you do make sense. I'll stay for one more drink."

Adelaide's face lit up. She cupped Vivi's face with her hands and gently kissed her on the lips. Vivi was startled and her breath caught in her throat. No friend had ever kissed her like this, but she didn't mind it. She didn't move away and Adelaide traced her finger down Vivi's forehead, nose, chin and neck.

"You are lovely," Adelaide said and leaned in and kissed her again. This time her lips were pressing more firmly.

Vivi placed one of her hands on Adelaide's waist and enjoyed the sensation of Adelaide's lips on hers. It awakened her body in the same way Bubba's kisses used to. This both confused and delighted her.

Adelaide stepped back. "Now. Do you feel better? I'm not going anywhere, and the night is still young so let's go enjoy it."

Vivi thought of Goldie and Bubba. She acknowledged the guilt that immediately arose, but chose not to carry it. Instead, she made a choice that would make her happy. "That sounds delightful," she said and followed Adelaide back to the hotel lobby.

***

The waning moon was still three quarters full and lit Vivi's way home. She needed time to think, and walked slowly, savoring the quiet and solitude. She was awash in the afterglow of her evening. Working backstage, promoting women's suffrage, the after party, and kissing Adelaide. What did that mean?

Adelaide had kissed her once more in front of the hotel as she left.

Her warm lips and body were a welcome contrast to the cool night air and Vivi had trouble pulling away. Had they done something wrong? Surely not. They just had a close friendship and were both elated from Adelaide's performance and the punch. They'd never kiss again, but this thought was immediately followed by the hope they would.

When Vivi got home the familiar kitchen smells grounded her in reality, but tonight had been real too. It'd only felt surreal because everything had vibrated with novelty, something she hadn't had in a long time. Had her desire to control life through routines inhibited her ability to feel alive?

Vivi put the flyers and her coat on the table and yawned. It was too late to think about this. She used the moonlight to navigate upstairs and peeked into Goldie's room. Bubba's snores rumbled from their bedroom and Vivi sighed with relief that they wouldn't have a confrontation tonight.

After changing into her nightgown, she slid into bed behind Bubba. His body was warm and Vivi molded herself to his back, and then pressed more firmly into him, full of the yearning that Adelaide's kiss had awoken. Bubba stirred, and then turned over. He pulled her into his arms.

"Vivi, you're home."

She answered by kissing him with an urgency that he easily returned. Tonight Vivi welcomed Bubba's caresses, and they made love for the first time in months.

CHAPTER 9

A heron honked its displeasure when Chapawee slid her boat into its slip at her dock. She'd been to town to buy some cornmeal, sugar and lard from the general store. It only took fifteen minutes to get home, but today she'd taken her time and fished Hungry Mother Creek. The speckled trout were moving back into the creeks for winter and she'd caught enough for her dinner, and Cora and Jeremiah's too.

Chapawee threw the stringer of fish onto her dock and unloaded her purchases. The water tapped gently on the side of her boat, and the fish flopped about in an attempt to find water. The older she got, the more compassion she had for dying creatures, and she almost threw them back in, but needed them for their protein.

Was that a horse neighing and stomping? Chapawee lifted herself out of the boat, and with the higher vantage point on the dock, she saw a horse tied to the hitching post in front of her home. Her heart rate increased and the hairs on the back of her neck stood on end. She didn't recognize the animal. Who was here? Someone that Mrs. Livingston had sent? It'd been over a week since her lettuce-stomping visit and Chapawee had hoped nothing would come of it. Should she take her boat around the bend in the creek and wait until they leave, or confront whoever was there?

The flash of baitfish beside the dock caught her eye. Chapawee looked into the tea-colored water, and remembered the time she and her sister Kanti jumped into the creek to hide when she was only six or seven. A group of men looking for runaway slaves had come to their property while their parents were out fishing. They'd heard the dogs before the men arrived, and ran into the shallow water and river grasses to hide.

Chapawee turned away from the water and walked towards her cabin, ignoring her instinct to hide this time. When she reached the end of her dock, a tall white man rounded the corner of her cabin. She immediately recognized him as the constable. He was young, probably early twenties, and had only had this job for a few months. Chapawee had seen him in town but never had any reason to talk with him. She stood in place and let him approach her. The mid-afternoon sun reflected off the gun resting against his hip. The constable nodded and stopped a reasonable distance from her.

Chapawee spoke first. "Afternoon, constable. What can I do for you?" Chapawee kept her voice strong and steady despite feeling vulnerable.

He removed a folded piece of paper from his pocket and then looked out towards the water. "Oh, you've been fishing," he said, noticing the trout lying on the dock.

"Yes. Caught some speckled trout for dinner." Chapawee took a couple steps towards her cabin. "I need to get them cleaned," she said, hoping this would speed up his visit.

He held up the paper. "I'm sorry to bother you, but I have a search warrant."

Chapawee's stomach turned. Mrs. Livingston must have wielded her pocketbook to make this happen. She stayed silent and maintained eye contact, knowing she had done nothing wrong.

"A community member has filed a complaint against you and . . ." the constable hesitated and then sighed. "And the magistrate said there was reason enough to issue the search warrant."

"What is the complaint and what are you searching for?" Chapawee asked, knowing the answer.

The constable took off his wide-brimmed hat and released his curly hair, the color of sand. He looked away, and then back at her. Chapawee smiled to herself. His discomfort was almost endearing. She knew he'd much rather keep talking about fish.

Finally he continued. "This citizen says that you're selling something that prevents women from getting pregnant."

Using his discomfort to her advantage, Chapawee asked, "It's against the law for a woman to not get pregnant?"

The constable blushed and broke eye contact with her. "Um, no but . . ."

Chapawee cut him off and took a step closer to him. "And I imagine there are many times a man is relieved when a woman doesn't get pregnant."

His blush deepened.

"So, I'm confused," Chapawee continued, "as to why you're here, seeing as not getting pregnant isn't against the law."

"But," the constable said regaining his composure, "the woman filing the complaint said you were selling her daughter some herbs to keep her from getting pregnant, and that is different than a woman just not getting pregnant."

"It is?" Chapawee asked. "According to who?"

The constable took a deep breath and stepped back from Chapawee. "The magistrate."

Chapawee sighed. The magistrate was probably firmly controlled by the Livingstons and the poor constable was just doing their bidding.

"So, I need to take a look around."

The fear of anything happening to her today dissipated, but she was concerned that things had gone this far. She swept her right hand towards her cabin. "Feel free. I don't own much so it won't take long." There'd be no way he'd find her hiding spot for the seeds, or even know what they were if he did.

"What's this?" the constable asked, pointing to the rue herb hanging from the edge of the roof.

"That's called rue herb," Chapawee said, walking to stand beside him. "Here." She took a bundle off its nail. "Smell this." He wrinkled his nose. "I dry it and make small packets to carry in my pockets in the summer to keep the mosquitoes away."

Satisfied, the constable nodded and Chapawee followed him to the front door of her cabin. She leaned against the door frame and watched him look aimlessly around. This search was useless with someone untrained in plant medicine. She could have left a bowl of the wild carrot seeds sitting on her table and told him it was to add to her bread and he wouldn't have known the difference.

It was unnerving to have someone looking through your things, Chapawee thought as the constable opened her cupboard, turned her pottery mug over and then patted the horsehair mattress lying in the corner. At least he was respectful of her property, unlike the slave hunters who'd let themselves into the cabin, knocking over her table, breaking the only dishes her family owned at the time. They'd even had the nerve to eat the biscuits that were supposed to be lunch for her and Kanti.

The afternoon was passing and Chapawee needed to clean her fish and put away her purchases from town. "Would you like to inspect my garden too?" she asked when he'd finished his circumnavigation of her cabin.

He hesitated, and looked outside and then back at Chapawee as if he wasn't sure if the garden should be part of the search.

They walked along the edge of the garden and row by row she identified each plant. When they approached the last few rows he asked, "What happened to your lettuce? Looks like something stepped on them."

Well, at least he knows what lettuce looks like. "Yes, as a matter-of-fact constable, something did crush my lettuce. It was Mrs. Livingston."

The constable took his hat off, ran his fingers through his hair again and looked at the ground. Chapawee continued. "Last Saturday she came here uninvited, and attempted to destroy my property, a more concrete reason to file a complaint than women not getting pregnant, don't you think? You can see the evidence with your own eyes, but I don't want to waste your time with this. I'm sure you have more important things to do."

The constable nodded and put his hat back on. "Yes, Ma'am. I do, and I'd best be going."

"What's your verdict on the search? Do I need to be worried?"

"No, Ma'am," the constable said as he mounted his horse. "Nothing seems out of the ordinary here. Have a good afternoon. And enjoy your fish," he added.

Chapawee watched him trot down her path to the road and hoped this would pacify Mrs. Livingston. Despite the fact nothing had been found, she knew Mrs. Livingston had made her the scapegoat for Lucy not giving her a grandchild, and until that changed, she needed to remain alert.

***

The school day was over and the classroom now quiet, except for the scratch of Goldie's pencil. Vivi sat back in her desk chair and yawned. She loved her job, but managing twelve children between the ages of six and fifteen for six hours was draining.

Goldie looked up from her paper. "Momma, is it time to go to Grandmother's?"

Today was Wednesday and they usually ate dinner with her mother and then went to Wednesday night church. At least her mother did. In the past few months Vivi's attendance had waned and she used fatigue, or Goldie's homework, as an excuse.

"We'll leave shortly. I need to clean up a bit and prepare for tomorrow."

"But I'm ready to go now," Goldie whined. "I'm tired of sitting in this room."

Vivi didn't like Goldie's tone of voice, but understood her desire to be outside.

"Finish the sentence you're on, pack your things, and you can go ahead to your grandmother's. I'll be there in about thirty minutes."

With a flourish, Goldie lifted her pencil and said, "I've just placed a period at the end of a sentence. I can go now." She grinned at Vivi, who could only laugh.

"OK. Run straight to your grandmother's. I'll be right there."

Goldie jumped up.

"And don't forget your jacket. It's cool and misty out there."

Goldie hugged Vivi quickly, grabbed her jacket from the peg, and ran down the steps from the second-story classroom. Vivi watched her from the window as she ran full tilt down Broad Street, her book bag clutched to her chest.

Vivi closed the window. The fresh air was needed with thirteen bodies in the classroom, but now it gave her a chill. A north-easterly wind had picked up yesterday and brought damp, gray weather, making a memory of the beautiful Indian summer they'd enjoyed for the past week.

The weather suits my mood, Vivi thought to herself. Saturday night she'd felt alive with the new experiences and feelings, but now she was back to her routine, hadn't seen Adelaide, and was pessimistic about the chances of anyone showing for the Equal Suffrage Association meeting next Thursday. But at least she and Bubba were getting along better. Ever since they'd made love Saturday night, he hadn't had anything to drink, was energetic, making jokes and spending more time with her and Goldie, like before his brother died.

Vivi neatened the rows of wooden desks and retrieved the broom from the closet. Had she made the difference in Bubba's mood, Vivi wondered as she swept the detritus of the day into a pile at the front of the room. Either it was her, or the sex, or both that made him happier, because Sunday he'd woken up different than his usual, hungover, irritable self.

That she could make him happy was a difficult concept to grasp. He'd always been her light, the one to bring her out of the dark. She didn't think she had that gift. Sure, she had it for Goldie, but she'd mostly relied on others to make her feel better since her father died; her mother, Bubba, and now Adelaide.

Vivi swept the pile of chalk dust, dirt, leaves, and the biscuit crumbs someone had dropped at lunch into the dustpan and emptied it into the trash. Could she have helped Bubba more after his brother drowned? Would he have stayed away from the alcohol if she'd been his light?

Vivi sat down at her desk, head in her hands. Today was the first time this thought had crossed her mind. Her focus had been on what Bubba wasn't doing for her and she'd lost sight of what she could do for him. But honestly, she'd only had something to offer him Saturday night because of Adelaide's kiss and attention.

This was too much to think about at the end of the day. The light was dimming in the classroom, and she needed to finish her chores and get to her mother's.

The cool, damp air made Vivi shiver and she hurried to the waste bin behind the general store. She emptied the basket and pressed the top layer of papers further down to keep them from blowing away. Vivi turned to go inside, then hesitated when she noticed a man standing with his back towards her. He was at the far end of the building and had his right arm extended, with the palm pressing into the wall. She took a few steps closer and simultaneously registered two things: the man was Art, Mr. Woodard's clerk and there was a young, light-skinned colored girl in front of him with her back against the building.

Vivi froze. The girl couldn't be much older than Goldie. Even in the dim light, Vivi could see the girl's eyes were wide and pleading. What would happen if she said something? Art was over six feet tall and his back as broad as the barrel where she'd just put her trash. He could easily back her up against the wall too. But here was a child, her hair neatly braided in two French braids on either side of her head. Her mother must have done that for her. Vivi's maternal instinct kicked in and erased her fear. Art, who continued to be oblivious to her presence, unbuttoned his pants.

"Art," Vivi said in her firm, teacher voice. She walked closer to him and made eye contact with the terrified girl. Art jumped at her voice and re-buttoned his pants. Vivi had no clue what to do next.

"Sneaking up on folks is not good manners, Mrs. Gibbs," Art said, looking her square in the eye with a look of defiance, like she'd done something wrong and not him.

Vivi stepped closer and planted her boots firmly on the ground. She took a breath to loosen the tightness that squeezed her vocal cords. "Art, I believe this little girl wants to go home. It's getting late and will be dark soon."

Vivi reached her hand out to the girl, who took it, but Art didn't move away.

"She doesn't want to go home," Art said, stepping closer to the girl who pressed herself tighter against the building. "She wants to be right here with me, don't you?"

The girl's hand tightened around Vivi's. Vivi's heart was pounding. She didn't expect him to resist. She'd thought he'd be filled with shame and let the girl go immediately, but was acting as if it was his right to have his way with her.

Art continued. "It's a good thing she likes me, because then we keep buying her daddy's flour for the store. Isn't that right, Pearl?"

Vivi connected the dots. Had this been going on for a while? The girl must be afraid that if she didn't do what Art wanted, her family would lose money. Surely Mr. Woodard didn't know this was going on.

"Art, she's only ten or eleven, the same age as my daughter and I know that spending time with men twice her age is not something she wants to do."

Art turned his body away from the building to address Vivi, and in that instant Pearl stepped over his foot and released Vivi's hand. She ran around the building towards the street, the green ribbons at the ends of her braids streaming behind her.

Vivi didn't take time to be relieved that Pearl was safe, because now she was afraid for herself.

The back door opened and Mr. Woodard yelled, "Art, where the hell are you? We need to close up for the day."

Vivi walked quickly towards Mr. Woodard and he immediately said, "Oh, I'm sorry for cursing, Mrs. Gibbs. I didn't know you were out here. Have you seen Art?"

Vivi looked back and Art was gone. He must have run around the side of the building when he heard the door open. She turned back to Mr. Woodard. Should she tell him?

"You're shaking, Mrs. Gibbs. Come inside. It's chilly out here. I'll look around front for Art."

Vivi followed him back into the store and without saying a word walked up the steps to her classroom. Her legs gave out and she sat down on the top step. The green ribbons at the end of Pearl's braids burned into Vivi's mind.

Vivi took deep breaths, one after the other, to calm herself. She was sweating and shaking at the same time, and her arms and legs were heavy and weak. The scene she'd just witnessed replayed in her mind over and over. What should she do about it?

Vivi wasn't sure how long she sat on the steps, but finally the cycle of flashbacks and questions slowed and she was able to think more clearly. Pearl was her first concern. Vivi needed to make sure she was OK and that her mother knew about the incident. A wave of nausea rolled over Vivi when she imagined someone telling her that this had happened to Goldie. It would be hard to hear, but as a mother she'd want to know, and imagined Pearl's mother would too.

But how would she find Pearl? She certainly couldn't go to the colored part of town knocking on doors until she found her, and definitely not tonight, because it was close to dark. Realizing the time, Vivi stood quickly. Goldie and her mother would be worried. Vivi threw her shawl over her shoulders and gathered her planner. Her flyers advertising the Equal Suffrage Association meeting were lying on her desk. She needed to get them to Sadie to see if she'd post them in her community.

Sadie! That was the answer. She was a teacher and most likely knew Pearl. Vivi would go to Sadie's school after she finished with school tomorrow. She'd take the flyers and talk with Sadie about Pearl, then figure out whether or not to tell Mr. Woodard or the constable.

At the bottom of the steps Vivi didn't look into the store to avoid the possibility of seeing Art, and rushed straight out the door. She pulled her shawl closer around her neck and almost ran the half-mile to her mother's. She needed to hug Goldie.

***

From the front steps of the general store, Vivi watched her students walking home. After what she'd seen yesterday, she didn't want to chance Art cornering one of them.

"Goldie, wait right here while I get my things and I'll walk you to your grandmother's."

Goldie jumped off the steps. "Momma, I've walked to Grandmother's a hundred times. I just did it yesterday. You don't have to go with me."

"Goldie," Vivi said firmly. "Wait here and I'll be right back."

"Yes, Ma'am," Goldie said and plopped herself down on the top step.

Vivi knew she was being irrational, but couldn't risk anything happening to Goldie. Together, they walked down Broad Street to her mother's. Thankfully, the wind had shifted west today and the sky was sapphire blue. A red maple leaf fluttered in front of them and Goldie stopped to pick it up.

"I'm gonna see if Grandmother has a big book we can press this in."

"That's a good idea, honey. Maybe you can find a few more leaves in her yard."

They were at the intersection of Broad and Church streets and Vivi could see her mother's house from here. "OK, Goldie. I'll stand here and watch you run on to your grandmother's."

Goldie cocked her head at Vivi. "Momma, what's wrong with you? Why do you all of a sudden think you need to watch me every second? I'm eleven you know, and I can take care of myself." Goldie put her hands on her hips.

Vivi's heart swelled with love for her independent daughter, so much like she had been at that age. She kissed the top of Goldie's head. "I'd like to think you need me for something, but you're right, you're a very capable eleven-year-old." Vivi neatened Goldie's ponytail. "I'm going to distribute more of these flyers and will be at your grandmother's by dark. We'll have dinner with her again, since your father is out fishing."

"OK," Goldie said, and began a slow jog towards her grandmother's. Over her shoulder she said, "See, I'm fine, Momma. You can go ahead."

Vivi waved at Goldie but stood there until she was safely in her mother's yard. Last night Vivi had gotten her mother alone and told her what had happened behind the general store, and now Etta was on the front porch watching for Goldie.

Vivi picked up her pace and walked west towards the edge of Oriental's town limits, where most of the colored people lived. On the way to Chapawee's, and the few times she'd ridden her horse to Bayboro, she'd seen a grist mill and small general store, but had no idea where the school was.

While she walked, Vivi rehearsed how she would talk to Sadie about what she'd seen. This was a delicate subject to discuss with someone she'd only met twice. And how would Sadie receive her, a white woman coming unannounced to ask for help? Vivi thought of the green ribbons at the end of Pearl's braids. No matter how nervous she was right now, it was nothing compared to what Pearl had experienced.

Vivi hesitated when she came to an intersection. The general store was on her left. Which direction was the school?

"Are you looking for someone?" a woman's voice said from behind her.

Vivi turned. There was a colored woman in front of her, probably a few years older than Vivi. They were almost the same height and their eyes met. The woman smiled kindly.

"If a white woman ever comes out here it's usually because her domestic didn't show for work."

Vivi took in the woman across from her. Her presence was calm and self-assured. She was dressed similarly to Vivi, and most likely hadn't been cleaning houses all day. Instead of a frayed bag full of flyers and a planner, like Vivi, this woman had a small, brown leather purse that hung delicately over her right elbow.

Vivi held out her hand. "I'm Vivian Gibbs, the grade schoolteacher in Oriental and I'm looking for Sadie," Vivi hesitated, "the teacher here. Is the schoolhouse close by?"

The woman shook her hand firmly. "It's nice to meet you Mrs. Gibbs. I'm Jacquelyn Williams, but everyone calls me Jack. The schoolhouse is to the left, and on my way home. I'm happy to walk you there," Jack said, and headed in that direction.

Vivi fell in beside her. "Thank you."

They walked in silence past small, wooden homes, most with porches. Jack called hello to an older woman sitting on her porch swing. Four boys about eight years old ran by chasing one another and laughing. Two men with sawdust flecking their hair and clothes, walked in the opposite direction on the other side of the road.

Vivi was aware that she was the only white person around. Not that she'd expected anything different, but this was the first time she'd ever been alone, outside her own neighborhood. Her heart rate increased, and despite the cool October air she was sweating. Why was she nervous? She wasn't threatened in any way. In fact, Jack was a comforting presence. Vivi thought of Pearl again, who really had been threatened, and ignored her own feelings. She was fine.

One of the men on the other side of the road called out to Jack, "Afternoon. Everything OK?"

"Yes. Everything's fine," Jack replied. "Have a good evening, Jasper."

Vivi blushed and Jack confirmed her suspicion when she said, "I'm sure he's wondering who you are and why you're here, but you seem harmless enough." Jack laughed and Vivi managed a smile.

"Oh yes," Vivi said, a little too quickly. "I just want to talk with Sadie about a student and to give her some flyers for a meeting next week about women's suffrage."

Jack stopped and pointed to the building on the left. "Here's the schoolhouse. Now what about this meeting?"

Vivi handed Jack a flyer from her bag and gave her a brief explanation of what she and Adelaide hoped to do.

Jack studied the flyer and then tucked it into her purse. She looked past Vivi and then raised her hand to wave. "Sadie," Jack called, "Mrs. Gibbs is here to see you."

Vivi turned and saw Sadie in the doorway of the schoolhouse shaking out a rug, cleaning at the end of the day, just like she'd done.

"Thanks for showing me the way, Jack. Maybe I'll see you next week at our meeting?"

Jack looked over Vivi's shoulder towards the school and then back at Vivi. "You're letting colored women attend?"

Vivi nodded. "Yes, that's why I wanted to give these flyers to Sadie, to help spread the word here."

"OK. Maybe I'll come then if Sadie does. Nice to meet you."

Jack didn't seem enthusiastic and Vivi wondered whether inviting the colored women was a good idea. She'd never asked Adelaide if that's what they did in Boston.

Jack tipped her head at Vivi and then continued walking west down the road. The sun was at the top of the tree line and Vivi needed to hurry to return home by dark. Sadie stood in the doorway, the braided rug over her arm. She hadn't said a word yet, and suddenly Vivi was self-conscious without Jack beside her.

"Hi, Sadie," Vivi said when she got to the stoop by the front door. "I'm sorry to come unannounced, but I'm worried about a young girl I saw yesterday in town. I believe she's one of your students. May I come in and talk with you about her?"

Sadie's stance relaxed slightly after hearing the purpose of Vivi's visit. "Sure, come on in, but I only have a few minutes."

Vivi followed Sadie into the small classroom that glowed in the late afternoon sunlight streaming in the west windows. The light also illuminated the cracks between the planks of the wall. This was no issue on a temperate fall afternoon, but Vivi remembered what Sadie had shared in the circle, and realized her students had little protection against a cold, damp winter morning. There was a pot-bellied stove at the back of the classroom and a chalkboard and large desk for Sadie at the front. In between was a mixture of seating, a couple desks like Vivi's students used, a rudimentary table made of a piece of plywood over stacked crates and six wooden chairs randomly placed around the room. Next to the door there was a bookcase that held the books Vivi had given to Sadie. Tacked directly on the wall by the bookcase were pictures of leaves that must have been drawn by the younger students. They were neatly labeled as maple, oak, and sweetgum, a similar lesson to what Vivi had done with her first graders.

Vivi's feet were throbbing after the twenty-minute walk in her school shoes, narrow-toed boots that laced to just above her ankle. "Do you mind if we sit down?" Vivi asked. "My feet are killing me."

"Sure," Sadie said, pulling a straight-back chair over to her desk. She motioned Vivi to it, and sat down in the one behind her desk.

Sadie's expression hadn't changed since Vivi's arrival, no smile or scowl, only a neutral demeanor that Vivi couldn't read. Vivi placed her bag on the floor and brushed some dirt off her skirt, all the while looking for the right words to start with.

Sadie slid to the edge of her chair. "So, you want to talk about a student of mine?"

"Yes," Vivi said, glad Sadie had ended her rumination. "I believe her name is Pearl and she looked to be about ten or eleven." Sadie nodded and Vivi sighed with relief. "You know her? Was she in school today?"

"Yes," Sadie said. "She's one of my 4th grade students."

"I'm glad she's OK."

Sadie leaned towards Vivi, "And why wouldn't she be OK?"

Heat rushed up Vivi's neck and her heart rate increased as she visualized the scene behind the general store. She took a breath. "Yesterday, at the end of the day I went behind the general store to empty my trash and I saw Art, Mr. Woodard's clerk, intimidating Pearl."

"Intimidating? What do you mean by that, Vivi?" Sadie's voice was tight with the first discernible emotion since Vivi's arrival.

Vivi relayed the details of what had happened just twenty-four hours ago and Sadie gripped the armrest of her chair as she listened. "So, the first thing I wanted to do was make sure Pearl was OK and that her parents knew what happened. I figured you could help with that part. I'm not sure what to do next. I think I should talk with Mr. Woodard. Art is a danger and shouldn't be working there."

Sadie stood when Vivi said that. "Oh, no. Don't say anything. We'll handle this ourselves."

Sadie walked to the west windows and looked out. "Nothing good will come of drawing attention to this, but I appreciate you letting me know. I'll talk with Pearl's parents and be extra attentive to her in school."

Vivi stood and walked to Sadie. "But Sadie, something needs to be done. It's a crime for a man that age to take advantage of a mere child. He should be punished so he doesn't do it again."

Sadie crossed her arms over her chest. "That's not how it works, Vivi," Sadie said with controlled force. "If you talk about this, Art will say Pearl wanted his attention and is old enough to make her own choices and that he did nothing wrong."

"But the constable, he'll believe me and will have Art punished."

Sadie threw her hands up in the air with exasperation. "Art is a white man, the constable is a white man. He'll take Art's side, especially since it's about Pearl, a colored girl. Then they'll stir up trouble for Pearl's family. Maybe Mr. Woodard would stop buying her father's flour."

Sadie paused. "Or worse."

Sadie's face was easy to read now, a mix of anger and fear, and maybe the hopelessness she'd shared in the circle. Vivi was quiet and processed what she'd just heard.

"But Sadie, that's so unfair."

Sadie moved one of the desks in alignment with the others. "I'm glad you feel that way, but until something changes and white men don't have all the power, that's the way it's going to be. We have to do our best to protect ourselves on our own."

"Things can change," Vivi said and moved to fetch her bag. "If women get the right to vote, then white men won't have all the power." She handed Sadie a flyer. "We're having a meeting next Thursday to organize a local chapter of the Equal Suffrage Association here in Pamlico County. Our goal is to raise support for a suffrage amendment to the North Carolina constitution."

There was silence while Sadie read the flyer.

"Would you be interested in attending?" Vivi asked. "I brought some flyers in case you're willing to put them up around here."

Sadie looked up at her. "Even if you passed this amendment, what makes you think we'd actually get to vote? Colored men have the right to vote, but the politicians passed the poll tax and literacy test making it impossible for most of them to exercise that right."

Vivi was silent because she didn't know about these practices, having only heard Bubba's version of his voting experience.

Sadie pointed at her desk. "Leave the flyers, but I can tell you no colored woman is going into town after dark, and most likely the Central Hotel wouldn't even let us in the door."

The light in the school room dimmed and the dissonance between Vivi and Sadie was palpable. Sadie was right. What had she been thinking? Just because she connected with Chapawee, Cora and Sadie in the circle, didn't mean they could easily mingle outside that space. Vivi chided herself for being naive and let the suffrage topic drop.

"Thank you for your help with Pearl." Vivi picked up her bag. "If there's anything else I can do just let me know."

Sadie took some keys from her desk drawer and she and Vivi walked to the front door. "I'll talk with Pearl's parents and we'll do our best to keep her away from Art." They stepped out into the cool air and Sadie locked the schoolroom door.

"And Vivi, thank you for coming all the way out here to tell me about Pearl. You could have ignored what you saw but you didn't."

Vivi nodded. "If it had been Goldie, I certainly would want someone to tell me."

Sadie met Vivi's gaze but her face had returned to a neutral expression that Vivi couldn't read.

"Have a good evening, Vivi."

"You too, Sadie."

They turned and walked in opposite directions. It was dusk now and Vivi picked up her pace to avoid being on the road in full darkness. She turned right at the general store and headed back to town. The western sky was a kaleidoscope of pink, cantaloupe and blue, but the colors were no comfort tonight. She was unsettled. Not because she was walking alone at dusk, but due to what had transpired that afternoon. She'd accomplished what she'd wanted in terms of telling Sadie about Pearl, but was acutely aware of the different worlds she and Sadie lived in.

The Baptist Church steeple was back-lit by the last glimmer of dusk when Vivi got to town. She looked around at the houses on either side of the street; some were similar to the ones in Sadie's neighborhood, but most were two or three times bigger, some with second stories. Vivi thought of the bookshelf in Sadie's classroom filled with her secondhand books, the sun streaming in through the cracks in the schoolroom wall, but mostly Vivi thought about Sadie's fear of retribution if she spoke about Pearl's abuse.

God forbid that Art would have done that to Goldie, but if he had, Vivi knew she and Bubba wouldn't have hesitated to talk with Mr. Woodard and the constable about it. They could seek justice on behalf of their daughter without fear, but Pearl's parents could not.

Her father's death had taught her that life wasn't fair. Everyone, colored, Indian and white, had to deal with death, but the inequity she saw today was specific to people who weren't white. The same set of circumstances would have vastly different outcomes depending on skin color. Vivi was almost running now, filled by anger at the injustice, and at herself for not seeing it sooner.

"Vivi. Vivi! Why are you running? Are you OK?"

Vivi stopped abruptly to avoid knocking Adelaide over. "Adelaide, what are you doing out in the dark?"

Before she said anything, Adelaide hugged Vivi tightly. "Looking for you. I'd stopped by your mother's to see you this afternoon, and she told me where you were and invited me to stay for dinner. She expected you back before dark. I got worried when it got late, and came out to find you."

"Thank you," Vivi said. "I'm fine I guess, but I'm troubled by something that happened today. It's made me realize more than ever that I want a voice in who's elected to office and the laws that they make."

"What happened?" Adelaide asked.

They arrived at her mother's yard. Vivi took a deep breath. "It's complicated. A lot has happened since I last saw you. I'll walk you back to the hotel after dinner to explain it all, but I have you to thank for stirring up my anger."

"Me?"

"Yes. You've opened my eyes to see the world in a new way." For an instant, Vivi wished her perspective hadn't changed because it had certainly complicated her life.

They stopped at the bottom of the front porch steps and Adelaide turned to face Vivi. "Well, I'm glad I've helped, but I hope you're feeling more than anger."

Vivi read Adelaide's body language and instinctively leaned forward to meet her lips. Suddenly her anger, the stress of her school day and thoughts of Pearl dissolved in the warmth of Adelaide's kiss.

The screen door squeaked and Vivi immediately stepped away from Adelaide, remembering where she was.

"Momma, there you are! We were worried." Goldie held open the door. "Come on, Grandmother has dinner ready and Miss Adelaide gets to stay too."

Vivi and Adelaide smiled at one another. "Yes. She told me. What a perfect way to end the day, with my three favorite women."

CHAPTER 10

Vivi sat in the parlor of the hotel, staring at the front door, while Adelaide prepared a pot of tea in the kitchen. The membership forms from the Equal Suffrage Association were stacked neatly on the table in front of her. Unable to keep still any longer, Vivi stood and walked to the window. The light from the front porch illuminated an empty street.

Would anyone show up? She knew Jack and Sadie wouldn't be there, but it was just as well. When she read the by-laws for the ESA, she learned that colored women weren't allowed to join. She'd always accepted that the lives of white and colored people were separate, but now it didn't make as much sense to her. Wouldn't it be better if all women worked together to get the vote?

Adelaide arrived and placed the teapot on the table in front of the couch and then patted the space beside her. She rested her hand on Vivi's thigh. "We need at least ten women to start a chapter here?" Adelaide asked.

"Yes." Vivi pulled on the ruffle at the end of her sleeve. "But you don't count, since you're not a resident of Pamlico County."

Adelaide laughed and leaned back against the couch. "Yes. I'm just the Yankee instigator."

"I'm glad you can laugh about it because that's what people are saying." Vivi left off that Bubba had used that phrase to describe Adelaide as well.

"Oh, it doesn't bother me, but I think a better phrase would be Yankee educator. After all, that's what I've done, educated you about the suffrage movement and shown you different ways to approach life."

Adelaide's hand was still on her leg and Vivi placed her hand over it. "Yes, but it was your idea to start a chapter of the ESA."

"You're right. I did instigate that." Adelaide paused. "But from the looks of it I haven't instigated much else."

Vivi sighed. "I only got permission to post the flyer in a few places and someone took down the ones in the tea shop and outside the general store. I announced it at church last night but no one was interested."

"Not interested, or against women's suffrage?" Adelaide asked and slid to the edge of the couch. "The few women I've tried to talk to about this were flat out against it. Said things were fine the way they were and women needed to focus on the home."

Vivi nodded. "Yes. It was the same at church. The ones who spoke up thought women voting was going against the way God meant things to be. They said they'd pray so I'll see the mistake I'm making in pursuing this."

"Well if they think you're going against God, I'd hate to hear what they think of me, a single woman traveling unaccompanied and singing for her supper."

Vivi stood and paced in front of the couch. "Maybe this is a mistake, Adelaide. Oriental may not be ready to fight for women's suffrage and I'm just wasting my time. If I was home right now, I could be—"

"Could be what?" Adelaide asked, cutting her off. "Doing the same thing you've done every weeknight for the past ten years?"

Vivi was about to take offense until Adelaide's hands enveloped her waist from behind. Adelaide rested her chin on Vivi's left shoulder and said, "Isn't it more exciting to be here with me, where you can't predict what will happen next?"

Adelaide's soft breath on her neck sent goosebumps down Vivi's left side. She leaned back into Adelaide and time stood still for a moment. She didn't answer Adelaide because she was right. Vivi knew exactly how tonight would play out had she stayed home.

The sound of the front door untangled Vivi and Adelaide. They looked at one another and smiled. Two people stepped into the foyer of the hotel, and Vivi immediately recognized them as women who'd taken a flyer at Adelaide's show.

"Kathryn, I'm glad you came." Kathryn was the mother of one of Vivi's students, but otherwise their paths didn't cross. Kathryn's husband managed the local bank, and she was in a different social circle than Vivi.

The other woman held out her hand and said, " I'm Eve Winthrop, Kathryn's mother." She had gray hair pulled back into a chignon, and was wearing a skirt that tapered just above her ankles and a deep purple jacket over her blouse. Vivi was wearing her newest navy-blue skirt, but felt plain next to Eve, and Kathryn, who was dressed similarly.

Vivi shook her hand and then introduced them to Adelaide. "This is Adelaide Thornberry, my friend from Boston. She's worked with the Boston Equal Suffrage Association for Good Government, and has offered her help as we get organized."

Eve leaned forward and looked into the parlor. "It doesn't look like there's much to organize. Do you expect anyone else?"

"Come. Have a cup of tea," Adelaide said and led the women into the parlor.

"I'm afraid this may be it," Vivi said once everyone was seated with their drinks. "The women we invited in person all declined, so we were keeping our fingers crossed that someone would show up."

Kathryn and her mother exchanged a glance. "We're not surprised," Kathryn said. "My aunt lives up in Asheville and has kept us up to date on what's happening with women's suffrage in North Carolina. The announcement at Adelaide's show was the first time we've heard it spoken about in Oriental."

Vivi nodded. "I talked with the president of the Oriental Women's Club, thinking they may have started some work on suffrage, but she said they hadn't taken that issue on."

"Kathryn and I are members, and did ask about suffrage last year," Eve said, "but they saw it as too controversial, and wanted to keep the focus on gathering books for a community reading room."

Vivi nodded. "My mother and I have occasionally discussed the right to vote, but until Adelaide talked with me about it, I'd never considered taking action either."

Adelaide leaned forward from her seat on the couch. "Well, we certainly can't wait around for the men in power to decide on their own to give us the right to vote."

"Exactly," Eve said and poured more tea from the pot Adelaide had left on the table. "But at the same time, it's hard to know how to make a difference. Last year over 5000 women marched for women's suffrage in Washington DC and still no federal amendment has been proposed."

Kathryn tapped her heel on the hardwood floor. "And Virginia and Maryland didn't pass their state amendments either," she added.

Adelaide stood up. "Now, ladies, we can't get discouraged. If every woman speaks up and takes action where she is, I know we can make this happen."

Everyone here was knowledgeable about the suffrage movement, Vivi realized. Maybe she wasn't the best one to be the organizer, but she pushed through her doubts and continued with the agenda. "What's happening now, is the Equal Suffrage Association wants to add a women's suffrage amendment to the North Carolina constitution. The first step is convincing our state legislators to pass this resolution, so our citizens can vote on it."

"Yes," Eve said. "My sister has said the focus is on gathering petitions in support of women's suffrage and giving them to our local senators and representatives."

"That's where we come in. Well, not me since I'm not from here," Adelaide added, and smiled.

Vivi put her hand on Adelaide's leg. "But we will use you as a resource since we've never done this before. My thought is that the three of us begin getting signatures for a Pamlico County petition."

"And maybe as we talk to women about suffrage, some will want to join our cause," Kathryn said.

"Some men will also. We have several strong male supporters in Boston."

The enthusiasm in the room intensified when they focused on actions they could take. Even though there were only two other women, it was a start and maybe she could convince Sadie and Jack to get signatures from the colored women. Even though they'd never be members of the Equal Suffrage Association, there was no reason they couldn't start their own petition. It couldn't hurt to include more signatures in the packet she'd send to Jordan Carawan, the state representative for Pamlico County.

Vivi slid a paper she'd received from the North Carolina ESA into the middle of the coffee table. "Here's a template for the petition the ESA sent me."

For the next hour and a half each woman created a petition and Adelaide coached them on how to talk convincingly to other women about suffrage. They ended by dividing the town of Oriental into thirds with each of them taking a section.

"OK," Vivi said. "We'll meet again in three weeks and see what progress has been made. Then we'll decide how to reach the other parts of our county."

All the women stood and hugged one another, bonded by their common goal.

"Thank you for calling this meeting, Vivi, and for all your help, Adelaide," Eve said and stepped onto the hotel's front porch.

"See you soon," Kathryn added. "And good luck to us all in getting signatures!"

The door shut and Vivi immediately hugged Adelaide. "Thank you!"

"For what?" Adelaide asked, keeping her hands on Vivi's waist.

"For waking me up. I've spent most of my time focused on what's happening in my life, which is important, especially my family, but it's energizing to broaden my perspective." Vivi paused and remembered what she'd shared in the women's circle about feeling disconnected. Her work on suffrage, and time with Adelaide were an antidote.

Adelaide tucked a piece of Vivi's hair behind her ear. "Sometimes when we focus on the bigger picture, our problems don't seem as big."

The heat from Adelaide's body and the delicate way she'd touched her hair made Vivi's knees weak. She wanted to kiss Adelaide again, but shouldn't she want to kiss Bubba and not her friend? Adelaide moved her head closer to Vivi, almost daring her to initiate a kiss. Neither of them spoke or moved and the charge between them intensified until their lips met, Vivi unsure of who initiated.

The kiss deepened and Vivi put her arms around Adelaide's upper back, pulling her as close as she could. She was lost in her body's response to Adelaide. Part of her wished it would never stop and another part wished it had never started. It didn't make sense to desire her best friend this way. Vivi pulled away to catch her breath and gather her thoughts.

Adelaide took her right hand. "That was nice," she said, smiling. "Why don't you come back to my room for a bit before you go home?"

Vivi hurried into the parlor, listening to her mind and not her body. She gathered her papers and purse. The grandmother clock in the parlor struck nine. "I need to get home." Vivi slipped her coat on and when she turned, she met Adelaide's gaze. There were tears in her eyes.

"I'm sorry I can't stay. It's just that I've got to . . ."

"Get home to your family," Adelaide finished for her. "I'll be fine. It just gets lonely here at night."

For the first time since they'd met, Adelaide appeared vulnerable. Vivi thought of her as confident and independent, and she was, but she was also hundreds of miles from her family, and besides interacting with the hotel guests, was alone most of the day.

Vivi gave Adelaide a quick hug, happy that her coat put an extra layer between them. "I'm going to start getting signatures for the petition Saturday morning. Why don't you come over for lunch that day and I'll let you know how it went and get pointers on how I can improve?" Vivi knew she wasn't giving Adelaide what she wanted, but it was the best she could offer right now.

Adelaide smiled, but without the usual light that accompanied it. "That sounds nice. I'll pick up some cookies from the tea shoppe for dessert."

The air was brisk and refreshed Vivi. She filled her lungs and exhaled deeply before beginning her walk home. She paid attention to the pressure of her feet on the dirt road, step, step, step. As much as Adelaide opened her up to new perspectives and feelings, she was only passing through, and Vivi needed to stay grounded in the life waiting for her at home.

**

"Good morning. I'm Vivi Gibbs," Vivi said to the balding man in his late forties who answered the door.

Before she could continue he inserted, "Oh, I know you. You taught my children, Liza and Frank Carpenter."

"Yes," Vivi replied, switching gears to recall the man's children. "I remember them. It's been a couple years since Frank finished school and Liza's been gone longer than that. I hope they're well."

"They're good. Liza's expecting our first grandchild any day now," the man said with a smile.

"That's wonderful news."

"Seeing as you're not teaching my children anymore, why are you here?" he asked. His tone was inquisitive, but not unkind.

Vivi held up her clipboard. "I'm gathering signatures on a petition to support women's right to vote. We want to send it to Jordan Carawan, our state representative, so he'll support a suffrage amendment to the North Carolina constitution."

The man, who'd been standing in his doorway, stepped onto the front porch with Vivi, leaving the front door ajar. "Women's right to vote?" he said with a snort and then stuck his hands deep in his pockets. "That's never going to happen. Women should focus on managing their home and raising children. I don't interfere with women's responsibilities, and women don't need to interfere with politics, which is a man's responsibility."

Vivi was ready for this argument. "But many laws about education and health have a direct impact on women and their families. Isn't it fair that they have a say in these matters?"

"I'm done talking with you, Mrs. Gibbs." He turned and went back into his house.

Vivi stepped closer to the door and said, "Perhaps your wife would have a different opinion."

Without looking back the man shut the door in Vivi's face. She stood there a moment, her heart thumping against her chest. The first time this happened she'd gotten tears in her eyes at the rebuff but now it made her angry. If the husband answered the door, she never even had the chance to speak with the wife. Maybe knocking on the front door on a Saturday wasn't the best tactic. The only signatures she'd gathered were from women she'd found outside hanging laundry and collecting pecans, but even some she found alone refused, and presented an argument similar to what she'd just heard.

It was almost noon and Vivi's feet were sore. Her black Sunday-best boots were fashionable with their ten tiny buttons, but the hard heels hurt her feet. Thoughts darted in her mind as she replayed her interactions. She mentally rehearsed new ways to talk about suffrage and formulated questions to ask Adelaide when she saw her for lunch.

***

"You're certainly deep in thought," Adelaide said.

Vivi blinked and saw she was standing in front of her house with no memory of how she'd got there. "I didn't see you sitting there. I was deep in thought. Sorry if you've been waiting long."

Vivi hadn't seen Adelaide since Thursday evening when she declined her invitation to go back to her room. She'd clearly hurt Adelaide that night and worried things would be strained between them today.

"Oh, no," Adelaide said, and patted the space beside her indicating Vivi should sit. "I've only been here a few minutes. I walked around back but didn't see Bubba or Goldie."

Vivi sat beside her, happy to give her feet a rest. "They're spending the day with Bubba's parents. Bubba's helping his father repair his barn and I'm sure Goldie is entertaining her grandmother."

"Well, I have to say I'm glad to have you all to myself. Now, tell me about your morning. Did you get some signatures on our petition?"

For the next twenty minutes Vivi shared her experiences, what had worked, what hadn't and Adelaide suggested some strategies that had been successful in Boston. The conversation flowed easily with no indication that Adelaide was hurt or angry.

"So, I should find a political issue that women would be interested in, open with that, and then talk about how the right to vote would give them more influence on that and similar issues?"

"Exactly," Adelaide said. "You mentioned health and education in general, but hopefully you can find a specific issue to present to them."

Vivi realized she'd need to stay better informed on state legislation. This afternoon she would purchase the *News and Observer* from the general store. It came from Raleigh, the state capital, and covered politics more closely than the local paper. But there was laundry to do, and she needed to have dinner ready for Goldie and Bubba when they got home. Vivi sighed.

"What's wrong?" Adelaide asked.

"I need more time. I want to read the paper from Raleigh to stay abreast of what's going on, but after you leave there are chores I need to do."

"What about tomorrow?"

"Goldie and I usually go to church with my mother." Vivi paused. "But I guess I could miss that. I'll take Goldie to Sunday School and then use that time to read the paper and next weekend I'll be ready to get more signatures." She rarely missed church, mostly out of obligation to her mother, but surely God wouldn't care if she was doing something that made her feel alive.

"You don't have to sit in a church to connect with God," Adelaide said, as if reading Vivi's mind. "Your enthusiasm about suffrage is God working through you, and taking action is sometimes more Christian than sitting in a pew listening to someone else's interpretation of God."

"I don't know if my minister would agree." Vivi's stomach growled. "But I do know I'm hungry. There's vegetable soup ready to heat up for lunch."

"That sounds good," Adelaide said.

With Adelaide's help it only took a few minutes to set the table and slice some apples to accompany their lunch. Vivi handed Adelaide a plate for her cookies.

"Making lunch is easier with you here to help. Bubba's either still out working, or sitting at the table waiting, and Goldie pitches in where she can, but I still do the bulk of the work."

Adelaide laughed and arranged the cookies. "Yes. I've found life much easier when I've lived with another woman."

"You mean your mother?" Vivi asked and walked back to the stove to check the soup.

Adelaide didn't answer and Vivi turned to look at her. Adelaide sat at the table and folded and unfolded the napkin at her place. "No, not my mother."

Vivi cocked her head at Adelaide's response and then turned to ladle the soup into bowls. Adelaide had lived with another woman, Vivi thought to herself. She'd never heard of that except for the sisters over in Stonewall who'd never married and lived together their entire lives.

"Thank you," Adelaide said when Vivi placed the steaming bowl in front of her. "It smells delicious."

Before Vivi could ask her question, Adelaide continued, "Let's have a moment of silence to give thanks before we eat." She took Vivi's hand. "It's the Quaker way," she said, and then bowed her head.

Vivi followed suit and stared at a carrot disc, floating in the soup. The warmth rising from the soup and emanating from Adelaide's hand wrapped her in comfort and she gave thanks for the moment. Adelaide squeezed her hand and Vivi lifted her head.

"Thanks. I've never started a meal like that, but I liked it. Reminded me of the silence we had in the women's circle."

Adelaide blew on a spoonful of soup and then, holding it midair said, "That's how we've always done it in my family. Everybody gives thanks in their own way rather than depending on someone else's words."

Adelaide swallowed her soup, giving Vivi the opportunity to speak. "So, you don't live with your parents when you're back in Boston?"

Adelaide dabbed her mouth with the napkin and said, "I prefer living on my own, but it's difficult to afford so I was living with a friend and we shared expenses."

This arrangement was foreign to Vivi. "Another woman who doesn't want to be married either?" Vivi asked incredulously. Adelaide was the first women she'd met who said she didn't want to marry and was bold enough to follow through with it. It was hard to imagine there were others like her.

Adelaide nodded. "Pauline is a secretary for an attorney in Boston. I kept the books for my father's business, did some work in the theater and we both spent time with the suffrage activities in Boston. Supporting a husband's career wouldn't allow us to do all that."

"Or having children," Vivi said, with an edge to her voice that she hadn't intended.

Adelaide smiled. "Yes, those two things do go hand in hand."

Vivi tried to imagine the life Adelaide described. Adelaide and Pauline discussing their days over dinner and maybe reading together before bed. Mornings must feel more relaxed without having to get a child ready too. Adelaide probably didn't even have to get up at a certain time. Maybe Pauline woke her before she left for work. A stab of envy pierced Vivi when she pictured this woman looking down at Adelaide sleeping.

"How is Pauline managing without you?" Vivi asked and crunched into an apple slice.

Adelaide blushed and put her spoon down. "I don't know."

"You haven't written one another?"

Adelaide sighed. "It's complicated, Vivi. Pauline and I." Adelaide took a sip of water and continued. "We ended our arrangement. We'd been living together for three years but it wasn't working anymore. That's part of the reason I took the job on the showboat. I wasn't ready to do the same things I'd always done in Boston, but without Pauline." Adelaide turned her head and looked out the back window to the water. Her eyes glistened with tears.

"I'm sorry," Vivi said, "but just because you can't live together doesn't mean you can't be friends with one another."

Adelaide turned back to look at Vivi and took a breath. "Vivi, we were more than just friends."

"More than friends?" Adelaide didn't respond. "Did you feel like sisters?"

"We loved one another," Adelaide paused. "The same way men and women love one another."

Vivi had just swallowed a bite of chocolate chip cookie and her throat constricted around it. She coughed and then took a sip of water.

Adelaide reached over and rubbed her back. "Take some deep breaths through your nose."

Vivi followed Adelaide's instructions and her throat relaxed but her thoughts continued in such a flurry she couldn't even formulate a question.

Adelaide stopped rubbing her back but kept her hand on Vivi's shoulder. "I know you're not familiar with this type of love," Adelaide said and then reached into Vivi's lap and held her hand, "but I think you understand what I'm talking about. Love has no boundaries. Only our minds and social customs limit it."

Vivi thought about how joyful and alive she'd felt these past few months with Adelaide. How Adelaide's eyes lit up when she saw Vivi. How Vivi yearned for the feel of Adelaide's lips on hers. Was this the love Adelaide was talking about?

Suddenly Vivi released Adelaide's hand and stood to clear the table. Adelaide picked up her soup bowl but Vivi waved her off. "No, no. I've got it. You don't need to help."

"Vivi, you're upset. We can clean up later. I think we need to talk about this. I know you're confused."

Vivi turned her back to Adelaide and set the soup bowl on the counter. She wasn't confused. In fact, things were more clear after what Adelaide had shared, and this scared her.

Vivi turned around. "I'm not confused," she said her voice rising. "It's clear to me that our lives are different. Living in a big city up north with your father's money to support you has given you options I've never had. You can choose how you spend your day, where you live." Vivi stomped past Adelaide and snatched her bowl from the table. "And even who you love."

"Believe me, my life isn't as easy as you think it is," Adelaide said and pushed her chair under the table, "but everybody has different opportunities based on the family they're born into. That's just the way it is."

Vivi's breath was shallow and she leaned back into the counter for support.

Adelaide continued, "But we can create new opportunities for ourselves. Just since I've been here you've learned more about women's suffrage, and are now taking this issue on."

A ball of heat welled in Vivi's chest. "Well, isn't it lucky for me that you came to open my eyes to the world," Vivi said sarcastically, and pushed past Adelaide to get the broom from the corner. With forceful strokes, she swept the cookie crumbs near the table into a pile. "I guess without you, I would have languished here in my ignorance."

Adelaide grabbed the broom handle and stopped Vivi from sweeping. "You're creating thoughts I've never had," Adelaide said, both of them still holding the broom. "Ignorance is the last word I'd associate with you."

Vivi snatched the handle from Adelaide and swept the crumbs out the back door. "And what is happening between us? You jumped on the showboat to stop thinking about Pauline and jumped off when you met me. Am I just another diversion so you don't think about her?" Vivi put the broom back in the corner and paced in front of Adelaide. "Sometimes I wish you'd never come to Oriental. Before you I was comfortable in my life. I didn't see all the unfairness in the world and didn't know there were options to being a wife and mother."

Adelaide retrieved her small handbag from the table. "Vivi, Pauline has nothing to do with the feelings I have for you, and now you sound like those women who don't support suffrage because it challenges the way things have always been. I felt safe being authentic with you, sharing my political ideas and the way that I love. That's all it was, Vivi," Adelaide said, walking to the back door. "Me, just being myself. I didn't set out to make you feel badly about your life, or to give you a heavier load to carry. That's all your doing and I don't appreciate you taking your frustration out on me. We both know you weren't comfortable in your life before I got here. You were looking for something to be passionate about and I gave you that, a cause to fight for and the feelings between us. All I did was show you that you have the power to change your life if only you'd use it."

Vivi stared at Adelaide who stood at the open back door. Her anger was spent and shame crept in. She hadn't acted like this since she'd been a teenager. Silence separated them. Vivi knew the right words would dissolve this wall. They'd embrace, and talk through this but still, no words came.

Adelaide stepped outside. "Since you have nothing more to say, I'm leaving, and if in fact you wish I'd never come here, perhaps it's best if I make arrangements to leave."

Adelaide's voice caught in her throat and for the second time that day, a door closed in Vivi's face. Immediately she melted to the floor, buried her head in her hands and cried. She wrapped her arms around herself and rocked back and forth, partly to comfort herself and partly to stay warm. The floor was cold, and cool air drifted under the door. Vivi's tears subsided. What had just happened and how could she make it right? The answer wouldn't be found sitting on the floor, so Vivi stood, grabbed her shawl and went outside.

When she got to the end of their dock, Vivi sat facing the sun to warm up. The blue water melted into the blue sky and the monochromatic panorama focused Vivi's thoughts.

What made her angry? Adelaide was right. She was taking something out on Adelaide, but what exactly? She thought of Adelaide's words, "I've only shown you that you have the power to change your life if only you'd use it." Before Adelaide, she had been waiting for Bubba to change so her life would improve, but Adelaide's encouragement and Vivi's own revelation at the circle reinforced that she could make things different, irrespective of what others did. Maybe she was angry with herself for not seeing this sooner.

A pelican swung low over the water and dove in after a fish. His pouch expanded and he gulped the snack with enthusiasm. Vivi watched him, aware of the knot in her stomach. She was also angry because she was afraid. After Adelaide's explanation, Vivi couldn't deny that she loved and desired Adelaide in a way that betrayed her vows to Bubba, but since Adelaide had come into her life she was happier and more alive. Should she sacrifice this to honor her marriage?

Vivi's thoughts tangled together with no clear answer. Inspiration seized her and she stood. She needed to write, something she hadn't done to soothe her emotions since her father died. This would be the only way to make some sense of what she was feeling.

CHAPTER 11

The upper branches of the trees clicked against one another and the river grass leaned northward in the strong southwest wind, unusual for November. Chapawee set her oyster basket down and put on her work gloves. The wind created a low tide and she wanted to take advantage of it to collect oysters. She walked gingerly to avoid rocks and shells until she reached a small oyster bed nestled in the curve of the shoreline. Her feet were numb from the cold mud, but the air temperature kept her from getting a chill.

Chapawee's family had harvested oysters from this spot for as long as she could remember. When she was young, her family always had an oyster roast at this time of the year. Her relatives living on the Coharie River would come in addition to the family from the Bay River. The women would meet in their circle, while the men collected and shucked the oysters and then the focus was on cooking, eating, and playing games.

Chapawee had taken those moments for granted when she was young, and now the memories were her companions. She picked up a healthy oyster, about the size of her palm, and popped off a couple smaller ones attached to it with her knife. It didn't take long for her basket to fill. There'd be plenty for her, with enough left over for Cora and Jeremiah if they wanted some.

The sun-warmed grass was a welcome contrast to the cold mud, and Chapawee stepped carefully on her numb feet. With all her effort, she lugged the full oyster basket to the table behind her cabin. Chapawee went inside for a bowl and when she returned Cora was there.

"I guessed you'd be collecting oysters," Cora said. "Perfect day for it."

"Yup," Chapawee agreed. "The sun shining on my head made the cold mud easier to tolerate. What are you up to today?"

"Went to church and just finished lunch. You have a minute to talk?"

Chapawee nodded and sat down in one of the cane chairs she kept by her workbench. "It gives me a minute to rest. Have a seat."

Cora pulled the other chair around and sat across from Chapawee. She took a small package wrapped in brown paper from her dress pocket. "Would you be able to take this to the post office when you go this week?"

"Sure," Chapawee said, taking the package.

"It's some of our wild carrot seeds I'm sending to Titus in Baltimore. Lord knows I'd love some more grandchildren, but he and Sylvia have only been married a year and it makes sense for them to save money before they start a family."

"When I mail this, it'll give me a chance to see if there's a letter from my daughter."

"Thanks," Cora said, leaning back in her chair. "Are things staying quiet around here? No more visits from Mrs. Livingston or the constable?"

"No, thank goodness. I'd like to think things have blown over, but Mrs. Livingston is an angry woman with nothing much to focus on besides not being a grandmother, so I'm staying alert."

"Well, your remedy isn't one hundred percent effective," Cora said, laughing. "Maybe Lucy will get pregnant and solve this issue for us."

Chapawee sighed. "Or Mrs. Livingston could try to understand Lucy's perspective and find another pastime besides waiting for grandchildren."

"I can understand where Mrs. Livingston is coming from though. Holding Abe's son when he visited this summer brought me more joy than I've had in a long time. I just wish things were different and they could live down here. How about you, Chapawee? Don't you miss your grandchildren?"

Chapawee looked towards the water. When her daughter, Tayen, left to marry 25 years ago, Chapawee grieved, but she'd still had her mother and sister here. In the beginning Tayen and her family would visit several times a year, but that tapered off as the grandchildren aged, and the two-day trip to visit them was more than Chapawee could handle alone. Tears filled her eyes when she thought of the two great-grandchildren she'd never met.

"Yes. I miss them every day, even the great-grandchildren I don't know yet."

"Why don't you move there with your daughter? I'd sure miss seeing you, but knowing you're with family would make me happy."

"Tayen would love that," Chapawee said, placing Cora's package on her workbench. "But I just can't. I'd be going there to die, and end up being a burden. I'd rather stay here, where I've lived most my life. Hungry Mother Creek, the Mother Tree, and the woods here are home, and it's where I want to end my days."

"I know you're independent, but don't let that keep you away from your family. You cared for your parents and it wasn't a burden. Why do you think you'd be one to Tayen?"

Chapawee slid Cora's package back and forth on the workbench. Cora made sense, but Tayen's mood could be volatile like her father's, and at her age Chapawee didn't think she could handle the stress of living like that again, no matter how much she loved her daughter and grandchildren.

When she didn't respond, Cora reached over and patted Chapawee on her knee. "Well, if you stay, you can count me as family, and now you have our circle for support too."

They hadn't spoken about the circle yet because Chapawee didn't want to pressure Cora. "The circle?" Chapawee asked. "Do I have a circle? It will only work if you and Sadie return."

Cora smiled. "You have a circle." Cora scooted her chair closer to Chapawee and into the sun. "Sadie and I talked about it after church."

Every muscle in Chapawee's body relaxed. She hadn't realized how much she was anticipating Cora and Sadie's decision. It would have been a huge disappointment if the circle hadn't come to fruition, because passing this on was one of the last things she was meant to do.

"This is great news," Chapawee said. She silently chided herself for even being worried. Her intuition to call the circle was strong, and she should have trusted it without question. "What made you decide to stay?"

"First of all, it's been a couple months and it seems Vivi and Etta haven't shared anything we discussed."

Chapawee interrupted Cora. "And I hope you'll feel safe sharing the whole truth when we meet next month at the solstice."

"Now, I regret that I wasn't truthful like the rest of you." Cora stood and walked over to inspect Chapawee's oysters. "But I've learned to put on an agreeable mask around white people and that won't change overnight."

"Cora, we all put on a mask sometimes, to please others, to stay safe, or even to hide the truth from ourselves. That's exactly why our circle is important. We need at least one place where we can take that mask off."

Cora took the knife lying on the workbench and pried open one of the oysters. "I've never hidden anything from you, Chapawee. Guess when you've known someone since childhood, it's easier." Cora detached the oyster from the shell and ate it in one gulp.

"And easier to help yourself to my oysters," Chapawee said playfully.

Cora smiled and laid the empty shell beside the basket. "And there's another reason we're comfortable returning to the circle."

"What is it?" Chapawee stood beside Cora and began shucking oysters into a bowl.

"Vivi came out to see Sadie at her schoolroom last week."

"She did? Why?"

"Out of concern for Pearl, one of Sadie's students. Vivi caught Art with Pearl behind the general store. Thankfully she arrived before anything happened, and Pearl was able to run away. Vivi wanted to make sure Pearl's parents knew, and went to Sadie for help."

Chapawee set the knife down. "That was good of Vivi."

"Yes," Cora said. "Sadie appreciated her concern."

"I imagine this wasn't the first time it's happened. I'm glad Vivi went to Sadie, but hopefully she didn't talk with Mr. Woodard about it," Chapawee said, wondering if Jack's last request for her remedy was for Pearl.

"I hope not. Art is Mr. Woodard's nephew. He'd never go against family to help a colored girl."

Chapawee continued shucking and neither spoke for a while. Over the years, many women had sought out her remedy after being raped. Even if they didn't share their stories, the desperation and shame she saw in their eyes revealed the truth. Chapawee took a few steps to Cora and put her arm around her waist. They didn't need to speak. She knew Cora was experiencing the same mixture of anger, grief and helplessness that she was. A thin white cloud covered the sun, and immediately the air temperature cooled.

After a few minutes, Chapawee returned to the oysters. "The best part of today is finding out that you and Sadie will return to the circle."

Cora took a deep breath and exhaled. "I'm still not completely comfortable with it, but always expecting the worst of white folk isn't any different than them always expecting the worst of us."

"And so far, Vivi and Etta have proven trustworthy."

"So far," Cora agreed. "Now, I'd better get home. Jeremiah will be up from his nap."

"Here, take some of these oysters," Chapawee said. "I can't possibly eat them all."

Cora picked up the bottom of her dress to create a container, and Chapawee dropped a dozen oysters in.

***

The southwest breeze blew Vivi's dress against her legs and encouraged a few tenacious leaves to release their hold. The sun and moderate temperatures countered the brisk wind, and Vivi hung her shawl over her left arm. She'd dropped Goldie at Sunday School, and returned to her mother's to write at her father's desk. She told her mother she had to meet with Adelaide about the suffrage association.

Vivi kept her head down to avoid eye contact with Mr. and Mrs. Midyette who were walking home from church. She didn't want to explain why she hadn't been there with her mother. The papers placed in the middle of her Bible fluttered in the breeze. She'd spent most of the night writing and rewriting . . . what would she call it? A letter, journal entry, or essay? She wasn't sure, but hoped it would serve as an apology to Adelaide as well as an explanation for her misdirected anger yesterday.

It took time last night before she was totally honest with what she wrote, especially about her feelings for Adelaide. Seeing her words on the page made it easier to discern the half-truths she'd been telling herself. She'd crossed things out, dug deeper into the feelings that scared her and then written them down. After midnight, the darkness and fatigue had weakened her defenses and the truth flowed more easily.

The front door of the hotel was unlocked and Vivi stepped inside. A man sitting in the parlor where they'd had their meeting on Thursday looked at her over the top of his newspaper. She nodded and walked towards Adelaide's room.

When she got to Adelaide's door, Vivi slid three folded pages from her Bible. The words they contained had changed her, but would they influence Adelaide and prevent her from leaving Oriental? Vivi unfolded the papers and looked at her writing, nothing but black ink on white paper, but each word was a tiny piece of her heart laid bare. Part of her wanted to run away, but her experience in the circle kept her in place. There was power in speaking honestly. Vivi took a deep breath and gently knocked on Adelaide's door.

Silence greeted her knock. Surely Adelaide hadn't found a way to leave already. Vivi knocked again with more force. "Adelaide, it's Vivi. Please let me in. I want to talk about yesterday."

Vivi put her ear to the door and heard movement on the other side. Adelaide opened the door just wide enough for her face. She looked at Vivi and then down the hall. "I'm still in my nightgown so come in quickly."

Adelaide's eyes were puffy and red-rimmed like Vivi's, and her auburn hair hung in waves down her back. She shut the door without making eye contact and then retreated to her bed. The room reeked of alcohol like the mornings after Bubba had been drinking. A silver flask beside the bed confirmed Vivi's suspicions.

"Aren't you supposed to be eating lunch with your family?" Adelaide asked, staring at a spot above Vivi's head. Her voice contained neither sarcasm nor affection.

Thank God Vivi had her written words, because her voice was once again unavailable. She lay her shawl and Bible at the end of the bed and handed Adelaide the folded papers.

"Adelaide," Vivi paused and swallowed, "please read what I've written. Yesterday my thoughts were a jumble, and I had to use my pen to untangle them." Vivi drummed her fingers on her thighs, and finally held onto fistfuls of her skirt to keep them still. "I stayed up all night writing and rewriting, and . . . just read it, and then we can talk." Vivi sat on the end of the bed.

Adelaide unfolded the papers and bowed her head to read. Vivi watched Adelaide's eyes move down the page and felt as vulnerable as she had giving birth to Goldie, with her mother and the midwife gathered around her open legs. The pages rustled when Adelaide laid the first paper on the bed. Vivi held her breath. Would her honesty help or be met by Adelaide's ridicule?

Vivi stood and walked to the window overlooking Hodges Street. Circus elephants could have paraded in front of her and she wouldn't have noticed. Her attention was focused three feet behind her.

"Vivi," Adelaide said. Her voice was the distant rumble of a summer storm, a sharp contrast to its earlier neutrality.

Vivi turned and reminded herself to breath. Adelaide's cheeks were wet.

"This is beautiful," Adelaide said. "You have a gift for writing."

Vivi relaxed at Adelaide's words, but it wasn't exactly what she wanted to hear. "Thank you, but . . ." Vivi paused and sat beside Adelaide on the bed. "Do you forgive me for yesterday?"

Adelaide opened her arms. Vivi leaned into them. "Of course," Adelaide said, her mouth beside Vivi's ear.

Adelaide released Vivi and took her hand. "You could have continued your life the way it was and never seen me again, but you didn't." Adelaide squeezed her hand. "You were honest with me, and most importantly honest with yourself, and that's the only way to create a life that's yours." She said the last word with emphasis. "And," she continued, more gently, "I'm glad you acknowledged that what's between us is deeper than friendship."

"You were right yesterday," Vivi said, relief allowing her words to flow more easily. "My life is more passionate since you've been part of it." Even with Bubba, Vivi thought, and then immediately felt guilty. All this talk about honesty and here she was deceiving her husband.

Adelaide lifted Vivi's hand and gently kissed her palm, and then the tender underside of her wrist. The delicate touch of Adelaide's lips was the last snowflake that set off an avalanche of desire. Vivi steadied herself on the bed with her free hand. Her physical need for Adelaide clouded her mind and banished thoughts of Bubba.

Adelaide locked eyes with Vivi and slipped out from under the covers to kneel at her feet. She unbuttoned Vivi's boots and gently removed them. Then Adelaide's hands moved under her skirt and up her leg until they reached the top of her stocking. Vivi caught her breath when Adelaide gently caressed her inner thigh, before rolling her stocking down and over her foot. She did the same with the other, and then Vivi stood, overcome with desire. With a delicate deliberation that aroused Vivi even more, Adelaide removed Vivi's skirt and shirt.

Before Vivi's shirt touched the floor they came together in a passionate kiss. The sensation of Adelaide's lips and the swell of her breasts pressing against her was more than Vivi could take, and she moaned. Her brain was unable to formulate a thought while every nerve ending in her body pulsed with need for Adelaide.

Adelaide pulled away from their kiss to look at Vivi. "Is this what you want?"

Vivi took a breath and tried to regain some composure. Adelaide was giving her a way out if she wanted it. She knew their relationship would either stall or progress based on this decision and that Adelaide may leave if she declined. Vivi couldn't bear the thought of that. She leaned in and kissed Adelaide gently in the curve of her neck.

"Yes. This is what I want."

CHAPTER 12

The laughter and chatter of the students diminished, and from the front porch of the general store, Vivi watched them scatter towards home. Ever since her encounter with Art and Pearl, this was her routine. Periodically she would look out the schoolroom window facing the back of the store, but hadn't seen Pearl since that day a month ago, and prayed nothing had happened since.

The students were keyed up for Thanksgiving, and a long weekend, and she'd let them leave early. But the truth be told, she hadn't been able to focus on school all week either.

Since Sunday, her every nerve-ending was tuned to what was pleasurable, beautiful and good. The past few years, she had just been going through the motions, but now her body, mind and spirit hummed with life. Her suffrage work, staying up through the night and writing from her heart on Saturday, and then her Sunday morning with Adelaide were the cause of her awakening.

The last three nights after supper, Vivi had worked on an editorial Adelaide had encouraged her to write for the Raleigh paper. It would expand on the sentiments in her letter to Adelaide about how her mind had opened to women's right to vote. If printed, they hoped it would resonate with rural North Carolina women who hadn't been educated about the suffrage movement yet.

Vivi climbed the steps to her classroom and leaned against the doorframe to watch Goldie dance on the other side of the room. She moved her arms, head and hips to a rhythm only she could hear, but Vivi recognized some of the movements from Adelaide's show last month. Goldie twirled around, saw Vivi, and held out her hands.

"Come dance with me, Momma."

"OK, honey. But then we have to clean up so we can go home. Want to help me make an apple pie for Thanksgiving tomorrow?" Vivi asked as she clasped Goldie's hands.

Goldie nodded her head and then swung Vivi's hands back and forth. Vivi had noticed that Goldie and Bubba's moods were also better this week, or maybe it just felt that way because she was happy.

"Mrs. Gibbs."

The melody in Vivi's mind screeched to a halt when she heard Mr. O'Neal's voice behind her. She dropped Goldie's hands and turned around.

"Looks like you're happy about the Thanksgiving holiday."

Vivi smoothed the front of her skirt. "Just a little break before I clean up," Vivi said, and walked to meet him in the middle of the room. "What can I do for you?"

"I was hoping to speak with you," he paused and looked over her head at Goldie, "alone."

Vivi knew she was being over-protective, but she didn't want Goldie outside the general store alone. "Goldie, take your book to the reading corner. Mr. O'Neal and I need to talk."

Thankfully Goldie didn't plead to run home or go to her grandmother's, and dutifully took *Anne of Green Gables* to the corner.

Vivi followed Mr. O'Neal to her desk. He pointed to her chair. "I'm fine standing. I do it all day," she said, preferring to look him in the eye.

"Mrs. Gibbs, I had hoped our conversation last month about your involvement with suffrage would be the only one we'd have to have, but it appears that's not the case."

Vivi's palms were sweating. "But Mr. O'Neal, you said my suffrage work shouldn't interfere with my teaching and it hasn't. I'm doing that at night and on weekends."

Mr. O'Neal exhaled loudly and sat on a corner of her desk. "Yes, that's what I said, but I work at the discretion of the school board and several disgruntled parents have complained about you."

"What?" Vivi said, more loudly than she'd planned. Goldie looked up from her book and Vivi continued with quieter intensity. "What are they complaining about? I haven't discussed this in the classroom."

"Word spread that you were gathering signatures for a suffrage petition. A few parents found out and contacted the school board."

Vivi neatened a pile of homework on her desk. "I know some people don't support it, but like I said before, I'm not bringing suffrage ideas into the classroom." Although I probably should, Vivi thought to herself.

"Yes, and I appreciate that, Mrs. Gibbs, but now the school board is involved . . ." He hesitated and looked over Vivi's head at Goldie.

Vivi leaned into the side of her desk for support, anticipating his next sentence.

"I have to ask you to stop your suffrage work."

Vivi inhaled sharply and Mr. O'Neal continued, "You're stirring up trouble and angering our parents and the school board won't tolerate it." He looked at his pocket watch and stood. "And quite frankly Mrs. Gibbs, this seems like a waste of your time. In order for women to get the right to vote, men must be in favor of suffrage, and I don't know any man who is."

Vivi finally exhaled and tried to juggle her feelings. She was angry, but also afraid of losing her job. What would Adelaide do? She always had a respectful way of asserting herself.

"Thank you for your input, but I don't see my suffrage work as a waste of time. What happens if I continue with my efforts?"

Mr. O'Neal's eyes narrowed and he looked at his watch again. He didn't seem prepared for this question. He assumed I'd nod my head and immediately agree with him, Vivi thought. She stood tall, drawing strength from her feet firmly planted on the floor. The tension mounted between them, and Vivi remained silent.

Mr. O'Neal took a step backwards towards the door. "Well, Mrs. Gibbs, if you choose to involve yourself with something the school board forbids, then," he took a breath, "then we'd have to terminate your contract."

Vivi sat in the chair behind her desk, more angry than afraid. It wasn't fair. Why did she have to choose between a profession she loved and a cause she supported just because the school board, all made up of men, didn't agree with it?

"I'll have to think about this."

"Talk with Bubba over the long weekend," Mr. O'Neal said. "I'm sure he'll help you understand the school board's perspective and I'll stop by next week to settle this matter."

Mr. O'Neal turned and left the classroom. Vivi remained seated at her desk and stared after him.

"Momma, what's wrong? Are you in trouble?"

Vivi put her arm around Goldie. "Mr. O'Neal's not happy that I'm using my free time to work on the women's right to vote, but don't worry, sweetie, we'll figure it out."

Vivi handed Goldie a broom. "Now, let's clean up. Then we'll go home and make an apple pie for tomorrow."

***

Tayen's letter warmed her chest. Chapawee buttoned it underneath her shirt to keep it dry on the way home. Before boarding her boat at the public dock, Chapawee reviewed her to-do list to ensure she hadn't forgotten anything. She'd been to the post office to mail Cora's package to her son and pick up Tayen's letter, and then exchanged some of her winter lettuce for a dozen eggs at the general store. That was all she needed to do.

There weren't many people in town today, the reason she came during the week and before the lumber mills released their workers. Two white boys about eight or nine ran past the wharf, chasing one another. Chapawee smiled. Vivi must have ended the school day early. She knew school was important for children, but personally thought making them sit at desks for hours at a time went against their nature. Time outside was where she'd learned the most; that, and time with her elders.

The boys almost collided with the constable and two other men, and this caught Chapawee's attention. She stepped down into her boat, stowed the eggs under the bench seat and untied her lines. If she could help it, she wanted to avoid crossing paths with the constable again, but he and the other men picked up their pace and walked directly towards her. Chapawee intuited that they were coming to speak to her and stepped back onto the wharf, squared her shoulders and stood calmly until they arrived.

"Constable," Chapawee said, starting the conversation. "It seems you're looking for me. What can I help you with?" Once the men were upon her, Chapawee recognized one as the postmaster with whom she'd just spoken.

The constable took off his hat, ran his fingers through his hair and said, "We just have a few questions for you. You know Franklin from the post office," the postmaster nodded at Chapawee, "and this is Percy, the magistrate."

The magistrate was only a few inches taller than Chapawee, with a receding hairline and the beginnings of a pot belly. He narrowed his eyes at her, and she wondered if the magistrate was doing the bidding of the Livingstons. "I'm happy to cooperate," she said. "What would you like to know?"

The postmaster took something out of his pocket and the magistrate immediately grabbed it. He stepped in front of Chapawee and held it under her nose. "Did you just mail this?"

It was Cora's box for her son, but it'd been unwrapped and then haphazardly taped back up. She didn't know why they were asking about this, but the postmaster had just seen her mail it so she couldn't lie. "Yes."

The magistrate nodded at the constable who stepped forward and said, "Ma'am, you're under arrest for violation of the Comstock Act."

Was she dreaming? Under arrest for mailing a box of seeds? "What?" Chapawee tried to catch her breath.

On the street, a small group had gathered to see what was unfolding by the wharf. Chapawee immediately picked out Mrs. Livingston standing with her arms folded across her chest. Their eyes met and the corners of Mrs. Livingston's mouth lifted slightly.

"You're under arrest," the constable repeated.

"But for what? I simply mailed this package to Baltimore. What's illegal about that?" Chapawee didn't want to implicate Cora in any way and left off that it was her package.

The magistrate poked the postmaster in his ribs and he said, apologetically, "Ma'am, the Comstock Act prohibits the distribution of birth control across state lines or through the mail."

"And it appears you are doing both," the magistrate added. "It's a federal law punishable by thirty days in jail and a $20 fine. Now Miss Chapawee, what is your last name? We'll need it for your arrest warrant."

Jail time? Chapawee was in a state of disbelief. Surely they wouldn't put her in jail? At almost seventy? An old woman? "Birth control?" Chapawee asked. "There are only seeds in that box. Show it to Dr. Purdy and I'm sure he'll agree. There're just seeds."

The constable looked back at the magistrate for direction. It was clear that he was running the show and Chapawee wondered how much money he'd been given to orchestrate this.

"We have evidence that these seeds are used as birth control," the magistrate said. "Our source says they're quite effective."

"So," Chapawee said, addressing the magistrate. "You're going to arrest me based on one person's belief that these seeds are used for birth control? Unless they're a medical expert, I don't see how you have enough evidence." And whoever's heard of the Comstock Act, she wanted to add. Chapawee clasped her hands in front of her to hide the shaking. She thought of her garden and the leftover oyster stew on her stove. Would she be able to return home tonight?

The magistrate shook the box of wild carrot seeds in front of her again. "Miss Chapawee, based on the information we have, you are breaking the law, and since we are responsible for enforcing the law, it is our duty to arrest you." The magistrate nodded at the constable who reached for his handcuffs.

Chapawee's knees went weak. This was happening. "There'll be no need for that. I'll go with you."

"And," the magistrate continued, "you can contact your attorney if you think we're wrongfully detaining you." He grinned at her.

Of course, Chapawee couldn't afford an attorney and the magistrate knew this. The crowd on the street had grown and Mrs. Livingston was at the front, not even hiding her smile now. Chapawee's fear morphed into anger. What was Mrs. Livingston thinking? That putting her in jail would magically bring her grandchildren? She'll be disappointed though. Chapawee knew Lucy had at least a six-month supply of seeds. Money had helped Mrs. Livingston get what she wanted over the years. but it wouldn't work in this situation. It's only going to make my life difficult, Chapawee thought.

The constable gently took her upper arm. "Come. We need to get you processed. The jail is only around the corner."

Chapawee knew where the jail was. She'd gone with Cora to visit Jeremiah before he was sent off on the chain gang. The magistrate and the postmaster led the way and she and the constable followed behind. Mrs. Livingston nodded slightly to the magistrate when they walked by. Chapawee scanned the crowd for a familiar face. She wanted to get word to Cora about what was happening and hoped she'd help get her boat home and take care of her garden.

"Chapawee!" Chapawee stopped when she heard her name and saw Vivi pushing herself to the front of the crowd. "What's happening? Are you OK?"

"This woman is being arrested," the magistrate said brusquely.

"Arrested?" Vivi said in disbelief. "For what?"

Mrs. Livingston stepped in front of the crowd and said, "For using her witch doctor medicine to interfere with God's plan." She put her hands on her hips and several people in the crowd bent their heads and whispered to one another.

Chapawee saw the struggle in Vivi's face. She bought the seeds so she knew about that, but didn't know it was against the law. Well, if Chapawee understood things correctly, selling her remedy was not illegal, but mailing it to another state was.

"OK. That's enough," the magistrate said. "Let's keep moving."

Chapawee kept her eyes on Vivi and when she passed her she whispered, "Please tell Cora about this. She'll know what to do."

Vivi nodded.

***

The three white men dwarfed Chapawee, and Vivi's heart broke as she watched them walk her to the jail.

Goldie clasped Vivi's hand tightly. "Momma, where are they taking Miss Chapawee?"

Before Vivi could answer, someone asked, "Do you know her?"

Vivi turned and saw that Mrs. Livingston had asked the question. The rest of the crowd had dispersed. She hesitated, not wanting to say anything that would incriminate Chapawee, especially to this woman, who seemed overly pleased with her arrest.

"So, do you take her magic potions too?" Mrs. Livingston asked. Before Vivi could answer, she bent down towards Goldie. "You don't have any brothers or sisters, do you?"

Vivi knew Mrs. Livingston indirectly through church, but had never been drawn to her, and now she knew why. She pulled Goldie closer and said, "Chapawee is a family friend."

Mrs. Livingston rolled her eyes and said, "Then I guess you won't be seeing your friend for a while."

Vivi ignored this comment and walked past her. She had too much on her mind to stand around talking to this mean-spirited woman. The urgency of the moment temporarily superseded her interaction with the superintendent. Right now, she had to get Goldie to her mother's, and then somehow find Cora's house to let her know what was happening. At the wharf, Vivi saw Chapawee's boat and this gave her an idea – but it would require Bubba's assistance.

"Come on, Goldie," Vivi said, "We need to help Miss Chapawee."

Vivi lifted her skirts, and she and Goldie ran in the direction of her mother's. If she hurried, she could get to Cora's before it was pitch dark.

***

Bubba led the way down Beards Creek in their jon boat, and Vivi followed closely in Chapawee's. After leaving Goldie with her mother, she'd run home, hoping Bubba hadn't been drinking and could help

163

execute her plan. He was sober, and agreed to help so readily that she threw her arms around his neck in gratitude.

"Hungry Mother Creek is coming up on the right," Bubba called back to her.

Vivi adjusted the rudder, and guided Chapawee's boat down the middle of the creek, thankful for the hours of instruction her father had given her on driving a boat.

It was close to sunset and the light was dimming, but Vivi made out the small beach area near the Mother Tree, and then the pier behind Chapawee's cabin. Bubba tied their boat at the end of the pier, and Vivi maneuvered Chapawee's into the small slip and quickly secured it.

She gathered her skirt in one hand, took Bubba's with the other, and stepped onto the pier.

"Do you have any idea where Cora's house is?" Bubba asked.

"No. Just that it's walking distance from here. I think there's a path through the woods."

Bubba lit a gas lantern and they walked to the front of Chapawee's cabin. Vivi paused to get her bearings. "Kershaw Road is to the left, the Mother Tree to the right, so let's look near the woods straight ahead, behind her garden."

In a few minutes they were walking on a worn path. Bubba held the lantern high to light the way, and soon the path ended in a clearing. There was a cabin there, larger than Chapawee's, with smoke coming from the chimney.

"That must be it," Vivi said and walked ahead of Bubba, anxious to talk to Cora.

At the bottom of the porch steps Bubba took Vivi's arm. "Stand over here while I knock on the door," he said, pointing to the side of the porch farthest from the door.

Vivi bristled at his instruction. This was her plan, after all. "They're not expecting us, and Cora's husband may not respond well to a white man showing up at his house unexpectedly."

Vivi hadn't thought about how they'd be received, only that she wanted to help Chapawee. "But Cora knows me. Wouldn't it be less threatening with me standing beside you, so Cora sees me?"

Bubba sighed and they approached the door together. Nobody answered after several knocks and Vivi couldn't hear any sounds from the cabin. They must be there though, because of the chimney smoke, she thought.

"Cora!" Vivi said loudly.

Before she could do anything else, Bubba said firmly, "We don't even know this is the right house, Vivi."

She ignored him. It had to be. She knocked again. "Cora, it's me, Vivi, and my husband Bubba. Chapawee's in trouble and we need to help her."

The door immediately swung open and Cora stood in the doorway, the man behind her clearly her husband. Although he had gray hair and leaned on a cane, Vivi sensed his muscles were coiled and ready to react if necessary.

"What's happened?" Cora asked, her voice laced with concern.

"Chapawee's in jail."

Cora took Vivi's hands and pulled her into the cabin and then motioned for Bubba to come in as well. The cabin smelled like cornbread and onions, and Vivi's stomach growled. The source of the dinner smells came from the wood-burning stove off to the right. A wooden kitchen table was immediately to her left, and there was a small sitting area near the back of the cabin. Behind the table was a door that must lead to their bedroom.

"This is Bubba," Vivi said.

"And Jeremiah." Cora motioned to her husband, now standing beside her.

Bubba and Jeremiah nodded to one another.

Cora's eyes never left Vivi's face. "Why in the world is Chapawee in jail?"

"I don't know the details, but it's connected with the remedy she sells. I think Mrs. Livingston may have something to do with it too. She seemed awfully pleased with Chapawee's arrest."

Cora put a hand to her mouth and sat down in a kitchen chair that Jeremiah quickly slid beneath her.

"We brought her boat back, and she told me to tell you what had happened because you'd know what to do."

"Heaven help me," Cora said, standing again. "How am I supposed to know?"

Bubba cleared his throat. "A lawyer would be a good place to start."

"Who's going to represent an Indian woman with no money?" Jeremiah added.

Cora ignored the men and said to Vivi, "I'm sure Mrs. Livingston has something to do with it. Listen to what she did to Chapawee's garden a few weeks ago."

Cora shared the details of Mrs. Livingston's garden-stomping visit with them all.

"Wow. She has some nerve, interfering with her daughter's life, trespassing, and destroying property."

Jeremiah opened his mouth to speak, then closed it. He turned sharply and walked to the window at the back of the cabin, the intensity of his demeanor juxtaposed against the delicate floral curtains.

"A lawyer could help," Vivi said, returning her focus to Chapawee, "but how would we find one?"

"And the money to pay him," Cora added.

Cora and Vivi brainstormed around the kitchen table while the two men stood silently at either end of the cabin.

"What about Lucy Potts, Mrs. Livingston's daughter?" Cora asked. "I wonder if she could convince her mother to drop the charges."

Lucy was in a different social circle than Vivi, and she only knew of her from a distance, but it was worth a try. "Cora, that's the best idea we've had."

***

Vivi removed the infuser from the teapot and poured herself a cup of chamomile tea. The heat and mellow sweetness was a welcome reprieve from an unusual day. She leaned forward and let the steam warm her face. It was only eight in the evening, but it felt like days ago that she'd let the children leave early for Thanksgiving.

After returning from Cora's, they'd eaten at her mother's before coming home. Now Goldie was upstairs reading, and this was the first moment Vivi'd had to process the day. The immediacy of helping Chapawee had pushed her conversation with the superintendent to the back of her mind, but she needed to tell Bubba about it.

A blast of cool air came in the back door with Bubba. "Everything's ready for roasting the turkey tomorrow." He hung his coat on a peg by the door and sat beside Vivi, who poured him a cup of tea.

Bubba leaned back in the chair, extending his legs under the kitchen table. "What a day. That's not how I thought I'd spend my afternoon."

"Me either. Goldie and I were going to make apple pie for our Thanksgiving dessert." Vivi reached over and squeezed Bubba's arm. "Thanks for your help today. You don't even know Chapawee, but you were willing to help her."

Bubba smiled. "I was helping you. I could tell you were determined to get Chapawee's boat home and talk with her neighbor. I didn't want you doing that alone."

Vivi looked away. He'd had no hesitation in helping her today, and a wave of guilt washed over her. Bubba wasn't perfect, but she still loved him – although now she loved Adelaide, too. They drank their tea in silence. Vivi moved her feelings for Adelaide aside and refocused on the moment. She needed to tell Bubba about the superintendent.

"Bubba, something else happened today that we need to discuss." Vivi unbuttoned the top of her high-necked blouse, took a deep breath, and shared everything Mr. O'Neal had said to her.

"Terminate your contract?!" Bubba stood forcefully and his chair almost toppled.

"Shh! Please don't yell. It'll upset Goldie." She motioned for Bubba to sit.

He leaned towards Vivi, hands on his knees. "Well, at least he's giving you a chance to stop your suffrage work before they fire you." His voice softened. "I don't think women need to vote, but I know you've enjoyed working for this cause. I'm sorry you'll have to stop." Bubba exhaled as if the problem had been solved.

"You're assuming that I'm going to stop." Vivi took her cup and saucer to the sink. "We haven't even discussed it yet."

"What's to discuss?" Bubba asked, joining her at the sink. "It's clear to me. You can't lose your job, so you must stop the suffrage work."

Disappointment hollowed Vivi's heart. He had easily given physical support to help Chapawee earlier, but was unable to support her on this. "But I'm the leader of Oriental's suffrage group."

"Honey, I'm sure you are a wonderful leader, but let Adelaide take over. You have your family to think about." Bubba kissed her on the cheek. "Let's go to bed. Tomorrow will be a busy day."

"I'll be up in a minute."

Vivi retrieved her ESA petition from her satchel and lay it on the kitchen table. Each name there was validation of her efforts so far. They were only signatures, but a small contribution to promote change for women. It made her feel useful, like she was harnessing what power she had to make the world a better place, especially for Goldie. Bubba didn't understand. He'd dismissed her suffrage work like a passing dalliance, and hadn't even considered options other than giving it up.

Vivi closed her eyes and rubbed her temples. She was too tired to be angry, or to think of other solutions, but tomorrow Adelaide would be there for support.

CHAPTER 13

The smell of onions, butter, and her mother's green bean casserole warming on the stove reminded Vivi it was Thanksgiving. After what happened to Chapawee yesterday, and her visit to Cora's last night, she was disoriented. The holiday halted progress in helping Chapawee, but she couldn't change that, and might as well enjoy time with her family and Adelaide.

Vivi drizzled melted butter into the pot with the potatoes and pressed firmly down with the masher. Although her father had been absent in her life for twice as long as he'd been present, he was never far from her mind, especially today. And as much as she enjoyed seeing her mother happy with Ben, Vivi was glad he was in New Bern having Thanksgiving with his son's family. She wasn't ready to add him to their celebration.

"Momma," Goldie called. "Come look at the table."

Vivi left the potato masher in the pot and went to admire the table her mother and Goldie had set. A pumpkin graced the middle of it with fall leaves radiating outward like an orange and red skirt. Her mother had brought ivy from her yard and wound it around the pewter candlesticks on either side of the pumpkin.

"Oh, my. It looks beautiful," Vivi said and put her arm around Goldie.

"And Momma," Goldie said, taking a shell off the table, "look how I wrote everyone's names on a shell so we'll know where to sit."

Vivi didn't know Goldie had done this. "What a creative idea, sweetheart. I love it. Miss Adelaide will be impressed with your beautiful decorations."

As if she'd talked her up, there was a knock at the door. Warmth spread across Vivi's chest. "Mother, can you add the salt and pepper to the potatoes? I'll let Adelaide in." She wanted a minute alone with Adelaide as they hadn't seen one another since their Sunday morning together.

Vivi quickly stepped onto the front porch and closed the door behind her. There was Adelaide. Her auburn hair glowed in the midday sun and her cheeks were rosy from the walk over. She smiled with delight the moment she saw Vivi.

"Am I invited in?" Adelaide asked, pointing to the closed door with a smile.

"Of course," Vivi said. "I just wanted you all to myself for a minute."

"Well, I can't argue with that." Adelaide stepped onto the porch, laid the loaf of bread she'd brought on the railing, and pulled Vivi into her arms. "Thank you for your letter and Sunday morning." Adelaide spoke softly into her ear. "I've been floating since then."

"Me too," Vivi replied, and quickly planted a kiss on Adelaide's lips. She stepped back from her, acutely aware that she was at home and not in Adelaide's room. "But a lot has happened since Sunday."

"You're working on your editorial, I hope," Adelaide said, retrieving the bread from the rail.

"I did a couple nights. But let me tell you what happened yesterday."

Vivi shared the events of yesterday afternoon, starting with her conversation with the superintendent and ending with the story of Chapawee and the evening visit to Cora.

Adelaide's eyes narrowed as she listened. The minute Vivi finished, Adelaide erupted. "This is ridiculous! I can't believe the school board is threatening to end your contract just because they don't agree with how you spend your free time. And poor Chapawee! The magistrate needs to arrest that scoundrel working at the general store, not her."

Vivi caught a whiff of the turkey Bubba was roasting outside, and knew they needed to finish preparing the meal. "I know. It was a lot for one day, but we can talk more about it later. I just wanted to fill you in on what Mother and Bubba already know. Come on," Vivi said, opening the door, "let's enjoy our Thanksgiving meal."

Vivi sat at one end of the rectangular table, across from Bubba. Adelaide was to her left and Goldie and her mother to the right. Their plates were full of turkey, mashed potatoes, deviled eggs, and green bean casserole. Adelaide's bread and a jar of persimmon jam sat beside the pumpkin.

Adelaide reached hands out to Vivi and Bubba. "Can we hold hands for grace, the Quaker way?" Adelaide asked.

"That's not how we say grace," Bubba said.

Before Vivi could respond, Goldie took her hand. "I like holding hands, but what's a Quaker?"

Vivi said, "It's a different way to worship God, kind of like the Methodists are different from Baptists."

Adelaide took Vivi's hand. "Well, a bit more different than that."

Vivi felt Bubba's gaze. She looked at him and smiled. "Bubba, can you please give the blessing?"

He nodded, and reluctantly took Adelaide's hand and then Etta's. They all bowed their heads. Vivi heard the rise and fall of Bubba's voice but his words didn't register because her attention was focused to her left. Adelaide gently rubbed the top of Vivi's hand with her thumb. Vivi scooted to the edge of her chair and raised her eyes. Adelaide was staring directly at her and they locked eyes for a moment.

Bubba said, "Amen," and Vivi quickly looked away and withdrew her hand.

"Thank you, Bubba. OK everyone," Vivi said, picking up her fork. "Dig in and remember to save room for the apple pie Goldie and I made this morning."

The Thanksgiving meal was accompanied by congenial conversation and laughter. Bubba relaxed and warmed to Adelaide when she directed her full attention on him, asking thoughtful questions about his fishing. Vivi looked around the table and felt deep contentment at having all the people she loved best within a few feet.

Adelaide laughed at something Bubba said and Vivi watched them while she ate the last of her apple pie. She was astonished at how she loved Adelaide, something she'd never conceived of, but was equally astonished at how their love had rekindled her feelings for Bubba. She kept looking at the two of them and her heart bloomed like a morning glory at dawn. It wasn't an either/or, it was both. She wanted Adelaide and Bubba to be in her life. That thought took her breath away and she took a drink of water.

"Honey, are you OK?" her mother asked, an expert in reading Vivi.

"Yes," Vivi said, pushing her plate away and leaning on the table towards her mother. "I was just thinking about how happy I am. This has been one of the best Thanksgivings since Daddy died, don't you think?"

"Yes. Adelaide may be from the north, but she fits in well."

"Having someone new at the table makes things more interesting," Goldie said.

Vivi smiled. "Are you getting bored with us, Goldie?"

"No," Goldie said with a sigh. "I'm just saying it's fun to have a singer from the showboat here for Thanksgiving."

Goldie stood and did a pirouette. "Miss Adelaide, can you teach me some of your dance steps when we're done?"

"I'd love to. Once you have the steps down pat, you'll be ready to travel on the floating theater with me," Adelaide said.

Bubba laughed. "Well, let's get her finished with school before she leaves."

"Daddy, you can come too." Goldie walked to Bubba. He spread his arms and hugged her tight. Vivi smiled. Her father used to hug her that way.

"Can I go outside and play?" Goldie asked, dancing again beside Bubba.

"Sure, honey," Vivi said. "You've been patient with all us adults. Don't forget to take your coat."

In a flash Goldie was out the door. Chapawee's shawl and blanket were in a basket beside the door, and they caught Vivi's attention. She'd retrieved them yesterday and wanted to deliver them as soon as she could. She thought of Chapawee, alone in jail. Had she eaten? Was she lonely?

"Mother, do you think we could take a plate of food and her things to Chapawee? I'm worried about her."

Before her mother answered Bubba said, "You better wait until tomorrow, because the jail is closed to visitors for the holiday."

Thoughts of Chapawee and yesterday's events resurfaced the decision the superintendent was forcing her to make.

"And what about you?" Adelaide asked, reading Vivi's mind. "The school board isn't threatening jail, but they're trying to take away your freedom of choice."

"Now, Adelaide," Bubba said. "That's a little dramatic. They simply don't want their teachers involved with politics."

Adelaide stiffened and said, "Vivi wants to work on women's suffrage and they say she can't. Seems obvious that's restricting her freedom to choose."

"I agree with Adelaide," her mother said. "They shouldn't be telling you what to do in your free time. Although, keep in mind the suffrage movement will come and go, but there'll always be children in Oriental who need an education."

"Exactly," Bubba said.

The pull between what others wanted and her own desires dissolved the contentment Vivi had savored a few moments ago.

"But she needs to take a stand," Adelaide said, her volume increasing.

Vivi held up her hand to silence Adelaide. "Let's not ruin the end of a delightful meal with arguing. I value all your opinions, but need time to make my own decision." Vivi saw Bubba tense. "And discuss with Bubba what's best for our family."

Adelaide's frustration was palpable and Vivi put her hand over Adelaide's. "Let's clear the table and join Goldie outside. Bubba, why don't you set up the croquet set?"

Thankfully croquet, and Goldie's presence, eased the conflict about Vivi's job. There was playful competition between them, and Goldie even learned a few dance steps from Adelaide.

Vivi put away the last of the dishes and listened to the murmur of Bubba and Goldie's voices upstairs. Most likely Bubba was telling her about one of his fishing adventures. She tiptoed upstairs and peeked into Goldie's room. Goldie leaned into Bubba's shoulder and he had one foot on the floor to prevent himself from falling out of the narrow bed.

The darkness in the hallway hid Vivi while she watched them. She wondered how much longer Goldie would let them tuck her in. She was at an uncomfortable age, sometimes wanting the comfort of being a child, and other times wanting the independence of an adult. Let her linger in her childhood, Vivi thought. After her father's death, she'd been thrust into adult responsibilities without any transition. Goldie's head rested on Bubba's shoulder. Goldie may have coloring like Etta, but her oval face and straight nose was almost identical to Bubba's. He pushed back her hair and kissed her forehead.

Vivi leaned on the doorframe. This was her family, sometimes monotonous, but deeply fulfilling. The connection and interdependence with Bubba and Goldie gave her life stability, but if she was honest, it sometimes became an unwanted anchor, keeping her from following her passions. With Adelaide, there was excitement, curiosity, and freedom from her roles of wife and mother. Connection and fulfillment versus independence and excitement. Her family gave her roots, and Adelaide gave her wings. How would she balance this and get the best of both?

Vivi sighed and Bubba looked up and met her gaze over the top of Goldie's head. He slid out of the bed and pulled the blanket up to her chin. Vivi walked in and kissed Goldie as well.

As soon as they shut her door Bubba pulled her against him and kissed her deeply. It was easy to respond tonight. The help he'd offered, the laughter they'd shared, and the gentleness she'd just witnessed reminded her of why she loved Bubba, and without his usual haze from moonshine, his need for her felt pure.

After their lovemaking, they lay in each others arms under the quilt. Bubba kissed the back of her head. "Vivi, something seems different with you."

Vivi tensed. "Relax," he said and rubbed her arm. "I mean it in a good way. It seems like since you've met Adelaide you've been happier." He nibbled her earlobe. "And more passionate."

Vivi wasn't sure how to answer so pressed herself more tightly against him in response.

Bubba continued, "After my brother drowned, I felt like I was losing you too, and it was more than I could take. I know I've been drinking too much, but moonshine was the only thing that eased my pain," he paused, and slid his hand around her waist, "until now."

Vivi brushed away her tears. She rolled over to face him. "You're right, Bubba. I wasn't there for you. You were lost in your grief, and then in your drinking and I felt abandoned. I withdrew and now I see now how selfish that was. You've always been the light in my life, but I never thought I had anything to offer you."

Bubba pulled her closer and said, "Vivi, you are my light too. How can you not see that?"

"I see it better now. My time with Adelaide, working on suffrage, and Chapawee's circle has energized me, made me happy, and I've seen how that's helped you," she paused, "and your drinking."

The last few months had been a revelation. She'd learned she could make herself happy without Bubba's help, and this seemed to improve their marriage, but did it really? How could their marriage be strong when she was hiding her affair with Adelaide? A wave of guilt washed over her. It was wrong to love Adelaide too, but she couldn't just turn off her feelings.

"And Vivi," Bubba said, bringing her back to the moment, "I know you've enjoyed your work on the petition, and the editorial for women's suffrage, but you're not going to jeopardize your job are you? We'd have trouble paying our bills without your salary."

Vivi slid her head off Bubba's shoulder onto her pillow. "Don't worry. I won't make a decision that would harm our family."

Bubba kissed her shoulder. "I knew you wouldn't. Good night, sweetheart. I love you."

"I love you too," Vivi said and leaned over to kiss him gently on the lips. "Now let's get some sleep. Tomorrow I've got to figure out a way to get Chapawee out of jail."

In a couple minutes Bubba's snoring provided accompaniment to Vivi's racing thoughts. Adelaide, the superintendent, Chapawee. When Bubba was sound asleep, she slipped out of bed, put on her flannel nightgown and wool socks and went downstairs. While she was awake, she might as well work on her editorial for the Raleigh paper.

***

The northeast wind was strong and pressed the late afternoon chill into Vivi's bones. She thought of Chapawee in her jail cell and hoped she was warm enough. Her second stop this afternoon was to deliver the blanket and shawl she'd collected from Chapawee's cabin.

Wednesday night felt like a long time ago after her busy Thanksgiving Day, but now Vivi was standing in front of Lucy Pott's house, ready to carry out the only plan she and Cora had devised. The two-story house had a long, covered porch, with the front door squarely in the middle. Vivi knocked. It was three in the afternoon, and she hoped Lucy was home. Lucy had moved to Oriental ten years ago, when her father started his lumber company. At that time she was in high school and Vivi was a young mother, so their paths had never crossed.

The tap, tap, of delicate footsteps kept Vivi from knocking again.

"I'm coming," a voice said. Vivi wasn't sure whether Lucy would answer, or a housekeeper, as she was certain they had enough money for one.

The door opened and there stood a white woman, about the same height as Vivi, wearing a simple brown dress with splotches of red, blue and green paint on the front. In the deep pockets of the dress were three paintbrushes of varying size. The woman's shoulder-length black hair was held back with a yellow ribbon. Could this be Lucy? Vivi thought. She'd been expecting someone more refined and intimidating, like her mother.

The woman smiled and then cocked her head to the right and Vivi realized she needed to speak.

"Good afternoon. I'm Vivi Gibbs."

"Oh, you're the teacher. I've been meaning to talk with you. I'm Lucy Potts." She released the door knob to shake Vivi's hand and a gust of wind blew the door back against its hinges. "Another blustery day," Lucy said. "Please, come inside where it's warm."

Vivi stepped into the entrance hall and then Lucy took her coat and led her into the parlor. "Have a seat. I've been painting all afternoon and apologize for my appearance," Lucy said, pointing to the paint stains on her dress.

Painting all afternoon, Vivi thought, momentarily envious of Lucy's ability to carve out time for herself. "Thank you for seeing me. I'll only take you away from painting for a few minutes." Vivi sat at the edge of the couch and wondered if the painting behind Lucy was one she'd done. "And I'm sorry to bother you on a holiday weekend. I hope you enjoyed your Thanksgiving yesterday."

"It's over, which is the best part. I'm actually glad you're here. I've been wanting to ask you something," Lucy said, and leaned back in the chair with her hands behind her head. "Do you need an art teacher for your students? I'd love to come in weekly and teach a class, or maybe several classes for the different age groups."

Vivi blinked and took a breath. Lucy acted as if she'd invited Vivi over instead of Vivi coming unannounced. "The kids would love that, but it would be up to the superintendent, not me." The superintendent. Vivi clenched her jaw.

"That makes sense. But where are my manners? I bombarded you with my question. Now, how can I help you this afternoon?"

This question was asked not with irritation or malice like Vivi had expected, but with genuine curiosity. "I mean no disrespect, but I've come to ask for help with your mother."

Lucy sighed loudly and looked up at the ceiling. "Oh no. What has she done now? Let me go ahead and apologize. She can be pompous sometimes."

"Well, it has to do with Chapawee."

"Chapawee?" Lucy sat up and leaned forward, resting her hand on her knees.

"Yes. The Indian woman who lives on Hungry Mother Creek and sells her remedy. I buy some from her, and I think you do too."

Lucy nodded solemnly and then stood. "What's happened? My mother is obsessed with me giving her grandchildren and there's no telling what she's done."

Lucy paced in front of the couch while Vivi shared the story. She started with the visit Lucy's mother made to Chapawee's, and ended with what Vivi had seen at the waterfront Wednesday.

Lucy shook her head and sat on the couch beside Vivi. "Miss Chapawee is in that cold jail right now because of my mother?"

"That's what I'm guessing. Could you talk with your mother? See if she'd recant her accusations? Maybe then they'd release her."

Lucy stood again, as did Vivi who wanted to keep this moving and get to the jail to see Chapawee.

"I'll do my best," Lucy said and looked directly at Vivi. "I hate that this happened, and feel horrible about her being in jail. Do you think she needs anything?"

"I don't know. I haven't talked with her since they arrested her, but I'm taking her shawl and blanket to her when I leave here."

"Follow me," Lucy said and walked back towards the foyer. "I have a loaf of bread and some honey. Would you take them to her?"

"Sure," Vivi replied. The kitchen was at the back of the house and Lucy retrieved some bread and a jar of honey from the pantry. The kitchen was twice as large as Vivi's with cabinets that went to the ceiling and an electric stove, but it wasn't very tidy. Plates and bowls were piled in the sink, mail and newspapers on the counter, and two empty mugs sat on the table nestled in the bow of a bay window.

Lucy must have noticed her appraisal and said, "Please excuse the mess. When I'm focused on a painting I tend to ignore my housekeeping."

"It's fine," Vivi said and watched Lucy scurry around her messy kitchen in her dress splotched with paint. Vivi admired her for putting time into what she was passionate about, and not just keeping house. The suffrage movement was a new passion for Vivi, but she only gave it attention after Goldie and Bubba were in bed, and the house was in order. Watching Lucy, she saw there was another way.

Finally, Lucy found a small burlap sack to put the food in. "Guess I shouldn't put a knife in to cut the bread should I?" Lucy laughed and handed the bag to Vivi.

Vivi smiled. "Thank you, for the food, and for talking with your mother."

"I'll speak with her first thing tomorrow and will let you know how it goes. Where do you live? Maybe I can stop by?"

Vivi gave Lucy her address and said, "Or you can stop by the school at the end of the day, when I'm cleaning up."

"Great," Lucy said. "And I'll send a letter to the superintendent inquiring about teaching art."

"I'd love to have you in the classroom with me." Vivi's throat tightened after she said this. Would she even be in the classroom in the future?

Vivi leaned into the wind and held Chapawee's blanket, shawl and the burlap sack close to her chest. The visit with Lucy had been completely different than what she'd expected. Lucy was warm and easy to talk to, and maybe she'd be interested in helping with their women's suffrage efforts, but would she be involved with that anymore? It wasn't fair, she thought, picking up her pace. Why did she have to choose?

CHAPTER 14

Chapawee sat on the makeshift bed, a metal shelf built into the wall and covered by a thin mattress. The cold from the brick behind her seeped into her back, despite the shawl Vivi had brought yesterday. There was no privacy when Vivi had visited, but when she presented the bread from Lucy, she whispered that Lucy was going to do her best to convince her mother to drop the charges. Chapawee doubted this would make a difference, but was grateful for the effort, and the food. She broke off a piece of bread and dipped it into the honey.

The only window in her cell faced southwest, denying her the warmth of the morning sunlight, and Chapawee drew her shawl tighter. It would be afternoon before she felt the sun on her face. It was hard to sit here, with long empty hours when there were collards to pick and pecans to collect at home. She scooted to the edge of the bed and took Tayen's letter out of her pocket. She examined the shapes that formed her name on the envelope, comforted by the familiar angles of her daughter's handwriting.

A key jostled in the door, and a few seconds later the constable came in. Chapawee was alone at night, but either he or the magistrate were here during the day.

"Morning, Ma'am," the constable said, and then threw his hat down on the wooden desk across from her cell.

"Morning," Chapawee said, without leaving the bed.

The smell of breakfast came in with the constable. No doubt bacon and eggs his mother had prepared for him as he still lived with his parents. Before taking off his coat he walked to her cell and offered a small package wrapped in wax paper through the bars. There was the smell of breakfast again. Chapawee accepted it, and the contents warmed her hand.

"Momma made an egg biscuit for you."

"Please thank her for me," Chapawee said, unwrapping it and taking a bite. "It's delicious."

Chapawee sat down and placed her daughter's letter at the far end of the bed while she ate. The constable's mother must be responsible for feeding the inmates because so far, the only food she'd eaten since Thursday came from her, and of course the bread Lucy had sent. Chapawee took small deliberate bites to savor the flavor and extend her breakfast time as long as she could.

The only sound in the jail was the creak of the constable's chair when he leaned back in it to stare out the window to the street. Chapawee wondered how much the town paid him, as it didn't appear he had much to do. She laughed to herself. Of course that was the case, seeing as a 70-year-old woman was the only criminal currently in the jail. Chapawee folded the wax paper neatly when she finished and picked up her daughter's letter.

The chair creaked again when he stood. "I'll take that wax paper home to Momma. She'll use it again."

Chapawee walked the paper over to him, still holding her daughter's letter.

The constable glanced at it. "I bet you wish you'd never gone to the post office on Wednesday, seeing as it landed you in jail."

He must be bored if he's making small talk with me, Chapawee thought. "I can't go back and change anything about the past, constable. What's done is done."

"You can call me Pete," he said and leaned against the wall across from her cell. "Who's your letter from?"

"It's from my daughter." She hesitated and then added, "She lives in

Sampson County, near the Coharie River."

"I don't know where that is. I've only been to New Bern twice with my father, but one day I'm gonna take the train all the way to Raleigh. See what big city life is like."

She smiled at his youthful exuberance. "You'd be far away from your parents like Tayen is."

"Yeah, but I could write to them like your daughter writes to you."

Chapawee stared at her daughter's handwriting again, the pattern of the letters and spaces like music she couldn't hear. She lifted her head and saw Pete looking intently at her. He held her gaze a minute and then said quietly, "Miss Chapawee, would you like me to read your daughter's letter to you?"

Chapawee looked away, and her eyes filled with tears borne of shame, but also gratitude for Pete's kindness. But was he being kind, or did he think there'd be incriminating evidence in the letter? Nothing Tayen wrote would have anything to do with why she was in jail. She hoped the letter was filled with good news, and not sickness or death, something she couldn't bear to hear sitting in this cell. She had too much time to think of all the awful things the letter might say. It'd be better to know.

Silently, Chapawee handed Tayen's letter to Pete. She leaned her head against one of the bars, clasped another with her right hand, and closed her eyes. It would take all her concentration to memorize her daughter's message. She heard the crinkle of paper as Pete unfolded the letter.

"Dear Heh-neh."

Pete's voice cracked and he cleared his throat. It was strange to hear her daughter's term of endearment spoken by this young, white man, probably the same age as her eldest grandson.

He continued. "All is well."

Chapawee sighed with relief. Her daughter began her letters this way to immediately let her know nothing tragic had happened. If her first words were, "I've got something to tell you," then Chapawee knew to brace herself.

Pete shared the details of Tayen's life over the past month, funny things the grandchildren had said, how her garden was doing, the goings on of the tribal council. Soon Pete's voice was replaced by Tayen's and Chapawee felt her daughter there with her, but the cold metal against her hand reminded her otherwise.

"Your loving daughter, Tayen," Pete finished.

Chapawee opened her eyes and looked at him. "Thank you. Would you mind reading it again so I can remember all the details?"

Pete nodded. "Heh-neh."

For another few minutes the differences in age, race, and gender slipped away and Chapawee and Pete were connected by Tayen's words.

***

Vivi kneeled next to Emily, her head tilted to listen to the hesitant voice. Emily was a first grader learning how to read.

"The fish is in the . . ." Emily paused.

"Sound it out," Vivi said gently.

Vivi heard the rustle of a skirt and turned slightly. Out of the corner of her eye she saw Adelaide leaning in the doorframe watching her. What was she doing here? Adelaide, in her classroom? Two disparate parts of her life intersected and it felt strange.

"R, r, river," Emily said.

Adelaide put her finger to her lips.

Vivi turned back to Emily. "Perfect. You're improving. Now take these sentences home to practice with your parents." Vivi wrote three simple sentences on Emily's slate and then moved on to the next student needing help.

For the next twenty minutes, Vivi was divided. Part of her finished up the school day as usual, and the other part was acutely aware of Adelaide watching her, and she felt exposed. Adelaide was seeing her teacher persona, something even Bubba had only heard about, but never seen. Vivi clarified each grade's homework assignments, reminded the students to gather their belongings and then dismissed class.

Chairs scratched against the floor and the children's voices burst forth in a cacophony of sound. Vivi thought of the superintendent. Would he show up now that school was over? Is that why Adelaide came? To speak her mind to him?

Goldie dashed past Vivi and made it to Adelaide first. "Miss Adelaide," she said, giving her a sideways hug. "Why are you at school?"

"You've come to see me sing, right?" Adelaide asked, and Goldie nodded. "Well, I wanted to see your mother teach."

Adelaide looked over Goldie's head at Vivi and she knew then, Adelaide wasn't here to argue with Mr. O'Neal. She was here to see her.

"And she has a special talent for it."

Goldie was unimpressed and walked away to whisper something to a classmate.

"Adelaide, this is a surprise," Vivi said and looked down the stairs, hoping Mr. O'Neal wasn't ascending them. "I don't have much time. I need to clean up, and the superintendent said he'd be back this week and could be stopping by today."

Adelaide took both Vivi's hands. "That's part of why I came. I know at Thanksgiving I was pressuring you to stand up for yourself, even if it meant losing your job, but I realized I wasn't honoring your passion for education. I thought seeing you in action would help me understand."

Vivi squeezed her hands and then released them when she noticed a coat hanging on a peg by the door. She snatched it up and yelled down the stairs, "Sarah, don't forget your coat!"

An adolescent girl at the bottom of the steps stopped and looked up at Vivi. "Just throw it to me, Mrs. Gibbs."

"Sarah, please come retrieve your coat. We don't throw things in the classroom."

Sarah trudged up the steps and without a word took the coat from Vivi.

Adelaide was doing her best not to laugh. "Mrs. Gibbs," she said playfully, "you're so strict."

Once Sarah was outside, they both burst into laughter. "I wouldn't want to be that age again."

"Me either," Vivi said, remembering the challenge of dealing with grief and puberty.

"What are you going to tell Mr. O'Neal?" Adelaide asked.

"I don't know. I told Bubba I wouldn't do anything to impact us financially, but," Vivi paused, "I don't want to stop fighting for women's right to vote. It's given me a sense of purpose that goes beyond the Oriental town limits."

"Could you do both?" Adelaide asked. "I mean, if you say you won't stop, would the school board really fire you? I can't imagine there are qualified teachers around here, lining up to take your place."

Vivi cocked her head. Was Adelaide right? If she called their bluff, would the school board really fire her and leave the children with no teacher? "Adelaide, I hadn't thought of that. If they let me go, it would take a while to find a replacement, maybe the rest of the school year. I would hope their anger at my suffrage work wouldn't outweigh the education of Pamlico County's children." It was a risk she was ready to take.

A weight lifted, and Vivi embraced Adelaide tightly. Adelaide had done it again, given her wings.

"Sometimes it's good to create your own answer," Adelaide said.

Vivi nodded and wondered what answer would solve the conundrum about how to balance her relationship with Adelaide and her marriage.

"Momma," Goldie said, interrupting Vivi's thoughts. "May I leave now and stop by Grandmother's on the way home?"

Vivi hesitated before she answered and Adelaide, who knew about Art and what Vivi had seen, interjected. "How about we walk together to your grandmother's?"

Goldie's eyes lit up. "Yeah! Can I, Mom? You can show me more dance steps as we go."

"Are you sure it won't interfere with your work at the hotel?" Vivi asked.

"No. We were full for Thanksgiving, but the last of those guests checked out this morning and my afternoon is free."

Goldie gathered her schoolbooks at her desk and while her back was turned, Adelaide kissed Vivi gently in the curve of her neck. "I'll go straight to the hotel after I drop Goldie off. Maybe you can stop by for a little while on your way home."

Vivi's skin burned where Adelaide's lips had been. "I'll come as quickly as I can, but I want to mail the editorial I've written for the *News and Observer* on my way over."

"Congratulations! Then we'll have something to celebrate."

"I'm just mailing it. They haven't accepted it yet." Vivi had enjoyed organizing her thoughts and writing the editorial, but couldn't imagine they would actually publish her words.

"Oh, but they will," Adelaide said with a nod of her head.

Goldie bounded back and stood beside Adelaide. "Bye, Mom. See you in a little bit."

"OK, honey. I can't wait to see the new dance steps Miss Adelaide teaches you."

Adelaide winked at Vivi, and then she and Goldie shimmied down the steps and pirouetted out the door.

"Vivi."

Vivi dropped the chalk she had been using to write a poem on the blackboard and whirled around to find Lucy Potts standing there. She was on edge, expecting Mr. O'Neal to show up and having to rush to the post office before meeting Adelaide.

"I'm sorry I startled you," Lucy said.

Vivi bent down to pick up the chalk. "That's OK. I was in my own world." Lucy had come about Chapawee, something she'd momentarily forgotten about. "Thanks for coming by. Have you talked with your mother?"

Lucy looked beyond Vivi to the blackboard and then back. "I did," Lucy sighed. "She is hell bent on seeing Chapawee punished, as if that will give her a grandchild."

Vivi's heart dropped.

"I don't know what's wrong with my mother," Lucy continued. "I told her that I don't want children right now, and Chapawee shouldn't be in jail because of my decision." Lucy walked to the blackboard and picked up the chalk. "She's so attached to her vision of how my life should be that she doesn't even hear me." Lucy began drawing. "I don't know why I'm surprised. It's been like that my whole life."

Vivi watched in amazement as Lucy drew. It seemed like magic, that from the piece of chalk she'd just dropped, a huge oak tree appeared, then a swing from the lower branches. For a moment Vivi forgot about the superintendent and Chapawee.

"Lucy, that's beautiful. I've never seen an artist create something before my eyes. What a gift you have."

Lucy placed the chalk in the tray and turned. Her cheeks were pink. "Oh. I'm sorry. I hadn't planned on that. Everywhere I go, I see art supplies." She smiled, picked up the chalk, and quickly added a young girl sitting on the swing with a butterfly hovering around her head.

When she finished she said, "But I do have good news, too."

Vivi stepped closer. "You do?"

"Yes. I've found another way to help Chapawee."

Lucy picked up the eraser and Vivi held up her hands and said, "No. Please leave your art. I want the children to enjoy it tomorrow. Now, tell me your plan to help Chapawee."

"My husband has a friend in Bayboro who's an attorney."

The afternoon was quickly evaporating, and Vivi swept while Lucy explained how she would paint a portrait of this attorney's wife in exchange for him representing Chapawee and getting her out of jail as soon as possible.

"He said it will take a week to get things taken care of, but at least she won't be in there for 30 days like the constable said."

Vivi leaned the broom in the corner. "Thank you," Vivi said. "You're going to a lot of trouble to help Chapawee and I know she'll appreciate it."

"It's the least I can do. I'll let you know when I have more details about when she'll be released."

"Sounds good. You know where to find me."

"Wait," Vivi said.

Lucy paused at the top of the stairs and Vivi continued. "I'm starting a chapter of the Equal Suffrage Association in Oriental, or will officially start one when I have enough women, but some of us are already gathering signatures on petitions. Would you have any interest in helping out with this? We're meeting again next Thursday evening."

Lucy tilted her head to look at Vivi. "Suffrage? Women's right to vote? I had no idea anyone here was working on that issue. I've been keeping up with it in the Raleigh paper. I'd love to help." Lucy laughed.

"My mother's already angry with me. Adding one more thorn in her side won't make any difference."

Vivi shared the details of the next meeting before Lucy left.

I guess I'm still working on suffrage, Vivi said to herself. The envelope addressed to the *News and Observer* lay on her desk, and provided more evidence of that fact. Now to get Bubba's understanding and support. The late afternoon sun slanted in the west window, reminding Vivi of the time. She quickly gathered her papers and the envelope and stuffed them in her bag. First stop was the post office, and then a few moments with Adelaide. She couldn't shimmy down the staircase like Adelaide, but managed to twirl at the bottom.

***

The call of an owl in the oak tree outside the jail brought Chapawee relief. Daybreak was only an hour away. It'd been a long night. She'd barely slept due to a cough that had taken hold, the body aches from eight nights on a flimsy mattress, and anticipation for her release today.

On Wednesday a lawyer from Bayboro swept into the jail, said he was representing her, and asked to speak with the magistrate immediately. Chapawee was surprised how quickly he'd arrived as it was only yesterday that Vivi had brought the paperwork for her to sign allowing Jonathan Pender to be her lawyer. Vivi told her that Lucy had no luck convincing her mother to recant her accusations, but had found another route to help. Mr. Pender was a friend of Lucy's husband and agreed to represent her in exchange for one of Lucy's paintings.

Chapawee stood and walked to the small window to look at the full moon, low in the western sky. The owl hooted again and she smiled, knowing the next time she stood in the moonlight and heard an owl she would be back home, home on her land by Hungry Mother Creek.

Thankfully her lawyer confronted the magistrate in the jailhouse so Chapawee could witness it. She didn't understand all the legal references, but the gist seemed to be there was only hearsay evidence that the wild carrot seeds were a contraceptive and that wasn't enough to hold a person in jail. This surprised her, as hearsay was exactly what put Cora's husband Jeremiah into jail, and then on a chain gang. Seemed like if a white person said something, it was fact, no matter what the truth. The magistrate resisted this line of defense saying the source was a fine, reputable citizen. He then leaned close to the lawyer and whispered something. Chapawee imagined he was bribing the lawyer with some of the money the Livingstons were paying him, but to no avail. The lawyer said something about statutes, regulations and district court and finally the magistrate relented.

Chapawee had hoped she'd be released immediately but the magistrate said it would take a couple days to process the paperwork and her lawyer didn't disagree. On his way out, Mr. Pender stopped in front of Chapawee, his first acknowledgment of her. She thanked him and he simply nodded his head and said he was staying at the Potts' for a couple days and would return Friday morning to ensure she was released.

By now, dim light glowed outside the window facing the street. It would be at least another hour until anyone arrived and Chapawee paced around the cell, ten laps in one direction, ten laps in the other, to stay warm and pass the time. The discomfort and helplessness she'd endured the past week was coming to an end, and she was grateful, but also angry it had taken white allies to secure her release. She knew there were hundreds of black and brown folk who'd sat in this cell much longer because no white person had come to their defense, and like Jeremiah, may have been put on a chain gang or sent to prison, losing years, or an entire life to a system designed to protect the white citizen's status at all costs.

The constable arrived earlier than usual and immediately handed

Chapawee an egg biscuit. "Better eat that quickly, Miss Chapawee," Pete said, waiting for her to return the wax paper it was wrapped in. "The magistrate will be here in a minute and thinks I'm feeding you the watered-down oatmeal we usually give the inmates."

Chapawee handed him the paper and quickly took a few bites. She would miss this part of her incarceration, a fresh biscuit that someone else made for her, but she'd give up breakfast for the rest of her life to wake up on the pallet in the corner of her cabin.

The jail door slammed behind the magistrate and Chapawee turned her back so he wouldn't see her chewing and then slipped the rest of her biscuit into her pocket. A few minutes later her attorney arrived and nodded when he walked past the cell. Chapawee couldn't hear what they were saying but Pete caught her eye and winked to reassure her. After a few minutes of conversation, some shuffling of papers and signatures, Pete unlocked the cell door. Chapawee made her mark on the paper her lawyer presented her and then Mr. Pender said, "You're free to go, Miss Chapawee." He turned and smiled at the magistrate, and Chapawee saw the enjoyment he got from outsmarting him.

"I'll see you out," Pete said. He took three long strides to the door and held it open. Chapawee walked into the morning light and took a huge breath of fresh air.

"Do you have a way home?" he asked, looking up and down the street.

"Yes. My neighbors have come to take me home."

Pete looked around. "Where are they?"

"I'm sure they'll be here in a minute," Chapawee said, knowing that Jeremiah gave a wide berth to the jail and lawmen since his experience.

"There they are." Chapawee took a couple steps in that direction and then stopped. She turned back to Pete. He watched some boys running past on their way to school and Chapawee imagined it was only a couple years ago that he'd done the same thing.

"Pete," Chapawee said, and his gaze moved to her. "Thank you. Thank you for your kindness." Her throat tightened when she thought of Pete reading Tayen's words. "And please thank your mother for her biscuits."

Pete smiled. "You're welcome, Miss Chapawee. I'm sorry this happened. I did my best to . . ."

Pete hesitated and she instinctively put her hand on his right forearm. "You did your best and I'm grateful for that." Chapawee leaned towards him. "People like you give me hope that one day things can be different."

Pete nodded, but Chapawee could tell he didn't fully understand her comment. He was kind and just being himself, not trying to change any social order. Pete went back inside and Chapawee walked to the end of New Street where Cora was waiting. The air was cold, but the sun warmed her back and Chapawee's speed increased. She was going home. Cora enveloped her in a tight hug.

"Sure is good to lay my eyes and hands on you, Chapawee," Cora said before releasing her.

"And it's good to see you, the sun, the trees, Jeremiah, and even old Drum," she added and rubbed the forehead of Cora's mule.

Cora climbed into the cart and then helped Chapawee onto the bench that was just long enough for the three of them. Jeremiah leaned forward and said, "Good to see you, Chapawee. I'm glad you didn't have to stay in there too long."

Chapawee nodded. "Thanks for coming to get me." Knowing all that Jeremiah had endured, she made a point not to complain about her week in jail. Cora understood this and didn't ask Chapawee about her time, but updated her on the state of her garden.

After that, they rode in silence and Chapawee spread her blanket over her and Cora's laps to keep them warm. Cora tucked the blanket under her hip and then asked, "Will you stop making your remedy?"

One of the front wheels of the cart dipped into a hole and Chapawee grasped Cora's arm for support. "I gave that a lot of thought," Chapawee said, still holding onto Cora. "We're pretty much done for this year anyway. Whoever hasn't purchased their remedy yet will probably stay away after hearing I was in jail. I'll keep our supply hidden in the cabin in case there's an emergency." She met Cora's gaze, both knowing what she meant by emergency.

They turned left onto Kershaw Road and Chapawee sat up taller. She took in the familiar fields interspersed with groves of pine and oak, with fresh appreciation.

"Chapawee," Cora said over the rattle of the cart. "I need to apologize."

Chapawee had hoped Cora wouldn't blame herself for what happened, because she certainly didn't. "There's no need to apologize, Cora."

"Yes. There is. The way Vivi explained things, you were arrested because you mailed that package of seeds to Titus. I was the one who asked you to do that."

"Cora, it's not your fault. You and I both know I was arrested because of Mrs. Livingston."

"But . . ."

"No," Chapawee inserted before Cora could add more. "There's no need to talk about this anymore. I'm out of jail now. We won't be selling our remedy for a while, and as far as I'm concerned everything is fine."

Cora sighed and put her arm around Chapawee as they turned down the dirt path to her cabin. "Thank you, my friend."

Jeremiah, who'd been quiet the entire ride, cleared his throat. "Chapawee, don't let your guard down too easily. Mrs. Livingston may be more determined after failing to get what she wanted the first time."

Chapawee knew Jeremiah spoke from experience. "I'll be careful Jeremiah, but I won't sell Lucy any more remedy, so Mrs. Livingston can't blame me much longer for her lack of grandchildren."

"Yeah, but it's more than that," Jeremiah said and pulled on the reins to slow Drum as they neared Chapawee's cabin. "For Mrs. Livingston you've come to represent what she doesn't have in her life. White folk do that all the time, casting their deficiencies onto us. It's more comfortable for them to hate us, and punish us, then it is to look inside and fix themselves."

"Amen," Cora said.

Chapawee knew Jeremiah was right, but wanted to focus on being home, not the threat of something else happening.

"Probably best if you stay to yourself this winter," Cora said. "I'll get whatever supplies you need, and I bet Etta and Vivi will help too, as much as you've helped them in the past."

"Thank you." Chapawee had to say this was a relief, not because of her fear of Mrs. Livingston, but because she was tired. She'd always prided herself on being independent, but wouldn't miss the cold, winter trips to town. If she were in a tribe, she'd be getting help out of respect for her status as an elder. They weren't related by blood, but Cora was definitely part of her tribe and she would accept the help with grace.

Jeremiah's warning slipped to the back of her mind when her home came into sight. Hungry Mother Creek threw a glint of sun in her direction, and over the top of her cabin she saw the upper branches of the Mother Tree swaying gently in the breeze. Smoke came from her chimney and when the cart stopped, Sadie stepped out of her cabin.

"Welcome home. I've got some soup ready for your lunch."

Chapawee quickly wiped a tear from the corner of her eye and gave Sadie a quick hug in appreciation.

"It's good to be home."

CHAPTER 15

"Thank you for coming out on a drizzly, cold night," Vivi said. Adelaide's hand gently enveloped Vivi's, which she'd unconsciously balled into a fist. Being in a leadership role was unfamiliar and she wanted to do it well. She uncurled her hand, and her fingers intertwined with Adelaide's for a moment. She welcomed Lucy to their group, but didn't need to introduce her, because Eve and Kathryn knew her from the Oriental Women's Club.

"Let's start by reporting on how our petitions are coming, and then plan our next step from there," Vivi said.

The front door of the hotel creaked and the women instinctively turned their heads to the foyer. Stella Aldridge stepped in bringing a blast of cold, damp air. "Sorry I'm a few minutes late. I hope I haven't missed anything."

Vivi hurried into the hall. "We've just begun. I'm happy you came," Vivi said, tilting her head to look up at Stella. She'd only seen her seated, and hadn't noticed her height then. She was probably taller than Bubba. Vivi took Stella's coat and hung it on a peg by the door. She must have come from work because she looked professional in an ankle-length forest green skirt and high-necked white blouse.

"Everyone," Vivi said when they stepped into the parlor. "This is Stella Aldridge. She's the telegraph operator at the train depot. I met her a couple of days ago when I went there to pick up a telegram."

Adelaide secured a chair from another room and the women expanded their circle so Stella could join. Adelaide said, "Vivi, why don't you tell everyone what your telegram was about before we start the meeting?"

Vivi blushed and looked down at the agenda she'd created for the meeting. Adelaide bumped her gently with her shoulder. "Go on."

Vivi couldn't contain her smile when she looked up at the women. "The telegram was from the *News and Observer* in Raleigh. There're going to publish an editorial I wrote about women's suffrage in this Sunday's paper."

Spontaneously everyone clapped and Vivi's blush deepened. "I wrote about my awakening to this cause in the hope it would help other rural women better understand what's at stake and join us." She touched Adelaide's leg. "If it wasn't for Adelaide, I wouldn't have had the courage to submit it."

"Oh, I can't wait to read it," Lucy said. "I guess it'll be next week before the train brings the Sunday paper here from Raleigh."

"It usually comes in on the Tuesday Swamp Lily train," Stella said.

"I appreciate your support, but let's get back to our agenda," Vivi said, wanting to get out of the spotlight. "Kathryn, why don't you start? How is your petition coming along?"

For the next hour the women discussed the progress with getting signatures as well as the challenges they'd encountered, similar to what Vivi had experienced. Adelaide suggested opening their conversations with a statement everyone could agree upon, like how efficiently women managed children and the household, before jumping into talk about the right to vote.

The addition of Lucy and Stella increased the energy and enthusiasm in the room compared to their first meeting. They didn't have a talking stick like in Chapawee's circle, and occasionally interrupted one another, but Vivi felt a similar power.

The grandmother clock struck the half hour. "It's 8:30, ladies," Vivi said. "Let's wrap up. Everyone know their next step?"

"Yes," Lucy said. "When I'm in Bayboro with my husband's family for Christmas, I'll do my best to get signatures from the women up there, and I'll start working on a suffrage postcard and get that to Vivi by next week."

Vivi nodded. "And thanks to an anonymous benefactor, we have money to cover the printing costs of the postcards." She'd gotten flustered with the attention about her editorial and forgot to share this earlier.

The women leaned in towards Vivi. "A benefactor?" Eve asked. "Who in Pamlico County would want to use their money to support women's suffrage?"

Vivi wasn't prepared for questions. She hated to lie, but wasn't comfortable sharing details about the philanthropic fund her father had left her. "The bank contacted me about an anonymous donation for the Pamlico County Equal Suffrage Association. They helped me set up an account so we can access this money."

"I wonder why they want to be anonymous, and not join our efforts to get the vote?" Lucy asked.

"Maybe they're well-known in town and concerned about public ridicule," Stella said.

"That's most likely it," Adelaide added. "We often get anonymous donations in Boston. Usually from prominent businessmen who support the cause but don't want any controversy."

Thank you, Adelaide, Vivi thought to herself and hoped the conversation would end here.

"How much did they donate?" Katherine asked. "Maybe we need a treasurer."

"Five hundred dollars." This was how much Vivi had transferred from the trust fund into the account she'd opened for their suffrage group. "That's a great idea. At our next meeting let's elect officers so we'll be organized as our association grows."

"Sounds good to me." Stella leaned forward and placed her teacup on the table. "Thanks for inviting me. I knew that women telegraph operators in other parts of the state supported suffrage, but didn't think anyone here did. I'm excited to help out, and I'll focus on getting signatures from the Kershaw area, where my parents live."

"And if we get a warmer day before our next meeting," Eve said, "I'll convince my husband to take me and Mom in our boat to the north part of the county, around Vandemere and Hobucken, and talk with the women there."

Vivi took a breath and relaxed against the back of the couch for the first time that evening. "Wonderful. Little by little we're reaching more of the county. I'll be in touch with the Equal Suffrage Association and find out when they want the petitions mailed into our representative. Oh," Vivi said remembering Sadie, "I'm going to talk with the colored schoolteacher to see if she'd work on a petition in her community."

Immediately there was tension in the room and Vivi saw Eve take a deep breath. Her instinct was to ease the awkwardness with words, but she held the silence in hope someone else would speak.

Eve cleared her throat. "Vivi, the topic of suffrage is controversial enough. I don't think it's a good idea to align with the colored women too."

Vivi slid to the edge of the couch and looked to Adelaide for guidance. Adelaide nodded slightly, indicating Vivi should speak.

Eve continued, pulling on the sleeve of her jacket as she spoke. "There's a reason the ESA won't allow colored women to be members. I think it would hurt our cause if people knew you included a petition from them."

Vivi's vocal cords were tight with the effort of restraining what she really thought. Eve was making a valid point though, but it wasn't fair.

"Eve," Vivi said, "our cause is procuring women's right to vote, and as far as I'm concerned that includes all women. We won't add the colored women as members, just combine their petitions with ours."

"Both your perspectives have merit," Kathryn said, her even, calm voice reducing some tension, "but based on what my aunt in Asheville has shared, the suffrage organizations don't include colored women to steer clear of the race issue. They even garner support for suffrage by arguing it would allow more white people to vote."

Vivi's face reddened at her ignorance for not knowing this, and that the cause igniting her passion was tainted.

"Ladies," Adelaide said and scooted closer to Vivi so their thighs were touching. "This issue has come up in Boston and no answer satisfies everyone. I suggest you focus on your common ground, and keep moving forward with the plans you've laid out."

Lucy stood and said, "That sounds good to me. I use the same strategy in my relationship with my mother."

That brought a smile to Eve's face. "I know your mother, Lucy, and imagine you're good at that." Eve turned to Vivi. "I'm sorry if I upset you Vivi, but I had to be truthful."

Vivi nodded and following Adelaide's advice, didn't object any further. They were making progress with new members and more signatures and she didn't want to derail this by focusing on their differences.

Everyone moved into the hallway. "I hope you all have a wonderful Christmas," Vivi said, wanting to end things on a positive note. "We'll meet again the second Thursday in January."

"And I can't wait to read your article," Kathryn said with one hand on the doorknob. The other women nodded in agreement as they tied their scarves, or pulled up the hoods on their winter coats. Kathryn, Eve and Stella stepped into the damp night with heads down to keep the mist from their eyes.

Lucy hung back and gave Vivi a quick hug. "Thanks for inviting me. I'll work on the postcard this weekend and get it to you next week. Maybe we could even get it published in our local paper."

"Thank you. I can't wait to see what you create." If they miss her editorial in the *News and Observer*, there'd be no hiding from the school board if the postcard was published locally, Vivi thought, with less trepidation than she would have expected.

Vivi rested her forehead on the door after she closed it behind Lucy. The cool wood grounded her. Things hadn't gone exactly as planned, but they were gaining momentum. She sighed. But what about the colored women? Could she promote women's suffrage and exclude them?

A chair scraped against the floor as Adelaide returned the parlor to its original configuration. Vivi joined her with the intention of collecting the tea things, but when Adelaide turned around and their eyes met, all of Vivi's repressed frustration escaped and she collapsed on the couch.

"Adelaide, how do you do it? How do you set aside racial equality while working on suffrage?"

Adelaide sat down and took Vivi's head into her lap. She removed Vivi's hair pins and wound her fingers in and out of Vivi's hair. "It's complicated. I try to be fair and kind, and speak up against prejudice, but our suffrage association in Boston doesn't include colored women either. It's a hard truth, but I believe we have a greater chance of gaining the right to vote if we don't add on the racial issue. After all, white men will be voting on suffrage legislation, and we want it to be palatable to them. Once we get the vote, then we'll have more power to help the colored women."

Vivi enjoyed the pressure of Adelaide's fingers in her hair, but removed them so she could sit up. "But, Adelaide, the colored women don't need our help," Vivi said, thinking of the intelligence and ingenuity with which Sadie did the same job as she, but with far fewer resources. "They need the freedom to live without fear, and the constant obstacles to success white people place before them. It would be an asset to have them as part of our suffrage movement."

Adelaide stood and placed the teacups and saucers on a tray. "I agree with everything you're saying and felt the same when I began my suffrage work, but like I said in our meeting, if you're going to make any progress, you have to steer clear of race, especially here in the south."

Teacups rattled in their saucers when Adelaide lifted the tray. Vivi sat silently and watched her disappear around the corner into the kitchen. She wrapped her arms around herself for comfort, and to contain her disappointment. Adelaide shouldn't compromise her beliefs like this. Vivi had fully expected her to support the inclusion of Sadie and the other colored women, but maybe she'd idealized Adelaide, and probably the suffrage movement too, her passion and naïveté clouding her judgment.

Vivi stood and walked to the window. Mist was suspended in the glow of the gas street light.

"Are you OK?"

Vivi turned quickly, startled by Adelaide's presence.

Adelaide put her hands on Vivi's shoulders. "I hope you don't give up on suffrage work because of this."

Vivi put her arms around Adelaide's waist. "No. I'm still committed to the cause, but hate we can't work for suffrage and include the colored women."

"Sometimes you can't have everything you want, and must pick your top priority." Adelaide pulled her closer. "Just like I've made you one of my top priorities."

Vivi looked away. Would she make Adelaide a priority over Bubba?

She couldn't make that choice, but Adelaide was who she was with right now. The energy intensified between them. A gust of wind threw rain against the window, but neither of them heard it.

CHAPTER 16

Steam, just visible in the soft light of dawn, flared from Lancelot's nostrils. Vivi dismounted, stomped her feet and rubbed her hands together.

"Sunrise in September is way more pleasant than December," she said to her mother who was tying her horse to Chapawee's hitching post.

"It could be worse," her mother replied. "At least it's not cold enough for frost."

Vivi's scarf had loosened on the ride over and she rewrapped it around her neck. "Mother, are we crazy for coming out here in the cold and half-dark? Bubba certainly didn't understand this morning, but I reminded him of the early morning hunts with his father and brother, and tried to convince him our circle was similar," she paused, "except for the killing part."

Etta laughed. "Yes. This does feel a bit crazy, but I was surprised at how meaningful the last circle was to me, and it will be good to see how Chapawee has fared since her release from jail. I still can't believe that happened. There have to be more important things to attend to in our town."

"I'm sure there are. I wonder if she'll talk about her experience in the circle?"

"How could she not?" Etta said. "I'm sure it's had a huge impact on her."

Vivi's stomach twisted when she anticipated holding the talking stick. She wanted to speak truthfully, but the details about her relationship with Adelaide and her marriage felt too personal to share, though they'd played a big role in her life since they'd last met. Could she honor the intention of the circle without disclosing everything?

"Etta, Vivi," a figure called from Chapawee's porch. Vivi recognized Cora's voice.

"Good morning, Cora," Etta called.

When they got to the porch Cora said, "Chapawee's already at the circle getting the fire going. Can you find your way OK? I'll wait here for Sadie."

"Sure," Vivi said and looked towards the woods. "We'll follow the glow of the fire."

Vivi and Etta stepped carefully through the underbrush to the clearing by the Mother Tree. Chapawee knelt by the fire. She didn't look up and fed the fire with small sticks, then larger branches and once the fire was strong, placed a couple logs on top.

The flames leapt and danced, adding light and warmth to the morning. Chapawee sat back on her heels and watched the fire a minute, and then went to stand. Vivi saw her hesitate and stepped over to offer her hand which Chapawee took.

"Thank you," Chapawee said, rubbing her back. "My body doesn't move as well as it used to, but I'm happy it's still moving."

Etta stepped forward. "Chapawee, it's good to see you. What an ordeal you must have gone through in jail."

"Oh, I'm fine, and I must thank Vivi for her help in my release."

Vivi still held Chapawee's hand and squeezed it gently. "All I did was pass a few messages along. It was Lucy and her painting that did most of the work."

"Morning," Sadie said when she and Cora entered the clearing.

After a few pleasantries, Chapawee directed them to sit in the same places they'd occupied at the fall equinox. Chapawee was on Vivi's left and Sadie to her right. She hadn't seen Sadie since her visit about Pearl and would check in about that after the circle.

Vivi settled herself on the quilt she'd brought to sit on, and held her hands to the fire. The yellow and orange of the fire mirrored the sky to her left as the sun approached the horizon. Winter silence blanketed the woods and the women naturally followed suit.

After a few minutes of quiet, which Vivi found less disconcerting than her first circle, Chapawee said, "The same principles apply as before, speak truthfully and only when you have the talking stick. I have no specific focus for today other than to share what comes to your mind when you pick up the talking stick."

Now Vivi was uncomfortable. Just speak what was on her mind? There was no guiding question like the last circle. Would she have anything of worth to share? Vivi took a breath and looked around the circle at the other women. Last time she'd shared the first thing that'd popped into her mind and it'd worked out well, and she'd trust that would happen again.

"Let's start with ten deep breaths together," Chapawee said and then placed the talking stick in front of her, "and whoever is moved to share may pick up the talking stick after that."

Vivi sent her breath deep into her lungs and then exhaled gently through her mouth, creating a small cloud in front of her. The cold morning pressed into her back, while the fire warmed her face, neck and arms. Her thoughts jumped to who would speak first, and she refocused on her last three breaths. When she finished, she lifted her gaze to see sunlight streaming through the bare trees on the other side of the creek. A few chickadees welcomed the light with their song.

Cora picked up the talking stick and everyone turned their attention to her. She kept both hands on the stick and leaned forward slightly. "What I'm going to share didn't just come to mind. I've been thinking about it over the past month." She paused and looked over the top of Vivi's head into the woods. "Today, I'm going to be more honest than I was at the last circle." She looked at Etta beside her and then across to Vivi and continued, "Please don't take offense, but the only white women I've known are the ones I've worked for. I acted friendly towards them, but was never friends with them. It was natural for me to put on an act and not be truthful at our last circle." She dropped the stick in to her lap and used her hands for emphasis. "I didn't lie about being content. There are quiet moments, especially with Jeremiah, where I feel exactly this way, but seeing what happened to Chapawee reminds me why I can never let my guard down. Things can change for the worse in an instant," she paused, and this time looked at Chapawee and Sadie, "especially if you're brown or black. So, I'm trying to keep the balance of appreciating the blessings in each moment while also staying alert." Cora lay the talking stick back in front of Chapawee.

Cora's words settled over Vivi. They reminded her of how she'd felt after her father died, unable to sleep or concentrate, waiting for the next bad thing to happen. But death did not discriminate based on skin color, and what Cora described, and Chapawee had lived through, wasn't a universal experience. Vivi had never feared being wrongfully jailed or physically harmed like Pearl. She'd go on alert for short periods of time, like when the superintendent came by school, or she saw Art behind the general store, but this was never a sustained feeling like Cora described. She could move about her day focused on who she was with and the task at hand without concern for her safety, something Cora, Chapawee and Sadie could not. Vivi moved her legs, uncomfortable in her position, and with the reality Cora had shared.

The sun gained altitude and warmed the morning air from cold to crisp. Vivi relaxed her shoulders and removed her gloves, but before she could retrieve the talking stick, Chapawee took it and rolled it back and forth in front of her like she was rolling out dough.

Chapawee sat with her back to the creek and faced the Mother Tree, staring at the trunk. "When we met at the fall equinox, I was in tune with the cycle of life, slowing and simplifying my life in response to my aging body and my need for quiet. I was embracing this season of my life and the season of the year, planting my fall garden, harvesting wild carrot seeds and collecting oysters."

Chapawee paused and looked around the circle at each woman. "And, as you all know, a routine trip to town ended up with me in jail for eight days at the end of November. I knew Mrs. Livingston had targeted me as the reason she wasn't a grandmother, but I let my guard down and went to town when I should have stayed at home, out of sight."

The wind picked up and the upper branches of the trees clicked against one another. Vivi looked away from Chapawee into the fire and felt guilty about the laughter, good food and games of her Thanksgiving while Chapawee was alone in jail.

Chapawee stopped rolling the talking stick and laughed gently. "Leave it to the government to interfere with the cycles of life." A kingfisher called out her agreement from a nearby tree. Chapawee continued, "I left the jail angry that the laws created by white men, enforced by white men and in this case, influenced by the money of a white woman, would put me in jail and like Cora said, I won't let my guard down again. But I also left the jail with hope, inspired by the kindness of my circle, Lucy Potts and her husband, and the constable."

Everyone's head turned towards Chapawee with this comment. The constable, Vivi thought. That was Peter, one of her students from five or six years ago. She didn't remember much about him except he was quiet and a decent student, but he was also one of the white men enforcing the law that Chapawee referred to.

"I know, the constable helped put me in jail, but he was following the orders of the magistrate, not his heart. How he treated me revealed his heart. Kindness from unexpected people brings hope. And whether it's inside a jail, or outside in a circle, when people create connection across vastly different life experiences, there is hope for a future with more equality and peace. It begins one person at a time." Chapawee rolled the talking stick away and put another log on the fire. The silence extended and she poked the fire with a large stick, adjusting the logs.

How does she do it? Vivi wondered. How does Chapawee balance her anger and hope; her need to be vigilant, with her desire to create connection? Maybe age has given her the wisdom to manage these paradoxes of life.

Sadie threw a twig into the fire and when Vivi looked up in response to her movement, their eyes met briefly and they both smiled. Vivi wanted to ask Sadie her thoughts about what Chapawee had shared and how they as younger women could embrace this wisdom in their lives.

The attention of the women turned to Vivi. She should go next since the talking stick was beside her, but was intimidated by the powerful words from Cora and Chapawee. What did she have to share? She remembered Chapawee's instructions and reached for the stick, trusting that what she needed to share would bubble up.

Vivi held the talking stick firmly in her lap with both hands. A tingle of energy circled her scalp, traveled down her neck and spread across her chest. She looked over at Chapawee. "You spoke of connection and that is something I've experienced more of since our last circle. It started with my new friend Adelaide. I've never had a friendship that's been so," Vivi paused, "intimate." She blushed at all she was leaving out, took a deep breath and continued. "Adelaide has educated me about women's suffrage, which inspired me to take up this cause. My work with suffrage connects me to suffragettes across the country, and it's also reconnected me to my writing." Her mother smiled at her across the fire. "But now the government, I guess you can call the school board part of the government, has stepped in and threatened my job because of my involvement with women's suffrage." She looked at Chapawee. "Government interference seems to be happening a lot, doesn't it?"

Chapawee dipped her head in acknowledgment.

"I'm grateful to the circle, because naming the disconnection in my life allowed me to make choices to change that." Vivi loosened the scarf around her neck, "I'm not sure what the future holds. The school board hasn't followed through with their threat yet, and I haven't stopped my suffrage work, or my writing. Although not knowing how things will work out is stressful, I have a greater sense of purpose in my life than I've had in a long time, and that feels good." But what didn't feel good was how her love for Adelaide required her to deceive Bubba. Although Vivi wasn't ready to share this truth with the circle, it was becoming harder for her to avoid.

Vivi dropped the stick between her and Sadie, and the support from the other women radiated towards her. The morning sun had climbed above the trees and now warmed Vivi's back. She unbuttoned her coat and took a breath. She hadn't known what to say, or exactly how she felt until she held the talking stick. Chapawee was right. Whatever came to mind in the silence was what needed to be spoken, or at least acknowledged, even if she didn't speak about everything. The words she'd just shared clarified her experience over the past few months. Her comfortable routine had become a rut that separated her from a fulfilling life, and stepping out of her comfort zone had been the antidote. Geese honked overhead and Vivi looked up to watch a pair flying over the creek. *But a side effect of the antidote was deception in her marriage.*

The sun illuminated the left side of Etta's face and she now held the talking stick gently in her lap. Vivi tried to think of her mother as a unique woman, with goals and dreams separate from her roles of wife and mother. This filter made Vivi consider what her mother had sacrificed for her. She was enthusiastic in her support of Vivi's writing and suffrage work, but maybe that was because she'd never had the opportunity to follow through with her dreams. Vivi was ashamed to admit she'd never thought of her mother this way, or bothered to ask about her aspirations.

"When I accepted Chapawee's invitation to the equinox circle, I wasn't sure if I'd return for a second meeting."

Vivi's took a breath to quiet her thoughts.

Her mother continued. "The concept of sitting with women I didn't know, outside, in a circle by an oak tree, was strange and uncomfortable. But, I'm here today, grateful to Chapawee for sharing this ritual, and amazed at the power it's already had in my life."

Etta smiled and tapped the talking stick gently on the ground. "After speaking out loud about my loneliness, I examined it more closely. I realized I was lonely primarily because I didn't allow people to get close to me, maybe out of fear of being hurt, and or maybe out of habit, but either way, I have the power to change this. It will take time to nurture new relationships, but I've made progress." Etta paused, and her blush told Vivi what she was going to share next.

"I've begun spending time with Ben, a man in my Sunday School class." A huge smile spread over her mother's face and the last reservations Vivi had about Ben slipped away. "He makes me laugh, and is interested in my thoughts and ideas. We enjoy our church activities, going for walks, and listening to music. I've been doing these things for years, but enjoy them more when I share them with Ben."

The fire shifted when a log burned through, and Chapawee placed another on top. Etta was quiet and watched the fire. She continued to hold the talking stick. The others remained silent and attentive. "After my husband died I thought I'd never love another man. And I won't love anyone the way I loved James, but as my feelings deepen with Ben, I realize I can love again. Love comes from an infinite source, and loving Ben takes nothing away from what I shared with James." Etta exhaled deeply and placed the talking stick in the center of the circle.

Her mother's wisdom resonated and Vivi's heart pounded against her ribs. That was exactly her experience too, that her love for Adelaide didn't diminish her love for Bubba, but of course her situation was different. The person she'd made vows to was still alive.

Sadie picked up the talking stick. The fire popped, and a spark landed in the dirt. Sadie quickly extinguished it with one end of the talking stick and then held it vertically in her left hand and gently tapped it on the ground.

Sadie began, "After our last circle, I was sad that 'frustrated' was the first word that came to mind to describe myself. I can't erase this feeling for it's justified, but like Cora who's finding balance between vigilance and contentment, I need to create balance between frustration and action. I'm trying to narrow my focus to where I have control, and take pressure off myself to solve all the inequalities in our community." Sadie paused and stared into the fire. "I've reminded myself of the power of education." She looked at Vivi. "And that not only do I wield that power as a teacher, but I transfer it to my students who take it into the world, and hopefully impact others in a positive way. Thinking of the long-term ramifications of teaching balances the minutiae I deal with like punctuation, fractions and writing a narrative essay."

A good reminder, Vivi thought to herself. Like Sadie, she often forgot the impact she was making and how it spread into the world.

Sadie took a deep breath. "Chapawee and Vivi, you both mentioned the government's negative impact in your life and I have the same experience. Many of the obstacles I encounter are placed there by the government. Before things improve for the black folk," she paused and looked at Etta and Vivi, "and even white women, things need to change in our government."

And that's exactly why women need the right to vote, Vivi thought.

Sadie redirected her attention to only Vivi. "I'd like to think this will happen if women get the right to vote, but even in the suffrage movement there are obstacles, since I can't join your Equal Suffrage Association."

This was said without malice, but shame crept up from Vivi's heart and blushed her neck and cheeks. She looked over at Sadie who held her gaze firmly. Vivi resisted the urge to look away, silently acknowledging what Sadie had just said.

"But as I mentioned earlier, I'm going to focus where I have control, and have convinced our Colored Women's Club to take up the suffrage issue, with me leading this initiative. My frustration can serve as fuel for action."

***

Sadie handed the talking stick to Vivi who passed it back to Chapawee. The spirit had led the circle this morning, Chapawee thought with gratitude. It'd been almost three weeks since her release from jail and she hadn't had the motivation to plan anything particular for the circle today. It probably turned out better that way. Each woman picked up on a theme from what others had shared, linking their stories and emphasizing commonalities, in the midst of their differences.

Chapawee crossed both hands over her heart and breathed deeply. The other women followed her lead. The pressure of her own hands across her heart was comforting, and she hoped the others felt it. After a few deep breaths, she reached her hands out to Cora and Vivi and the women all clasped hands to close the circle, physically intensifying the energy between them.

"Thank you for your honest contribution to our circle today. Powerful truths were shared emphasizing the importance of acknowledging the darkness in the world and in our lives, while using our light to overcome that, whether it's through connection," she paused and looked at Vivi, "love," which made Etta blush, "action," Chapawee nodded at Sadie, "gratitude," she said squeezing Cora's hand, "or hope."

The sun warmed Chapawee's back and illuminated the lower portion of the Mother Tree. She marveled at the trunk. It was the width of her seven-year-old wrist when she first saw it and now the circumference was as wide as two barrels side by side. Chapawee smiled at the paradox of nature. Her strength and stature was diminishing with age, while the Mother Tree's grew.

Chapawee squeezed Vivi's and Cora's hands and then released them. "Please hold the sacred silence until you reach my cabin. I'll take care of the fire and be there shortly."

The other women unfolded themselves to standing and quietly moved away from the circle. Chapawee sat still, and listened to the crunch of leaves as the women walked the path towards her cabin. She wished that sound was bringing her mother and sister to her. How she missed them. She was happy for her new circle, but sitting here, where she'd been many times with her mother and sister, intensified their absence in her life.

Chapawee picked up a stick, separated the larger branches in the fire, and then pushed some of the ashes over the lingering flames. The morning sun beckoned, and she scooted around to face Hungry Mother Creek. How many times had she watched the sun dance on this water? Thousands? Millions? The beauty was always noticed and appreciated by her. Chapawee rested her chin on top of the stick and closed her eyes. This was home, and even if she were blind, she'd hear, smell and feel the comfort of it.

Strong hands clasped both her shoulders from behind, startling her. She must have dozed off.

"Chapawee?" Cora asked with concern. "Are you OK? I was worried when you didn't come back."

Chapawee reached up to her shoulder and covered Cora's hand with her own. "I'm fine. Just enjoying the sun on my face."

"And looking at the backs of your eyelids?" Cora laughed and sat beside her.

"Well, maybe so, but I'm in no rush."

"Me either," Cora said, sitting beside her.

CHAPTER 17

The rustle of newspaper pages, the clink of Adelaide's teacup in her saucer, and the occasional pop from the fireplace had been the only sounds in the past ten minutes. Vivi exhaled and rested her head on the back of the chair, pleasantly fatigued after their passionate start to the morning. This had been the routine since Christmas. Vivi arrived at Adelaide's room after breakfast, they had tea, read and talked for several hours, before walking back to Vivi's for lunch. Goldie had stayed with Bubba's parents after their Christmas celebration last Friday and they'd pick her up tomorrow on New Year's Day. Bubba was repairing nets this week, which left Vivi time for herself.

It was easy being with Adelaide, and Vivi enjoyed their moments of extended silence as much as their conversations. And what of their passion? She knew she was betraying Bubba, and would vow to end that portion of their relationship, but the moment Adelaide touched her, her resolve vanished. And other times she rationalized it wasn't betrayal because Bubba always knew when she was with Adelaide. He'd even joined them for lunch the past few days and most importantly her marriage had improved since meeting Adelaide. If her relationship with her was wrong, why would that have happened?

Vivi looked over at Adelaide propped up in bed reading, wearing only her chemise. The love between them amazed her because it was so different. Her relationship with Bubba was like wearing her comfortable bath robe, the one she couldn't wait to put on after Goldie went to bed and they sat by the fire alone, but her relationship with Adelaide was like wearing a party dress, not comfortable, but it made her feel pretty, special and the center of attention.

Vivi chuckled, imagining herself wearing a dress with embroidered tulle draped over silk to the general store. That would never fit in around here, even at the fanciest party.

"What's so funny?" Adelaide asked.

"I was just imagining myself in that dress," Vivi said, pointing to an advertisement on the back page of *The Boston Globe* Adelaide was reading. "I'd cause quite a stir at the general store." Vivi didn't share what she'd really been thinking to avoid a conversation about their relationship. She wanted to enjoy their last morning together, as Goldie returned tomorrow.

"If you came to Boston with me, there'd be plenty of places to wear it."

Vivi met Adelaide's gaze for a moment and then looked at the fire. After a beat of silence, Adelaide turned back the pages of her newspaper and slid it towards Vivi. "Here's an editorial written by the president of the Boston Equal Suffrage Association for Good Government. Maybe it will give you some ideas for your articles for the ESA."

Vivi leaned forward in her chair and retrieved the paper from the end of the bed. Just Monday, she'd received a letter from the North Carolina ESA. They'd seen her editorial in the *News and Observer* and wanted her to be their eastern North Carolina reporter, submitting editorials to local newspapers and reporting on suffrage events in this part of the state. She hadn't accepted the offer yet, but Adelaide certainly thought she should.

Vivi read the first few paragraphs and then looked at Adelaide. "Do you think I'll have enough to say if I write for the ESA, and how will I have the time to attend local suffrage events to report on them?"

Adelaide slid to the end of the bed, across from Vivi's chair. "You don't have to reinvent the wheel. Submit your *News and Observer* piece first and then when new events happen, you'll have new thoughts to share. And you don't have to go to every event. You could contact a local suffrage leader and they could report back to you, or I bet Lucy or Stella could even go, gather the information and then you write it up."

"Oh, I hadn't thought of that," Vivi said.

"I know. You keep thinking of why it won't work, instead of why it will. And count me in to help. The winter here is beginning to bore me, and soon the regular hotel manager will be back and I'll have nothing to do. I'd love to hop on the train and go somewhere new."

"Isn't that cheating if others help?" Vivi asked, thinking of the ethical standards she expected of her students.

"Of course not," Adelaide said and stood to pour herself another cup of tea. "We'll be the sources, bring you the information and then you'll weave it into an article that will captivate and persuade readers."

Vivi had to smile at Adelaide's enthusiasm. "Thanks for believing in me."

"Well, I'm right, aren't I? You didn't want to send your editorial to the *News and Observer* but I knew they'd love it and they did. Now take my word. You should accept this offer."

Vivi held her cup out to Adelaide. "Well, the ESA did offer a small payment for each piece I submit which would help if the school board ends my contract."

"And if that happens, you'll have more time to write and travel."

Vivi leaned forward and kissed Adelaide gently, to avoid spilling her tea. "Thank you for focusing on how it can work. I'll need these insights to help persuade Bubba to let me take this position."

Adelaide stood, walked to the fireplace and put another log on. "May I give you one more piece of advice?"

Vivi nodded.

"Don't ask for his permission. Share your decision to take this offer and then ask for his support."

Vivi didn't say anything and let this sink in. This would be a new way of handling things. Their entire marriage she'd told Bubba what she'd like to do, but there was always a question mark at the end until he gave his approval or dissent.

Adelaide continued. "He doesn't ask you for permission about where he goes fishing or who he hires to work on his boat, does he?"

"Well, no, but I don't know anything about his job."

"Exactly," Adelaide said. She pumped the bellows to stoke the fire. "And he doesn't know anything about being a writer. As long as you're still contributing financially, I don't see what the problem could be."

Vivi hadn't thought of it like that. The flames leapt with Adelaide's efforts and she retook her position on the bed with another edition of *The Boston Globe*. Vivi returned to the editorial Adelaide had given her but the words were only black marks on the page, and what she saw instead was herself, hopping on a train, or perhaps a steamer, heading to Goldsboro, Wilmington or maybe north to Elizabeth City, to attend a suffrage event.

She loved teaching, but was confined by the four walls and schedule. Her stomach filled with butterflies at the freedom, adventure, and novelty that working for the ESA would provide. Could she make a difference in the world as a writer and not a teacher? She'd still be educating and expanding minds, just in a different way.

What about Goldie? She'd ask her mother to help with Goldie if she was gone overnight when Bubba was out fishing. It may be a while before she'd need that help though. She wouldn't leave her teaching position until they found her replacement. Her student's education shouldn't suffer because of her choice.

Her choice! Her thoughts and visions clarified her position. She would accept the ESA's offer.

"Adelaide!" Vivi said and dropped her paper on the floor. "I'm going to do it. I'm going to write the ESA today and accept their offer."

Adelaide's eyes lit up. Simultaneously they stood and embraced.

Adelaide rubbed her back and said, "Look who's the instigator now."

They separated and Vivi laughed. "I don't know about that. I'm just following my heart and the path that energizes me." Vivi paused and took a breath. "Well, if I'm honest, not all that energy is fueled by excitement – some of it comes from fear, too."

"Perfect! That's what happens when you're pushing against your edges and creating room to grow."

Vivi thought about times she'd experienced this before, leaving for the teacher's training school, marrying Bubba, finding out she was pregnant, and even her first time at the women's circle. Adelaide was right. All these experiences made her stronger, wiser, more loving. Prior to the women's circle she hadn't felt this way in a long time. She'd become complacent in her routine. Staying busy in her roles of wife, mother and teacher, had crowded out opportunities for her personal growth.

Adelaide put on her bathrobe and stepped into the hall.

"Where are you going?" Vivi asked.

"To search the kitchen for something to toast your decision with. I know the hidden cabinet where Ben keeps the brandy."

Vivi laughed and picked up the paper she'd dropped on the floor. "It's probably moonshine, not brandy, and let's hold off on that toast until I ask Bubba," Vivi hesitated, "for his support."

"OK," Adelaide said. "Let's go talk to him now. It's almost lunchtime anyway." She removed the bathrobe and reached for her blouse.

Vivi remembered how much she'd enjoyed removing Adelaide's blouse earlier, and a wave of desire washed over her. She'd never talk with Bubba if she kept thinking about that. Gently, she said, "I know you want to support me, and I appreciate that, but taking this job will be a big change for our family. It's best if I have this conversation with Bubba alone."

The spell of the morning was broken. The laughter, embraces, and connection they'd had were erased with the two words, our family. Adelaide's smile evaporated and she turned away.

Vivi regretted her choice of words. She could have made her point without excluding Adelaide. This was a pattern. They'd savor their moments together, until the reality of Vivi's life interrupted.

Adelaide handed Vivi her coat. "Let me know how it goes," she said. Her voice matched the cool air seeping into the room from the hallway.

Vivi walked home slowly and tried to stop worrying about Adelaide. She needed to focus on Bubba, and how she'd talk with him about her decision to write for the ESA. But she couldn't forget the look in Adelaide's eyes when she left. Beneath the carefree and adventurous persona, was a lonely woman who could never have a family that would be accepted by others. Many times, she'd suggested that Vivi should come to Boston, and Vivi knew if she ever agreed, Adelaide would have them packed and on a north-bound train within a week's time. If she kept refusing, would Adelaide give up on her and leave? Would she even stay through the winter? Vivi both hoped and feared that Adelaide would leave without saying goodbye, thus ending the strain, but also the exultation of living in two worlds simultaneously.

The physical exertion and sun directly overhead created enough warmth that Vivi took her coat off. She turned right on Midyette Street, and as she neared home, it became easier to focus on the conversation she wanted to have with Bubba. She mentally rehearsed the arguments in support of her choice.

Vivi walked to the back of the house to look for Bubba but he wasn't there or on his boat. She found him in the kitchen, seated at the table, cleaning his rifle. He looked up when she entered and then cocked his head to one side when she closed the door behind her. "Adelaide isn't with you?" he asked.

"No," Vivi said and hung her coat up. "I thought it'd be nice for us to have some time alone before we pick up Goldie at your parents' tomorrow."

Bubba nodded and bent back over his rifle. Vivi stepped closer to the table and discerned the smell of alcohol. Her heart tightened into a fist. She hadn't noticed Bubba drinking since she'd been on Christmas break and had hoped he was done. No glass or bottle was on the table, but the outline of a flask in Bubba's pants pocket revealed the source. What made him drink today? And while handling a gun. That wasn't safe. Thank God Goldie wasn't home. She opened her mouth to chastise him and then stopped. Her judgment wouldn't help him heal. This was the pattern they'd had since his brother died and it wasn't working.

Vivi sat, but Bubba kept his head down, intent on oiling the rifle barrel.

"Bubba," she said, trying not to sound harsh.

He looked up and his eyes glistened. "Don't start in on me, Vivi. It's the holiday and I've hardly had a drink the last few weeks." He dragged his arm across his eyes and his wool sweater absorbed the wetness.

Vivi swallowed her well-practiced reprimand and tried the approach of curiosity instead of criticism. "What made you want to drink today?" she asked.

Bubba was silent a moment and seemed unprepared for her question. "I don't know. Just wanted to relax a little."

Vivi even surprised herself when she said, "That sounds like a good idea." She took a glass from the cabinet and placed it purposely in front of Bubba. "May I have a little?"

Bubba's shoulders relaxed. He smiled and put a hand on Vivi's forehead. "Are you OK? You're not acting like yourself."

Vivi swatted his hand away. "Sometimes it's good to change things up," she said and then took a sip of the moonshine he'd poured for her. It burned her lips, throat and belly, but that quickly deescalated into warmth. "Are you going bear hunting at your parents' tomorrow?" she asked, since he was cleaning the rifle he used for that.

Shortly after they were married, Bubba's parents left Oriental and built a home on the Bay River. His father said Oriental was getting too crowded, with too many laws. Now his parents' home was surrounded by hundreds of acres of forest. Before his brother died, they would hunt there. Suddenly Vivi knew the reason Bubba was drinking.

She took a small sip, and when the burn subsided she asked, "Are you sad because you can't hunt with your brother anymore?"

Adelaide had taught Vivi to speak more directly, but as the silence lengthened, she wondered if she'd made a mistake. Would Bubba slam his rifle on the table and walk out, or would he answer her?

Bubba's shoulders shook and fat tears splashed on the barrel of his rifle. Vivi froze. She'd never seen Bubba cry like this, and it frightened her. Yet she'd shed many tears for her father and Bubba had the right to grieve too.

Vivi walked behind Bubba's chair and draped herself over his back, nestling her head into the crook of his neck. He put the rifle on the table and took her hands in his. A small sob escaped his mouth and Vivi kissed his neck.

"I should have gone out looking for my brother that day," Bubba said. "The way the water was pushing in from the northeast, and the clouds were rolling, I knew the storm would be bad."

"But you didn't even know he was still on the water." Vivi sat down next to Bubba.

She remembered that September day clearly. She and Goldie were aware of the unusual weather and stood on the dock for several hours, screaming with relief and waving their arms when the bow of Bubba's fishing boat came into view. The wind was gaining strength and as soon as his boat was secure, the crew raced home to help their families prepare for the hurricane. Goldie was sent inside, and then she and Bubba tied down anything that could become a life- threatening projectile.

Bubba didn't respond and Vivi continued. "You were taking care of our home, me and Goldie. There was no time to see if your brother was safely home."

"But Ray was my brother. I should have known that he needed me."

Vivi understood. How many times had she thought about what she could have done to save her father. Even now, when she logically knew nothing would have saved him, she occasionally reimagined the last minutes of his life, where she was the hero and somehow breathed life back into him. Vivi's throat tightened.

"It would be nice to think we have the power to save our loved ones from death, but we don't." Vivi realized she was talking to herself as much as Bubba. "That storm ended up being a hurricane and you got your crew home safely. If you'd gone out looking for your brother you would have risked their lives. Your mother would have lost both sons, and Goldie would have grown up without a father, like me."

Bubba wiped his eyes and took a drink from Vivi's glass. "Ray taught me everything I know about fishing and being on the water. I don't understand why he didn't get home sooner that day."

Vivi sat back in her chair. "Bubba, you can rewrite the events of that day a thousand more times but it won't bring your brother back. It only keeps you in the past," she paused, "and in the bottle."

He held her gaze but didn't say anything. Vivi continued. "I should know. I've been doing it since I was eleven. I realize now that I used your attention and playfulness as balm for my sadness about my father, and when you descended into your own grief, my support was gone.

Instead of comforting you, I was angry you weren't there for me." Vivi knelt in front of Bubba, wrapped her arms around his waist and lay her head on his chest. "I'm sorry."

Bubba stood and pulled Vivi to her feet. He kissed her on the lips and then held her close. "You're here for me now, and that's all that matters." Bubba caressed her hair and then loosened his hold to look at her. "There's nothing to be gained by criticizing yourself for something in the past. Is there?"

Vivi smiled up at him. "I couldn't have said it better myself."

After lunch, Bubba did some work on the boat and Vivi washed clothes. She wanted to get the clothes on the line for a few hours before the sun went down. She pinned her petticoat, Bubba's shirt and one of Goldie's dresses up. The house was quiet without Goldie, and although she'd enjoyed the free time while Goldie was gone, she'd be happy to see her tomorrow.

Today hadn't gone as planned, but she was happy that she and Bubba had talked about his brother and she had apologized for being self-centered when he'd needed her most. The gulf between them since his brother's death had narrowed with a single conversation. God, why hadn't I helped Bubba talk about his feelings before this? Vivi thought to herself. We could have saved a year of heartache. *Stop.* The only place she had power was in this moment and she was using it to be the supportive wife Bubba needed. The wind picked up intensity and Vivi walked to the other side of the line, with her back to the water, so the clothes wouldn't flap in her face.

Bubba's boots clomped down the pier and she smiled when his hands encircled her waist. She pinned the last piece on the line and then leaned back into his broad chest. Where Adelaide was soft with curves, Bubba was firm, with angles. The thought of Adelaide distracted her. Was she OK? It was New Year's Eve. Should she go back to the hotel and invite her for supper?

Bubba released her and said, "How about I build us a fire? You make some tea and we can play a game of rummy."

"Rummy," Vivi said, picking up the bag of clothes pins. "We haven't played that in ages." When they were courting and first married they frequently played rummy, but life had gotten too busy, and they hadn't brought out the cards in several years.

"I know," Bubba said and pushed her playfully on the shoulder. "Are you scared you're out of practice and may lose?"

Vivi laughed. "Oh, no. I'm ready to beat you anytime."

They walked back to the house and Vivi pushed away thoughts of Adelaide. She'd stop by the hotel on Sunday when they returned from Bubba's parents.

Vivi lost two out of three of their games because her mind wasn't focused. Instead, it was deciding whether to have the conversation about her ESA job. All afternoon things with Bubba had felt like they used to, and she hated to ruin their connection, but preferred to have this discussion before Goldie got home.

"That was fun," Bubba said. He neatened the cards and then put his arm around Vivi's shoulder. In a quiet voice he said, "It's been a while since I've had fun."

"I know." Vivi leaned into him.

"But you've been having more fun since you met Adelaide."

He said this casually, with no accusation, but Vivi supplied that herself. Her relationship with Adelaide was a betrayal. If it wasn't, she'd feel comfortable sharing everything about it with Bubba.

"Yes. We get along well," Vivi said, realizing she had to say something. "Which is surprising given how different we are."

"Yeah," Bubba said. "She's not married, has no children and is a Yankee. And she's a suffragette. I bet you wouldn't have become involved with that movement if you hadn't met her."

"You're right." Here was an opening, Vivi thought. "Do you mind that I'm doing that?"

Bubba was silent and from the corner of her eyes she saw him staring into the fire. "It seems you've been happier since you started working on suffrage, and for that reason I support it, but . . ." He paused and took a breath. "I think it's a waste of your time. The vast majority of people don't see the need for women to vote."

Vivi slid to the edge of the couch and turned to Bubba. "And that's exactly why I need to educate people about women's right to vote, because most have never considered this as an option."

Bubba took her right hand. "I haven't seen you this passionate in a while, which is a benefit of you doing this work." He released her hand and rubbed her thigh gently. "And it's made you more passionate in other ways too."

Vivi ignored this comment and tried to contain her frustration at Bubba's trivialization of something important to her. "Bubba, this cause means a lot to me. It's not a fleeting interest. I want the world to be different for me, Goldie and our granddaughters one day."

"Yes, but that's what scares folks, that the world would be different."

Bubba stood and put another log on the fire. When he sat down Vivi slid next to him. "But change doesn't automatically mean things would be worse. Maybe they'd get better."

Bubba put his arm around her. "You have a point."

"And Bubba?" Vivi's heart was pounding. "I have a new way to promote suffrage." She carefully chose her words. "I'm going to write for the Equal Suffrage Association and cover eastern North Carolina. I'll write editorials, report on local suffrage events and get paid for each piece I submit."

Vivi felt the muscles in Bubba's arms and shoulders tighten. He didn't say anything immediately, and Vivi continued, not wanting to give him time to think of arguments against this.

"It'll mean extra money for us, and I'll earn it doing something I love."

Bubba removed his arm to look at her. "I hope you'll make enough money to cover the teaching salary you'll lose once the school board sees your articles."

Vivi swallowed the lump in her throat. "I hope it doesn't come to that, but I'm not going to let the school board bully me into giving up something I value."

Bubba stood. "It seems you've made this decision without bothering to ask me."

Adelaide's voice played in her mind. "I'm sharing my decision now."

"Well, I don't think it's the right one. You'll jeopardize our income." Bubba paced in front of the fireplace. "And I'll be the butt of jokes among the men. They'll think I'm home taking care of the house while you're out getting the vote for women."

Vivi stood, propelled by anger at Bubba's narrow-mindedness. "Bubba, that's ridiculous, and this isn't about you. Don't you want me to be happy and fulfilled?"

Bubba looked over her head out their front window. Vivi continued. "I was getting your input, not your permission. I plan to accept this job and deal with the consequences."

"Fine," Bubba said, walking into the kitchen. "Do what makes you happy." He slammed the back door.

Vivi paced the kitchen, several times pausing at the back door. Part of her wanted to run after Bubba and say she'd give up her suffrage work, just to keep the peace. That would mean giving up a part of herself, a part she was proud of, and what type of role model would that be for Goldie?

It was dark now and close to dinner, but she had no desire to cook for Bubba. There was only one place she wanted to be right now, and that was with Adelaide. Unlike Bubba, Adelaide wanted her to grow and be fulfilled. Vivi dashed off a quick note and left it on the kitchen table. *Going to see Adelaide. Back in a few hours.*

The walls of her house were closing in, and stepping outside into the cold air was a relief. Vivi ran most of the way to the hotel, fueled by emotions and adrenaline. Adelaide was reading in the parlor. She looked up. "Vivi, I thought you were home, having family time with Bubba."

Vivi stepped into the room and when Adelaide saw her face, she stood and opened her arms. Vivi fell into them. The tick of the grandmother clock and the pressure of Adelaide's hands slowed Vivi's breath.

They separated and Adelaide said, "I take it that Bubba didn't respond well when you shared your decision?"

"No."

"Would you be available then to join me for New Year's Eve dinner here at the hotel?"

Vivi knew she'd hurt Adelaide this afternoon by not including her in the conversation with Bubba, but here she was, accepting her back with no hesitation. "I'd love that." Despite her intention to be home earlier, Vivi brought in 1915 with Adelaide. She peeled herself away from Adelaide just after midnight only to sleep alone, while Bubba slept on his boat.

CHAPTER 18

Everything took longer than it used to. Just a couple years ago she'd have grabbed her fishing gear and made it to the pier in one trip. Chapawee didn't trust her balance and now it took three trips, one to carry the wooden bucket she'd use for a seat, one for the fishing pole and bait, and one to get the hat she had forgotten, but finally she was settled.

After four days of cold rain, the sun and lack of wind enticed her into the chilly air to try and lure some fish from their winter lethargy. She reached into the bowl beside her and pinched off a piece of the cornmeal bait her father had taught her to make. She formed a ball around her hook and dropped it near one of her dock pilings. Hopefully the warmth of the sun would energize the fish and they'd be ready to eat. Other times of the year they wouldn't give a ball of cornmeal a second look, but in winter, with dwindling bait fish, Chapawee hoped they'd be enticed.

It was almost noon and she positioned herself to face south and take advantage of the sun. If she didn't catch anything, at least she'd be revitalized by the time outside. She remembered sitting here with Father, the winter before he died, waiting patiently for the fish to bite. By then her husband had passed away and she was spending most of her time helping her parents as they aged. And now, here she was, close to the same age her father had been, but without a daughter to help. She'd have support if she went to live with Tayen, but navigating Tayen's moods, the family dynamics, and the politics of a tribal council, didn't feel worth the price of relinquishing her home on Hungry Mother Creek.

Chapawee closed her eyes to fully appreciate the warmth of the sun and the winter quiet. The gentle lap of water against the shore and the intermittent call of a kingfisher farther down the creek was all she heard. Compared to the cacophony of birds, bugs, squirrels and jumping fish in the other seasons, winter was serene, at least today with the calm winds.

The minutes passed in quiet meditation. I'll catch some peace, even if I don't catch dinner, she thought to herself. She took a grateful breath of the fresh air, the damp and stagnant jail cell still fresh in her memory. The pounding of horse hooves interrupted her serenity, and she turned towards land. Who was coming out here in the middle of a Tuesday? Could it be Mrs. Livingston intent on making her point?

Pete emerged from the woods and answered her question. He lifted his hand in greeting when he saw her, and then tied up his horse. Chapawee smiled and waved, immediately pleased to see him, but then recognized he most likely wasn't making a social call, and his visit could mean trouble. She brought in her line and threw the remainder of the cornmeal ball into the water. She stood and walked to meet Pete.

"Afternoon, Miss Chapawee," Pete said, doffing his cap when she reached him. "Are you able to catch anything in that cold water?" he asked, pointing out to Hungry Mother Creek.

"Not yet," Chapawee said, brushing cornmeal off her hands. "But I still have a few more hours to try. Now what brings you here? I'd like to think it's a social visit, but I'm worried there's trouble."

Pete looked out at the water and then back at Chapawee. "Let's call this a social visit because I'm not here officially. Please don't say anything about me being here today."

Chapawee took a breath. This didn't sound good. "Sure, you have my word."

Pete continued, "I'll be coming back this week or next with the magistrate and Joseph Allegany."

"The man who owns Magnolia Bend?"

"Yes," Pete said and looked over his shoulder towards his horse. "I wanted to warn you so you'd be prepared."

A chill swept down Chapawee's spine and out to her arms. When Chapawee was a child, her father and the owner of Magnolia Bend Plantation had made a verbal agreement, allowing them to live on this land. Mr. Allegany was the new owner and not part of the family her father had dealt with. She shivered and drew her shawl around her. This could only mean one thing and Pete confirmed this with his next sentence.

"Mr. Allegany plans to charge you with trespassing on his land if you don't leave."

Chapawee caught her breath. No doubt Mrs. Livingston was behind Mr. Allegany's sudden interest in her.

"I'm sorry. I wish there was something I could do." Pete removed his hat and ran his fingers through his thick hair.

"No need to be sorry, Pete. I appreciate you coming out here. Just doing that was a risk."

"But what will you do?" Pete asked, putting his hat back on.

"Don't worry about me. I'll figure things out. The good thing about being my age is I've had plenty of experiences coping with unexpected challenges." Chapawee hoped her words comforted Pete, but they did little to assuage her fear.

"OK," Pete said. "I better get back to town."

"Thank you for coming."

Pete walked to his horse and then Chapawee called to him, "Wait! I have something I want to give you."

Scurrying into her cabin, she wasn't sure what to give him, but wanted there to be an exchange for his kindness and his mother's biscuits. Ah, this will work. She picked up a tiny basket she'd woven from the river grass and dumped the dried parsley it held onto her table. She'd easily make another for herself.

Pete was standing right outside her back door and she almost collided with him. "Here," she said, handing him the basket. "It's a small token of my appreciation for you and your mother. Please give this to her and let her know it's perfect for storing dried herbs."

Pete smiled. "Thank you. I'm sure Momma will love this."

The energy between them strengthened and Chapawee knew if circumstances were different, she would have hugged him. Instead, she took a moment to appreciate their connection. Pete stood quietly with her and then walked to his horse.

The patience to fish was gone. Chapawee walked the trail into the woods to keep pace with her racing thoughts. It was mid-afternoon and the sun, still well above the western tree-line, was warm. Chapawee walked directly to the Mother Tree and stood with her back against the trunk. The palms of both her hands rested on the undulating bark of the live oak and she took deep breaths to slow her thoughts and ground herself. There was no way to devise a plan when thoughts of the past, present and future were tumbling over one another.

Chapawee looked out at Hungry Mother Creek and could see her and Kanti swimming unclothed in the water on a sultry summer day, her father cleaning fish on the dock and her mother in the garden. She saw a similar scene, years later, except this time Tayen and her cousin were swimming, she and her sister were helping her mother in the garden and all the men were out on the boat. Often, when her father returned and the fish were plentiful, Cora and Jeremiah would join them for a fish fry and their boys played with Tayen and her niece. And then there were the quiet times, just the four of them again, she, her parents, and Kanti, after her daughter and niece married and moved to the Coharie River.

The creek, cabin, garden, the woods bordering it all, and everything in her sight was home, where her memories lived, where she'd cried in joy and sorrow, bled in childbirth and sweated in toil. Who would she be if this land was taken from her? Where would she go?

The intensity of this pressed into Chapawee and she sank to the ground, still leaning into the Mother Tree for support. The tears flowed freely and she didn't try to stop them. A sob escaped and she wrapped her arms tightly around herself.

Chapawee didn't know how long she cried or when she stopped. A small lizard sunned itself on top of a rock that edged the circle. A pelican crashed into the creek searching for fish and the empty branches of the black gum and oak clicked against one another in the breeze. Soon Chapawee's emotions and thoughts synchronized with her surroundings. Her breath was even, eyes dry and her thoughts were coming one at a time. A solution would only come to her if she were quiet and still, so she leaned her head against the Mother Tree. A hawk called out his support from deep in the woods.

***

Small, wet snowflakes fell without a sound and melted as soon as they touched the ground. There probably wouldn't be any accumulation, but it was enough snow to drive Vivi's students to distraction and she released them a few minutes early. From the porch of the general store, she watched the children scatter. Goldie and her best friend, Nan, ran full speed down Hodges St. to Nan's house, with plans to build a snowman. The flakes melted instantly on her mitten, and Vivi smiled at the girls' optimism. It was more likely Goldie would come home covered in mud and not snow, but they'd have fun no matter.

With the children safely on their way home, Vivi picked up her satchel and walked towards her mother's. She should stay and grade a few papers, but wanted to finish an article about an ESA meeting in Kinston last week. It would have been just as easy to go home to write, but Vivi concentrated better sitting at her father's desk. At least that's what she told herself. If she were honest, part of the lure of this arrangement was to be away from Bubba. On a day like this, he'd probably be at home making it difficult to focus.

Things had been tense between them since she'd told him about her job with the ESA. He never forbade her to do it, but he acted as if it wasn't happening. His angst had escalated when her *News and Observer* editorial was also published in the *Pamlico Enterprise*. The ESA paid her for that article and distributed it as they saw fit. She didn't know it was in the local paper until last Wednesday when she came home and found the paper folded back to her editorial and left in the middle of the kitchen table. Vivi had picked it up and was immediately filled with pride and disbelief at seeing her name in print again. Vivian P. Gibbs. Her celebration ended with the thought of how to face Bubba. He came in while she was cooking dinner, and once she explained that it was a surprise to her too, and she wasn't hiding it from him, he'd let it drop. She was relieved to avoid an argument, but hurt he never voiced any congratulations.

A gust of wind from the northeast funneled down Broad Street breaking the hold of a few determined, brown, oak leaves. Vivi pulled her scarf tighter around her neck and turned towards her mother's. The grass now wore a sheen of white. Maybe Goldie and Nan had willed the snow to stick with their desire for a snowman.

"Vivi! Vivi!"

Vivi stopped on the corner when she heard Adelaide's voice. Adelaide was doing her best to run in her stylish, heeled boots and hold the hood of her coat down on her head. Vivi changed direction and walked quickly towards her. "Is everything OK?"

Adelaide stopped with her hands on her hips and didn't answer while she caught her breath. "Everything's fine," Adelaide said. She held out her hand to catch a few snowflakes. "What is this? White rain? I've never seen snow like this before."

Vivi laughed. "I guess you can call this snow. It's not cold enough for the full-fledged version, but once the sun goes down and the temperatures drop, it may transform into the snow you're used to up north." Vivi linked her arm in Adelaide's, and turned them so their backs were against the wind. "Why are you out in this weather anyway?"

"I was looking for you, and went to the school room but Mr. Woodard said you'd let the kids out early. I figured you'd be going to your mother's."

Vivi nodded. "What's going on?"

"Can we walk back to the hotel to talk? I'm getting a chill out here."

"Sure. But only for a minute. I want time to work on my next article before Goldie gets back."

"I promise. I won't keep you long."

Vivi knew that wouldn't be the case. When she was with Adelaide, time melted away as quickly as these snowflakes.

Once they were warmly ensconced in the hotel's parlor with a cup of hot chocolate, Vivi asked, "OK. What's so important?"

Adelaide set her cup down and clasped her hands in front of her. "We're going to Raleigh next week!"

Vivi choked on her drink. "What? Why? I can't go to Raleigh. I have to teach."

"You have to. It's already decided and I've gotten us reservations at the Yarborough hotel."

"Adelaide," Vivi began but Adelaide held her hand up.

"Hear me out. There's a good reason to be there. On Saturday a suffrage amendment was introduced in both the house and the senate."

"How do you know this?" Vivi asked. She'd been scouring the local paper and *News and Observer* on the weekends for suffrage news, but hadn't heard about this.

"Stella told me. Many of the women telegraph operators are staunch suffragettes. One from Raleigh put the word out."

"I'm glad there are men in the legislature supporting us, but why does that mean we need to go to Raleigh?"

Adelaide stood and paced in front of Vivi. "Because next week there will be a public hearing to debate the amendment and you should be there as a reporter for the ESA." Adelaide paused but when Vivi remained silent, she continued. "There needs to be a strong show of support from women of North Carolina, plus, Anna Shaw, the president of the National American Woman Suffrage Association is speaking. I've heard her before and she's brilliant. It's slow here at the hotel, and there's no problem with me being away a couple of days."

Heat flushed Vivi's face and her heart rate picked up. For a moment she embraced the possibility of being in Raleigh to witness the legislative process. With her presence, and then her words, she could show her support for suffrage. But who would teach the children and what about Bubba and Goldie?

Adelaide sat beside her and took Vivi's hand. "Don't think about why it won't work out. Let's focus on how this can happen. It's a once in a lifetime opportunity," Adelaide paused, "and a special memory for us to share."

Vivi slid to the edge of the couch. Thanks to Adelaide's prompt, her mind filled with solutions. "I'm sure Mother would help with Goldie, and I could use money from the trust to pay my expenses."

Adelaide interjected, "I bet Lucy would be a substitute teacher if you left her plans, and you're prepared for your contract not to be renewed anyway, so it won't matter if the school board finds out."

Now Vivi's voice was infused with enthusiasm. "I'll talk with Mother today."

"And I'll find Lucy, talk with her and have her come see you at school tomorrow."

If she were Goldie, Vivi would have jumped up and down, but instead she stood and looked out the window. The snow was sticking to the grass and branches. She turned to Adelaide. "When would we leave?"

"Sunday," Adelaide said, joining her at the window. "I'll take care of all the travel arrangements. All you have to do is meet me at the depot at eleven Sunday morning."

They hugged briefly and then Vivi left for her mother's. Every nerve-ending in her body was activated and she ran to expend this energy. She was a suffragette, a writer, and a reporter for the ESA, and was going to Raleigh. She couldn't wait to tell her mother, who'd be proud of her. A conversation with Bubba would have to happen, but she set that aside for now to enjoy her excitement. When she reached her mother's yard she stooped and gathered some snow into a snowball. She threw it into the street just for the fun of it.

***

Two weeks had passed since Pete had delivered his warning, and Chapawee continued her routine, but without the usual focus and enjoyment. Half her attention was on alert for the sound of horses. She took a bundle of dried goldenrod from the basket beside the stove and dropped it into the boiling pot of water. The water looked insipid, but in an hour when she dipped some out, it would be the color of liquid sunshine, or gold, or butter, depending on the hue of last year's goldenrod crop.

Chapawee stepped out her front door into the cold air. She held her breath and was still, but didn't hear any horses, only the drip of moisture left by the morning fog. Not only was she on the lookout for Pete, but she was also expecting Etta who was bringing her eggs and flour. Since she'd been released from jail, the women in the circle had brought what she needed to keep her from being seen in town.

Her tactic of staying out of sight to let things blow over hadn't worked. She sighed and stirred the boiling goldenrod flowers. Jeremiah was right. Mrs. Livingston was determined to harass her, as if grandchildren would magically be created from Chapawee's suffering.

The hair on the back of Chapawee's neck stood up and she immediately went to the window. She didn't see anything but when she cracked the door the sound of hooves confirmed her instinct. She closed the door and watched from her window as two horses exited the wooded path into her yard. It was the magistrate, and the other man must have been Joseph Allegany because he was broad and thick and definitely not lithe, like Pete. The two men dismounted, but Pete never appeared, which intensified Chapawee's anxiety. Even though he couldn't change what would happen, he was a silent ally and witness.

Chapawee paced the floor. Should she go out and meet them or wait? Let them come to me and stand inside my home, she thought. They'll feel uncomfortable in the home of an Indian woman which could work to her advantage.

The fire in her stove was burning low and she added another piece of wood. The men passed by her window, and immediately after there were three staccato raps on the front door.

Thank goodness Pete had warned her so she'd had time to mentally prepare for this visit. "Good morning, gentleman," Chapawee said, doing her best to keep her voice even.

"Morning, Ma'am," the magistrate said. His hands were thrust deep in his pockets and his arms pressed tightly against his body for warmth. In contrast, Mr. Allegany's body was relaxed under his thick winter coat, and his hands, encased in leather gloves, were clasped loosely on the mound of his stomach. Chapawee had never met him before, but thanks to Pete's warning knew who he was. Where was Pete? she wondered and looked beyond the men to the path but didn't see him.

"Could you step outside and speak with us for a moment?" the magistrate asked.

Chapawee opened the door wider and said, "It's too cold for my old bones out there. Please come in my cabin where it's warmer."

The two men looked at one another. "We'd prefer for you to step outside."

"If you'd like to speak with me, you're welcome to come inside where it's warm." Chapawee stepped back into the cabin and hoped she wasn't pushing her luck.

The magistrate stepped inside and immediately removed his hands from his pockets and rubbed them together. Mr. Allegany took several steps into the cabin, and returned to his former posture, leaving on his gloves. He hadn't said anything yet, but his presence expanded to take up most of the room and Chapawee hoped she hadn't made a mistake by inviting them in. She watched them appraise her small cabin. She didn't know where the magistrate lived, but had been to Magnolia Bend, Mr. Allegany's plantation home, with her father when she was a girl, and knew her cabin was barely the size of his living room. Their eyes took in her pallet of blankets on the floor, the bundles of herbs drying on nails behind the stove, and the small wooden table under the window that looked out onto Hungry Mother Creek.

Mr. Allegany tapped a foot and the magistrate eyed the pot on her stove. Maybe Mrs. Livingston had convinced them she was a witch and they thought she was boiling a potion right now. This made her smile, and she stood silently, waiting for them to speak.

"Miss Chapawee," the magistrate finally said and edged closer to her stove. He eyed the pot and continued. "We've come to discuss your living arrangements here on Hungry Mother Creek."

Mr. Allegany removed his gloves and unbuttoned the top two buttons of his coat. Before the magistrate continued he interjected, "This is my property and you're trespassing."

Even though she was prepared for these words, her whole body tensed and she turned toward the goldenrod dye to regain her composure.

"Here." The magistrate thrust a paper towards her. "You're being charged with trespassing and we're giving you until spring to remove yourself and your possessions from this land."

A wave of relief washed over her. Pete hadn't given her any time frames and her worst fear was she'd have to leave immediately. "Trespassing?" Chapawee asked. "My family has lived here for over sixty years."

"Trespassing for sixty years is the truth of the matter," Mr. Allegany said. "This land has always been part of a fifty-acre tract that's deeded to Magnolia Bend, which I now own."

"Mr. Allegany, my father had an agreement with Mr. Wade that we could live here in exchange for my father's labor during tobacco harvest. When he died his son upheld that agreement, even after my father was too old to work."

The magistrate, who'd been peering into Chapawee's pot of goldenrod dye jerked to attention and said, "That agreement has no legal standing, especially since Magnolia Bend is no longer owned by the Wades."

Mr. Allegany inched backwards to the door, clearly ready to be done with this. Undeterred, Chapawee took several steps towards him. "Mr. Allegany, I'm asking you to extend this agreement. Two years have already passed since you purchased Magnolia Bend and I've been here without issue. I'm old and my time is short. What would a couple more years of me living here hurt? Once I die, you can do whatever you want with this land."

Mr. Allegany probably didn't even know she'd been living here. The plot containing her cabin and garden was the only usable land in the tract. The rest was marshy, prone to flooding and not suitable for farming. Maybe that was the reason it had never sold off with the rest of the plantation land belonging to Magnolia Bend. Chapawee knew Mrs. Livingston, and maybe even her husband, were pressuring Mr. Allegany to do this. But what was he getting out of it? He was probably more wealthy than the Livingstons, so their money wouldn't motivate him like it did the magistrate.

"This is clear cut, Chapa . . ." He struggled with her name as he jammed his gloves back on, clearly irritated now. "You're on land I own, and I'm telling you to leave. There's no room for agreements, discussion or compromise."

He was doing this to exert his own power, Chapawee thought, but took heed of his anger. Cora's friend, who worked as a housekeeper at Magnolia Bend, said that Mr. Allegany's anger quickly escalated into rage that he often took out physically on his wife, Nellie. Chapawee wondered what he and the magistrate would think if they knew Nellie used her remedy. The remedy wasn't always effective, and Nellie had given birth to a son earlier this year. Now Chapawee worried about his fate.

Mr. Allegany opened the door and strode to the horses, his coat tails flapping in the wind he created. The magistrate hustled behind him and then turned back to address Chapawee. "Miss Chapawee, you know what the jail cell is like. I suggest you figure out a plan to be off this land by spring."

What exactly did he mean by spring? When the weather warmed up, the official first day of spring? Chapawee didn't press him and hoped the ambiguity would give her more flexibility. "I understand," she said, knowing that her words wouldn't make a difference.

The magistrate hesitated and looked back to the pot on her stove. "What's that you're boiling in your pot?"

"Nothing but goldenrod dye for my wool, but you can drink it as tea, too. Care for a cup?" Chapawee asked. At least she could enjoy one moment of this encounter.

"No. No," the magistrate said and backed out the door, still open from Mr. Allegany's departure.

Chapawee followed him and before he stepped off her porch asked, "Where's the constable? He's usually with you."

"Not that it's any of your business, but he's home sick with the flu."

In the distance, Chapawee saw Mr. Allegany mount his horse and trot down the path towards Kershaw Road. The magistrate pumped his short legs in his version of a run to get to his horse and catch up.

On the way to her table, Chapawee tossed the trespassing paper into the fire and then sank into her chair. She belonged to this land, just as much as the Mother Tree, but who was she kidding? White men thought land was a commodity, something to be divided up and parceled out, not something to be shared, honored and cared for. Chapawee brushed away a tear. She may have to leave Hungry Mother Creek, but no manmade law would limit the power of nature, and this thought gave her some peace.

The smell of goldenrod brought her back to the moment. The dye was certainly ready by now and she needed a diversion. She took the pot outside and removed the flowers and stems. When it was back on the stove, she dropped her wool into the pot and stirred it into the dye.

A knock at the door startled Chapawee and she dropped her wooden spoon on the floor. She'd forgotten Etta was bringing eggs and flour.

Chapawee opened the door and Etta immediately asked, "Is everything all right? I passed the magistrate and some other man on my way here."

"That was Joseph Allegany," Chapawee said and opened the door wider so Etta could come inside. "He owns this land." The words burned Chapawee's throat and she paused to swallow. "He's charging me with trespassing and I have to be off the property by spring."

"What?" Etta asked, putting the eggs and flour on the floor beside the stove. "But your family has always lived here."

Chapawee and Etta sat at the table as Chapawee shared the details of what had transpired. Speaking the truth of her situation made her predicament real. She would have to leave the only home she'd ever known.

CHAPTER 19

The lobby of the Yarborough Hotel vibrated with the energy of several hundred women, escalating Vivi's excitement, and banishing her fatigue from the long train ride to Raleigh yesterday. She slipped her hand into Adelaide's and they worked their way through the crowd, towards the door. They wanted to get to the Capital early and secure a good seat in the gallery.

"Oh, there's Anna Shaw," Adelaide said, releasing Vivi's hand. "Wait here. I'm going to say hello."

Vivi stepped back against the wall and watched Adelaide thread herself through the women until she reached Anna Shaw. The two women shook hands, and then bent their heads together in conversation.

A lump formed at the back of Vivi's throat. With Adelaide across the room, she felt out of place. Clusters of women laughed and talked, and occasionally there was a call of recognition across the room. Most of the women, including Adelaide, were wearing their suffragette uniform, long white skirts and long-sleeved white blouses, some with high lace necks and some with starched pleats down the front. The women wore gold sashes with 'Votes for Women' emblazoned across their chests or a yellow rose pinned at their shoulder.

Vivi's mother would have made Vivi a beautiful suffrage outfit, but there hadn't been time, and she made do with a long navy-blue skirt and simple white blouse. This morning while dressing, Adelaide had surprised her with her own sash.

Vivi chided herself for being self-conscious. Her worry about fitting in took away from the magnitude of the moment. She deserved to be here as much as anyone; after all, she was one of the reporters for the ESA. Her family and Lucy were sacrificing so she could be here and she owed it to them to make the most of her time.

Her mother and Lucy had been thrilled about her opportunity to go to Raleigh, but Bubba had not. After she'd taken care of the details of being gone for several days, she talked with Bubba and presented her plan, along with her travel itinerary. He listened without a word, but his body revealed his feelings, the angle of his chin, his rapid breath and wide stance. He asked her once not to go, citing her safety as the reason. With her most persuasive arguments she tried to allay his fears. When he nodded and withdrew to his boat, she knew he'd conceded, but it was an empty victory without his support and enthusiasm.

This past week they'd maintained a good rapport in front of Goldie, but every night in bed he turned his back to her. She couldn't determine the reason for his silence. Did he disapprove of suffrage, threatened by her passion for something outside the family, or was he worried about their income if she lost her job? To keep their marriage convivial, would she have to avoid talking about her suffrage work and not share an important part of herself with him?

Vivi caught sight of Adelaide walking her way. Thank God for Adelaide, who saw more in Vivi than she saw in herself. Why couldn't Bubba?

"Oh, Vivi, Anna remembered me from our work together in Boston. She hopes this year that Massachusetts will take up a state suffrage amendment again."

"Again?" Vivi asked.

"Yes. There was an unsuccessful referendum twenty years ago."

Vivi's eyes widened. Twenty years ago? Suffrage efforts had been going on that long and she'd been mostly in the dark until a few months ago. Well, she was here now and that's what counted, but she needed to research and add more information about women's right to vote in her older students' curriculum, that's if she had a job after today.

Adelaide reoriented her sash that had slipped when she traversed the room. "It feels like home to be here, in a city, with all the suffragettes."

Adelaide was lit from within, similar to how she looked on stage. She took Vivi by both shoulders and planted a firm kiss directly on her lips. "I'm happy we can share this."

Adelaide's enthusiasm and love cleared Vivi's thoughts of Bubba and not fitting in. She slipped on her gloves and linked her arm in Adelaide's. "Let's go to the Capital."

"You've got your pen and paper?" Adelaide asked.

She lifted her handbag and said, "Of course. I'm a reporter after all."

Adelaide graced her with a smile that made Vivi feel like the only person in the room. "Yes, you are, my dear."

The street was a river of white, flowing to the state Capital several blocks away. Occasionally there was a woman with a red rose in place of the gold, indicating she was an anti, someone who opposed the suffrage amendment. The throng of women, tall buildings lining the street, and the rumble of car engines, were a dream to Vivi. Such a different environment from Oriental with its harbor and tree-lined streets, but the contrast enlivened her.

"Come on," Vivi said to Adelaide. "Let's pass a few of these women so we're sure to get a good seat."

Adelaide smiled at her. "Lead the way."

Vivi stepped into the street and picked up her pace. Removed from the crowd, she could see the state Capital building straight ahead. The building was made of granite and had four columns in front that were two stories high. It was shaped like a cross, and where the wings met was a huge dome. The only structure this large that Vivi had seen was a steamer that came regularly to Oriental's harbor.

Hundreds of times in the past ten years she'd walked to the general store and unlocked the school room to start her day, but she'd never been as excited as she was today for her job as a journalist. Instead of reading about what happened at this hearing, she was going to witness it and other people would read her words. She ascended the first set of steps to the lawn and looked up at the Capital building. Her eyes filled with tears.

Adelaide slipped her arm around Vivi's waist. "Are you OK?"

Vivi nodded and took a breath to regain her composure. "I wish my father were alive to see me now. I think he'd be proud."

"Of course he would," Adelaide said. They stood there a moment looking up at the building and Vivi took in every detail, the gleam of the sun off the granite, the swish of suffragettes' skirts, the pressure of Adelaide's hand on her waist. Besides capturing the details for her article, she wanted this moment to be etched in her memory.

They were able to get a seat in the third row of the gallery that looked over the chamber for the House of Representatives. The legislators filed in, along with Anna Shaw and the five other women who would speak today.

"There's Barbara Henderson, the president of the North Carolina Equal Suffrage Association," Vivi said and scooted to the edge of her seat to see better. "I met her briefly last night at the reception."

The woman in front of Vivi turned around to look at her and Vivi realized that her knees were pressing into the woman's back. "Oh, I'm sorry," Vivi said and slid back on the bench.

Adelaide laughed. "I've never seen you this excited. I like it."

For a few more minutes Vivi let herself take in the surroundings and adjust to the close proximity of suffrage leaders as well as the state legislators. She craned her neck to see if she could pick out Jordan Carawan, but had only seen a picture of him and never seen him in person.

The speaker of the house pounded his gavel and called the hearing to order. This was Vivi's cue to settle down and focus. She opened her writing pad to a fresh page and readied her pen.

After several hours of taking notes and doing her best to capture the most powerful quotes, Vivi's hand and mind were tired. Despite the cool temperatures outside, the upper-level gallery was warm from the body heat, and Vivi wished for water. The women around her though, seemed content. They sat quietly, with straight backs and hands folded in their laps. Even when a speaker made an especially strong point, either for or against suffrage, they showed decorum at all times.

Adelaide leaned over and whispered, "I think Barbara Henderson is the last speaker."

"Good," Vivi said when she saw her walking to the podium. "I'm thirsty and need to move around a bit."

Adelaide patted her leg. "This is a part of suffrage work too, waiting, missing meals, being uncomfortable." Adelaide paused and looked around, "And biting your tongue when someone makes a ridiculous anti-suffrage statement." Vivi giggled quietly. She glanced at the stoic women around her and imagined they were also holding back retorts and cheers for the sake of being ladylike.

Barbara Henderson stepped to the speaker's podium. She was petite with curly black hair pulled into a loose bun. She placed her hands on either side of the podium and dove right into her speech. "As Abraham Lincoln said, government of the people, by the people and for the people shall not perish from this earth. Possibly you do not consider women people." From her first sentence, Vivi was mesmerized and took notes furiously.

When the hearing ended, the suffragettes poured out of the Capital. They took their first inhalation, and into the brisk winter air released all they'd held in during the hearing. Voices rose and fell in laughter and jubilation. Vivi and Adelaide held hands to avoid being separated.

"Everyone's excited," Vivi said to Adelaide when they paused at the edge of the crowd. "Do you think we have a chance of passing this amendment?"

"I don't know, but don't focus on the outcome yet. There's power in speaking up for what you believe in, whether you do that with your voice, like the speakers, or with your presence like us, and that's what's igniting this crowd. It sounds like the House and Senate will vote in a few days, and you can deal with the results then. Now, let's enjoy the celebration."

When they returned to their room, it was close to 5 o'clock. Vivi immediately took her shoes off and flopped onto the bed. Adelaide drew the curtains and turned on a lamp to chase the gloom away.

"While they kiss one fair hand, and snatch the ballot from the other," Vivi read from her notes. They both dissolved into the laughter they'd held onto during the hearing and Adelaide joined Vivi who was now propped up on the bed. Vivi held her stomach. "Barbara Henderson was amazing. Her points were brilliant, funny at times, and difficult to argue against."

"All the women were brilliant," Adelaide said. "You have a lot to be proud of here in North Carolina. Your suffrage leaders are on par with the ones in Massachusetts. I didn't expect to be impressed."

"Me either," Vivi said. "It's the first time I've ever seen women speak with such intelligence and confidence in front of a group of men."

"It won't be the last time, and hopefully once we get the vote, women sharing their opinions, ideas and analysis will be accepted as normal."

There was a gentle knock at the door. Vivi looked at Adelaide. "Are you expecting someone?"

"No, but it may be the housekeeper. Come in," Adelaide said.

The door opened and a colored girl stepped into the room. She couldn't have been more than fifteen or sixteen. "May I build a fire for you?" she asked and motioned to the fireplace.

Vivi stood and in her stockinged feet walked over to the fireplace. Everything they needed was there. "Oh, thank you, but it looks like we have everything we need. I can start it for us."

Behind her Adelaide said gently, "But Vivi, that's her job." Adelaide directed her voice to the young girl. "Yes, we'd love to have a fire."

Vivi watched while the girl carefully laid the fire. It was uncomfortable to not help, and why was this girl working? She was only a few years older than Goldie.

"Vivi, come sit down. She doesn't need you looking over her shoulder."

Vivi took her notepad and pen from the bed and sat in the chair by the window. In a few minutes the fire was crackling and the girl turned to leave.

"Thank you," Vivi said and the girl nodded. Adelaide was dozing on the bed and didn't stir when the door quietly closed.

Vivi tapped her pen on her pad and stared at the door. All day long she'd been caught up in the excitement and novelty of the day and the absence of colored women hadn't even registered. In fact, it felt normal to only be surrounded by white people. Until the young girl came to lay the fire, she'd blocked out the uncomfortable fact that the suffrage movement was excluding colored women.

Sadie had begun to work for suffrage back home, and Vivi imagined there were plenty of other colored women in North Carolina doing the same. There were over fifty signatures on Sadie's petition in support of suffrage, half of which were men, significantly more men than had signed Vivi's petition. Not even Adelaide knew that Vivi had quietly included Sadie's petition with the ones she and the other women had completed. She mailed them directly to Jordan Carawan, the state representative for Pamlico County, but was dubious as to whether he'd reviewed them and the carefully crafted letter she'd written.

Today, the all-white, male legislators listened to persuasive arguments supporting women's suffrage from women who looked like their mothers, sisters and wives, and still there was resistance. She could only imagine the opposition would have been exponential if colored women were also present. Was it right to sacrifice the voice of the colored women, to win the right to vote? And what were the men afraid of? Vivi thought to herself. They kept referring to the valuable contributions women made to their homes and family, and this was especially true of the colored women who not only took care of their own families, but frequently oversaw the homes and children of many white families. The men should be able to extrapolate that women would also provide valuable contributions to the political realm.

Thoughts, words and sentences rolled in on a high tide and Vivi wanted to grab them before they receded. Before she knew it, she'd written the first paragraph of her report on today's events. Adelaide sighed in her sleep. They should be dressing for dinner, but she couldn't stop now.

***

Three huge chandeliers cast a warm glow over the dining room of the Yarborough Hotel. Vivi unfolded the linen napkin, hoping it would protect the deep purple silk dress from any spills. Adelaide had kindly loaned one of her dresses to Vivi, and the day before they left her mother had altered it. She felt out of place in such a fashionable dress, sitting at a table with a setting that had more utensils for one person than she'd use for three.

Money from her father's trust fund was paying for this extravagant meal. Adelaide had assured her it was simply the price of suffrage work, but the guilt was still there. With this type of cost, only the affluent had the ability to participate. Vivi looked around the room at the women dining and wondered if there were other suffragettes somewhere in a boarding house, eating a simple meal brought from home. If it wasn't for her father's money, she wouldn't have been able to be here. She looked across at Adelaide studying the menu. The same was true for her.

"Ladies, may I take your order?"

The waiter's voice startled her, and Vivi retrieved the menu from the table. It was like reading a foreign language. None of the foods were familiar except for the flounder stuffed with crabmeat. She looked up and saw Adelaide watching her.

"How about I order for us?"

Vivi blushed and lay the menu down. The entire trip she'd vacillated between euphoria at being a part of history, and embarrassment at her naïveté of proper, big-city etiquette.

"We'll start with the cream of celery soup," Adelaide said and handed both menus to the waiter. "And then we'll have the roast beef with mashed potatoes and asparagus for our entrees." The waiter listened without writing anything down, nodded his head, and silently retreated from their table.

"You'll love the celery soup," Adelaide said. "It's one of my favorite dishes."

"Thank you for ordering," Vivi said and took a sip of water from the crystal goblet. "This is a new environment for me."

Adelaide waved her hand. "It's my pleasure to introduce you to this world. You've done the same with me in Oriental, helping me understand the southern culture, food, and crazy winter weather, 60 degrees one day and wet snow the next." Adelaide reached under the table and took Vivi's left hand. Vivi tensed for a moment, but the tablecloth concealed their affection. The dining room was mostly filled with women who weren't paying attention to them anyway.

They released hands and sat back when the waiter served their soup.

Vivi stared at the row of spoons on the right side of her place setting. Out of the corner of her eye she saw Adelaide take the one on the outside, and followed suit. They ate their soup in silence and as soon as Vivi finished hers, the waiter appeared at her right elbow and whisked the bowl and saucer away. She knew she was paying for the hotel staffs' assistance, but after years of helping her mother, and taking care of Bubba and Goldie, it was difficult to accept.

"Do you ever feel guilty?" Vivi asked.

"Guilty about what?"

"All of this," Vivi said and swept her hand in front of her. "The waiter, crystal, someone cleaning our room for us. Most people in Oriental couldn't even afford the train ticket here, much less this dinner."

"What are you saying, Vivi? We shouldn't be here because everyone can't?"

"Well, no."

Adelaide leaned back in her chair. "We're here because we can be, and using our presence to change the laws so our country can be more equitable. Isn't that better than staying at home and doing nothing?"

Vivi let that thought settle. She agreed with Adelaide up to a point, but the hotel and meal were still decadent to her.

The waiter slid their plates of roast beef in front of them and the aroma made Vivi's mouth water.

"Enough talk about guilt," Adelaide said and lifted her fork in the air. "Let's enjoy our dinner and you can tell me about what you were furiously writing before we came down."

"I thought you were asleep."

"I was dozing, but when I saw your head down and heard the pen scratching, I stayed quiet to give you time to write."

"Thank you," Vivi said, appreciating Adelaide's ability to give her that space, something she had difficulty creating in her home with Bubba.

She couldn't wait any longer. The smell from her plate was too tantalizing. She took a bite, and closed her eyes to savor the tender meat and then watched how Adelaide approached the asparagus, something Vivi had never eaten.

The conversation flowed easily the rest of the evening, and meandered from stories about Adelaide's childhood and growing up with three brothers, to Vivi's time at the teacher's training school, to what they'd get for dessert. Vivi relaxed into the moment and focused on Adelaide, the taste of her meal, and the hum of women's voices in the background.

"I will always remember this, Adelaide, sitting here with you, under the chandeliers after witnessing history at our state Capital." Vivi wondered if they'd ever share a moment like this again.

"If you come with me to Boston, we'll have more occasions like this." Adelaide was thinking of their future as well.

"Or you could stay in Oriental, and we'd come to Raleigh whenever you needed a taste of the big city." Adelaide frequently mentioned Vivi moving to Boston, but this was the first time Vivi had suggested Adelaide stay.

For a moment, the background noise of the restaurant faded away and Vivi was only aware of the silence that hung between them. Adelaide drummed her fingers on the table and her neck was blotched with red. Finally, Adelaide said, "That would work well for you, wouldn't it, Vivi?"

Vivi tensed at the tone of Adelaide's voice, now regretting her suggestion.

Adelaide continued, "If I stayed, you could have it all, your marriage and family, and when you were bored, or your husband wasn't supportive enough, I'd be there for you." Adelaide pushed away her dessert plate. "But what about me, Vivi? Don't I deserve to be the most important person in someone's life?"

A vice tightened around Vivi's chest and she took a sip of water. "I'm sorry Adelaide. You're right, that wouldn't be fair. I was just trying to find a way to stay in each other's lives." Vivi looked away, ashamed she hadn't even thought of it from Adelaide's perspective.

"You've never met anyone like me before," Adelaide said in a gentler voice. "I imagine it's difficult to understand, but my needs and dreams aren't any different than yours. I want someone to share my life with, and grow old with, not just a series of affairs."

Vivi sat back in her chair. The option of two women in a lifelong relationship similar to a marriage didn't seem possible, and she'd made the assumption Adelaide would have to settle for less. "I'd never thought of it that way," Vivi said. Now she realized for Adelaide to get what she wanted, their relationship would have to change. "Adelaide," Vivi began. Unsure of what to say next, she simply said, "I love you."

"I know," Adelaide said and placed her hand on Vivi's thigh. "Let's not ruin this perfect evening with more talk. There'll be plenty of time for that later." Adelaide's palm and fingers were warm honey that created a rush of desire in Vivi.

Adelaide signaled the waiter and signed for their dinner. As soon as they closed the door to their room, Vivi pulled Adelaide into a passionate kiss. For the rest of the evening, Vivi did her best to make her feel like the most important person in her life.

***

Brown, barren fields rolled out to meet the cornflower-blue horizon. A young boy in denim overalls sprinted beside the train for a few seconds, laughing and waving. Vivi waved back and thought of Goldie who'd be waiting for her at the depot in Oriental.

The train car was a liminal space for Vivi. Yesterday, she'd witnessed history at the state Capital as a suffragette reporter, and spent a magical evening with the woman she loved. Now, she was returning to Oriental and the roles of mother, wife and teacher. Could she embody both worlds simultaneously?

The clack of the train's wheels echoed, disrupting Vivi's barrage of questions, and prompting her to look out the window. New Bern was behind them and they were crossing the bridge over the Neuse River.

"Look, Adelaide," Vivi said and nudged her foot with her own. "You can't see the tracks. It's like we're skimming on top of the water."

Adelaide glanced out the window, smiled, and then returned her attention to her book. With her travels, Adelaide must be accustomed to this, Vivi thought as she continued to enjoy the peaceful view, a momentary diversion from her thoughts.

Tall cypress tress lined the shore and a heron flew upriver, her afternoon perch disturbed by the train. With a small thump, the train transitioned to solid ground and back into Pamlico County, the only home Vivi had ever known. She was unfamiliar with the land in the county, spending the majority of her time in the few square miles of Oriental, but she'd traveled along most of the county's shoreline by boat with her father, and then Bubba.

Vivi looked at the blank page in front of her. She hadn't written anything in the last fifteen minutes. The knot that had lain quietly in her belly since boarding the train expanded the closer they got to Oriental. What was wrong with her? She should be excited to see Bubba and Goldie and to return to her students tomorrow.

The train blew its whistle and slowed as it approached Bayboro. Vivi closed her eyes and rested her head on the back of the seat. Next stop was Oriental. What if this was the most exciting thing she'd ever experience, and now it was over? A one-time trip to Raleigh had been challenging to orchestrate, and she couldn't imagine coordinating this type of travel on a regular basis. She wished for a bigger life, the one Adelaide had introduced her to, but then felt guilty at being unappreciative of all that she had. She was a mother, and Goldie's needs should come first. Maybe the best she could do was make sure Goldie didn't set limits on her life.

Adelaide stood to stretch when the train stopped. "Almost home," she said and peered into Vivi's lap at her notepad. "Doesn't look like you've written much."

"Not since we crossed the river. I can't focus. Too many questions getting in my way."

Adelaide sat down and stowed her book into her satchel. "Questions about what?"

Vivi tapped her pen on the notebook in her lap. "My life. Questions I wouldn't have to answer if I stayed on the train." Vivi paused and watched the Bayboro passengers disembark. "Part of me doesn't want to go home," she said, surprising herself with this statement. "Not that I don't love my family," she quickly added.

"Really?" Adelaide asked. "I know you enjoyed the hearing at the Capital, but you also seemed uncomfortable at the hotel. I thought you'd be ready to be back on familiar ground."

They were sitting across from one another, and Vivi leaned forward to hold Adelaide's hand. "You're right. I was uncomfortable, but all those new experiences," Vivi stroked the top of Adelaide's hand with her thumb, "and being with you, made me feel more alive." She exhaled and looked out the window at the familiar landscape. "Now I'm back to all the things I know by heart."

Adelaide touched her knee. "You can be with me as much as you want if you choose to, that doesn't have to end." Adelaide's statement hung in the air like a challenge.

Vivi pressed her palm into the cold windowpane and didn't meet Adelaide's eyes. Love for Adelaide and love for her family pulled her heart in opposing directions. Her father's death taught her that losing a love could break your heart, but now she knew adding a love could as well.

The train slowed outside Oriental and Vivi still hadn't responded to Adelaide.

"Oh my goodness!" Adelaide said and grabbed her arm. "Look."

Stella, Lucy, Kathryn, and Eve all stood on the depot landing. They were dressed in white like the suffragettes in Raleigh. Stella and Lucy held a banner between them that read, "Welcome Home Pamlico County Suffragettes." Goldie held a poster, which she must have made herself, that read, "Pass the Suffrage Amendment." Her mother and Ben each waved a small pendant that said, "Votes for Women." Vivi smiled when she saw Bubba standing off to the side of the group. He looked at the ground, left and right over his shoulder, and then up to the train. Well, at least he was here.

Vivi lowered the train window and waved. "Oh, Adelaide, can you believe the welcome for us? I never imagined this would happen." The unexpected homecoming was a real diversion and Vivi pushed Adelaide's challenge about their relationship to the back of her mind.

Adelaide said quietly, "This isn't for us. It's for you. You're the Pamlico County suffragette."

Vivi looked back out the window and watched the entourage walk down the platform to align with their car. Her family and friends were here to celebrate her, even Bubba in his quiet way. In the past few months her web of connections had expanded, and it felt good.

"They're proud of you," Adelaide said. "One of their own has gone to

Raleigh to help change the course of history."

"Oh Adelaide," Vivi said and pushed her gently. "It's not quite as dramatic as that."

"Of course it is. Don't underestimate your contributions." Adelaide motioned for her to disembark first. When Vivi stepped onto the platform a camera flashed, Goldie ran to her for a hug, and the women gathered around and peppered her with questions about the hearing. Out of the corner of her eye she saw Bubba gather their bags from the porter. Despite her misgivings on the train, it felt good to be home.

Vivi kept one arm around Goldie's shoulders and hugged her mother with the other, all the while sharing some of the memorable quotes of the hearing with Stella, Lucy, Kathryn and Eve. Adelaide stood quietly behind her, letting Vivi be the focus of attention.

"OK everyone," her mother said. "Let's get these ladies back to my house for a home-cooked meal."

"Momma, we're having a party for you and Miss Adelaide, and I made the pecan pie for dessert."

Vivi kissed the top of Goldie's head. "Thank you, sweetheart."

"Pecan pie," Adelaide said. "A southern homecoming sure tastes better than a northern one."

Suitcases thumped to the ground behind her. Vivi turned, knowing Bubba was there.

"Hey, Bubba," Vivi said.

He gave her a warmer hug than she'd expected. "Glad you're home safely."

"Me too, and what a homecoming."

"Yes. You've drawn quite a crowd," Bubba nodded in the direction of the depot, "including the school superintendent."

Vivi looked behind her and saw Mr. O'Neal. He wore a black overcoat and stood stiffly with arms crossed over his chest, a stark contrast to the women in white, waving banners. He motioned her over.

"Is that the superintendent?" Adelaide asked and placed a hand on Vivi's arm.

Vivi was suddenly warm, and unbuttoned her navy-blue coat. Before she could answer Adelaide, Bubba interjected, "Yes. That's Mr. O'Neal and I doubt he's here to welcome you back."

Since accepting the job with the ESA Vivi had prepared for this moment, but still, she was nervous. Her choice to work for suffrage made some parents, the school board and Bubba unhappy, but this choice brought her alive by reconnecting her to writing and giving her another way to contribute to the world. Would she have the courage to stay the course?

Adelaide stepped beside Vivi. "Bubba, if he's here to fire Vivi, it doesn't matter. She has another job with the ESA anyway."

Bubba picked up the suitcases, glared at Adelaide, and didn't say a word.

"You're an amazing writer and will be fine without your teaching job," Adelaide said softly in her ear, and then snatched her suitcase from Bubba and marched over to walk with Etta and Ben.

On her way to Mr. O'Neal, Vivi was intercepted by Goldie, who'd been helping Stella and Lucy roll up the banner. "Come on, Momma. Let's go to the party."

Vivi looked to her left and saw the others leaving the train platform. "Run and catch up to your grandmother and Miss Adelaide," Vivi said. "I need to talk with Mr. O'Neal, and then your father and I will be right there."

Goldie looked at Mr. O'Neal and back at Vivi. "Is everything alright? Are you in trouble?"

Vivi met Bubba's gaze over Goldie's head. He stepped forward and squeezed Goldie's shoulders. "Everything is fine, sweetheart. Now go help your grandmother prepare for dinner. We'll see you in a minute."

"Thank you," Vivi said, relieved he hadn't revealed his displeasure to Goldie.

Mr. O'Neal was now walking in her direction. To counter her anxiety, Vivi strode confidently to meet him halfway. Bubba followed and stood beside her.

"Bubba. Mrs. Gibbs," Mr. O'Neal said, nodding his head. "I imagine you know why I'm here." He removed a newspaper from the interior pocket of his coat. "Between this," he said holding her editorial in the *Pamlico Enterprise* in front of her face, "and this," he said, pointing to the departing group, "you are clearly still working on suffrage, which the school board has asked you not to do." Mr. O'Neal put away the newspaper and took a deep breath.

Vivi's heart pounded. "Yes. I've made the choice to use my personal time and writing skills to fight for women's right to vote."

"And except for taking a few personal days this week, which she rarely does, her suffrage work hasn't interfered with her teaching," Bubba said.

Bubba's voice startled Vivi. She hadn't expected him to speak, and especially not in her defense. Did he really support her, or was this a desperate effort to help her keep her job and income?

"I'm surprised at you, Bubba," Mr. O'Neal said. "Do you think women should be in politics now? This isn't about taking time away from her teaching, it's about the example Mrs. Gibbs is setting." He directed his focus on Vivi now. "A teacher is a role model for her students, especially the girls. We don't want them thinking about voting. We want them to be prepared to manage their homes, raise their children and support their husbands. Women shouldn't soil their skirts in politics and traipse off to attend legislative sessions."

Anger, not anxiety, now churned in Vivi. "Mr. O'Neal." Bubba must have sensed the tone in her voice and squeezed her elbow. "I understand that's your perspective, but I think a woman standing up for what she believes in, and asking to be treated equally in the eyes of our government is a fine role model for young women." Vivi thought of the satisfaction her suffrage work had brought into her life. "And this may be startling news to you," she had nothing to lose at this point, "but sometimes women need more than a home and family to make them happy."

Bubba's head dropped to his chest and Mr. O'Neal's cheeks blazed red. He looked at Bubba. "See what this suffrage work has done to her? Made her unappreciative of the good life you've given her, and for the job the school board entrusted her with. If it were up to me, I'd terminate your contract immediately, but we haven't found a replacement teacher yet. You'll receive the official paperwork in a couple days stating that your contract will terminate as soon as a teacher has been hired in your place."

Mr. O'Neal turned quickly, and his coat tail lifted into the air.

Vivi watched him walk away and surprised herself by not being upset. She actually felt free of the threat that'd been looming over her. Now it was done and she would deal with the consequences, one of which stood beside her.

"Bubba . . ."

He picked up her suitcase and walked towards the stairs down to the street.

Vivi caught up to him and took his arm. "Thank you for what you said to support me, but I know you're upset about this."

"Yes, but I can't talk about it right now." Bubba kept walking and Vivi exhaled. She didn't want to discuss it either, and ruin the celebration her mother and Goldie had planned.

"Let's try and enjoy the evening, and nothing is going to change immediately. We have time to figure out a plan."

Vivi kept her arm linked in Bubba's and although they walked in silence, he never pulled away. When they reached her mother's yard, Goldie stepped onto the front porched and waved.

"Hurry! We're waiting for you."

Adelaide stepped into the doorway, and the smile immediately left her face. Vivi dropped Bubba's arm, and Adelaide disappeared into the house.

***

"Momma, tell me again about all the women walking down the street to the Capital," Goldie said as she slipped her nightgown over her head. "I wish I could have been there with you and Miss Adelaide."

Vivi patted Goldie's bed. "We'll talk about it more tomorrow, and maybe there'll be a picture in the Raleigh paper this weekend, but now you need to go to sleep. We both have school tomorrow."

Goldie pulled the quilt up to her chin and Vivi sat on the edge of her bed. "Thank you for being good while I was away," Vivi said, and tucked a lock of Goldie's ashen hair behind her ear. "It sounds like you were a big help to Miss Lucy and your father. I'm proud of you."

Goldie reached up and hugged Vivi tightly around her neck. "I'm almost a grown up so it wasn't hard and besides, I just did what you would have."

Vivi laughed. "You have a few more years before you have to worry about being a grown up." She leaned down and kissed Goldie's forehead. "Sleep tight and I'll see you in the morning."

"OK, Momma."

Vivi gently closed Goldie's door and lay her head against the door frame. Earlier today she'd complained to Adelaide about returning home where she knew everything by heart, as if that were a bad thing, but loving Goldie was something done by heart that she never wanted to give up.

The back door shut and the sound of wood tumbling onto the hearth echoed up the stairway. Vivi heard Bubba stacking it, and then the crackle when he threw a new log on the fire. They'd barely talked since her return. He tolerated the celebration dinner with mostly good humor, but never directly asked her anything, allowing the women to drive the conversation. On their walk home tonight they focused on how he and Goldie had fared on their own, and Goldie's exuberant presence eased the tension between them. But now, they needed to talk. They couldn't avoid the topic of her suffrage work, and their marriage.

Bubba was on the couch staring into the fire when Vivi got downstairs. She sat beside him, alert for the smell of alcohol, but it wasn't there, only silence. Vivi stared at the fire with him and tried to find the right words to start their conversation. She opted for something positive.

"Thank you for all you did for Goldie and around the house while I was gone."

"It wasn't hard. It was only two nights." His face softened into a smile and now he looked towards her. "And Goldie seemed to like being the woman of the house. She took charge of cooking our meals and even told me to slow down when I was eating."

Vivi laughed. "Just like I do."

"Yes. Just like you."

"She's a good girl."

"Yup," Bubba said. "We must have done something right with her."

"We must have, but she's changing all the time and it seems we have to keep learning new strategies."

"Kinda like marriage," Bubba said, holding her gaze.

"Yes." Vivi paused. "What strategy do we need now, Bubba? I know you're angry that my suffrage work caused me to lose my job but we need to face this together." Together. Vivi thought of this conversation from Adelaide's perspective and it looked like she was making a choice. Truthfully, she had day dreamed about choosing a life with Adelaide, but when she imagined life ten years from now, she could only picture living here, by the Neuse River with Bubba and Goldie.

Bubba stood and put another log on the fire. The muscles in his upper back and shoulders tightened. "And now that you've lost your job, how will we manage?" he asked, his voice taut with emotion. "Freelance writing about suffrage won't bring in steady money."

His words threw daggers into the air and Vivi cringed.

"We need your salary to pay the bills." Bubba made a fist with his right hand and slammed it into his left palm. "Dammit, Vivi. I work as hard as I can. Sometimes going days without sleep when the fish are running, and we still need your money to help. A man should be able to work hard, like I do, and make enough to take care of his family without his wife having to work." Bubba turned away from her and shoved both hands into his pockets.

Now she understood the tone of his voice. The condemnation wasn't for her, it was for himself. "That's why you've been angry about the potential loss of my job? Not because I'm doing suffrage work, but because you feel your income isn't enough for our family?"

Bubba turned, met her eyes briefly and then looked away. "If it's that important to you, I could take fewer days off in the spring and fall. I'd make more money that way, but haven't done it because I didn't want to be away from you and Goldie."

Vivi stood and took Bubba's hands in hers. "Bubba, I'm proud of how hard you work. You provide the bulk of our income, and for your crew and their families."

Bubba's shoulders relaxed and he ran his fingers through his hair. "Thanks. Sometimes I forget that my efforts contribute to other families too."

"And Bubba," Vivi said and sat back down. "We could make it on what you bring in from fishing if we watch our expenses and put less toward Goldie's college fund." She needed to tell him about the trust that could help with college, but now wasn't the time. "But that's beside the point, because no matter how much you make, I still want to work and contribute to our family and the community."

Bubba sat down beside her and took a deep breath. "I'm surprised you were willing to give up your job. I always thought you loved teaching."

"I didn't give up my job, the school board took it away, but just because I don't work for the Pamlico County schools doesn't mean I have to stop teaching." Vivi scooted closer to Bubba so their legs were touching. "I'll probably get to teach until the end of this school year, and then I'll advertise my services as a private tutor. That could supplement the income I get from writing for the ESA."

Bubba took her left hand between both his palms. "What about how folks will treat you when they know you're working for the ESA? You may lose some friends. Not many people around here support women's right to vote."

Vivi appreciated Bubba considering this aspect. "I'm not worried about that. I'm tired of making choices based on what others think is right, and the truth is, I only had acquaintances before meeting Adelaide and getting involved with suffrage. This work has connected me to women like Kathryn, Lucy and Stella, and we're becoming friends." Vivi paused. She looked into the fire and thought about the women in her circle as well. "Saying yes to new opportunities the last few months has created connections to some amazing women." And these women were here in Oriental, not in Boston, she thought to herself.

Bubba laughed. "I only met the others today, but I know Adelaide, and I can think of a lot of other words to describe her besides amazing."

"Like what?" Vivi was interested in Bubba's perception of Adelaide.

"Well, sassy and outspoken for one," he said without malice.

Vivi smiled. "She'd probably take that as a compliment." Why had she brought Adelaide up, because now all she could think about was the look in Adelaide's eyes when she left with Bubba and Goldie tonight. After all Adelaide had done for her, the last thing she wanted to do was hurt her, but Vivi knew she had.

Bubba interrupted her thoughts. "I don't understand your passion for getting women the right to vote, but that work brings you alive, and I won't stand in your way."

Vivi had to erase thoughts of Adelaide before his words registered. "Thank you." She leaned sideways into his shoulder. "We'll work together to figure out the money without you changing your fishing routine."

Bubba took her chin in his hand and leaned down. Just before his lips reached hers, he whispered, "My wife, the writer and suffragette." Then he kissed her deeply.

Vivi returned the kiss, but her mind was on Adelaide, alone in her room. Part of her wanted to run to the hotel to be with her. She'd always thought that more love was better, but loving two people at the same time wasn't. Being with Adelaide was easier when she and Bubba were in conflict, but now, the Bubba she'd fallen in love with was returning.

When the kiss ended, they both stood and Bubba pulled her into his arms. He pressed himself against her, and gently traced her spine with one hand. Vivi rested her head on his chest and closed her eyes. She knew Bubba by heart, too.

***

After their lovemaking, Bubba and Vivi lay entwined. Soon Bubba's breathing slowed and she watched him sleep. A lock of hair fell across his forehead. His drinking had angered her, but then she hadn't given him space to share his grief. She'd also been angry that he didn't support her suffrage work, when all along his reticence was mostly due to his belief he wasn't a good provider. None of these things were done to intentionally hurt her. Shame lay on Vivi's chest making it difficult to breathe, and she slid from under Bubba's arm. He turned on his side and began snoring.

Travel weary, and with a full school day tomorrow, she should be sleeping too, but the inner turmoil she'd either ignored or tamped down the past few months was unavoidable. Sleep would elude her tonight, so Vivi gently slipped from the bed.

A few embers glowed in the hearth and she used these to build a fire, giving herself warmth and light. On the couch, she curled her legs under her and pulled a wool blanket across her lap. Pen and paper lay at the ready on the end table, but she didn't need to clarify her thoughts through journaling. Her recent conversations with Adelaide and Bubba had done that. Her love for Adelaide hurt Adelaide by not giving her everything she deserved, and hurt Bubba by betraying their marriage vows. Vivi had used the fact that Adelaide was a woman, and Bubba was drinking and unsupportive, to justify her affair with Adelaide, but that was wrong.

The fire popped, and Vivi stretched out on the couch and positioned a pillow under her head. Tears fell silently. The circle had taught her the power of speaking her truth, and now she needed to do that with herself. Since her father's death, she'd used others to fill the space he had held, first Bubba and then Adelaide, but this pattern now hurt people she loved. The first step to rectify things was to end her affair with Adelaide.

With this thought, relief and sorrow simultaneously coursed through her. Vivi wrapped her arms around herself and gently rocked side to side. After a few minutes she scooted to a sitting position and reached for the pen and paper. *Dear Bubba*, she began. Unsure of whether she'd ever share this letter with him, tonight Vivi needed a place to explain how the affair happened, and how she'd never let it happen again.

CHAPTER 20

"As much as I love my home on Hungry Mother Creek, it's nice to have a change of scenery," Chapawee said when they turned right onto Kershaw Road. This was the first time she'd left her property since her release from jail at the end of November.

"Get along." Cora slapped the reins gently against Drum's neck. He swung his head around to look at them, but continued to walk at his own pace. "I guess old Drum doesn't want to rush this morning."

"That's OK. It's a beautiful day and I'm not in a hurry." They weren't going all the way into Oriental, only as far as the colored general store to mail her letter to Tayen and get some eggs and sugar.

The fields on either side of the road were waiting for the corn and soybeans that would be planted come spring. Spring, Chapawee thought to herself. She wouldn't be here to see this year's crop. Of course she could look at the fields in Sampson County where Tayen lived. Four seagulls called out and landed in the field to her right. But there wouldn't be seagulls.

Chapawee put her hand to her chest and felt the edges of the envelope through her shawl. Tayen had been asking her for years to move, and the letter Cora had helped her write was to finally accept this offer. She asked that Tayen and her husband come for her at the beginning of April so she could have one more circle at the spring equinox.

Cora looked over at Chapawee. "Part of you doesn't want to mail that letter."

Chapawee removed her hand from her chest and looked straight ahead at Drum's head dipping with each step. "Of course, but I have no choice. I'm focusing on the fact my daughter wants me to be with her and that I'll have time with my grand and great-grandchildren." She paused. "I hope they see me as a resource and not a burden." She also hoped Tayen's changing moods had mellowed with age.

Cora secured Drum to the general store's hitching post. Once inside, it took a minute to adjust to the dim light. The walls were lined with shelves filled with hardware, fishing supplies and basic home items like candles, cast iron skillets and even a homemade quilt. In the middle of the store were the grocery items.

"Cora! Chapawee! It's good to see you." Jack came from behind the counter and gave Chapawee a hug.

"Chapawee, how are you? I heard about your time in jail. What a ridiculous waste of taxpayers' money. Makes no sense for the magistrate to punish you like that."

Cora interjected, "Jack, when has what the white folk do ever made sense?"

Chapawee appreciated their outrage on her behalf, but didn't want to talk about her jail time any more. She threw the small bag she'd crafted out of a flour sack onto the counter. "Here's the last of this year's remedy in exchange for some sugar and eggs," she pulled the envelope from under her shawl, "and postage for this."

"Sure," Jack said. "I'm taking mail to the post office in town this afternoon."

Chapawee slid the letter towards Jack who whisked it away and under the counter. That was it, Chapawee thought to herself. In two months she'd be gone. She walked down a row of canned goods, to regain her composure.

"Grab a couple cans of pinto beans and tomatoes too. I know I'll sell all this remedy for more than the postage, sugar and eggs."

"Thanks," Chapawee said and put the cans on the counter. "And how are things with Pearl? I hope she's been able to stay away from the general store in town."

Jack leaned over the counter and lowered her voice, despite the fact they were the only ones in the store. "They never told Pearl's father what was happening for fear he'd get himself killed trying to defend her, but Sadie offered Pearl a job helping her clean the school room each afternoon. It's five cents a month that Sadie can barely spare, but it was enough for Pearl's father to release her from her responsibilities at his mill."

Chapawee and Cora simultaneously sighed in relief.

"Thank goodness for Sadie," Cora said.

Jack held the bag of wild carrot seeds. "Is this all you have until the fall?"

Thankfully, Cora remained quiet. Chapawee didn't want to tell anyone she was leaving until she told her circle at their equinox gathering. "Yes. But don't forget the rue weed we planted behind the store last year. If you run out of seeds, you can use the rue herb tea instead."

"That's right. Do y'all have a minute to come out back? I want you to show me again how much to use for each serving of tea."

"Cora, you're the driver. Do you have time?"

"Sure do, and it's probably good for me to have a refresher too."

Chapawee held Cora's gaze. Cora would continue her work once she moved to Tayen's and now Jack would help as well. The patch of rue herb they'd planted last spring had thrived and the plants were already several feet high, but most of the leaves had died in the winter and dropped to the ground.

Chapawee knelt beside the woody stems. "This isn't the time to harvest, but I'm glad we came out anyway, because it's time to prune and prepare for the spring growth."

Jack knelt beside her and Chapawee broke off the top of a stem. "Cut them back to about this height and by the end of March you'll see new growth and then flowers by the end of April."

"Ok, I'll do that tomorrow morning. And then this spring I'll use these leaves if I run out of your remedy."

"Yes." Chapawee picked up a handful of dead rue leaves from the ground and held her hand open for Cora and Jack to see. "Use about this much for each serving of tea. Near summer's end when the plant is thriving, you can pick some stalks to hang and dry for later."

"You have some bundles at home, don't you?" Cora asked.

She sat back on her heels. "Yes. I'll bring some by the next time we come, Jack, and show you how I make tea."

"Thank you. I'm honored you're sharing this knowledge with me." Jack stood and extended her hand to Chapawee who used it to steady herself to standing.

"I may have knowledge," Chapawee squeezed Jack's hand before she released it, "but youth has the strength."

The women laughed companionably and walked slowly back to the store to collect Chapawee's items. Jack loaded the sugar, cans, and a dozen eggs carefully into a cardboard box.

"I'll only use my rue herb if you're out of remedy. I don't want to encroach on your business."

"Don't worry about that. I don't consider what I do a business, just an exchange. I give women a choice as to how they live their life in exchange for food, so I can live mine."

Cora slapped her hand onto the counter which made Chapawee jump. "I just had an idea! What if, when Jack sells her rue herb she keeps the money separate. It could be an emergency fund for any woman who needs help." Chapawee and Jack nodded and Cora continued. "And this fall, we'll contribute our wild carrot seeds and they can be sold to help the fund too."

It was a brilliant idea, Chapawee thought to herself. She'd be gone and wouldn't need to exchange the remedy for staples. Cora could do the fall harvest alone, and then bring it all here.

Jack's face lit up and she squeezed Cora's arm. "I love this idea. We'll use the fund for emergencies, and when it grows, maybe we could help a young woman with continuing her education."

"What a perfect idea," Chapawee said. "Use the gifts of mother nature to help women with family planning, which in turn creates funding to support colored women." Chapawee nodded slowly. "And never forget," Cora and Jack leaned closer to hear her, "that it all started with gifts from the earth."

The day had warmed up and Chapawee dropped her shawl onto the floor of the cart. Cora was talking non-stop about the women's fund as she was now calling it. Drum absorbed Cora's excitement and walked more quickly compared to their outbound trip.

Cora's voice rose and fell and Chapawee nodded when appropriate, but her attention was elsewhere. She mentally repeated what good could come out of living with Tayen and her family, but it did nothing to ease the sadness of leaving. Here she had a purpose, growing her own food, cultivating the remedy, leading the circle. What role would she have on the Coharie River?

After Cora took her box of food inside and they'd said their goodbyes, Chapawee sat on her porch steps. To her right a cluster of green shoots caught her attention. An impatient daffodil was ready to make an appearance. Chapawee gently brushed the palm of her hand over the firm leaves. The season was changing, in nature and her life.

***

The anticipation of talking with Adelaide this afternoon made the school day feel interminable. Vivi was happy to be outside now, even with the light drizzle and cool temperatures.

"See you in a little bit, Momma," Goldie said and ran in the direction of her grandmother's.

"I'll be there soon. Ask your grandmother if you can help with any chores." Goldie lifted her hand in acknowledgement but kept running.

Exhaustion enveloped Vivi like a suit of armor. She'd barely slept the past two nights. The night of her return from Raleigh she'd been up until dawn writing the letter to Bubba, and last night she'd stayed up past midnight incorporating the latest developments into her article for the ESA. Stella had come over just before dinner with news she'd gotten through the telegraph operator network. Both houses of the General Assembly voted against the suffrage amendment. To top that off, Representative Carawan had said, "It would be a sad day in North Carolina when women were allowed the ballot." Adelaide, and several of the women she'd talked to in Raleigh had somewhat prepared her for this outcome, but it was still disappointing. These events didn't deflate her passion for suffrage though, and had provided some respite from her sadness.

She couldn't put off her conversation with Adelaide any longer and walked in the direction of the hotel. The feel of the earth under her feet grounded Vivi's conflicting emotions, part of her heart was breaking and another part was relieved. At the hotel, she expected Adelaide to be at the reception desk preparing for the weekend guests, but she wasn't there. Vivi walked to her room and knocked gently on the door. There was movement inside, but Adelaide didn't answer.

Vivi knocked again. "Adelaide, it's me. I hear you in there. Is everything OK? May I come in?"

The door opened a couple inches and Adelaide pressed herself in that space so Vivi couldn't see into the room. "I wasn't expecting you," Adelaide said through the crack. "I figured you wouldn't have time for me until tomorrow."

Vivi tensed at the tone of Adelaide's voice. She sounded angry already. Did she intuit what Vivi was here to talk about? "What do you mean by that? I had a lot to catch up on at school and last night worked on my article about the hearing." Vivi elevated onto her tiptoes to look over Adelaide's head but could only see the fireplace. "Did Stella tell you about the latest developments?"

"Yes. She came by last night," Adelaide said, no emotion in her voice. "I'm sorry the house won't vote on the amendment."

"Come on, Adelaide." Vivi swallowed to loosen the vice around her throat. "We need to talk about our relationship," her voice cracked but she continued, "and we can't do that through this crack in the door."

Vivi placed her palm on the door and took a step into the room. Adelaide reluctantly moved to the side to avoid a collision. Suddenly, there wasn't enough oxygen in the air. Vivi placed a hand on her chest to catch her breath. The dresses Adelaide performed in were neatly folded and stacked in a trunk on the floor. Her other belongings were strewed across the bed.

"What's happening?" Vivi asked, dropping her satchel to the floor. "Why are you packing?"

Vivi knew the answer before she'd asked the question. Their trip to Raleigh must have clarified things for Adelaide too.

Adelaide stepped in front of Vivi and began folding the clothes on the bed. "I need to get back to Boston. The Boston Equal Suffrage Association for Good Government is focused on getting a suffrage amendment on their ballot in October, and I want to be there to help."

Vivi collapsed into the chair by the fireplace while Adelaide continued to pack. Her heart crumbled, and the pieces stuck in her throat. She'd been prepared to end the affair with Adelaide, but not for Adelaide's departure. "Would you have said goodbye if I hadn't come today?"

"There's barely been time, Vivi. When I returned from Raleigh, I learned that the hotel manager was coming back next week. That was confirmation it was time for me to move on. I started looking for transportation north and just this morning, found out that a steamship is leaving tomorrow for Norfolk."

The image of Adelaide on the deck of a steamer, leaving Oriental, made it hard for Vivi to breath.

Adelaide, still packing with her back to Vivi, filled in the silence. "You can't be that surprised I'm leaving. I've asked you ten different ways to come to Boston and you've always deflected the question." Adelaide paused and turned to look at Vivi. "At dinner at the Yarborough, I was clear about what I wanted from our relationship, and for a few hours that night I let myself believe it could happen. I let go of that fantasy though as soon as you stepped off the train to greet your family and friends. Your home is in Oriental."

Vivi took deep breaths to quell her emotions. "You're right. I was coming here today to tell you that, and to end our affair." She slid to the edge of the chair. "It was selfish to lead you on like I did. I felt so much more alive when we were together, and I didn't want that to end. I'm sorry."

Adelaide sat on the end of the bed to face her. "It's not all your fault." Her voice was soft now, without the edge it had when Vivi arrived. "From the beginning, I've known deep down that you belonged to Bubba and Goldie, but when you and I were together, it felt like your other life didn't exist. It was just us, and for the past six months I've lived for those moments with you." Adelaide's voice cracked. "But it's not sustainable, and it's not fair to me, or to your marriage."

One after the other, tears dripped from Vivi's eyes, down her cheeks and onto her hands. She made no attempt to stop them. "I wish things could be different," Vivi said and pulled the bottom of her skirt up to wipe her face. "that you could stay and we'd be friends, but . . ." That would never work. Her heart caved in at the thought of Adelaide hundreds of miles away. How would she have the courage to sustain her new life as a writer and suffragette without Adelaide?

Vivi stood, needing to move her emotions through her body, and Adelaide followed suit. "It won't feel the same here without you." Vivi had difficulty processing what was happening. This might be the last time she'd see Adelaide.

"It won't feel the same here either," Adelaide said placing her hand over her heart, "but Vivi as much as this hurts me now, being with you in Oriental was worth it."

They fell into one another's arms and Adelaide nestled her head in the crook of Vivi's neck. There was so much Vivi wanted to say, but words were superfluous. Vivi paid close attention to the feel of Adelaide's breath on her neck and the warmth and pressure of her body. They held one another, unaware of time passing until the faint chime of the grandmother clock in the parlor alerted them to this fact.

Vivi released Adelaide, and when she opened her mouth to speak Adelaide put her fingers over her lips. "Shh. Don't say anything."

Adelaide backed away and Vivi picked up her satchel. The three steps to the door were like walking the plank, carrying a huge boulder.

Vivi took the long way to her mother's, walking past the riverfront where the Neuse River stretched five miles wide. The river had brought Adelaide to her on a showboat and tomorrow would take her away on a steamer. She paused and watched the water, rippled by the gentle breeze. Would it have been better if Adelaide had never come? *Stop.* Just like with her father's death, rewriting the past wouldn't change anything. Adelaide had come, and now, she must take what she'd learned about herself, both good and bad, and move forward.

CHAPTER 21

It'd been two weeks since Adelaide's departure and the heaviness had lifted enough that when Vivi was engaged with teaching, writing or Goldie, she momentarily forgot that Adelaide was gone. Now she sat on the bench outside their back door with a letter Adelaide had posted from Norfolk. She'd saved it to read alone while Bubba walked Goldie to Sunday School.

Vivi slid her thumb under the lip of the envelope, aware that Adelaide had been the last to touch this. The sight of Adelaide's round, curling script reinforced that words made by pen and paper were the foundation of their relationship now, no voice, caresses or laugh to accompany them. The words blurred on the page. Vivi dabbed the corner of her eyes and began reading. Adelaide kept the letter light with tales from her travels, and advice for the next suffrage meeting in Oriental. She asked how Vivi's story on the women suffrage amendment had been received and where it'd been published. She shared the names and address of several newspapers in coastal Virginia, as well as the address for the *Boston Globe*.

And Vivi, Adelaide had written, *I know when you read that last sentence your first thought was that your writing isn't good enough for out of state papers, but believe me it is. Suffragettes from other states can learn from what happened in North Carolina. One person at a time, you can change people through your writing, on suffrage, or whatever topic you choose. Please, Vivi, never underestimate the power of your words.*

Vivi paused. She could say the same about Adelaide. Her words, though sung not written, had changed Vivi that night on the showboat, and been the impetus for introducing herself to Adelaide. As their relationship had grown, Adelaide had helped her feel again, sometimes love and excitement, sometimes anger and fear, but experiencing this range of emotions had brought Vivi back to life.

She dearly loved Bubba and Goldie, but these loves, although authentic, were expected. The feelings she had for Adelaide were totally unexpected, confusing and delightful. Opening up to a new way of loving with Adelaide had also opened Vivi to new opportunities, sharing honestly in the women's circle and pursuing her passions for suffrage and writing, things she would have denied before Adelaide.

Vivi was lost in thought, and jumped when Bubba sat beside her on the bench.

"Is that a letter from Adelaide?"

Vivi nodded and Bubba put his arm around her. "Part of me is glad she's gone so I have more of your time, but I know you'll miss her."

Vivi neatened the stationary on her lap. "Yes. I've never had a friend like Adelaide." And I'll never have another like her, Vivi thought to herself. Only she and Adelaide would know the truth about their relationship.

"I know," Bubba said, gently massaging the back of Vivi's neck. "Although I resented some of the time you spent with her, I'm glad she came into your life, because you've been happier and," Bubba paused, "more like the Vivi I first met."

Vivi leaned into Bubba who pulled her closer. "Everything about Adelaide was new and different, and she helped me get out of the rut I'd been in the past few years."

Bubba interjected, "The rut we've both been in because of my drinking."

"And your brother's death, Bubba, but you seem more like yourself too, and you haven't had a drink since Christmas."

"I know. And your mood and attention has helped that."

Vivi rested her head on Bubba's chest and watched the sunlight sparkle on the water like sequins in a spotlight. Her time in the women's circle, writing and doing suffrage work had all improved her mood. They fulfilled her in a way that motherhood and marriage couldn't, but that was okay.

Bubba pulled her closer and Vivi slid her arm around his waist. She'd chosen Adelaide for a season, but Bubba was who she chose for the rest of her life, the person she knew by heart, the father of her child, the person she'd grow old with. Maybe having a choice while Adelaide was here helped her see more clearly what she wanted. She wanted a life here, on the Neuse River with Bubba and Goldie, not a life that only filled a single role, but one that allowed her to express her creativity and explore her interests. This was the lasting gift Adelaide had given her.

Bubba tilted Vivi's chin towards him and kissed her gently on the lips. "I have some work to do on the boat for a bit, but let's leave in an hour and walk by the waterfront on the way to your mother's for lunch."

Vivi nodded. "Yes, let's."

The sun was higher now and Vivi moved from the bench to the back steps to stay in the warmth. She reread Adelaide's letter and then slid it under the stationary she'd brought out with her. *Dear Adelaide,* she began and then paused, allowing the grief to flow and then ebb. Adelaide was gone, back home in Boston by now, but as she put pen to paper, Vivi knew they'd always be connected by their words.

***

It was a perfect morning, cerulean blue sky, cool temperatures, and no wind. Vivi lifted her face to the sun and felt the promise of spring in its warmth. She, Bubba and Goldie hurried to the train station. The white skirt Vivi's mother had made, peeked out from under her winter coat. She now had the full suffragette ensemble.

"Momma, did you remember your 'Votes for Women' sash?" Goldie asked when they were beside the tracks.

"I did, sweetheart. I'm not sure all the women at the convention support suffrage, but they'll know that I do."

"As the reporter for the ESA, I doubt they'll be surprised." Bubba said and then handed her bag to the porter.

Vivi was going to New Bern to attend the state convention for the North Carolina Federation of Women's Clubs. She'd be reporting on the keynote speech tonight by Walter Clark, the chief justice of the North Carolina Supreme Court. As an outspoken supporter of women's suffrage, he would be the first man Vivi had heard speak in favor of women's right to vote.

"Thanks for taking care of your father." Vivi winked at Bubba and then hugged Goldie, whose head now reached Vivi's shoulder.

"Don't worry Momma. We'll be fine," Goldie said confidently.

The train whistled.

"You better board the train." Bubba hugged her, and Vivi lingered for a moment, enjoying the pressure of his arms around her.

"Please be careful," Bubba said, keeping one hand on her shoulder. "Someone is meeting you at the New Bern station, right?"

"Yes. A member of the New Bern Women's Club will be there, and show me the way to Griffin Hall, where Mr. Clark is speaking."

Vivi kissed Bubba on the lips. "I'll be fine, and home by dinner tomorrow."

"I'll be interested to hear what a man has to say about votes for women."

"And I'll be happy to share that with you," Vivi said with a smile.

Bubba put his hand in the small of her back and walked with her to the train.

"I'll see you tomorrow." Vivi waved goodbye to Bubba and Goldie and then entered the train to find her seat.

From her satchel, she removed the notes she'd already made on Walter Clark. The train left the station and Vivi began preparing questions for the private interview she had with him tonight after his speech.

At the edge of town the train whistled again. Vivi paused her writing and looked out the window. In the background was familiar farmland, and in the foreground she saw her reflection. Her face was framed by the high collar of her white blouse and her thick brown hair, today pulled back in a chignon like Adelaide had taught her. She was a journalist, heading to New Bern alone, to report for the Equal Suffrage Association. Vivi smiled back at herself.

Tomorrow, she'd return to her roots in Oriental, but today she was flying on her own with the wings Adelaide had helped her find.

***

The daffodils beside her porch nodded their jaunty yellow heads at Chapawee. She paused and nodded back, understanding they would continue to bloom and multiply long after she was gone. Spring officially began in a few days, but the woods already glowed golden green in the morning light. The smell of fresh turned dirt pulled Chapawee to her garden, and the collision of seeds in her pocket emphasized each step.

Last weekend, kind Jeremiah had tilled a small patch of her garden. Even though she'd be leaving with Tayen in a few weeks, Chapawee wanted to do her early spring planting and have one last opportunity to commune with the soil that had been a generous provider to her family for the past sixty-some years.

Had it really been that long? Chapawee thought. She clearly

remembered the first time she saw this plot of land. Her father had scouted it alone, and then brought her and her mother and sister to make it their home. The day they arrived was warm, sometime in late spring, and she and Kanti had immediately jumped into the creek to swim, familiarizing themselves with the tea-colored water they'd now play in and eat from.

Chapawee carefully lowered herself to the edge of the garden. She looked at the tilled soil and mentally mapped the configuration of rows to accommodate the collards, turnips and potatoes. A gentle rain had fallen yesterday so the soil was moist and ready to accept her seeds. She pressed her finger into the earth and dropped a potato seed in the indentation. The muscle memory of sowing seeds engaged, and Chapawee merged with the process, punch a small hole, drop a seed, cover with dirt, slide to the next spot and repeat. Thank goodness she was physically up for work today. The past week her chest had been heavy and her breath more labored, emotional symptoms of leaving. She hoped the antidote would be embracing her great-grandchildren for the first time.

The potatoes and turnips were done. Cora would be here soon to help her get water from the creek, but she needed to rest before she finished with the collards. Chapawee scooted out of the dirt onto the grass. The sun was almost directly overhead and warmed her shoulders, neck and back. She consciously tried to slow and deepen her breathing. Maybe Cora could plant the last of the seeds when she arrived. She'd be tending the garden anyway. Chapawee leaned forward with her elbows on her knees to better catch her breath. Although she wouldn't benefit from her garden, cultivating it before she left was a small act of defiance, and a way to honor the cycle her family had maintained since they arrived on this land.

Her breath wasn't improving and now her chest was heavy, like a barrel was sitting on it. Chapawee lay back on the ground. It was too much effort to hold herself up. The earth was warm and after a few minutes the dampness of yesterday's rain seeped into the back of her dress. She moved her hands gently back and forth across the ground and her palms were tickled first by tufts of grass, and then by the granular, sandy soil.

A hawk made lazy circles in the cobalt blue sky and she watched it to distract from the heaviness in her chest. Her vision narrowed and the hawk morphed into her mother. Tears slid from her eyes, down her cheek and into the soil. The vision of her mother moved closer, and now Chapawee saw that her sister and father were with her.

"Chapawee! Chapawee!"

Cora's voice sounded far away, but when her head was lifted into her lap, she knew she was with her.

"Chapawee, can you hear me?" Cora's voice was tight with concern and Chapawee wanted to tell her not to worry because she was feeling better.

Chapawee was aware of the pressure of Cora's hand as she caressed her head and temples, but all she could see was her family, now standing quietly at her feet. There was moisture on her forehead from Cora's tears.

"Chapawee? Is this it? Dear friend, do what you must, but I will miss you."

It took all her concentration, but Chapawee opened her eyes to look at her. She reached out and Cora took her hand, black and brown fingers entwined. "You are a good friend, Cora," Chapawee said quietly.

Cora squeezed her hand. "Our lives haven't been easy, but your friendship was one of its greatest gifts."

Chapawee blinked her eyes in agreement. "Cora?"

Cora leaned down so her face was only a few inches away her friend's mouth. "You must call the circle at the equinox. Don't let it end with me."

Cora nodded and then sang in a low, husky voice, all the while cradling Chapawee's head. The rhythm of Cora's voice washed over her and then began to fade. Chapawee closed her eyes and left Hungry Mother Creek on her own terms.

AUTHOR'S NOTE

Calling the Circle, is a work of fiction, but I did my best to be historically accurate in my portrayal of eastern North Carolina in 1914 and 1915. There are times, though, when I adjusted historical facts, or invented circumstances for narrative purposes.

Choices for women were more restrictive than portrayed in *Calling the Circle.* There was a marriage bar in the United States during this time that prevented married women from working in clerical and teaching jobs. Because rural areas had a greater need for teachers, they were more likely to hire married women. It is possible that a married woman like Vivi could have been a teacher, but I found no record of a married school teacher in Oriental in 1914. The marriage bar officially ended when the Civil Rights Act was passed in 1964. Unmarried women also had employment restrictions, and the James Adams Floating Theater prohibited unmarried women from being a part of the cast or crew. In the fictional world, I gave Adelaide the opportunity to perform on the showboat as an unmarried woman.

I took the liberty to adjust the schedule of the James Adams Floating Theater. It only stopped in Oriental May 4-9, 1925, and April 17-22, 1939. The closest it got to Oriental in 1914, the first year it was in use, was when it was in Aurora, North Carolina, March 19-21.

The women's suffrage history contained in *Calling the Circle* is all based on historical facts with two major exceptions. I found no documentation of any suffrage organization in Oriental or Pamlico County. However, I did take the name Stella Aldridge from a list the Oriental History Museum compiled of the first women in Oriental to register to vote. In Vivi's last scene, I adjusted the date Walter Clark spoke in New Bern to the North Carolina Federation of Women's Clubs, from May 8, 1913, to February 27, 1915.

Several details about Oriental were also adjusted. Vivi and Adelaide would not have boarded a train in Oriental and gone directly to Raleigh. They would have taken a train to New Bern, and then a coach to Chocowinity where they would have boarded a train to Raleigh.

In 1914 the school for white children was above the Paris Woodard General Store, but in 1915, the first graded school began in a specially built schoolhouse on Church Street. I found no documentation of a school for African Americans in 1914. In the early 1920s there was one built on Town Road, and in 1921 the Holt's Chapel School was built by the Rosenthal Foundation.

The instructions and dosages for the Wild Carrot remedy were taken from the Museum of Conception and Abortion, https://muvs.org/en/topics/t-plants/wild-carrot-en/, but there is very limited research on the safety and effectiveness of this wildflower for preventing pregnancy. Please consult with your physician regarding birth control, and do not follow any instructions in this book.

My research for *Calling the Circle* reminded me of the progress we have made in addressing women's rights and racial injustices and it also illuminated how many things remain the same. There is still work to be done.

ACKNOWLEDGEMENTS

My name is on the cover of *Calling the Circle,* but it would not be in your hands, or on your e-reader, if it wasn't for the love, support, and knowledge of many others. This novel is my first historical novel, and before I began writing, I researched the social, racial, and political environment in Pamlico County and North Carolina, during 1914 and 1915. I am indebted to the Pamlico County Heritage Center and the Oriental History Museum for their help anytime I stopped by to research. Diana Bell-Kate from the North Carolina Museum of History provided insight into the clothing. Thank you to Anastasia Sims for her book *The Power of Femininity in the New South. Women's Organizations and Politics in North Carolina, 1880-1930.* I returned to this book hundreds of times to ensure I represented the suffrage history correctly. I gained specific details about the James Adams Floating Theater in C. Richard Gillispie's book, *The James Adams Floating Theatre.*

I extend deep gratitude to Ann Fitzmaurice and Gaye Hill, for serving as beta readers, but most importantly for being a constant source of love, support and fun in my personal and writing life: #wearewriters! To Lynn Murray for being the first beta reader for *Calling the Circle* and providing insightful feedback and unconditional support. To Amy Rogers, from the North Carolina Writers Network, for her developmental editing that strengthened the characters and plot. To my helpful author group, Padgett Gerler, Leslie Tall Manning, Tracie Barton-Barrett and Michelle Garren Flye, for providing feedback in later drafts and for sustaining my writing practice through the pandemic with laughter, love and inspiration. To Elizabeth Ward for her keen copy editing. To Terry Halpern for her meticulous proofreading that put the finishing touches on *Calling the Circle*. To Nathan Bauer for formatting the print and e-book versions. To Kylie Sek for the beautiful cover that turned out just as I had imagined.

All of my novels contain strong relationships between women which honor the amazing women in my life. Thank you to my original women's group for over 25 years of love, support and positive role modeling. To my Oriental women's circle for your wisdom, honesty and belief in me. To my "Little Book Club," you know who you are, for critical and lighthearted book discussions amongst laughter, love and support. To Sev Tok, for helping me see beyond my limits and bringing good energy into my life. To Julia Brandon for being my best cheerleader and anam cara. To Tracy Pardieu for your love, support and deep friendship since the fifth grade. To my mother and father whose unconditional love and support provided the foundation for me to live authentically. To my sister Christie for always listening and understanding, and for our precious early morning runs together.

I am immensely grateful to my husband Bobby for your unwavering belief in me, willingness to talk about characters, plot, and marketing, and for standing beside me without complaint at festivals and book signings. By far the best decision of my life was marrying you. Thank you to Moonpie, the calico cat who found me two years ago. You've taught me that love has no limits, (who knew I could love a cat) and that the best days are full of play and naps.

And finally, thank you to my wonderful hometown of Oriental for its continued support of *Hungry Mother Creek* and *The Mother Tree*, and anticipation for *Calling the Circle*. Nautical Wheelers, Inland Waterway Provision Company and the Front Porch Music Festival have all allowed me to sell my books locally, and are enthusiastic in their support. Thank you to local book clubs and readers for supporting a local author. I'm immensely grateful for friends, acquaintances and strangers who stop to say they have enjoyed my books and to inquire about my progress on *Calling the Circle*. Your interest, support and positive feedback mean more than you will ever know.

QUESTIONS FOR DISCUSSION

1. The novel alternates between Chapawee and Vivi's perspectives. Which character did you connect with more? Why?

2. Chapawee feels strong connections to the land on Hungry Mother Creek, her ancestors, and the cycles of nature, while Vivi initially feels disconnected from most aspects of her life. Why do you think there is this difference? Does Vivi feel a greater sense of connection in her life by the end of the novel? What things are you most connected to?

3. Chapawee was reluctant to move away from her home on Hungry Mother Creek to the Coharie River where her daughter lived. What factors contributed to her desire to stay in Pamlico County? Is there a place you have a strong connection to that would make it difficult to leave?

4. Chapawee and Cora harvest Wild Carrot (Queen Anne's Lace) to prevent pregnancy after unprotected sex. Compare and contrast women's access to family planning in *Calling the Circle's* time period to today.

5. After the first circle Sadie and Cora have some reservations. Sadie says "…it seems idealistic that the five of us sitting in a circle as equals will make any difference in the larger world." Chapawee answers "…change has to start somewhere, and it might as well be with us." Do you agree more with Chapawee or Sadie? Why? Share a personal example of where a change in one person positively impacted others.

6. Vivi loves both Adelaide and Bubba. Do you think it's possible to be in love with two people at the same time? Why or why not?

7. What is your reaction to Vivi's affair? Do you think she would have had an affair if Adelaide had been a man?

8. Should Vivi have told Bubba the truth about her relationship with Adelaide? If she did, how would Bubba have reacted? Do you think it's acceptable to not share the truth if it will hurt someone? Why or why not?

9. Vivi's father died in front of her when she was eleven. Discuss the role this played in her life.

10. Bubba appears angry and unsupportive about Vivi's suffrage work. Were you surprised that his feelings came from self judgement about his ability to provide for his family? What other factors may have contributed to his difficulty in supporting Vivi's work on women's right to vote?

11. How did Vivi's work in suffrage change her? What causes outside your family and career are you passionate about?

12. Vivi, Bubba, and Chapawee are grieving the death of loved ones. How does each character cope with their loss(es)?

13. Vivi feels that her family gives her roots, with stability and connection, and Adelaide gives her wings, with excitement, new perspectives, and freedom. Is it possible to get all these needs met by one person? Is it even healthy to look to others for these things?

14. What role did the women's circle play in Vivi's awakening, both personally and to the disparity between white women and women of color? Who are the women in your life that help you grow and introduce you to new perspectives?

15. What was your reaction to how the novel ended for Vivi and Chapawee? Would you have written it differently? Why?

ABOUT THE AUTHOR

Heather Cobham is the award wining author of *Hungry Mother Creek* and *The Mother Tree*. She grew up in eastern North Carolina and now lives with her husband in Oriental, North Carolina. In addition to being a writer, Heather is a licensed clinical social worker and works as a counselor. She fights writer's block and manages her own stress by running, paddle boarding, yoga and reading. Visit her at www.heathercobham.com

Made in the USA
Middletown, DE
28 May 2023

31041447R00184